Blind Defence

Also by John Fairfax

Summary Justice

Blind Defence

John Fairfax

Little, Brown

LITTLE, BROWN

First published in Great Britain in 2018 by Little, Brown

1 3 5 7 9 10 8 6 4 2

All characters and events in this publication, other than those clearly in the public domain, are fictitious and any resemblance to real persons, living or dead, is purely coincidental.

A CIP catalogue record for this book is available from the British Library.

Hardback ISBN 978-1-4087-0875-0
Trade paperback ISBN 978-1-4087-0876-7

Typeset in Sabon by Palimpsest Book Production Limited, Falkirk, Stirlingshire

Printed and bound in Great Britain by Clays Ltd, St Ives plc

Papers used by Little, Brown are from well-managed forests and other responsible sources.

MIX
Paper from responsible sources
FSC® C104740
FSC www.fsc.org

Little, Brown
An imprint of
Little, Brown Book Group
Carmelite House
50 Victoria Embankment
London EC4Y 0DZ

An Hachette UK Company
www.hachette.co.uk

www.littlebrown.co.uk

To Keith and Marie-Edith Cameron

Laws are like cobwebs, which may catch small flies,
but let wasps and hornets break through

A Critical Essay on the Faculties of the Mind,
Jonathan Swift

March 2000, HMP Codrington

'Your name's Benson, isn't it?'

'Yes.'

'So why call yourself Rizla?'

'Because I've always got a cigarette paper in my pocket.'

Meersham leaned forward and shoved a cassette into a portable TV video player. The machine whirred and tiny squares of fluorescent light appeared in his black eyes. He pointed at the screen and Skagman, who was standing behind him, tattooed arms afloat, made a guard dog's grunt. Gulls screeched. Waves crashed in the distance.

'Are you short?' said Benson, his tongue sticking to his palate. 'I've got loads.'

'I don't smoke. You should know that by now. I own this place.'

Benson had been on C Wing for a month, two'd up with Andrzej something-or-other, a scrawny lad from Warsaw who spoke no English. They were getting on fine. Andrzej lay on his bed, crying or sleeping. Benson studied medical or legal journals, evading a scream that would twist his guts if he thought about the lock in the cell door. Five minutes earlier, he'd been reading 'Children, trauma and evidence: the potential suppression of truth' by T. Maddison et al., in the *International Quarterly of Forensic Psychology*. Children, it seemed, sometimes dealt with trauma by reporting an event like a bystander rather than a participant. In the process, critical information known only to the child could be left undiscovered. Benson had just been wondering if Maddison et al. had missed the point – because the same could surely be said of adults – when, after twenty-two hours of bang-up, the cell door had swung open and Skagman's drooping mouth appeared two inches from his own.

'You're wanted.'

Terry Meersham was in his late twenties. Pale and wiry, and short enough to look stunted, he was slouching on a stool, a gold dressing gown draped over his shoulders. His scrappy black beard suggested a youth trying to persuade the world he was old enough to buy his own lager but his eyes – watchful and still, like those of a cat – glittered with experience beyond his years.

'What you in for, Rizla?'

Even after seven months inside, he wasn't used to the word. 'Murder,' he said.

'Respect, man, respect. How old are you?'

'Twenty-two.'

'Is that all? You're just a kid, aren't you, Rizla?'

'Yes.'

'Who smokes.'

'Yes.'

'What did you do?'

According to the jury, he'd murdered Paul Harbeton. As for Benson, like the children studied by Maddison et al., he'd partly removed himself from the trauma. There'd been a fight between two men outside the Bricklayers Arms on Gresse Street in central London. One of them, four hundred and ninety-nine days ago, had fallen to the pavement, his cheekbone fractured by a headbutt, blood pouring from his nose. Benson seemed to look at the prostrate figure as if he was that confused bystander. But he was the one lying on the ground.

'I'm told Paul Harbeton gave you a Glasgow kiss,' said Meersham.

'Yes, he did.'

'And then you followed him into Soho and cracked his head open from behind.' Using a remote, Meersham rewound the video and began another viewing. The same gulls screeched all over again. The same waves crashed on the same shore. 'That wasn't very nice, Rizla.'

Benson agreed.

'Skagman here always lets people know he's coming, don't you, Skagman?'

'Yeah.'

'Looks them in the eye. Look him in the eye, Skagman.'

Skagman did. And Benson found neither light nor shade; just a dull sheen like pond water. He stepped slowly back, colliding with another prisoner who'd just entered the cell, a squat figure with short arms and a shaved scalp. The bones on one side of his face were larger than the other, giving the impression of permanent swelling. In his hands was a cardboard box. Benson's cardboard box.

'This is everything,' he said.

'Say hello to Crazy Joe, Rizla.'

Benson did as he was told. After a sigh, Meersham cut the video. Leaning forward, thin legs wide apart, he started taking items out of the box, talking to Benson at the same time.

'Do you know why he's called Crazy?'

'No.'

'Have a guess.'

'Really, I don't know.'

Meersham was holding a photograph of Benson's parents, Jim and Elizabeth. He threw it aside and reached in for another.

'I said have a guess.'

'Because he's crazy?'

'Bingo. Though I wouldn't say that again if I were you. What's wrong with your brother? This is your brother?'

He was holding a picture of Eddie, aged ten, sitting in his wheelchair.

'Yes,' said Benson. 'He's paralysed from the waist down.'

'What happened?'

'He was hit by a car . . . he was on his bike and he—'

'Was he wearing a helmet?'

'No.'

'Brain damage?'

'Yes.'

'Serves him right.' Meersham tossed the photo onto the floor. 'What the hell is this lot?'

Meersham had found the journals. They too went on the floor, followed by the books: Charlesworth and Percy on *Negligence*, Clerk and Lindsell on *Torts*, and finally Smith and Hogan's *Criminal Law*. Meersham looked at this last as if it was full of bad jokes.

'You wanna be a lawyer?'

'Yes.'

'When you get out?'

'Yes.'

'You haven't got a chance in hell.'

Benson's defence counsel, Helen Camberley QC, had voiced a similar opinion. So had George Braithwaite, his solicitor. But Tess de Vere, the student on work experience, had urged him to go for it. She'd told him to persevere, and take the knocks until he'd made it back into court.

'Nothing can stop me,' he said.

'Clear up the mess,' said Meersham, not seeming to have heard.

Benson crouched down and placed the photos, the journals

and the books back in the cardboard box. As he stood up, Meersham rose too, and slowly, allowing his gold dressing gown to slide to the floor. Straining for height, his long neck made a light crack.

'I don't care about your plans,' he murmured, teeth clenched. 'What bothers me is that you smoke. You've brought poison on to my wing. Do you know what smoking causes?'

Benson nodded.

'Do you?' said Meersham, his fine lips stretched thinner. 'You've heard of peripheral vascular disease?'

Benson nodded.

'Furring of the arteries?'

Another nod. Benson hadn't, but he daren't say no.

'Weakening of the oesophagus?'

Benson didn't react. Meersham was staring at him, white with rage.

'Brain aneurysms. Cellulite. Stained teeth. And I haven't even mentioned damage to the vessels that supply blood to the meat and two veg, have I?'

'No, you haven't.'

'Or the cancers.'

'No.'

'You've got seven days.'

Benson frowned. 'For what?'

'To get off this wing. If you're still here on Saturday morning, I'll have your kneecaps. Now get out.'

When Benson got back to his cell, he stopped dead at the entrance. Andrzej was leaning on the sink, dabbing at his smashed nose and mouth with toilet paper. He turned to Benson, muttering an explanation in Polish, and though Benson understood none of the words he knew what had happened: Crazy Andrzej had tried to stop Crazy Joe from taking Crazy Benson's property. But something else had happened, too, and Benson couldn't begin to express his gratitude. Because in this lawless, inhuman, noisy, filthy, forgotten universe, he'd found someone who'd do anything to cling on to his humanity. He'd found a friend, if only for a week.

PART ONE

Four days before trial

1

The Rt. Hon. Richard Merrington MP, Secretary of State for Justice, folded the *Daily Telegraph* in half and laid it on the breakfast table of the family home in Highgate, a terraced Georgian gem on Pond Square. He'd purchased it during his wilderness years, when, as a political journalist, he'd dreamed of being the one written about, rather than the one who'd done the writing. A headline had been brought to his attention by the use of a thick black marker. If his twenty-year-old son, David, hadn't been smiling he'd have sworn out loud – not at the item circled, but the desecration of his paper. Instead, he tried to sound merely disappointed.

'Yes, I know. That silly woman sent him the Blood Orange murder. I suppose the show starts all over again. No doubt you'll enjoy yourself enormously.'

'That's sexist for starters.'

'What is?'

'"Silly woman". Her name is Tess de Vere.'

'It's no different to "silly man".'

'The register's different. And it's patronising, too.'

'Really? Oh, I'll mind my—'

'Morning, darling.'

Merrington's wife, Pamela, breezed into the room, stopped, swung a glance between husband and son and said, 'Have you had another row?'

'Just warming up, my love. You know how it is' – he

spoke while buttering some toast – 'you get washed and dressed, you come downstairs, reasonably happy, and you find your paper vandalised by . . . God, how do I describe him? My son, I suppose, but that misses the point. Let's try a designer radical who finds the erosion of orthodox values not just amusing but—'

'He's pissed off that Benson's got a second big trial.'

'Don't swear, darling, please, it's frightful on the ear.'

'Oh, don't be silly, my love,' cooed Merrington. 'This is the rousing speech of a dissident.'

'I'm anti-establishment. There's a difference.'

'Really? In my dictionary—'

Pamela raised her voice. 'Benson's representing that awful man?'

'Yes, my love, and I see you're thrilled to bits. The underdog gets to bark once more. I wonder who gets bitten? Ah . . . hang on a moment . . . dear God, I never thought of that, it might just be me. Coffee, darling? Fresh orange juice?'

'The trial's next week, isn't it?'

'Yes, dear.' Merrington looked up as if startled, agreeably, by an outrageous idea. 'Thinking of attending? We could go together.'

The Hopton Yard killing had been bad enough. Merrington had come home to find his wife appalled by the stance he'd taken in relation to Paul Harbeton's family. His son had come home for the weekend appalled by the stance he'd taken in relation to William Benson. They'd formed a double act of indignation, which became a trinity when his mother finished reading the *Church Times*. None of them had remotely understood the delicacy of Merrington's position. And of course, he could hardly have revealed his various motivations, because they'd been, quite simply, ignoble. The appearance of Benson – a man with a *conviction* for murder – defending a woman *charged* with murder had been, he'd thought, a godsend for a newly appointed Justice Secretary. He'd joined his voice to the public outcry. An online petition calling on him to shut the likes of Benson down had prompted him to announce the necessary emergency legislation. Who on earth would want to oppose such measures? He'd been on to a winner. He'd presented himself as a man who listened to the voice of the people. Unfortunately, though, *other* people had spoken out. A second online petition had appeared, this one framed in terms of redemption. It had been called 'Everyone Deserves a Second Chance'. Which had, inevitably, attracted those inclined to think beyond what they might feel. To his astonishment, in tandem with Benson's performance at the Old Bailey, the mood of the country, and even the House, had threatened to turn against him. To avoid a climbdown within months of taking office, Merrington had nudged the proposed Bill sideways. He'd been compelled to meet a grieving mother and her four remaining sons, and tell them a promise is an elastic term in politics.

'We'll get there, Mrs Harbeton, I assure you. We just need to be patient. Choose our moment. Then strike with the sword of justice delayed. Not denied, please note; just delayed.'

He'd sounded as if he'd actually done something. They'd trooped out, consoled and deceived. Thereafter, it seemed as if the gods had cut him some slack, because Benson's career had gone mercifully quiet and other, more pressing, questions had occupied his Ministry. The journalists had gone after other fish; and not for the first time, Merrington had been grateful for the forgetfulness of the media industry, who liked their scandals fresh, not to mention flapping. Insofar as Merrington had given the matter any further thought, he'd hoped that Benson would either tire of humdrum crime or – preferably – starve, forcing him to leave the profession.

Regrettably, neither outcome had transpired. Benson's name had appeared once more in the press. This time, however, the issue was not so much the notoriety of the advocate, though that was ever present, but the tragedy of the victim. The Blood Orange murder had captured the public imagination.

'It really is an awful business,' said Pamela, pouring herself a coffee. 'That poor woman leaves Dover and comes to London wanting a better life, and then her nauseating jilted boyfriend, or whatever he was, tracks her down and . . . takes her life away.'

The *Sun* hadn't been so diffident: he'd drugged her, jammed a blood orange in her mouth and then strung her up by an extension cable, hoping it would look like suicide. And it wasn't all about having been dumped. By killing her he stood to net sixty grand from a joint inheritance. Money and bruised feelings were behind so many crimes, thought Merrington, dabbing his mouth. And protectiveness. Let's not forget protectiveness. Most people, if the stakes were high enough, would do anything to shield their family from harm. Even a Member of Parliament.

'I feel so frightfully sorry for her,' Pamela continued, adding milk. 'She'd been in London just over a week. She'd planned so many things. She'd bought a bike from a Red Cross shop. She'd got away from a dreadful place and a dreadful man and—'

'There's nothing dreadful about Dover, darling,' said Merrington.

'Well, every time we've gone there, somebody has sworn at you.'

'Spat, darling.'

'That happens everywhere, Mum.'

'David's right, you know. As my reverend father used to say, "Foxes have their holes . . ."'

And David, groaning, finished off the worn-out line: '". . . but the Son of Man has nowhere to lay his head." That says it all. You think you're some kind of Messiah.'

Merrington demurred, lightly. Then he picked up the *Telegraph* and turned to the obituaries hoping to unearth some good ideas for his own.

'Do you think Benson will pull out?' said Pamela, sitting down. 'It's such a sordid case.'

'He can't pull out, Mum,' said David energetically. 'He's bound by the Cab Rank Rule. All barristers are. If a brief lands on his desk he has to take it, regardless of what he thinks and regardless of the consequences.'

'But the man's guilty.'

Merrington looked up. 'Darling, we've been over this—'

'You don't know that,' said David, taking back control. 'The Crown says they're convinced he is. It goes no further. Now they have to prove it. Beyond reasonable doubt.'

'You're telling me Benson can't just tell him to own up?'

'My dear—'

'Of course he can,' David went on. 'He probably has done. But if the guy insists he's innocent, then Benson has no choice. He'll have to do everything in his power to undermine the evidence presented by the Crown . . . even if he personally finds it convincing.'

Merrington's eyes drifted towards his son. There'd been no swearing. No slang. He'd trotted out the tired explanations reserved for anyone puzzled (or outraged) by the mechanics of the criminal law. That Pamela still couldn't grasp the importance of the Cab Rank Rule came as no surprise to Merrington. He'd tried countless times to enlighten her. It was her special charm not to understand. What struck him now was David's phraseology. And the delivery. That 'regardless of the consequences' sounded vaguely middle-aged. Possibly self-important. It sounded like a quotation. As did 'evidence presented by the Crown'. And David was reading Greats. He was meant to be quoting Homer. Or Virgil. Merrington suppressed a smile. His son had been talking to a lawyer. Probably a silk. Maybe someone seeking preferment.

'Well, I'm delighted to note that a vandal knows something about life at the Bar. It may have escaped your notice, David, but the administration of justice is my remit.'

'Haven't you told your father?' said Pamela.

'No. Not yet.'

'Well, you must,' she enthused. 'Go on.'

David had the same jet-black hair as his mother, only his was longish and tangled, while hers was short and neat. They had the same fine eyebrows, the same soft mouth. But David possessed his father's mind – by Merrington's humble judgement, sharp and clean – along with his appetite for unsettling the complacent, though he was yet to discover the true pleasures of causing outrage.

'A friend of mine's mother is a barrister,' he began. 'We went to watch her in court.'

'And?'

'It was incredible. I met her afterwards and we talked.'

'No doubt she recognised your surname?'

'I kept it back.'

'What on earth for?'

'It's a distraction.' David used the word as if he meant 'embarrassment'. He shifted in his seat. 'I'm thinking of coming to the Bar after Oxford.'

To conceal his delight, Merrington pretended to finish reading a sentence. 'Not a bad idea.' This was promising. For once they were speaking the same language. Until now, when considering future employment, David had spoken of homeless charities, revealing that engaging moral alarm which he shared with his mother. Rashly, Merrington had praised the impulse but questioned the potential outcome, the underuse of his talents, which hadn't gone down well at all. Why? Because he'd denigrated the marginalised and those determined to help them. Merrington had been nonplussed. He loved Ralph McTell. So this talk of the Bar came as sweet honey from the rock. An appealing sincerity had settled upon David.

'I enjoy the argument,' he said.

'I'd noticed.'

'And there's always something in the balance . . . it's serious. Win or lose, it matters.'

Merrington feigned casual support. But mentally he was thinking of his grandfather's wig. It would be Merrington's gift to David. The imagined ceremony – a father and son moment in the drawing room – almost made his voice crack. 'I've numerous contacts at the Bar. I could make a few calls if you like. Can't promise anything.' Which, of course, was untrue. As he well knew, outcomes – the desired kind – came with power.

'No, it's okay.'

'I'd recommend one of the leaner commercial sets. Like Carnforth Buildings. Lord Wollman is Head of Chambers. He's an old—'

'I want to do crime.'

'Oh God, I wouldn't do that. There's no money it. Not any more. I've slashed the fees.'

'I don't care about the money.'

'You'll be the first criminal barrister who doesn't.'

'It's crime that interests me, Dad.'

'Are you sure?'

'Yes. But not with one of your conventional set-ups. They're just part of the establishment.'

Merrington hadn't got a first at Cambridge for nothing. He'd hadn't worked his way to a ministerial department without acquiring various rarefied skills. Back-stabbing a friend in the name of moral necessity was one of them – it had secured him his current position – but by far the most effective – and harmless – was an ability to read people's minds. Anticipating their next move and acting accordingly. And Merrington now knew why his earnest son had said nothing of the Bar; and why he was now moving cornflakes around his bowl, not daring to meet his father's eye. There was no doubt about it. After completing his studies in *Literae Humaniores* at Balliol College, Oxford, the son of the Secretary of State for Justice and Lord Chancellor (a combined position) would enrol on the Bar Professional Training Course, sit the end-of-year examinations, do brilliantly, because he was clever, and then seek a pupillage in a set of chambers that had somehow turned its back upon convention. Merrington only knew of one. And it only had one member. William Benson.

'Don't forget the homeless too quickly, David,' said Merrington, as if he'd glimpsed a light. 'They too need advocates.'

When Merrington got to Petty France he sat at his desk, looking at the chairs that had once been occupied by the Harbeton family. And he thought, with cold satisfaction, that he might well be many things, but he wasn't a hypocrite. The advice he'd given to that grieving household was the advice he'd give to himself: be patient and choose your moment. In the meantime, however, he'd act. Because the stakes were high and, like every other parent and potential criminal, Merrington would do anything to serve the best interests of his family. He picked up the phone and dialled a private number.

'Good morning, Bradley, it's Richard. We'll be needing your man with the gloves again.'

2

'I'm in a fix,' said Tess.

'You've dressed for the occasion,' said Sally.

'I've dressed for the job.'

'With Chanel No. 5?'

'You're unbearable. Can't you hear me? I'm not happy about this.'

They were seated in the Days of the Raj Tea Shop in Chelsea. Tess was there because it was a haunt of her friend and soulmate Sally Martindale. And Sally went there because there was an integrated Browhaus and Ministry of Waxing salon, offering treatments of such consequence that she thought they should be available on the National Health.

'Then you should never have instructed him in the first place,' said Sally.

'So you keep bloody well saying.'

'Because you keep bloody well complaining.'

'I don't. And for the last time, strictly speaking, I didn't instruct him. The client insisted.'

'Strictly speaking, you instructed him. And deep down you're pleased. You just daren't admit it to yourself.'

They'd met for breakfast near Sally's place of work, the Etterby Gallery, because Tess had a client conference with Benson nearby, at HMP Kensal Green. Sally had opted for the porridge, Tess for some toast. Tess's mind, however, lay elsewhere. A pending trial. And the renewal of her association with William Benson. Six months previously, magistrates in Tottenham had committed Brent Stainsby for trial at the Old Bailey for the murder of Diane Heybridge, remanding him into custody. News of the case had spread quickly. The facts, simple and brutal, had roused pity and disgust among Londoners and throughout the south-east. He'd started getting hate mail. He'd been beaten up by his own cellmate. In a panic, and irrationally, he'd sacked his solicitor and called Coker & Dale, wanting to speak to Tess. And it became abundantly clear during the initial conference that by instructing Tess he thought he'd be getting Benson as well – their two names were twinned in his mind because of the Hopton Yard killing – and he wanted Benson and no one else. He wanted Tess and no one else. So Tess's room for manoeuvre had been limited. In due course, she'd taken instructions and sent the brief to Archie Congreve, Benson's clerk. At that point, the tabloid press had opened fire. Having campaigned to shut Benson down at the outset of his career, and failed, they'd now returned to the fray, ostensibly as champions of Stainsby's tragic victim, their goal to denigrate Benson, the killer who'd trumped a Justice Secretary. And so Diane Heybridge had become a story. As had Benson. Again. All that aside, it was a distressing case made all the more difficult by the attitude of the accused.

'Stainsby won't admit anything,' said Tess. 'Not unless he absolutely has to. He seems to think that Benson is some sort of magician . . . that he's going to pull off a mind-boggling trick once the trial is underway. But that isn't going to happen. Stainsby's going to get life.'

'He's no chance?'

'Well, I can't see any.'

Tess didn't know where to begin. And she had to admit that for the first time as a lawyer she was having real difficulty grafting herself onto her client's case. Like everyone else, she felt for the woman he'd allegedly murdered. Diane Heybridge had been a simple girl without much of a past and not much of a future. She'd been bullied and browbeaten and shoved aside by Stainsby since the day they'd met. Every witness had said so. She'd never really lived. She'd never really been happy. It was hard to look at the autopsy photographs – a wad of unforgiving close-ups – without thinking that a deeper injustice had taken place. Something monumental. Tess and Sally had suffered their ups and downs, some of them grave, some of them heartbreaking, but they'd each enjoyed a golden upbringing, with countless opportunities to develop themselves, with friends and family nearby to help manage the rougher terrain. What of Diane? A woman just like Tess or Sally. She'd never had a chance from the moment she was born.

'He started off denying he'd driven from Dover to London, and then he was shown the CCTV footage. He still denied he'd gone to see Diane, until a witness put him outside her flat the night she was killed. He denied buying a takeaway until the receipt was found in his coat pocket. He denies smoking in the flat, even though a cigarette butt was found by the body. His DNA is on the electric cable that was tied around her neck. He's picked up by the CCTV cameras heading home. He won't discuss the detail because he's hoping the witnesses will back off. He's—'

'Thick?'

'No, in a strange way this guy is clever. But he's an egotist too, blind to the importance of other people: those close to him, and those who aren't, but who might help him.'

'Except for Benson,' said Sally. 'He's not blind to Benson.'

'No. You're right there.'

Which wasn't entirely surprising. Leaving aside Benson *qua* putative magician, he'd wanted London's most controversial barrister for another reason. Stainsby had been a fisherman. Likewise his father and both of his grandfathers. They'd all been part of the ancient fishing industry in Kent, or what remained of it, operating only a short distance from the waters fished by Benson's father off the Norfolk coast. For Benson, too, came from a fishing background, though he'd abandoned the nets and lobster pots for a degree in philosophy. If he'd ever thought of going back to sea with his father after graduation, that possibility had been overtaken during the tense days he'd sat in the dock at the Old Bailey watching Helen Camberley QC trying to save his life. He'd fallen for the Bar. Plato and the rest had been shown the door. And now, after an impossible journey from a prison cell to his own chambers, Benson was representing Stainsby, who seemed to think their shared background would make him try that little bit harder. Tess said:

'Hopefully, after this last conference, he'll plead. Failing in that, we'll have a hopeless trial.'

Sally savoured her porridge. 'Which means that T de V will be shoulder to shoulder with WB.'

'Yes.'

'Leaning over the same desk. Examining important documents.'

'Oh lay off.'

'Sharing an awful journey.'

'I can't bear it.'

'He's dark and dangerous and demonised. What more do you want?'

'God, you're tiresome.'

'And he's got a boat. A brightly painted barge or something. With an Aga. Do you want my advice?'

Tess closed her eyes. She'd been drowned in advice. Getting anywhere near Benson attracted advice like flies to jam. All of it the same: get out of there.

'My advice comes for free,' said Sally.

'I don't want it.'

Sally became serious. 'Go back to your investigation.'

'What?'

This sudden shift from mischief to gravity was Sally's modus operandi. On first meeting as undergraduates at Oxford, Tess, fresh from rural Ireland, had thought this

English gal superficial – entertainingly so – and mildly eccentric, particularly in relation to her choice of clothing, which, back then and since, had often been referential – to forgotten fads, past revolutions and lesser-known paintings. Everything she'd worn had prompted a question. And Tess had asked them. Which had been the beginning of her enlightenment. For Tess had soon learned that this playful brunette was, in fact, deeply serious . . . a sort of desert ascetic with a taste for Liebfraumilch, indifferent to existentialist thought and intolerant of German words for various kinds of suffering.

'When you walked back into his life after sixteen years—'

'He walked back into mine, remember. He lured me to that barge with an article in the *Guardian* telling his story, explaining that he'd opened his own set of chambers. He knew I'd read it. He knew I'd come offering help.'

'And you offered help. You needn't have done. You walked back into his life. And you remained there on one condition: that you'd find out once and for all if he was innocent. We were getting somewhere, Tess. And you're only in a fix because you don't know the answer.'

Sally seemed to shift position. Her voice, with its crisp respect for consonants, became ponderous:

'He told you that he didn't kill Paul Harbeton. He told the world that he did, and he said he only lied in order to get rehabilitated. Because that was the only way to come to the Bar. Where he could fight the good fight. With people like you.' She paused to sip her Darjeeling. 'I wonder where the truth lies. If you knew the answer to *that* one, you wouldn't be sitting here wringing your hands – your cuticles are advancing, by the way – you'd be on that barge—'

'You're wrong, Sally. And you've forgotten something. We found the first great lie and I don't want to find any more.'

'Then you should never have sent him that brief. But you did.'

They fell silent. And in the interlude Tess had to admit a truth she'd been attempting to suppress: quite apart from any issues of trust, she wanted to watch Benson in court again, hear the change in his voice, feel the electricity in the air . . .

'Stainsby will plead next week,' she said sharply. 'I'll go my way, Benson will go his. And our investigation into his trial remains closed. Okay?'

'Indubitably.'

Sally finished her Nightrunner's of Bengal Slow-Acting Porridge and Tess her Maharaja's Toast. There wasn't much else to say.

Tess parked her cherry red 1964 Mini at the mouth of a street near to the Green. She then walked to a huge dented door in the prison wall, where she'd agreed to meet Benson. This entrance was for legal visitors only. Graffiti climbed up the metal door, spreading over the bricks on either side. The gateway to hell had to look something like this. Even now, after so many years, she hated prison visits, passing from an ordinary street into the constant noise and that awful smell that she somehow associated with rotting food.

Tess checked her watch. Benson was late. Looking around, she adjusted her velvet hat. She bent over to give her new shoes a rub with a tissue. She came upright and felt oddly exposed. And she wondered where Benson might be.

3

And there he was, in his old blue duffel coat.

Benson was trying to not run, which made his rapid walk faintly ludicrous. Tess thought of Charlie Chaplin. And she thought of the rumours. That interest in Benson generated by the Hopton Yard killing had faded. Sure, he performed well in other cases. But basic crime was basic crime. It didn't take a genius. And given Benson's baggage, you could never work out if he'd lost a trial because the jury didn't trust him, or because the evidence was too strong. As a result, solicitors were instructing him less and less. Tess had heard he was on his way out.

'I can explain,' said Benson, panting, arranging his tie. 'I overslept and then I was late for a meeting with my bank – actually, it's a building society, a cooperative – which made me late for you, and it shouldn't have happened' – he began tidying his hair, making a side parting with his fingers – 'I should have taken the Tube. Or a taxi. I'm sorry. We'd better go straight in.'

'Yes, I think we better had.'

'I'm not that keen on prison visits,' he said, ringing the bell.

'Me neither.'

'I might as well tell you now, I get flashbacks.'

'I understand.'

'It's nice to see you again.'

'You too.'

'It's been a while.'

'Yes.'

'Almost a year.'

'You haven't changed.'

'Neither have you.'

Having instructed Benson, Tess had then neatly avoided the subsequent client conference. Rather than attend, she'd sent along Basil, her assistant, who'd also stood in for the preliminary hearings. With the trial itself now imminent, she'd finally turned up. Boots struck the ground on the other side of the wall.

'About being late, I'm sorry. Truly.'

'It's okay.'

'It won't happen again.'

'No problem.'

'Did I tell you I have a new cat?'

'No.'

'He's called Traddles. He'd eat a horse if it came in a tin.'

'Bicycle clips.'

'Pardon?'

Tess pointed down to Benson's ankles. 'You'd better take them off.'

Benson pocketed the clips and then, anticipating the arrival of the guard, he began to fidget and bite his lip, shifting from foot to foot. (According to Basil, Benson had behaved in an identical manner while waiting for the first conference.) But what alarmed Tess now was not so much Benson's quirks, or the clanging open of the door, or the jangling of keys on a chain hanging from the guard's belt, or the sudden and awful contraction of the horizon to a cramped courtyard of stained brick topped with razor wire, or the relentless clanging and shouting, or the strange smell of decay. It was that Benson had turned up empty-handed. He'd come running without the brief or any means of taking notes.

Tess watched Benson expectantly.

He was seated, eyes closed, breathing deeply, not even trying to hide his panic. He winced at every noise. Perspiration gathered on his brow. He was trembling. And then it happened, just like Basil said it would. As the door handle moved, seconds before Brent Stainsby entered the room, Benson opened his eyes and became a totally different man.

'Take a seat, please, Mr Stainsby,' he said, nodding towards a chair bolted to the floor on the other side of the bolted-down table.

Stainsby, however, could barely contain himself. Still standing, anonymous in grey jogging bottoms and maroon T-shirt, he tipped out words that no one else would listen to:

'You've got to get me out of here. People have knives. There's a stabbing every week. And there's drugs everywhere. The screws are scared to hell. The place is run by gangs. They'd gut you for a burn. A headbanger killed himself two days back. There's still blood all over—'

'Please sit down, Mr Stainsby,' said Benson. 'We've a lot of ground to cover. The trial is going ahead and this time you have to answer my questions.'

From the beginning, Stainsby had refused to give detailed instructions; foolish and suspicious, he'd been holding out, hoping the Crown would drop the case. But they hadn't.

'Didn't you hear me?' he growled.

'I did. Take a seat.' Stainsby didn't move, so Benson relented. 'I understand you're on the Numbers. Rule forty-five?'

'Yeah, but so what? I'm still at risk.'

'You've been segregated. You're safe.'

'I'm not safe anywhere . . . you've got to get me out. I've been warned. Someone's out to kill me.'

'Then you'd better remain on the Numbers. In my day, we called it "Cucumbers". Have you heard of that one?'

'I want out. The place is going to explode.'

Tess smiled reassurance, but inside she regarded Stainsby with dismay. He was heavily built, with sloping shoulders. His hair had been recently clipped, leaving black bristles over his scalp. His mouth hung slightly open. He looked brutal and stupid. Pointing with authority at the chair, Benson said:

'I can't get you out. That's up to the jury. If they don't accept what you say, you'll spend at least fourteen years in places just like this. Some of them worse. If you plead, you'll get credit from the judge. Which means less time inside. Have you given any thought to our last—'

'I'm not pleading, okay? Because I didn't kill her. Look, I've told you. Diane was weak. Weak in the head' – Stainsby was tapping his skull with a thick, dirty finger as he sat down. 'She topped herself, okay? She was on all sorts of tablets and she overdosed and she hung herself. It's simple.'

'If only it were, Mr Stainsby.'

Stainsby made a guttural noise like a trapped animal. 'I didn't kill her, Mr Benson. What else can I say? I'm not clever like you, all right? I can't think up any arguments and reasons. I can only tell you the truth.'

'Well, that will help a great deal,' said Benson. 'Why did you deny going to London? Deny seeing Diane? Deny bringing her medicines? Deny buying a takeaway? Deny—'

'Because they were after me. The pigs weren't listening.'

'"The pigs" being the police?'

'Yeah, who else? As soon as they arrested me it was all over and done with, like the Birmingham Six. They wouldn't listen to anything I said. It's not what they say, Mr Benson. It's how they look at you. It's how they speak to you. And I could tell they were going to put me down for this one, even though I had nothing to do with it.'

'But why lie?'

'I was scared, right? I didn't want to tell them anything, because they were after me, okay?'

'"They", I assume, is DCI Goodshaw?'

'Yeah, and his mates. They came to Dover on the Sunday, the day after they'd found the body, okay? Did they say, "We're sorry to tell you your girlfriend's dead"? No, they looked at me like I was dirt and searched the bloody flat. They'd decided I'd killed her before they'd even met me. That's why I told them nothing. Not a damned thing. And now they're using it against me. I told them and I'm telling you: it's suicide. Diane was weak in the head. It's simple, but they want to pin it on me.'

Tess wrote down all these replies. But she wasn't really listening. Stainsby's way of speaking, especially about Diane, disgusted her, like it must have disgusted DCI Goodshaw, and like it would certainly disgust and alienate a jury. Tess glanced at Benson. He was concentrating fiercely.

'Tell me about Diane's mother, Rosie Heybridge.'

'She's a cow.'

'Why?'

'She never liked me.'

'Why?'

'Because of my mum and dad.'

'To be clear, you're talking about Caroline and Frank Stainsby?'

'Yeah.'

'I don't understand why Rosie would dislike you because of your parents.'

'Because Diane was close to my mum. And when she died and my dad went to pieces, Diane was there for him. They'd have a curry every Friday night. Rosie was jealous. She took it out on me.'

Benson nodded as if he'd jotted down all the details. He seemed to turn a page in his mind.

'What about the Dover Five?'

'A bunch of women.'

'That's not especially helpful.'

'Diane's friends. They've all been left on the shelf. With Diane gone, there's only four now.'

'Yes, I suppose there are. That would be Samantha, Angela—'

'Cathy and Jane, yeah.'

'Did you get on with any of them?'

'Nah.'

'Why?'

'They were jealous of Diane. Because Diane had a fella – me. It's simple.'

'I see. Were these close friends?'

'Well, she saw them every Saturday night.'

'Was Diane closer to any one of them in particular?'

'Yeah, Jane Tapster. Best friends since they were thirteen. Weighs about six tons. She's the biggest loser of the lot.'

Benson assumed a mandarin calm, but only for a moment. The severe attention to detail soon returned.

'But not for Diane,' he insisted. 'For Diane, Jane was special?'

'Yes, I suppose so. They both worked at Greggs. They'd see each other on their own sometimes, you know, apart from going out as a fivesome. Listen, you've got to get me out of here. Even the screws are scared. They're not in control. There are drones bringing in drugs as if they were pizzas. You just—'

'I can't help you in prison. I can only help you in court. Your father died on the thirty-first of July 2015. The will was read out by Mr Hargreaves, your solicitor, on the twelfth of August. Was that the first time you'd heard about the Aviva life insurance policy?'

'Bloody right. My dad never mentioned it.'

'Diane had been left your mother's jewellery too?'

'Yeah.'

'The pay-out on the policy was £63,400. Your dad wanted that sum divided equally between you and—'

'False. Stop right there.' Stainsby had squared his shoulders. 'We don't know what my dad really wanted because when my dad signed that will, me and Diane were together. An item. She left me that night, the night she found out about the bloody money.'

'And so you went to see Mr Hargreaves the next morning – the thirteenth – and said, "I'll do time before she gets anything from my parents."'

'Yeah.'

'And he explained that, legally, Diane was a beneficiary and you couldn't prevent her from receiving the bequest?'

'Yeah, that's right.'

'On the seventeenth an altercation took place at Greggs, Diane's place of work. You made a scene and said, "You won't see a penny of that policy and you will never, ever wear my mother's jewellery."'

'Sounds about right.'

'The police were called. You were arrested and given an informal warning.'

'Yeah. I was told to keep away from Diane, and I did.'

'Friday the eighteenth of September, a month later: probate comes through. When informed by Mr Hargreaves that the policy can now be paid out, and that Diane is entitled to a half share, you say, "I'll choke her first." Correct?'

'Nah. And if I did, I didn't mean it. I was off my head.'

Benson nodded. He introduced a new topic:

'Stainsby's Seafood Locker Ltd. You set that up in 2007?'

'Yeah.'

'To deliver fresh seafood from the south-east coast?'

'Using all my contacts, yeah.'

'The business barely broke even.'

'I did my best, okay? Christ, I wasn't going to go on the dole.'

'Which meant you were financially dependent on Diane?'

'We were a couple.'

'Okay, let's sum up. You and Diane are together for fourteen years. Your father dies. Diane discovers she's going to receive about £30K. That same evening, she leaves you. You make various threats over the next few days. Notwithstanding

Diane's legal rights, you make it clear she will never touch the money or your mother's jewellery.'

'That's it. You've got it.'

'Thank you.' Benson seemed to have finished. His face was expressionless. Tess, watching him closely, pen poised, became gradually uncomfortable. The silence was almost threatening. Stainsby felt the chill.

'What's wrong?'

'Nothing, Mr Stainsby,' replied Benson. 'I'm just puzzled.'

'By what?'

'The great change.'

'What great change?'

'You tell me, please. What happened between ten-fifteen a.m. on Friday the eighteenth of September, when you told Mr Hargreaves that you'd do time before Diane received anything, and eleven a.m. on Monday the twenty-eighth of September, when you turned up at Mr Hargreaves's office saying you'd had a change of heart. Not that the change would make any difference, because the money and jewellery would have gone to Diane anyway. That's eight days. Give me the explanation.'

'I cooled down. It's simple.'

'No, you didn't. You're still angry now.'

'I'm angry because I've been banged up in hell over this business. I'm angry with Diane for killing herself and putting me here.'

'You went to see Mr Hargreaves for another reason.'

'And what might that be?'

'You wanted Diane's address. And he wouldn't give it to you.'

Stainsby was leaning forward, his eyes were bloodshot, his skin moist and pale.

'No, he wouldn't.'

'And so you went to Cathy Dawson, one of the Dover

Five. And you told Cathy that you wanted to make up with Diane, but that it was all to be a secret. Having got the address, you—'

'I've had enough.' Stainsby stood up, his fists clenched. 'You're my brief, you're meant to be fighting for me.'

'Do sit down, Mr Stainsby. If you can't handle someone who is on your side, you won't handle this trial, when everyone's against you. Take a deep breath and answer my questions. The evidence suggests you went to London because you'd decided to kill her. You needed the money. All of it. Because your business was going nowhere. You were furious. Because Diane, the only girl with a fella, had dropped you as soon as she could afford to get away.'

'But I didn't, Mr Benson. I didn't kill her. I swear . . . on my mother's life. Look, you've got to get me out of here. The place is going to blow.'

4

Tess examined her notes. And she saw the pattern. Benson had dealt with the key relationships and was now moving to the crime scene. He'd planned his approach meticulously and he didn't need the papers. He'd memorised them. Just like he was memorising Stainsby's answers. Writing it all down, Tess couldn't escape a growing sense of dread. Stainsby was describing his arrival in Tottenham at around 7.30 p.m. She could see him slouching outside the flat, the first floor of a grim building, 15C Heston Road, off Broad Lane, just a few hours before Diane died with an electric cable tied around her neck. Stainsby was speaking, his rough hands making rough gestures. Like he'd told the pigs (he said), he'd come all the way from Dover to make up. He'd bought a curry, because it was a Friday night. It's what Diane had always done with his father, so it was a kind of peace gesture. He'd wanted her to relax. Not feel threatened. He'd bought some cans of beer. He'd brought his mother's jewellery. He'd rung the doorbell and said sorry. And Tess felt her heart judder.

'What was Diane's reaction when she saw the jewellery?' asked Benson.

'She was sad. She cried. She went into her bedroom to put it all on.'

'Why the bedroom?'

'She wanted to see herself in the mirror.'

'Did you follow her?'

'No.'

'So, she came back wearing earrings, a bracelet and a pendant on a chain?'

'Yeah.'

'Still crying?'

'Yeah. Well, sniffing.'

'And then you ate?'

'Yeah.'

'Off plates or out of the cartons?'

'Plates.'

'Drank beer?'

'Yeah.'

'Listened to David Bowie?'

'Yeah.'

'What did you talk about?'

'Nothing much. My mum and dad. Good times in Dover.'

'Did you smoke?'

'Nah.'

'Not just during the meal, but at any time while you were with Diane, up to the time you left?'

'Nah.'

'The witness who found Diane's body the next day says she could smell smoke in the air.'

'Not me.'

'Ash was found on an armchair.'

'I didn't sit on no armchair.'

'A cigarette butt was found in the bedroom, at Diane's feet.'

'Not mine.'

'The brand is the brand you smoke.'

'So what?'

'Durand. French. They're not that common. I checked every shop in Tottenham and no one sells them. I went to Dover. I found them in three—'

'I didn't go anywhere near Diane's bedroom. That butt has nothing to do with me.'

'It has. Your DNA is on it.'

'Then someone planted it.'

'Who?'

'The pigs.'

'Why?'

'How the hell would I know? Ask Goodshaw. He's the one who's after me.'

'What happened after the meal? Give me all the detail. Leave nothing out.'

'We said goodbye. I wanted to get back to Dover. It was late.'

'What time was this?'

'Getting on for eleven.'

'Did you kiss her?'

'Nah. Why?'

'These things usually happen after a reconciliation. With most people, anyway.'

'Not me. We were finished. She'd moved on. It's simple.'

'Did you at least shake hands?'

'Nah.'

'Can you explain how two of your hairs came to be found on her cardigan?'

'No, I can't.'

'Or one of them on the inside of the sticky tape wrapped around her wrists?'

'Sorry. No idea.'

'Did you sit on the armchair nearest the window?'

'I already told you, I didn't sit on no armchair.'

'Because a single hair was found on the headrest.'

'Not mine.'

'It is.'

'The extension cable around Diane's neck has your DNA on it. How—'

'Never touched it.'

'You did.'

'I didn't. Didn't even see the thing.'

Maybe he *is* thick, thought Tess. If you're going to kill someone and lie, then you might as well lie about evidence that will help your defence. She understood his denying he'd smoked, because that tied him to the fag end. But Stainsby had refused to explain the hair. And all because he couldn't admit to any sign of affection between himself and the woman who'd dumped him. God, he was awful. Tess just wanted to get out of the room. Benson seemed to feel the same way because he stood up and went to the barred window, looking outside, towards the clean blue sky. Quietly, he said, 'Carry on. Remember, leave nothing out. I want every detail.'

'I put on my coat. I picked up the cartons and the cans. And I left.'

'What did you do with the rubbish?'

'I threw it in a bin, twenty yards from the flat.'

'Why not use Diane's? It was five yards from the dining table.'

'Look, I was trying to be nice, okay, clearing up, all right? Christ, what's wrong with that?'

'You left a can behind.'

'Yeah, Diane's, because she hadn't finished. I tidied up and I left. That's it. End of story. It's simple.'

'Are you sure?'

'Yeah. Why?'

'What about the jewellery? I asked you to leave nothing out.'

Stainsby, until now twitching constantly, became eerily still; Benson, speaking slowly, returned to his chair. 'She'd put on the bracelet and the earrings, and the pendant on a chain. How did you get them back?'

Tess could hardly follow the answer. Stainsby was scratching the side of his scalp with his stubby, nail-bitten fingers, saying Diane hadn't wanted to keep them. He said he'd put them in his jacket pocket just before leaving for Dover. He mumbled something else, only Tess had finally lost her concentration. She'd been stunned by a grotesque vision: the sight of Stainsby removing each item from Diane's body while she struggled with death. Had Benson seen the same appalling moment? Tess wasn't sure. He moved on relentlessly. Another mental page seemed to turn.

'Diane kept her medicines in a shoebox,' he began. 'And when she went to London, she left the shoebox behind. Why did you bring it with the curry and the beer and the jewellery?'

Stainsby looked at Benson as if he'd only half a brain. 'Diane's been taking pills for years. I thought she might need them. I was going to chuck it out and then I thought she might go under again. She was soft in the head, you know.'

'Yes, so you keep saying.'

'But she was. She'd walk around with bags under her eyes and say nothing.'

'I see. Do you know how many brands of medication were in that box?'

'Seven or eight? I don't know.'

'Six. There were six. Do you know the names of any of them?'

'Nah. Why would I? I don't need stuff like that.'

'Did Diane ever tell you that particular medicines had made her feel ill? That she'd suffered disturbing side effects?'

'No. She never talked about her pills or whatever. She kept all that to herself.'

'She never mentioned Betripline? Or its full name, benzotriptyline? It's an antidepressant. Very powerful.'

'Nah. Never.'

'It's the drug they found in her stomach. Along with the curry. And the beer.'

'She must have taken them after I'd gone. It's simple.'

'Even though she knew they'd give her double vision, make her dizzy and send her to sleep?'

'It's what she did.'

'What about Fluvopram?'

'Never heard of it.'

'That, too, was in her stomach. This one made her weak and sweaty.'

'News to me.'

'The problem is, Mr Stainsby, it doesn't quite make sense. If Diane wanted to hang herself, she wouldn't take a couple of drugs that would make the task all the harder to perform . . . if not impossible. Medication that should never be taken with alcohol.'

Stainsby groaned as if he'd seen through a ruse. His bleary eyes swung between Benson and Tess. He jerked his head as if to wink, only he didn't. 'I ain't pleading, okay? I don't have the answers to your clever questions, but that doesn't mean I killed Diane. It means I'm in a corner. It means I need a good brief. Are you going to fight for me or what?'

Benson stood up, nodding to the guard on the other side of the window. 'Tooth and nail, Mr Stainsby. Tooth and nail. Oh, by the way' – the door handle moved – 'did you ever see Diane eat a blood orange?'

Tess, trying to read Stainsby's coarse features, turned cold. Either a nerve flickered at the corner of his mouth or he gave the hint of a smile.

'Never, Mr Benson. Not once.'

'He just raised fit-up for the first time,' said Benson. 'Until now, he's never suggested that Goodshaw could have planted evidence in the flat.'

He'd walked Tess to her Mini. They'd each been lost in their thoughts. For Tess, unpleasant ones, dark stains in the mind that would still be there when she stepped out of the shower later that night.

'He's making it up as he goes along. I don't take it seriously.'

'And he talked about pills. The drugs mixed in the food came from sachets. They were in powder form.'

'Doesn't mean a thing. There were pills in the box.'

Benson didn't react; then he said, 'Anyway, what do you make of—'

'He's lying,' snapped Tess. 'He killed her and he's got no remorse. There's no grief. There's no pity, no compassion, no regret . . . nothing. Just self-obsession. He still doesn't know why she left him; and I've no idea why she ever went with him. He's the reason she needed fistfuls of antidepressants. What a creep. That's what I make of him.'

Benson removed his bicycle clips from his pocket and began turning them around in his hands as if preparing to throw a horseshoe.

'I was going to say, what do you make of the missing witness?'

'What missing witness?'

'Jane Tapster, "the biggest loser of the lot".'

Tess thought for a moment and then coloured slightly. She'd missed something. Benson seemed to be taking aim.

'It's intriguing,' he said. 'The best friend who knows the most is the only member of the Dover Five who didn't provide a witness statement. The person who cared the most has said nothing.'

Tess didn't answer. Benson had done it again. He'd brought the case alive. Taking Tess's silence for a hint, Benson immediately obliged:

'Well, enough of that. I'd better hit the road.'

'Yes. Me too.'

'See you on Monday, I suppose.'

'Yep. Number Two Court. Ten a.m.'

After an awkward shuffle, Benson set off to retrieve his bicycle. She watched him walk along the street, empty save for a tatty blue van, keeping himself wide of the prison wall, his gaze averted. A hunched figure surrounded by graffiti and litter. An ex-con who was somehow still inside. On the Numbers. And Tess felt a stab of longing: that life, and relationships, might be simple. She was confused. She wanted Benson out of her life and she wanted to give him a lift. Take him back to chambers. Have a bite of lunch. She'd warmed – again – to his contradictions. He was so broke he couldn't afford a taxi or the Tube. And yet he'd gone to Dover on the trail of obscure French cigarettes. All for a misogynist and liar who'd been charged with a murder he said he didn't commit.

5

Benson pedalled furiously, flogging himself through Pentonville and Shoreditch onto Bishopsgate. He was nearly there; nearly at Congreve Chambers, where fish and seafood had been sold for a hundred and seventeen years, until Archie had steered the family business into bankruptcy, landing himself a custodial sentence for tax fraud in the process.

What the hell was he racing for? Because he'd seen that blue van? No, he was used to being tailed, used to people winding the window down to shout abuse at him, or chuck a half-eaten sandwich in his face. Was it the desire to open a fresh brief? It couldn't be; he didn't have one. And his attention wasn't even fixed on the road. It lay with Tess de Vere's worn velvet hat, and that expression in her eyes when she'd turned to greet him. He could still see the anxiety when he walked into the clerk's room.

'Mr Edgeworth. How very nice to see you again.'

Only it wasn't.

Mr Edgeworth was the manager of the Whitechapel Building Society. He was also an old friend of George Braithwaite, the solicitor who'd represented Benson in his murder trial. More to the point, he'd been appointed the sole trustee of funds subsequently advanced, anonymously, to effect Benson's transition from a prison cell to the Bar. Those funds had been handled by Mr Edgeworth. And when Benson had decided to go it alone, it was Mr Edgeworth who'd granted him a loan of £18,000 to convert a fishmonger's into a set of chambers. That was last year. They'd met a few hours ago to discuss Benson's overdraft and yet another default on his loan payments. And yet another extension had been granted.

'I didn't call Head Office,' he said, after following Benson into the Gutting Room, his study. 'Head Office called me. Just after you'd gone. They want immediate action. You see, we're struggling, too. As a small outfit, we're not going to survive unless . . .'

He was passing the brim of his grey trilby through his fingers.

'Look, I don't like doing this, Mr Benson. I have to take your chequebook. You can only draw out thirty pounds a day. We'll honour existing standing orders and direct debits.'

'I imagine that's thanks to you, and not Head Office.'

'It is.'

'I'm grateful.'

'But there's one condition. You see, Head Office came up with a solution we hadn't thought about.'

'And what might that be?'

'Sell your barge.'

Benson laughed. 'It's my home.'

'To them it's an asset. And assets can be realised to pay off debts. I'm sorry. Very sorry.'

Benson was adamant. 'They can't make me sell *The Wooden Doll*. They don't have the right.'

'No, they don't. But they don't have to offer you financial services either. If they withdraw them, you're finished. No bank or building society will take you. Either you get quick money from some other source, or you liquidate the only asset you've got. Once the loan has been repaid, we'll be back to normal. We can both forget about Head Office.'

Benson couldn't help but think of Friday nights when he played Monopoly with Archie, his four sisters and CJ, their ancient father. Unlike the Head Office people, the Congreve women were ruthless from the moment they were owed anything, and they'd force you under even if your only debt was two quid for landing on the Old Kent Road. Benson couldn't believe Mr Edgeworth's employers could match them for brutality; but there was something in that troubled man's expression that told him he was very much mistaken.

'If your houseboat isn't on the market within a week, Head Office will start proceedings. They'll get a writ of control. You'll get seven days' notice and then a High Court enforcement officer will turn up at Seymour Basin and sail your home down the Albert Canal and sell it for less than you'd like. Grasp the nettle, Mr Benson. I am very sorry about this. Truly.'

Benson hardly acknowledged Mr Edgeworth's departure, or the entry of Archie and Molly, the Cockney clerk and Geordie typist whom Mr Edgeworth had described only that morning – though politely – as excess baggage. Given that they were both on the ample side, the image had at least been apposite. But that was where the accuracy of the remark ended. These two figures, both in their sixties, were essential to Benson's well-being. The usual distinctions of the workplace didn't apply. There was no hierarchy of importance. They were friends, not colleagues. Musketeers without a king. And, as always, these friends had taken advantage of Benson's need to leave his door ajar – a habit formed since leaving prison. They'd tuned in:

'What's a writ of control?' asked Archie, big hands in the pockets of his baggy corduroy trousers.

'A fi fa,' said Molly, smoothing her apron. 'A writ of fieri facias.'

'What's one of them?'

'They're used to enforce a judgment in the High Court.'

'And the enforcement officer?'

'A sort of bailiff. They seize and sell goods to the value of the judgment.'

Archie was still troubled by the Latin. 'What the hell is going on?'

Benson slumped in the chair at his desk. Until now there'd been a certain comedy in his dealings with Mr Edgeworth: the back and forth had come to feel like a game without consequences. He'd been deceiving himself. Archie took a step forward.

'Tell me, Rizla, what's happened?'

'You can't call me that, Archie. That was my prison name. We don't share a cell any more. And—'

'What's all this about a loan?'

'It's nothing.'

'Nothing? Do you think I'm—'

Molly placed a hand on the heavy raised arm. The much smaller of the two, she nonetheless commanded complete authority. 'Mr Congreve, I'm not just a typist: I know a thing or two about wrestling. And when you've just been floored by a Damascus head and leglock, you don't want to answer any questions. You need to get off the canvas first.'

Molly quickly left the room and Archie sat down in an old leather armchair, one of two picked up for twenty quid from the Salvation Army. The kettle rattled in the distance, and presently Molly, always a busy mover, returned with a pot of tea, mugs and a plate of biscuits. Finally seated, she took a deep breath and spoke while exhaling:

'Now, Mr Benson, to quote Mr Congreve: what the hell is going on?'

And so Benson explained how he'd borrowed the capital to refurbish the building, knowing full well that Archie would think it had all come from Benson's benefactor. How he knew that Archie was broke; that his family wasn't far from broke. How he could never dream of allowing Congreve's, a building steeped in family pride, to be subject to a mortgage that Benson might fail to repay. How he'd risked, it turned out, *The Wooden Doll*.

'I've not been pulling enough work in,' said Benson. 'It's as simple as that.'

'You should have told me, Rizla.'

'I couldn't.'

'After all we've been through?'

'You'd have gone to your dad and you'd have gone to your sisters and they'd all have said, "We can sort this." You'd have said the same thing.'

'Dead right.'

'And Head Office would now be after this building. Your history, and theirs. Sorry, Archie, I couldn't take that risk. I thought I could grind down the debt, but I haven't.'

Molly's tone suggested she wouldn't take no for an answer. 'Have a digestive, Mr Benson.'

'We share the debt, Rizla,' said Archie.

Benson felt so much better. Having spoken of his doubt the attendant anxiety had lost some of its grip. And he'd underestimated the importance of friendship. He managed a smile.

'I'm not worried,' he said. 'Head Office can't take my barge. It's my home. So it's not a chattel. And the scope of the writ doesn't include—'

'It does,' said Molly. She touched her hair as if getting ready to have her photo taken. And for a moment, Benson understood the management committee of Latchford Chambers. Forty years of typing up opinions dictated by its top QCs had given Molly a certain acumen, which she'd flaunted when correcting the work of junior counsel. She'd come to Benson unappeased by a generous redundancy package. '*Chelsea Yacht and Boat Co.* v. *Pope*,' she said smartly.

'Come off it.'

'Predictable outcome, really. A houseboat was held to be a chattel even though it was joined to the land by service pipes, cables, ropes and all sorts.'

'Why's that predictable?' said Archie.

'Well in *Cave* v. *Capel* – this is a funny case – a bailiff seized a caravan, but the owner was still inside, and—'

'Okay, I'm off the canvas,' said Benson, raising his voice. 'If they seize my boat—'

'You can stay upstairs,' said Archie.

'But you live upstairs.'

'There's a box room. I'd take it, but I wouldn't fit it. I've eaten too many pies. We'll sort this, Rizla. We're going to survive. We've beaten worse odds.'

They had. Professionally and personally. Benson didn't know what to say. On coming to the Bar he'd had rubbish dumped at his gate. He'd been beaten up. He'd been sworn at. He'd had countless doors slammed in his face. But the Congreve family had come to his side, and, excepting the grubby fight for wealth on Friday nights, they'd stayed there. God alone knew if they'd been abused for their open hearts; their fidelity. They'd never tell him; and they'd never walk away. To suppress a surge of feeling, Benson laughed, saying:

'Mr Edgeworth's solution is to make the Tuesday Club a going concern.'

'You're joking.'

'I'm not.'

'He thinks a bunch of ex-cons who meet for a pint once a week can charge for their criminal know-how?'

'Yes.'

'That's completely bonkers.'

'Off the wall.'

'There's only one solution, Mr Benson,' Molly said. She had stood up and was reaching for the biscuits. 'You've got to make a big impression with *R* v. *Stainsby.* I watched some of London's finest grow from pupils to giants. It takes time. It takes luck. And it takes a few big trials that people can't forget. And then you'll be a household name.'

'I'm already a name and it doesn't help.'

'Nonsense. Mick McManus made it, and he was known as "The Man You Love to Hate".'

'I'm a lawyer not a wrestler.'

'Show me the difference.'

'The fights aren't staged.'

'Trust me, Mr Benson,' said Molly, walking to the door, 'the Hopton Yard killing wasn't enough. This case is what you need.'

'And if I lose?'

Molly turned around. 'Succeeding at the Bar isn't just about winning, Mr Benson. It's about making people trust you, even if they hate you. You can win the jury and the public and still lose the case.'

Benson liked the idea. It was noble. It was true. But it wouldn't save his skin. 'To be "The Man Everyone Loves to Hate", I've got to win cases where everyone knows the defendant's guilty, and you don't want to win, and you shouldn't win, but somehow you do. Only I don't know how to do it because sometimes you just can't get past the evidence.'

'Then make yourself Diane's defender.'

'But I represent Stainsby.'

'Stainsby the man?' Molly was enigmatic; she was no longer talking about the client. 'He can go to hell.'

That evening, after instructing Barlow's Waterside Property Specialists to sell *The Wooden Doll*, Benson shrugged on his duffel coat and began the short ride home, intending to meander along back streets to avoid the rush of late evening traffic on the City Road. First, though, he bought a packet of Pall Mall cigarettes. He lit one and threw the rest in a builder's skip behind Liverpool Street Station. Pedalling slowly and thinking of the boat he'd shortly lose, Benson wasn't ready for what happened next. Not that being prepared would have made any difference. The blue van swept past him and came to a sudden halt about thirty yards up the road. Two thickset men in balaclavas appeared from the passenger side of the vehicle. One opened the rear doors, the other came directly towards Benson, meaty hands in the air, ready to stop him if he didn't slow down.

'Get in the back – now.'

6

'I've something to say,' said Gordon, after they'd ordered the set menu. The lights were subdued. A candle flickered. 'This isn't easy for me, Tess, because it's a delicate subject.'

Oh God, thought Tess. He's going to make a declaration.

'I've been hesitating for months, thinking it best to say nothing, but in the end, I've decided to take the risk.'

'Take it, Gordon, I won't bite.'

Tess had spent the afternoon reviewing files, dictating letters and phoning clients. But thoughts of Benson had plagued her concentration. She kept returning to the way he asked questions – always short and rapid, never torturous; his memorisation of the brief; his attention to the smallest of details; and the energy that had filled the room when he'd paused, not to deliberate, but to put Stainsby under pressure. Come late evening, she'd thrown on her coat, as if the conference had just ended, when Gordon Hayward, head of the criminal law department, had put his bald head around the door.

'You've not forgotten, have you?'

'Of course not.'

Which had been an outright lie. A week back, Gordon

had invited her to the Bleeding Heart Bistro just around the corner. He'd been characteristically intense, while trying to be casual. Now, in the candlelight, he was being confidential. His paunch pressed against the table, he breathed in slowly, as if to savour air for the last time.

'You've guessed what I'm going to say, haven't you?'

'No.'

'Honestly? You've no idea?'

Gordon's interest in Tess had been sparked the day she'd arrived at C&D. Within a week he'd been sporting various bright ties and wide braces, loud shirts and chunky cuff-links. He'd gone for a more assertive brand of aftershave. And he'd invited her to almost every type of restaurant, untroubled by refusals, not appearing to notice her resistance to attention. He tugged a starched sleeve into view and Tess thought it was time to shift gear.

'Okay, let's both be honest,' she said. 'If this is hard for you, Gordon, then it's even harder for me. If you've picked up a certain coolness, it's—'

'I have. But I don't care what people say. You have my support.'

Tess paused, her glass held in mid-air. This was not the declaration she'd expected.

'There are people in the firm who aren't happy with you, Tess. That's why they're cool. Freezing, in parts. They think you played the management committee. And to be fair, it's understandable. Add it up yourself: you were on a consultancy last year and you went and instructed Benson. You gave him oxygen. The partners made it clear they weren't happy. You then dropped him. At which point, you get appointed full-time. But what did you do the following week? You went and instructed him again.'

'I didn't drop him to get the job, Gordon.'

'Appearances matter, Tess. And it looks like you gave him

more oxygen, just when he might have died off. And again it's a high-profile case. And again the firm is put under the spotlight. And again we're pulled into the debate about Benson.'

'That's a lot of agains, Gordon.'

'Exactly.'

'And – again – that's not what happened. I would never deceive an interview panel. I dropped him because . . .'

Because Tess had discovered that Benson, unknown to the prosecution and the defence, had known his victim and had been looking for him for more than a year before their confrontation. Which meant that the meeting in the Bricklayers Arms prior to the killing had not been accidental. She said:

'. . . because it's my job to choose counsel for any given case. And in this Blood Orange business, the client insisted on Benson. What else could I do?'

'Nothing. Which is why you have my support.' Gordon had shaved too enthusiastically and his skin was chafed. He paused to stroke his chin. 'But there is something else you might consider.'

'Leave the firm?'

'Hell, no. If you did that, it would look as if you'd been moved on; and the partners don't want that either.'

'What, then?'

'Truth is, you're trapped, Tess. Leave or stay, the problem remains. I'm suggesting you go back to the beginning. The very beginning.'

'What do you mean?'

'Benson's conviction. That's the real problem.'

The waiter returned, but Tess didn't even notice what was on her plate. She couldn't even recall what she'd ordered. She reached for a glass of wine, a bit too quickly.

'Benson went down on circumstantial evidence, didn't he?' said Gordon.

'Yes.'

'There'd been a fight between Benson and Paul Harbeton outside a pub?'

'Yes.'

'They went their separate ways?'

'Yes.'

'Harbeton is then found dead shortly afterwards in Soho?'

'Yes. And Benson is found in a parallel street covered in evidence.'

'That had come from the earlier fight.' Gordon tasted his wine. 'No one actually saw him kill this bloke, did they?'

'No.'

'And no murder weapon was ever found.'

'No. But so what? He wasn't arrested until a week later. He'd had plenty of time to get rid of it . . . whatever it was. A metal bar. A piece of wood. God knows.'

Gordon put his glass down.

'The problem with circumstantial evidence is that the pieces on the table can mean anything. You know the score. We switch them around, trying to find a more convincing explanation . . . and in Benson's case, the defence didn't find one. All they had was his story, but it wasn't enough. And who knows, he might have lied . . . but that doesn't mean he killed Paul Harbeton. You know as well as I do, you can't just rely on what the client tells you.'

Tess had to agree. Clients often had secrets. Clients frequently harmed their own defence. Clients always needed someone to look further than their own instructions.

'Forget Benson's story,' said Gordon, leaning back. 'Look instead at everyone else's. Maybe something was missed.'

'Are you suggesting I reopen his case?'

'Let's put it this way: you're tied to C&D and you're tied to Benson. Your only way out is to prove that Benson is innocent. Pull that off and your problems are over.'

'Gordon, you're forgetting something. He might be guilty.'

'Do you trust him or not?'

Tess opened her mouth but, not knowing the answer to the question, she stalled.

Try the wine,' said Gordon. 'It's remarkable.'

7

'No thanks,' said Benson.

The two heavies had remained outside the van. The driver had reached a thick arm between some curtains into the back, offering Benson a cigarette.

'No hard feelings, okay? I just want to talk.'

Benson's fear – instinctive and sharp – had quickly evaporated. He was familiar with the preamble to genuine violence and the excitement shown by violent men – there's a very specific atmosphere created by the fusion of the two . . . like the ignition of lust – and there was something amateur about this backstreet operation. These men posed no threat.

'There are easier ways,' said Benson, 'like making a call.'

'No way. This has to be face to face.'

'Then why the masks?'

'Because I don't trust no one. Because I want to stay alive.'

The back of the van was rusted and dented – Benson had seen that much before the doors were slammed shut. And he recognised the smell: engine oil and the sea – not something fresh and bracing, but the heavy stench of nets and salt and shells and weed and dead fish. No amount of cleaning would take it away.

'He killed her, right?'

'Who?'

'Stainsby. He bloody killed her. It's simple.'

'I'm sorry, let me out. If you have something to say, go to the police.'

'Okay, calm down. I'm just telling you what you need to know. Because this case is bigger than Diane, right? I know what I'm talking about because—'

'Get your big friends to open the doors. Now.'

'Just listen. I can't go to the pigs. I'm telling you, because you're not part of the system, okay?'

Benson was seated on a wheel arch, legs apart, his elbows on his thighs. Panic was tightening the pit of his stomach. And it had nothing to do with his current predicament. Confined spaces summoned another life. Distant noises rose in his mind, coming closer and closer. He could hear the crash of cell doors, the shouting, the jeers and the swearing. Someone begged for help . . . and it was Benson, Benson as a boy, because that was all he'd been when they'd locked him away. He took a series of deep breaths. All he could see was the outline of the driver against the grubby yellow curtains. He, too, was a big man.

'Are you sure you don't want a smoke?'

The arm appeared again, and this time Benson snatched the cigarette. His own had been dropped on the road when he'd been manhandled off his bike.

'Why can't you go to the police?' he said through his teeth.

'They wouldn't listen. Not to me.'

'Because you've got form?'

'Because I've fed them rubbish in the past. It's simple.'

If only it were, Mr Stainsby. The reply had sounded over the growing racket in Benson's mind. That one, short phrase – it's simple – had evoked his client, and Benson was now sure that the big guy behind the curtain knew him. That

Stainsby had been the stronger of the pair. That he'd done the talking while the other, his subordinate, listened. It was simple. Benson quickly struck a match. The rust and peeling paint appeared in the flare of light and vanished with a flick of Benson's wrist.

'Open the doors or I'll scream.'

'Are you some kind of girl?'

'I know more men who've screamed than women, and none who've screamed as loud. Open the doors. I won't run. Remember, you've got your mates outside. I just don't like being locked in. Let's say it disturbs my concentration.'

After a shout through the window, a lever swivelled and one of the doors opened an inch. A shaft of pale light struck Benson and he sucked in the cool evening air. Gradually the tightness in his jaw relaxed. He stilled his trembling hand by holding the cigarette to his lips. The smoke hit his guts and he let out a low sigh.

'You can't say a word about this case,' he said at last.

'I don't want to. That's not why I'm here. I'm here to tell you about another.'

'Involving Stainsby?'

'You're interested now, aren't you?'

'That depends.'

'He's not told you, has he?' said the man, his tone mocking. 'He's left you in the dark.'

'Look, maybe I'm just old fashioned, but I don't like being assaulted. And false imprisonment – which is what this is – probably upsets me more than a good kicking. So, say what you've got to say, and let me go.'

'Be patient, Mr Benson. This is worth knowing, right? Stainsby's not what he seems. He's—'

'Get on with it.'

'2009. Seven years back. He got lifted for GBH. Beat someone up in a nightclub.'

'Where was this?'

'Dover. It nearly went to court. There was going to be a trial and everything, right? He was going down, but they had to let him go.'

'Actually, it's time you let me go. Thanks for the burn. I'm fascinated by what you've said, and I'll bear it in mind, but—'

'His alibi was Diane. She got him off. And she was backed by her mate Jane Tapster. Diane said he'd been at home. She's the reason he walked. And now she's dead.'

Benson glanced at the curtain. The speaker had turned and Benson could see his profile.

'Yeah, that's what I'm saying. The alibi's been put down. Like a dog.'

'But the police have made no connection.'

'Are you stupid or what? They don't know the alibi was false, do they?' He took an angry drag on his cigarette; when he next spoke, after a long moment, his tone was softer. 'Diane was a good kid, all right? She didn't deserve this. So if you're going to get Stainsby off a murder rap, you might as well know what really happened.'

He shouted out of the window, and the two heavies climbed back into the van.

'Don't take the registration number,' he said as Benson clambered out. 'I'm here for Diane, okay? And if you care about right and wrong and that sort of thing, you'll make sure he goes down.'

The registration number was, in fact, barely legible. Benson didn't even try to distinguish the letters and numbers. Instead, he fixed his gaze on the driver's wing mirror, where he got a clear and unobstructed view of the frightened guy who felt for Diane. He was heavily bearded, with dark, thick brows and a sloping forehead. As the engine spluttered into life their eyes met, very briefly . . . and Benson frowned at the look of appeal: a boy's desperate wish that a grown-up would mend his broken toy.

'Tess? This is Benson.' He called her from home after feeding Traddles. 'We might have a problem.'

8

'I presume you asked?' said Benson.

Tess had come to Congreve Chambers straight from home, skipping breakfast, and now she was seated in the Gutting Room. She loved this place. The arched alcoves had been shelved and were now packed tight with books. Benson's desk, salvaged from a ship captain's cabin, stood on oak flooring thought – according to Congreve lore – to have been retrieved from a captured Spanish galleon. The ornate plasterwork came from the era of empire and self-conscious classicism. The walls were covered with prints of old Spitalfields. A world long gone. Benson, in his lawyer's suit, seemed to belong there. He was standing by the window, gazing into the rear yard. Archie, in baggy brown trousers, was leaning on a large iron radiator, arms folded. Molly, brisk and silent, poured the Earl Grey and left the room.

'I specifically asked him if he'd ever been in trouble with the police,' said Tess. 'I nailed it down. I wanted to know if he'd ever been arrested, interviewed, charged, cautioned, anything, and apart from the time he went into Greggs and got arrested, he said no. He said his past was clean.'

'Odd he should say nothing.'

'Is it? He didn't give us full instructions until the last

minute. He keeps his cards close to his chest. Even the ones we need to see.'

Benson returned to his desk, where he'd been reading the Stainsby brief when Tess had arrived. He'd been courteous and attentive, taking her hat and coat, offering her a seat, but his dark brown eyes – after initial contact – had kept away from hers. The effect of his shyness was endearing: he seemed to be looking for something on the floor. So was his personal disorganisation: he'd held out a plate of biscuits, revealing a paperclip in place of a cuff-link. But once the work had begun, his attention shifted entirely onto the case. No detail had been mislaid.

'At least we now know why Stainsby mentioned fit-up,' he said. 'He's thinking of saying the police in London framed him in 2015 because the police in Dover had to let him go in 2009.'

'Do the police in London even know what happened in Dover?' asked Archie.

'Yes. So does the CPS, and so will my opponent on Monday. After Diane's body was found, the SIO – DCI Goodshaw – will have tapped her name into the Police National Computer, and he'll have seen that she'd been Stainsby's alibi in a case that never went to trial. He'll have contacted the police in Dover and checked out the details. If there was any potential connection between 2009 and 2015, he'll have pursued it. But he hasn't done. As the guy in the van reminded me, they've no reason to think the alibi was false.'

'Slow down a minute,' said Archie. 'This guy says that Stainsby killed Diane to silence her?'

'Something like that,' said Benson.

'Meaning she was threatening to open up about 2009?'

'Possibly,' said Tess. 'Or to cover himself if ever she did.'

'We don't know, Archie,' said Benson, getting tetchy. 'And

none of this matters, because none of this is evidence in the trial. The guy in the van isn't a witness. And everything he said is probably hearsay or conjecture. The Crown's case is that Stainsby abused her for years and then murdered her – and I quote – "out of spite and for money". Our defence is suicide. But that doesn't mean that an alleged GBH in 2009 isn't a problem. It is.'

'Why?'

'Because if Stainsby even hints that the police might have framed him, the prosecution can apply to bring details of 2009 into the trial, not to prove a propensity for violence but because he's attacked someone's character, or because he's created a false impression . . . there are seven "gateways" where stuff like this can end up in front of the jury. And if it does, persuading them that he murdered Diane would be that much easier. The rules apply to me too. Whatever I say is deemed to have been said by Stainsby. One false move and 2009 becomes public knowledge.'

'Well, whatever happened is no secret,' said Archie. 'The police know. The guy in the van knows. Stainsby knows.' He glanced around the Gutting Room. 'We're the only ones who don't. Hadn't we better find out?'

Benson went to fiddle with his cuff-link but found the paperclip. 'Absolutely.'

'I'll go back to the Green this afternoon,' said Tess.

'No, don't.' Benson pulled his jacket sleeve down. 'Let's hold off on that. He's kept 2009 to himself. I want to know why.'

'So what's to be done?' said Archie

'Tess, would you speak to Tapster? Ask her about the fight in the nightclub and why she's kept out of the investigation into Diane's death.'

'Sure.'

'Then we decide if we say anything to Stainsby.'

'Okay.'

'And Archie, get the Tuesday Club on it. The usual stuff. Background check any names. See if there's any chat on the inside. Any rumours. Cross-refer with Tess once she's seen Tapster. Then, if necessary, do the same thing all over again.'

'Will do.'

Tess could see that Benson was ill at ease. She spoke quietly. 'What's wrong, Will?'

'This guy in the van. He held something back. I could sense it. He had more to say – much more – about his dealings with Stainsby, only he daren't open up. He's only told me half the story . . . because he's scared, scared for his life.'

'All the more reason to find out what happened in 2009, then.'

'Yes. But I fear that will only give us half the answer.' He leaned back in his chair, turning aside from the spread of papers on his desk. 'And there's something else. That blood orange. It stands out . . . like a message; only I can't imagine what it might mean.'

'I suppose it depends who put it in her mouth,' said Tess, 'Stainsby or Diane.'

She'd been struck by the same nauseating detail but hadn't wanted to dwell on it. Neither, it seemed, did Benson. He stood up and moved away from the open brief as if to get some distance between himself and the photographs of Diane's body.

'I think we're done,' he said, reaching for his duffel coat.

'Where are you off to, Rizla?'

'Dear God, Archie, it's—'

'All right, Mr Benson.'

'I want to see where Diane died. Get a sense of her last week alive. The landlord has finally agreed to let me in.'

'Do you want a lift?' The words had slipped out before Tess could grab them back.

'No, it's okay,' said Benson, just as quickly. 'I like to do this kind of thing on my own. Thanks. Really. That's very kind.' He was by the door now. 'Call me if anything significant turns up. 'Failing that, Monday morning, Number Two Court.'

Archie coughed. 'Don't forget. It's Monopoly tonight,' he said; and Benson's face hardened.

'Bloody right it is. By nine o'clock I'll own two hotels in Mayfair . . . and God help your sisters.'

After Benson had gone, Molly returned to clear away the tea things, head down, not speaking. And because Tess lingered, so did Archie. When they were alone, she said, 'How's Benson doing? I mean professionally.'

'Thriving, Miss de Vere.'

'Come on, Archie, it's Tess. And he's not thriving.'

'Then why ask?'

'Because I'm concerned.'

Archie almost smiled. 'But not concerned enough to send him work.'

'It's not that simple.'

'I know. That's what everyone says. But I wouldn't worry, he understands. There's no ill feeling.'

Tess blushed. What could she say? She'd dropped Benson. Confusion followed the rush of blood, because she liked it here; this Gutting Room of books and history; she liked Archie, and the lobster in the clerk's room, installed in a glass tank over a hundred years ago by Archie's grandfather. She liked Benson, if only he—

'He's having to sell his boat, you know,' said Archie. 'He shouldered the debt without saying anything and now he's the one who has to pay. It's not right, is it?'

'His boat? In Seymour Basin?'

'Well, he hasn't got another one.'

'I suppose not. But that's his home.'

'Actually, it's a chattel.'

Tess had to get out. The walls were closing in. 'I'll be in touch after I've spoken to Jane Tapster. Goodbye, Archie.'

Confused and burning with guilt, she moved quickly into the clerk's room, where Molly opened the door onto Artillery Passage. She said nothing, but Archie did, and he seemed to speak for them both. The old friendliness had gone:

'Goodbye, Miss de Vere.'

9

'I don't understand myself.'

Tess had offered him a lift and he'd said no. They could have hit the road together, but Benson had opted for the bus. They could have made up some of the lost ground.

'Why did I do that?'

Taking her hat and coat, he'd glimpsed the sea in her eyes. Moments later, unable to look up, he'd focused on the delicate wrist bone that had emerged when she'd reached for her cup of tea; to see it again, he'd offered her a biscuit. And then, when she'd sat back, it had gone; and all he'd been able to think about were the eyes he'd dared not meet. He thought about them now, all the way to Tottenham.

After dismounting, he lit a bent Pall Mall retrieved from the skip behind Liverpool Street Station, his eyes on a building at the junction with Heston Road, some thirty yards down Broad Lane. The ground floor was occupied by Alan's Kebabs, a shop the size of a corridor, and North London

Computers, whose windows were now blacked out with paint. Benson had been here before. At 10.30 on a Friday night a month ago, after the search for Durand cigarettes. He'd bought a kebab from a girl called Tracy after queueing with punters from the Stag's Head on the other side of the road.

'Why did I do that?'

Benson crossed over, dodging between cars, heading towards the building, and a bulky man in a trapper hat talking to a boy wearing a padded coat, beanie, scarf and gloves.

'Mr Benson?'

'Yes. I imagine you're Mr Nesbit.'

'None other.'

P. Q. Nesbit, Esq. ran Homebird London Rentals. As far as Benson could learn, he specialised in cheap and nasty property, offering low rents to low-income tenants. The website made it sound like a public service. Diane's flat occupied the first floor of the building.

'The lad's not with me,' he said, nodding to the boy. 'He's the son of another tenant. Shouldn't be hanging around here, really. Go on, push off. This isn't for your eyes.'

The boy kicked an imaginary football towards a low wall and sat down.

'He's from the Horn of Africa,' said Nesbit confidentially. 'Eritrea or somewhere. Nice enough family. Never late with the lolly. But the kid has nowhere to play. Who'd want to leave the sun and come here, eh? They're not used to the cold. Just look at him.'

Benson stubbed his cigarette on the edge of a rubbish bin and dumped two others.

'Trying to stop?' asked Nesbit cheerily.

'Shall we get started?'

'We? I'm not going in there. Not on your life. It's open.

Head on in. I'll wait here.' Nesbit glanced over his shoulder. 'I thought I told you to clear off!'

Benson opened a tatty white door.

Nesbit had assured Benson that everything was exactly as Diane had left it. The sitting/dining room had a round table, two armchairs, a coffee table and a small flatscreen television. There was a white Formica shelf with a CD player on it, the flex hanging down by a socket. The carpet, a washed-out green, was stained with the vestiges of different seating arrangements. There were three sash windows. The two facing Broad Lane rattled with every wave of traffic. On the wall was a poster of Big Ben.

Benson looked down the short corridor towards another door.

Diane had pushed it open, entered her bedroom and put on Caroline Stainsby's jewellery. She'd come back crying, and then she'd sipped beer and eaten a takeaway at the round table, talking with Stainsby about good times in Dover.

It didn't ring true, even to Benson. Good times? They'd eaten, yes. But there can't have been much to say. She'd dumped him not even two months earlier. The Dover Five must have been whooping. And Stainsby must have sat there seething. David Bowie had filled the dreadful silence. Or maybe Stainsby had managed that distinctive flicker of a smile . . . looking at Diane wearing his mother's jewellery, poor Diane thinking she'd won the fight when, before the night was out, she'd have no need for memories, or sentiment, or the ornaments that kept them alive.

You're for the defence.

Stainsby maintained he'd left Diane 'getting on for eleven'. Which was over three hours later. Three hours of chat? Listing the fun memories, after Frank's wife had died and his business collapsed? And the rest? That was Benson's case.

Stop.

Benson walked into the bedroom.

On the wall was a poster of a red double-decker negotiating Piccadilly Circus. To his immediate left was a dressing table. The top edge had a cigarette burn, on the side nearest the door upon which Diane had been found hanging. The SOCO people had found a Durand cigarette end on the carpet, immediately below the burnt edge. The Crown's case was that after drugging Diane, Stainsby had helped her lie down on her bed and then returned to the sitting room where he'd waited, smoking patiently. Once he was sure she was incapacitated, he'd returned, placed the burning cigarette on the dressing table, and then set to work. Benson's skin prickled. This is where Stainsby had taken her hands and—

Your case is suicide.

Benson returned to look again at the armchair used – allegedly – by Stainsby while he'd waited for the drugs to work. A hair had been found on the headrest; flakes of ash had been carefully lifted off the armrest. The chair itself was two feet from a wall, two yards from the flatscreen and three yards from the sash window above the kebab shop. There wasn't a lot of space in the flat. It was a small, soulless world.

This is your argument.

A bus rushed past . . . and all at once Benson imagined poor Diane, sitting here alone, staring real life in the face, thinking it just hurt too much. He saw her crying. He watched with ruthless concentration. He fleshed out his fantasy: Stainsby had just left the flat; this time he was gone for good; and, strangely, Diane didn't feel any relief; then the truth crawled over her like flies on a corpse. The great dash to London hadn't worked. She'd bought the posters but the longed-for happiness was still out of reach . . . and always would be. She looked at the shoebox full of medicines that had never worked. She looked at the extension cable.

Benson snapped out of his reverie. If it wasn't for the forensic, it would be a good story.

Back on the pavement, Benson left Nesbit to secure the premises. The boy from Eritrea was still sitting on the wall; he'd refused to clear off. He looked inquisitive. And mischievous. The boy slipped to his feet just as Nesbit returned, keys jangling.

'If you know of anyone interested in a cheap let, give us a call, will you?' he said, pocketing the keys. 'Not good for business, this' – he tilted his head, presumably at Diane's tragedy – 'no one wants the flat. I mean, I half understand it, but—'

'Do you read, Mr Nesbit?'

'Oh yes.'

'Any preferences?'

'True crime, to be honest. What the Krays got up to. And the Richardsons. Nailing people to the floorboards.'

'Really?'

'Dead right. The Yardies too. That kind of thing.'

'Well, I suggest you try the Landlord and Tenant Act 1985. Section eleven. It'll scare your brains out.'

Nesbit took a step back as if slapped, swore, and then walked quickly away. Once he'd driven off, Benson's eyes fell on the rubbish bin. Two mangled Pall Malls were in there. And he wanted to get them back. But the boy was watching him. I can live with this, thought Benson. I've swallowed much worse. He reached inside.

'You shouldn't smoke, you know.'

Benson nodded, pocketing a wrecked stub like Nesbit had pocketed the keys, possessively, and without shame.

'They cause wrinkles,' said the boy, coming closer, dribbling an imaginary ball.

'I know.'

'And weak bones.'

Benson slowly turned around, his mouth dry, his throat tight. The boy could only be twelve or so.

'They'll turn your skin grey and they'll double your chance of heart attack.'

'Yes, I know.'

'And they can stop you being a dad too. Are you a dad?'

'No.'

'Well, if you stop smoking, and wait twenty years, you might not get head or neck cancer. And you can have some children, if you want.'

'I'll never have any children.'

'Why not?'

'Because no one would want . . .'

Benson left quickly. A species of fear had come over him that he hadn't felt in sixteen years. When he next passed a waste bin he threw the twisted stub away as if it were on fire. Then he ran for a double-decker, leaping through the doors just as they closed.

He'd calmed by the time he was back in Spitalfields. He ambled along Bethnal Green Road, telling himself that HMP Codrington was another world; that Terry Meersham and his minders were out of his life. But the memory of powerlessness and the threat of violence remained, ruining what might have been an otherwise pleasant experience: purchasing top-drawer assets . . . not two hotels in Mayfair, but a set of cuff-links from the Crypt Trust charity shop – a couple of fish etched in silver.

10

'Nothing is planned,' said Sally. 'A little boy walks around the corner and a millisecond later' – she clicked her fingers – 'the moment is caught in time. It's as though it was meant to happen. That it had to happen. But it was simply chance.'

Sally had organised an exhibition of Cartier-Bresson's photographs at her gallery in Chelsea. She'd given a brief talk on how the great man would prowl around a certain place for days, sensing a picture, waiting for all the elements to fall into position and then, suddenly – snap – he'd capture a moment of wonder. A boy carrying bottles of wine. A kiss watched by a dog. A man shouldering a coffin.

Nothing had been planned.

The thought stayed with Tess throughout the evening as she watched Sally take people from print to print, pointing out the perfection of chance. When everyone – enlightened and enthralled – had gone home, they sat down at a small table, bought from a restaurant in Paris when Tess and Sally had been students. Getting it back to London had been hell. And not because the thing was heavy. Gendarmes, responsible citizens and customs officials had all been convinced they were thieves. Again and again, from Paris to Calais, Sally had been obliged to call the proprietor to verify the transaction. It was only when they'd got to England that their troubles were over. No one seemed to find it odd that two girls were travelling with a table. Now it was a priceless fixture, heavy with memory.

'Absolutely fascinating,' said Tess.

'Thank you.'

'Really, I'd never thought coincidence could have such *meaning*.'

'That's the point. We're surrounded by a mysterious coherence.'

'Making sense of things, if only we could see it.' Tess clicked her fingers.

So did Sally. She'd dressed in a striped top with a pleated belt and a beret, copying a woman in one of the photographs. And now she filled their glasses with claret decanted into an old bottle, another special touch that had added charm to the evening. Tess felt she was in another world. She glanced around at the prints of Paris in the fifties and sixties: an old woman was looking for loose change, a man was breathing fire, couples were kissing . . . at a table, beneath a tree, beside a gargoyle, over a motorbike, by a Métro station. Her eyes came to rest on two women seated among empty vegetable crates at the Fontaine des Innocents. They were old friends. And they were talking, confidentially.

'I've had a mysterious experience, recently,' said Tess.

'You're being facetious. It's unbecoming.'

'No, I'm being serious.'

'Truly?'

'Yes. It was a surreal happening that disclosed with crystalline simplicity the hidden order of my existence.'

'I knew it. If we're not talking guns and knives and ligatures and dead bodies, you're just not interested. The only chance you've got of spotting a deeper meaning is if someone gives it an exhibit number. And even then, you'd think they'd got the label wrong. I feel sorry for you. Yours is a universe without miracles, great or small.'

Tess found the argument compelling. But hers was too. Unperturbed, she resumed its presentation:

'Last Thursday we met for breakfast.'

'We did.'

'And I was preparing to see Benson.'

'You were.'

'And I was ill at ease, and you said we ought to go back to our investigation. To find out if Benson was innocent or not. Because if that question was sorted, I'd be sorted.'

'I don't think I'd use that turn of phrase, but yes, I said as much.'

'Well, that evening, I was invited out to dinner.'

'Were you?'

'I was. By Gordon Hayward, at work. Have I introduced you? Flashy dresser, balding, single?'

'No.'

'But I've mentioned him.'

'You have.'

'Well, this is the dreamlike bit. There we were, sitting at this table, not much bigger than this one, and guess what he says? He says, in effect, that I should reopen my investigation into Benson. Because if I did, all my problems would be over. Isn't that extraordinary? Twice in the same day. Two people who've never met each other say the same thing. It was a man shouldering a coffin moment. If I believed in little miracles, I'd have thought that was simply amazing.' Tess sipped some wine. 'But I'm a label girl. I add up evidence. And I—'

'Okay, I called him.'

'You called my boss that morning? Out of the blue? And had a chat about me and Benson and what you think I need?'

'No. I spoke to him six months ago.'

Tess couldn't immediately reply; and Sally, taking advantage of the silence, rose and stepped back from the table, as if to place her old friend in perspective.

'Now listen,' she continued. 'I couldn't let the matter drop. Not after seeing what doubt and confusion had done to you. So I continued the investigation from where we left off. All I needed was professional guidance.'

'You continued the investigation?'

'I did.'

'You went to Gordon?'

'I had lunch with Gordon, who has no sense of colour, but he's a darling. And he put me on the right road. He told me what to do.'

'Six months ago?'

'Yes. And I've made what I think you labelling types call significant progress.'

Tess closed her eyes; she wanted to get away, but she couldn't escape Sally's voice. Which itself was alarming. Because, without seeing her, Tess noticed there was no fun in it; no sense of caper or irreverence.

'A man followed you, Tess. And he asked you to give a message to Benson, do you remember? He asked you to thank him for killing Paul Harbeton. He said he wished he'd done it himself . . . that if Benson hadn't done it, someone else would have done, eventually. This Harbeton was not a nice guy, Tess. That's what Benson knows. And for some reason he wants it kept secret. That's why he denied knowing him. But that doesn't mean he killed him. Benson is trapped, just like you.'

Tess opened her eyes. 'I don't want this, Sally.'

'Well I'll do it on my own.'

'What the hell are you talking about? What have you been doing?'

'I've taken Gordon's advice. I've turned my attention from Benson to the witnesses. And I've found something, Tess. It's not much, but it's a thread, and—'

'You leave it alone.' Tess was in control of herself now, and she was scared. 'You don't pull it. Because God knows what might happen.'

'But you've nothing to lose.'

'Oh yes, I have.'

Watching Benson at work, both in the conference and in chambers, had been electrifying, and she was now impatient for the beginning of the trial, and what would surely be a riveting performance. But aside from professional considerations, she liked the way he couldn't hold her gaze. She liked his bicycle clips and the missing cuff-link. She was drawn to his lonesome world, shared only with a cat.

'Sally, if we found out he'd killed Paul Harbeton I'd lose what I have now.'

'But all you've got is uncertainty and confusion.'

'And I'd rather have confusion and uncertainty than nothing. Don't you understand? Sometimes people settle for less because the little bit they've got is like one of your miracles. They don't understand it . . . but it changes a small part of their world. Makes it wonderful.'

If Sally was moved by this declaration she didn't show it. Instead she came back to the table she'd bought in Montmartre. They'd gone to Paris at the end of their first year. They'd sat outside Le Consulat on the rue Norvins, eating *moules frites*, while Tess banged on about some guy who'd just been given a life sentence for murder. He'd been with them for most of the trip. Seated together, once more, that distant moment came alive again, suffused with everything that had happened since. Sally spoke quietly, as if fearful that other diners might be listening.

'My world is art. But art is life, Tess. And life is about relationships. I know about those.'

It was true: she did. Apart from selling prints and English watercolours, Sally ran a discreet business advising individuals on their relationships and human resources managers on staff recruitment. Her approach was novel, relying not on conventional psychological tools – tests, questionnaires and the like – but the study and interpretation of handwriting. Tess couldn't take the discipline seriously. But she wasn't so foolish as to dismiss out of hand her general reading of human relations.

'Benson got under your skin when you were young, Tess,' she said. 'That's when injustice burns deepest . . . and you cared. You really did. And it marked you. You watched a frightened boy go under and there was nothing you could do. But then, eleven years later, he surfaced . . . and it's no wonder you no longer know what to think or feel. He's not the same person, and yet, in a way, he is. Same for you. You're not who you were . . . and yet it's not that straightforward.' Sally leaned over the table, arms folded. 'Tess, it all began with strong emotion, emotions that easily lead to a strong attachment . . . maybe an attachment for life. They've settled down, now, to a confused attraction that won't go away. And that's why you need to know what's going on and where you're heading. Because compassion without limit can feel like love. It can wear the same clothes, and say the same things . . . but it's different. It leads to friendship, deep friendship. Whereas love . . . well, it's compassion's bolshie best friend; the one who makes you ill and lose weight.'

Tess averted her gaze, wanting to escape into a picture. But the street scene was crowded; a trader's stall blocked half the pavement. And Sally wouldn't let her go.

'Go back to the beginning, Tess. Find out if Benson is innocent. Find out if he relied on you, or if he used you.' She took Tess's hand. 'If you bring clarity to your point of departure, you'll discover where you want to go from here. And if he turns out to have been innocent after all, well, you can take a closer look . . . see if compassion borrowed her best friend's clothes. The alternative is to remain at sixes and sevens, holding on to a little miracle, forever scared it might just turn into a nightmare. Let me help you. I can—'

'Drop it, Sally.' Tess drew her hand away as if to hide her nakedness. She felt cold. 'Do this for me, will you? Whatever you're on to, leave it. Please.'

Sally examined Tess as if her jacket didn't quite match her trousers.

'Okay,' she said, drawing back. 'But you're making a mistake.'

When they'd finished off the wine they tidied up and turned off the lights. Outside on the pavement, they were quiet for a while. There was a distance between them, and while Tess needed the space, she ached, too, for the time they'd dragged that table along the streets of Paris. When they'd been young and adventurous. When they'd never imagined having to live with doubt and disappointment; and the trauma of compromise with those we love. Tess said:

'I'm grateful, Sally.'

'What for?'

'You've always listened. You've always cared. You're always there for me, even when I don't need you.'

Sally gave a shrug and hailed a passing taxi. When she was in the back seat, she opened the window.

'Tess, I'll drop the investigation, but that's not where the argument ends. Can't you see that this Harbeton business is so much bigger than your needs? Have you never considered that without you – and what we'd set out to do – Benson will remain an outsider for ever? He'll be hated and reviled. When he might be freed and rehabilitated. For real, and not just on paper. Is that what you want? Because his being there at all, in your life, is a little miracle?'

She closed the window and the driver pulled away. That made two kicks in the teeth: one from Archie and one from her best friend. They weren't planned, of course, but they felt connected. She walked home, unable to forget those captivating images of life in Paris. A mischievous boy. A big man carrying a coffin. And a man with a cigarette in his hand who'd leaned over a table to snatch a kiss.

11

Benson was nervous. He paced around Bethnal Green in the dark, trying to find some courage. Finally, he came across a mental ploy. He imagined he was in a Lancaster bomber. The fuselage was ablaze and the aircraft was losing height, heading towards a cauldron of flame in Dresden, a fire he'd helped start and a crime that would never burn out. In a panic, Benson almost ran into Selby Street. Without another thought, he seemed to leap and pull a ripcord. The buzzer screamed.

'Take a seat, Will.'

She was extraordinary. Dr Abasiama Agozino, a clinical psychologist specialising in battle stress, spoke as if she'd seen Benson only last week. That a year had passed seemed to be of no consequence. As usual, her appearance was unique and surprising. Beads of coloured glass and carved wood had been threaded into plaits, creating tails that had been woven around lengths of pale blue silk. As usual, there was a box of tissues and a large cactus on the table. As usual, she didn't seem to breathe. And, as usual, she didn't mind if Benson spoke or not. Her natural habitat was silence.

'I've got a new cat,' he said, after a long pause. 'He's called Traddles.'

'A good name.'

'When he's hungry his body itches all over and he leans on things and people until you produce the goods.'

'You understand each other.'

'It's not reciprocal.'

'How so?'

'I can't work out if it's me he likes or the tins I open.'

'Motivations are always mixed.'

'Yes.' Benson dried up; and when Abasiama didn't help, he made another leap: 'Look, I thought I could get by.'

'That's fine.'

'I went solo.'

'That's fine too.'

'I didn't let you know. I'm sorry. That was rude.'

'It was. But why have you come back, Will? You've been able to fly solo for years.'

'Because there's more to life than staying in the air. I want to understand myself.' Benson looked at the cactus and the tissues. They were there as alternatives. But he didn't know why, and he didn't want to either. He said, 'I've been instructed in the Blood Orange murder. To fight my case I must believe in something that's almost certainly untrue. I don't mean actually believe, I mean borrowing all that usually comes with belief – passion, conviction, commitment, determination – and present the lot to a jury as if I was being honest, when I'm not.'

Abasiama said, 'And what don't you understand?'

'I find it very easy. I shouldn't, but I do. I just turn away from what's true and live another life as if it was real. It comes to me naturally; and it's unnatural.'

Benson froze. Abasiama was silent and still, but she might as well have spoken. Benson had stumbled into woods far darker than those involved in defending the guilty. What he'd said wasn't simply true of his work; it was true of his day-to-day existence. And while Abasiama didn't say so, they both knew this was the reason for Benson's return. Mysteriously, he'd taken up where they'd left off almost a year ago: the danger of turning away from reality, which he found so very easy. She said:

'Did you write down your confessions?'

'Yes.'

'Every day?'

'Yes.'

'Short and to the point?'

'Yes.'

'Were you honest?'

'Not at first. But I'm getting better every day.'

'You've maintained the discipline?'

'Yes. I write a few lines every night, and every morning I put them in the shredder.'

Abasiama had suggested the practice as a way of helping Benson approach the truths he couldn't face. Truths about Eddie, his brother, trapped in a wheelchair. Truths about the fight with Paul Harbeton. Truths hidden by lies and evasion. Hidden out of fear; so much crippling fear that Benson was now trapped by his own secrets. He could never tell them, not now. Too much had happened after the first terrified lie. But Abasiama had disagreed. She'd said you can at least tell yourself.

'Does it help?' she asked.

'Yes. But it's made things far worse.'

'How?'

'Before, I didn't want anyone to know the truth; now I want *everyone* to know – not just me. But I can't go there. I can never go there.'

Abasiama didn't contradict him, which somehow warned Benson that the question remained open; and that at some point he was bound to return to it, whether he liked it or not. Then she said:

'Are you going to continue the practice?'

'Yes.'

'Even though it makes things worse?'

'Yes. Because for eight hours or so, after the writing and before the shredding, I manage to live with myself. It's there on a page. We're in the same room. And in the morning, it's a kind of suicide. I throw myself in the bin.'

The person who went to work only came truly alive – almost violently – in court. This was something Benson couldn't fathom. It was a given, and he daren't question it, just in case the magic failed. As soon as he put on his wig and gown he was a different man. The heavy guilt just disappeared.

'What else don't you understand, Will?' asked Abasiama.

Benson hadn't intended to talk about what he said next. In fact, in coming to see Abasiama, he hadn't planned to talk about anything at all. His objective had been to re-establish contact, nothing more. To say he needed a navigator. But, as usual, the unexpected happened.

'Occasionally, I wake up and I can't get out of bed. It's as though I've been steam-rollered into the mattress. Traddles is trampling all over me, wanting breakfast, and I just can't move. I've been late for conferences and late for court, and I just don't know what's going on.'

Abasiama asked numerous questions, all of them practical, none likely to expose the dark workings of the unconscious. But shortly a pattern emerged. Benson had been steam-rollered every time he was due to meet Stainsby, or due in court in relation to his trial. There had been two conferences and two preliminary hearings. He'd been late for them all.

'That's never happened before. I'm always early.'

'Are you unsettled by your client?'

'No. Though I should be.'

'Are you troubled by what you must do to defend him?'

'As I said, it comes naturally. And even if it didn't, I believe in the system. Someone else prosecutes.'

'Are you anxious about going into court?'

'Yes. You know that. I always have been. I'm always sick. That's par for the course.'

'Then there's only one other constant, common to you and your client.'

'What's that?'

'Not "what". "Who".'

Benson frowned. 'My solicitor . . . Tess de Vere? But she only attended the last conference.'

'But that's not what you expected, is it? You thought you were going to see her on each occasion.'

'Why would I be unsettled or troubled by Tess de Vere?'

'How would I know?'

With that, Abasiama moved on to explore Benson's half-hearted attempts to shut doors and lock them, and his dubious strategy to stop smoking.

Traddles welcomed Benson on board with the usual obsequiousness. He brushed against his legs, leaning hard, and purring seductively. But Benson wasn't taken in. The blighter just wanted more to eat. Ignoring the attention, Benson wrote some confessions – just a few lines, because he was tired – and then set about his usual pre-trial preparations. He ironed a shirt and collar, starched a fresh pair of bands, polished his shoes and chose a tie to match his cuff-links. He read through the brief one last time, letting his eyes move swiftly over the pages, taking note of the passages he hadn't underlined. And then, tripping over Traddles, who knew the meaning of perseverance, if not tact, he went to bed, leaving the aft door wide open. Almost instantly, on turning out the light, Benson had an epiphany.

He knew why he'd flogged himself all the way from the Green to Spitalfields. He hadn't been cycling to the caseload that wasn't there or away from the blue van that was. He'd been cycling towards Monday morning, when he expected to see Tess de Vere. Which, as a revelation, could only be described as marginally illuminating, because it shed no light on his subsequent impulse to avoid her.

Drifting off to sleep, his final thoughts went to Diane

Heybridge, who'd either killed herself or been murdered. He saw her face angled on the autopsy table, a blood orange in her mouth. He grimaced wondering if this awful death might have a meaning, and just as consciousness slipped away, like the last grains of sand in an hourglass, Benson seemed to hear Molly's voice:

'Make yourself Diane's defender.'

PART TWO

The case for the prosecution

Benson's personal officer, Mr Phillips, was sympathetic. Told of the threat, he arranged a transfer to C Wing. There, Benson was handed over to Mr Lewis, who led him to his new pad where he was two'd up with another lifer, Owen 'Manchester' Kennedy.

Manchester was a burn cat. He smoked almost every minute he was conscious. Benson put him in his late fifties.

'What you in for, Rizla?'

'Murder.'

'Snap.'

He was a huge man with huge lungs and day in day out he pumped smoke around the cell, wheezing and coughing between burns. When it got too much he'd spit in the sink or reach for the Ventolin.

'You're the first not to complain,' said Lewis, coming over.

Benson was gazing at the chip-net strung between the landings. He'd been banged up for twenty-three hours a day for over a month.

'And that's impressive.' Lewis rested an arm on the railing. 'It means you're serious about doing your bird. Do you want a job?'

'What kind?' Benson would do anything to get out of that cell.

'I can have word with the library.'

It was as if sunlight had got past the flaking walls. Even the crashing and the shouting seemed far off. The smell of locked-in bodies seemed to lose its force. What could he say?

'Leave it with me,' said Lewis.

* * *

That night Benson lay with his hands behind his head. The walls weren't so thick; the cell door wasn't so locked; the air wasn't so heavy. His mind fizzed and he couldn't sleep. He felt like a chat.

'Manchester?'

'Yes?'

'Do you have any family waiting for you?'

'Sure I do.'

'You married?'

'Oh aye.'

'What's her name, then?'

'Julie.'

'Any kids?'

'Just one.'

'Come on, Manchester.'

'A lad. Christopher Steven Kennedy.'

'How old is he?

A match struck and a gasp of light flared from the bunk below.

'I hear you've landed a job,' wheezed Manchester.

'Yes. It's a peach.'

Manchester coughed and spat and coughed some more. 'Be careful, Rizla,' he said, scraping out the words.

'What do you mean?'

'I've been inside twenty-two years, lad. I've seen everything. And I'm warning you. Don't ever trust a screw.'

12

Merrington opened his desk drawer and took a beta-blocker from a tin that had once held mints. Thirty minutes later, after some calls, emails and a bout of dictation, he turned to the four graphs. They depicted life behind bars between 2010 and 2016.

The first graph showed the number of assaults between prisoners and prisoner-on-staff. A blue line swung upwards describing a 62 per cent rise, averaging out at sixty-five attacks per day.

The second graph showed a yellow line. It too swung upwards, mapping a 42 per cent increase in self-harm and a 78 per cent rise in suicides.

The third graph – this one had a green line – showed a fall in the number of frontline prison staff. Viewed as a drawing, it was the precise opposite of the other two.

And it was obvious why violence, self-harm and suicide had risen, and why staff had fallen: £900 million had been taken out of the budget. No other explanation was required. And this is what Merrington loved about the job. He had to avoid making that connection in public. He had to find another analysis for the self-evident, even if it strained reality. And if it strained reality, then that too needed masking. You had to be a magician.

The phone rang.

'Greg Rawlings from the Prison Officers' Association wants to know if you can bring forward next week's meeting to this week. He suggests Wednesday.'

'What's the diary like?'

'There's an hour in the morning.'

Merrington glanced at the rising blue line: 27,775 assaults up to last June, 5954 of them on prison officers. But the beta-blocker had done its work. He spoke normally. There was no tremor in his voice. His breath was regular.

'Could we meet sooner?' He wanted to trump the union's concern.

'Not without some cancellations.'

'Let's make it happen.'

'Of course.'

Merrington didn't need to ask why Rawlings wanted an earlier slot. He was going to repeat what he'd been saying since their first meeting last May, when Merrington had moved to the Ministry of Justice. A meltdown was underway in the prison service. The minister was presiding over a bloodbath. This time, though, Merrington expected a threat of industrial action. Beta-blockers couldn't stop that sort of thing. He turned to the fourth graph. This time the line was red and jagged.

The phone rang.

'Bradley Hilmarton's arrived.'

Merrington stood at the window, hands clasped behind his back, looking towards St James's Park and the tired trees, ready for the long sleep of winter.

'This time we're dealing with a private individual, not a colleague,' he said.

'That's no problem.'

'I'm relying on your absolute discretion.'

'This is my business, Richard. My work is untraceable.'

If Merrington couldn't stop Benson from practising through legislation, then he'd look to the Bar Standards Board. Which meant, in the first instance, supplying them with sufficient dirt to merit convening an independent disciplinary tribunal.

'I'm after the truth about someone.'

'I'll find it.'

'His name is William Benson.'

'The barrister with the murder conviction?'

'The same.'

Merrington had his eye on three possible charges: engaging in conduct which was dishonest and discreditable to a barrister; engaging in conduct which was prejudicial to the administration of justice; and engaging in conduct which was likely to diminish public confidence in the legal profession, the administration of justice, or bring the profession into disrepute.

'What exactly do you want to know?' asked Hilmarton.

'He admitted his guilt but the world and his wife knows he only did so to get parole and qualify as a rehabilitated man. He's turned the system upside down. I need information that'll put things the right way up.'

'What sort of information?'

'Examine his life since leaving prison. Find out if he's done anything remotely dishonest.'

'Okay. Anything else?'

'Yes.' Merrington visualised Artillery Passage – a charming narrow alley in Spitalfields where Benson had opened his unconventional chambers; chambers his own son threatened to join. 'He had a benefactor. I'd like to know who it was and whether the money was clean.'

'Consider it done.'

'Thanks, Bradley.'

Hilmarton let himself out without a word, and then Merrington went back to his desk and that last graph. The jagged red line showing the unprecedented rise in the prison population. It was steeper than the assaults or the suicides and was the mirror image of nothing. Which meant things could only get worse. And quickly. Prisoners were pouring into an already flooded system. He looked towards the window, roughly in the direction of the Old Bailey. He tried to block out a desperate thought, but failed: the irony was irresistible. If Benson won the Blood Orange murder, at least there'd be one fewer prisoner in the mix.

13

Benson hadn't conducted a trial at the Bailey since the Hopton Yard killing. The bread-and-butter work that had come afterwards had seen him appearing at other crown courts, often at the extremities of the circuit. The limelight tends not to fall on places like Croydon Magistrates' Court when you're defending a layabout for handling a stolen bicycle. So stepping into the robing room of the Bailey for a major trial in the full glare of the media wasn't simply intimidating for Benson, it was completely nerve-racking. It was back to the staring, the whispered comments and the ambiguous nods of acknowledgement, glances that could mean he was either damned or praised, and if praised, only because he'd had the guts to remain at the Bar when no one wanted him around. Approaching the building had been bad enough: the cameras had snapped to the sound of jostling, someone had called his name for a face-shot, as if he was a star, or a demon, while, on the other side of the road, Paul Harbeton's family, a mother and four sons, were standing in a line holding a banner: WE HAVE NOT FORGOTTEN.

'Neither have I,' said Benson, putting on his wig. 'And neither has anyone else.'

With his brief under his arm, Benson swapped the robing room for the toilets, where he promptly vomited. Then, his stomach still in spasm, he took the clockwise quartered staircase, his mind on the great advocates whose feet had smoothed its marble steps. The pupils who had become giants. Those legends of fierce independence, whose careers had begun with a little luck and a lot of determination.

'Are you Benson?'

He looked up and the ghosts fled. Standing in front of him was a sharp-eyed man in his mid to late forties. His wig was old and his gown was torn, indicating both experience and vanity, because the tear could easily have been repaired. He was expressionless.

'I am,' said Benson.

'You're for Stainsby?'

'Yes.'

'I'm Andrew Yardley. I prosecute. Can I have a word?'

Until now, the Crown had been represented by Hannah Carey, who'd attended both preliminary hearings. Benson had found her easy to get on with. He'd looked forward to a trial without any of the difficulties that come with difficult people.

'Hannah's case has run over in Leeds,' said Yardley, when they'd stepped into a conference room. 'The brief's been returned to me. I have a slightly different take on things. In the first instance, perhaps you can help me. Is Stainsby going to plead after all?'

'No.'

'Why not?'

'He says he's innocent.'

'I hope you've advised him properly.'

'I wouldn't worry about my advice.'

Yardley smiled as if Benson had only recently completed his pupillage.

'I've seen the proposed witness list,' he said. 'I'd like to make a few changes.'

'And they are?'

'I want a sense of narrative.'

'Which means?'

'Calling witnesses that Hannah was going to read.'

'Which ones?'

'From the discovery of the body to the attendance of the SOCOs.'

Benson had seen the trick. Yardley knew about 2009. And

he also knew a desperate defendant on a second rap could easily be pushed to say he'd been framed. With that in mind, Yardley had isolated the only window of opportunity, because once the scenes of crime officers were in the flat, planting evidence would have been impossible. Yardley was planning to rile Stainsby. And if Stainsby took the bait, which he would, Yardley would ask for the jury to be sent out. He'd point to a defence statement that made no reference to fit-up. He'd observe – courteously – that even Benson had failed to raise the matter when he'd had the chance to do so. And he'd ask if her ladyship would kindly open one of the seven gateways. Which she would. As it happened, exploring the undisclosed defence suited Benson's purposes. He couldn't advise Stainsby to drop the argument until he'd shown him it couldn't have happened. He smiled:

'Do I call you Andrew or Yardley?'

'As you feel comfortable.'

'Well, Andrew, if you feel moved to waste time, don't let me stand in your way. Go ahead.'

'You've no objection?'

'Call whoever you like.'

'Thank you, Benson.'

Again, once in court, Benson felt light-headed.

He'd felt the same flush of excitement when he'd defended Sarah Collingstone in Number 1 Court. Now he was in Number 2 Court, another packed oak-panelled arena where legendary fights had taken place, literally to the death, because that was what had been at stake. The abandoned gallows were still downstairs, at the end of a long, arched corridor that got narrower and narrower as it approached the final doorway. The dice had been cast in this room and others like it. Microphones, laptops and mobile phones couldn't erase the memory of crippling tension as men like

Stainsby sat mute while men like Benson fought to save a life in the balance. Men, already condemned, claiming to be innocent. The public gallery was restive. Journalists were hunched, many of them covering the proceedings in real time for their employers' websites. Too many of them were staring at Benson . . . or Archie, who was seated behind him.

'Court rise.'

Mrs Justice Fleetwood came on to the bench and Benson felt his mind turn sharp. His stomach settled and his anxiety vanished, as did the tapping hacks and the observing public. He felt like an athlete waiting for the sharp snap of a starting pistol, only this was no sprint; it was a run that required stamina and pacing and tactical discipline. He emptied his mind, breathing slowly and deeply, following Abasiama's instructions. The jury was sworn in and the clerk read the single charge on the indictment: that on Friday the 2nd of October 2015, Brent Stainsby murdered Diane Heybridge.

'Ladies and gentlemen, we begin this trial with some guidance and warnings,' said the judge. 'No doubt you have followed the media coverage of this case. You may have argued with your friends and family. You will have overheard conversations at work and in the street. You must now very carefully, and quite deliberately, exclude anything you have heard or thought from your mind. They are all grave distractions. Do not research the case on the internet. Do not seek assistance from Facebook or Twitter. The trial of Brent Stainsby starts today, in this room. You are the jury. Nothing must sway your judgement but the evidence you will hear. Mr Yardley – when you're ready.'

'I'm grateful, my lady.' Yardley paused as if he faced a door he'd rather not open. Then he entered, bringing the jury with him, making introductions, first himself and then Benson, moving respectfully on to his opening speech. He seemed to stand before a body in a morgue. His features were soft and mobile, adding tone and depth to his words. One hand moved occasionally, and slowly, as if he was laying out pictures of Diane on a table. Snapshots of a ruined life. Even Benson was captivated.

14

Tracing the only Jane Tapster in Dover had been easy enough. Basil had obtained her home address, working hours and mobile number, along with a photograph sourced from Facebook. Getting her to speak, however, was another matter. After one cut call, all the others had been diverted to voicemail. So Tess opted for a home visit, a decision that was shelved the moment she saw Tapster entering a supermarket near the block of flats where she lived, and from which she emerged minutes later carrying a plastic bag and a folded copy of the *Sun*, waddling to Pencester Gardens in the centre of town, and a bench overlooking the River Dour. There she sat down, lit up and opened her paper.

'Nasty case,' said Tess, sitting beside her.

She nodded at the spread on the Blood Orange murder. There was a picture of Diane smiling, and another of Stainsby, as if he was about to land a punch.

'Yeah,' said Tapster.

'Poor kid.'

'Yeah.'

Tapster flicked her unfinished cigarette onto the grass and edged away, getting ready to leave.

'Is that all you've got to say, Jane? This is Diane's moment. Stainsby's in the dock.'

'Oh God, it's you.' Tapster crumpled her paper and grabbed

her plastic bag, but her morning snack fell out and a can of Coke hit the ground and rolled down the path. She scrambled after the can while Tess picked up the Mars bar and the egg and bacon bap. Tapster snatched them, backing off. 'I'm not talking, right? No comment, okay? Just leave me be.'

She stumbled off towards a pavilion shaped like a witch's hat, but Tess called out:

'Come back, Jane. I'm not here to ask you about Stainsby's trial. I'm here to talk about your false alibi in 2009. When you set Stainsby free to kill your best friend.'

Tapster was beaten.

Like Diane, perhaps she always had been. She wasn't used to winning anything. That single unwarranted remark from Tess had broken her resistance: the woman who'd lied for Diane had been felled at the throw of the first stone. She sat on the bench, leaning forward, head down, her arms folded tight around her waist. Anyone passing by would think she'd just been kicked in the stomach. A faint breeze disturbed her hair: the purple highlights looked tired, and the brown roots were showing. Thirty yards or so away a group of youths with a dog had gathered round another bench. They were popping open cans of beer, and swearing and spitting, all in fun. The dog barked, joining in.

'Who told you? Gary bloody Bredfield?'

'I'm not prepared to say.'

'You can't trust him. He's blown his brains with spice. And half of that was bleach.'

'It doesn't matter who told me.' Tess made a mental note of the name. 'I just want your side of the story, Jane. Not Bredfield's or anyone else's. I don't want to shop you.'

With the threat gone, Tapster was confused. 'Then why would I talk to you?'

'Because you owe it to your best friend.'

'You're not for her. You're for Stainsby.'

'That's true, Jane. But the truth about Diane's life belongs in that courtroom. The truth doesn't take sides. Just tell me what happened. Then I'll leave you alone.'

Tapster remembered the date for the lie: Saturday, 6th of February 2009. Diane had been watching a DVD at Tapster's and hadn't gone home until after eleven. If asked by the police, Tapster was to say Diane had left at nine, which would have put her with Stainsby at 9.30 p.m.

'I thought the Dover Five went out on Saturdays?' said Tess.

'We did, but Angela and Cathy were ill, so Diane came over to mine.'

'And Stainsby had gone to a nightclub?'

'Yeah. The Twisted Wheel. A real hole.'

'Where he got into a fight?'

'More than a fight.'

Tapster held herself more tightly. The dog, an Alsatian, had bounded over, the dirty rope round its neck flying in the air. It was jumping and snapping. One of the youths came running and kicked it away to whistles and laughter.

'Didn't Bredfield say?' asked Tapster. 'He'd nearly killed him.'

'Who?'

'An off-duty copper.'

'Are you sure?'

'Of course I am. I was interviewed, wasn't I? They told me. Said he'd knocked him out from behind or something. I didn't want to listen, okay? I just shut my ears. I didn't want to know what that psychopath had done. They were showing me photographs and everything and telling me this was my chance to do something good. But I just wanted to help Diane. She'd had it bad enough with Stainsby as it is. If I didn't back her up she'd've been on her own . . . and she was scared of him. Always had been.'

Once again, Tess wondered why Diane had accepted the fear and the domination for so long; why she'd drugged herself with antidepressants rather than get away. There was a kind of courage to her self-destruction. Tess came back to that Saturday night at the Twisted Wheel seven years ago:

'Do you remember the policeman's name?'

'Yeah. John Foster.'

'So you and Diane put Stainsby back home round about the time Foster was attacked?'

'That's right.'

'Why did Stainsby go for him?'

'No bloody idea. The police didn't know, Diane didn't know and I didn't know. Even Bredfield didn't know. It was crazy.'

'Had Stainsby ever met him before?'

'No. That was part of his defence, wasn't it? He said he had no motive.'

'Had Stainsby ever been lifted?'

'No, never. Though he should have been. Him and Bredfield. It was just an unprovoked attack. There weren't no reasons. He must have battered him for the hell of it.'

Tapster had relaxed, but only slightly. She fumbled for a cigarette and dragged in the smoke.

'Anyway, the case was dropped. And it was my fault. And Diane's. We set him free.'

'Why do you say that? There must have been other evidence.'

'It's what the police said to Diane after they'd let Stainsby go. They said it was down to me and her. The case had been looked at by some big lawyer in London and they'd said there wasn't enough evidence and that the real problem had been Diane and me because we'd no reason to lie and we were good characters or something.'

Holding the cigarette at the side of her mouth she opened

the Mars bar. She was comfortless. The smoke and the sugar just didn't hit the spot.

'What do you want to know all this for anyway?' she said, chewing hungrily, not caring about the sight of her gorging. 'It's got nothing to do with Stainsby's trial.'

'Why do you say that?'

'Because I knew Diane, right? She was my best friend.' She spoke like someone turning a corner, getting away from the bullies. Her tone was defiant and confident. 'She never judged me or laughed at me or said I was a fat cow or a loser or a waste of space. I know all that – just look at me. I don't need anyone to tell me. But Diane told me other things. Nice things. She liked my eyes. And the sound of my voice and the way I laughed. She liked all that, okay? She said I was funny. She preferred being with me to the others. She said we were the Dover Two and nothing would ever come between us. She loved me. She told me stuff she'd never tell anyone else. And I know that bastard didn't kill her.'

'Everything you've told me is important, Jane . . . but this is especially important. What exactly are you saying?'

Tapster had gradually changed. The unhappy eating had turned into a feast at a wake. Her grief had a smile. She'd found a good side to dying.

'I'm saying Stainsby's right. Diane killed herself.'

'Are you sure?'

'I'm the only one who knows.'

The Alsatian was back and barking, that filthy rope making loops with every jerk of its neck. Tapster threw her egg and bacon bap into the Dour and the beast dived in, splashing after it, hysterical with expectation. Tapster walked off, to jeers from the drunken crowd and with Tess calling her name, a devouring goddess who knew that for once in her life she was a winner, and a big one. Because Jane Tapster had won the lottery. And now she was the only person in the world who could save Brent Stainsby, that bastard who'd called her a loser.

15

'We've all seen Diane Heybridge before, ladies and gentlemen,' said Yardley. 'On the bus. In a queue at the bank. Posting a letter. She's the ordinary person we fail to notice because she's just like ourselves. Her hopes were like yours. Her troubles like yours. The only difference is that none of you are involved with someone like this defendant. At some time between nine p.m. and eleven p.m. on Friday the second of October last year he murdered her. Why did he do it? This trial will answer that question.'

Benson didn't know whether to admire Yardley for his oratory or despise him for his methods. He'd evoked the very picture of Diane presented by the media just after the judge had urged the jury to erase it from their minds. With that prejudice revived, he now turned to the life of the defendant.

And, paradoxically, it was a sympathetic portrait.

Stainsby had been born into four generations of fishermen sailing out of Dover and Ramsgate. Frank, his father, had been a legend, employing up to seventy-five people. The family home was a detached property on a slope outside Dover. Named The Grove, the windows had sea views above the slate roofs of the houses down below. There were two apple trees in the garden. Frank's wife, Caroline, supplemented the family income at Thunderbolt Taxis, where she took calls and organised the drivers. They were a happy, relatively well-off family.

'But this comfortable existence was coming to an end,' said Yardley. 'The defendant wouldn't have noticed. When he was two, Frank Stainsby (Ramsgate) Ltd went into liquidation and the remaining business, Frank Stainsby (Dover) Ltd, was forced to reduce its working boats from nine to three. When the defendant left school, aged sixteen, he'd thought his future was secure, boasting he'd no need for qualifications. He didn't know that his father could barely make ends meet as fishing quotas and frozen foods squeezed the life out of the industry.'

Benson recognised the description. His own father had faced the same relentless pressures. Even now it was a struggle. He had one boat left, and he ran it alone. Because he'd let his son go. Told him to follow his heart.

'2002 was a catastrophic year for the Stainsby family,' said Yardley. 'For the defendant, aged twenty-four, things began well. He met Diane Heybridge, who worked at Greggs in Crompton Road. He thought about buying a flat. He bought a car. He couldn't have imagined that before the year was out his mother would be dead from breast cancer and his father would be declared bankrupt, with The Grove, his wife's jewellery and his son's car sold at auction to pay off debts accumulated in secret. By 2003, Frank was destitute, living in a property owned by the Dover Seamen's Society and the defendant was living with Diane, in her council flat, mocked on Friends Reunited by the classmates who'd earned those pointless qualifications. All that remained of the family company was a two-floor boat shed near the harbour, a shell of a business with nothing left inside except a broken toilet.'

Yardley dwelled on this outcome like the doctor who'd found the first damaged cell or the accountant who'd first recognised the deficit could never be turned around. Because these two events, coming in quick succession, were the turning point in the defendant's life. This was the year he became an embittered and angry man.

'One can only applaud his efforts to rebuild his life. He sought work on other fishing boats, and for the next four years – 2003 to 2006 – he moved around Kent, Suffolk and Norfolk taking what jobs he could, a deckhand who'd always seen himself as a captain. It was an itinerant existence, which came to an end in 2007 when, at the age of twenty-eight, he formed his own company: Stainsby's Seafood Locker Ltd. Using the old boat shed in Dover as a registered office, the defendant bought a second-hand refrigerated van and began making deliveries of seafood from coastal ports to inland restaurants and supermarkets. It was a brave venture, but it failed. The pressures on the fishing industry had been transferred to its dependent trades. The company became a front for damaged pride. Without Diane, the defendant couldn't have put a litre of fuel in the tank.'

Benson glanced at Stainsby in the dock. He was dressed in a borrowed blue suit that was a size too small, giving him the appearance of a bouncer who wants you to know he's been to the gym. He was glaring at Yardley as if he might hit him: perhaps as hard as the guy he'd battered in that Dover nightclub – an event neatly passed over by Yardley, who'd now turned to Diane's story. Benson's red pencil scored a line in the margin of his notes. The Crown had begun it very late, skipping her childhood.

'Throughout this tragic year, Diane nursed Caroline until she died. And after Frank's financial collapse she was there to help him when he turned to drink. She was the one who the police called when he caused trouble in town. She was the one who took him home. And she was the one who brought him an Indian takeaway on Friday nights. It became a tradition. A tradition that this defendant was to exploit when he planned the murder of his girlfriend.

'And that had been after fourteen years of abuse. Diane had made her bid for freedom the week that Frank died. At the reading of his will she discovered that Frank had maintained an Aviva life insurance policy which now generated a sum in excess of sixty thousand pounds, to be divided equally, under the terms of the will, between herself and the defendant. And, in recognition of her relationship with Caroline, Diane was to receive all that remained of her jewellery: a pair of earrings, a bracelet and a pendant on a chain. That very evening Diane left the defendant, left her own flat, and moved in with a friend, Jane Tapster. But her eyes were on London. Within a week, she'd enrolled on a secretarial course in Harringay, applied for part-time work in Finsbury Park and taken a flat sight unseen in Tottenham. A month later – on Wednesday the twenty-third of September, 2015 – she left Dover. And that should have been the beginning of Diane's great adventure. Only it wasn't to be. She never started the secretarial course. She never started the work. She only made it to Tottenham.'

Because – said Yardley – this defendant wouldn't let her go. He looked at him across the silent courtroom.

'He followed her to London. And when he got there, he turned up on a Friday night with an Indian takeaway spiked with medication – medication that Diane had needed to cope with her previous life; medication she'd left behind. When she was incapacitated . . .'

Benson knew the Crown's case. He knew about the hanging and he didn't want to hear Yardley spell out everything that had happened beforehand.

'He murdered her, ladies and gentlemen,' said Yardley. 'And three days later he asked his solicitor if he had any claim on her share of the policy. Such is our case. Mr Benson will argue that Diane killed herself. I leave it to him to elaborate why. You will have to choose between the two explanations and you will need to be sure you are right. It is a stark choice, ladies and gentlemen. Bring your hearts and minds to the task.'

Mrs Justice Fleetwood thanked Yardley. And Yardley turned a page in his file.

16

Yardley didn't call every witness from the finding of the body until the arrival of the SOCOs. Just key personnel: a police community support officer, Constance Walcott, and the duty inspector, Katherine Taylor. The effect was chilling. The detail – from the receipt of an emergency call to officers attending and the securing of the scene – was clinical, in stark contrast to the human story being investigated. First aid not being required, Diane's body had been left hanging in the bedroom. Benson listened carefully, checking the chronology he'd prepared:

03.10.2015	Saturday
12.13 p.m.	999 call received from neighbour: MILENA SIBHATU
12.32 p.m.	2 PCSOs arrive at 15C Heston Road: GRAHAM O'CONNELL and CONSTANCE WALCOTT. Property secured.
1.03 p.m.	Duty inspector arrives: INSPECTOR KATHERINE TAYLOR. Logbook opened recording entry and exit to premises
1.20 p.m.	TAYLOR speaks with SIBHATU and calls Tottenham CID
1.49 p.m.	DCI STUART GOODSHAW arrives.

2.15 p.m.	DR AGGARWAL, divisional surgeon, arrives. Given lividity and rigor, time of death: 9.00 p.m. to 11.00 p.m. on 02.10.2015.
3.00 p.m.	SOCOs take over crime scene.

Walcott and her colleague had met Milena Sibhatu on the pavement at Heston Road. After a brief examination of the premises and the body, Walcott had called the duty inspector and then remained outside with Sibhatu. All doors had been closed. No one with access to the site smoked. Benson rose:

'Do you know this area, Miss Walcott?'

'Very well. It's my beat.'

'Do you get people gathering outside Alan's Kebab's on a Friday night?'

'Yes. Lots. From the Stag's Head across the road. And locals.'

'Saturdays too?'

'Yes.'

'Would you have rented this flat?'

'No way.'

'Why not?'

'Where do you want me to begin?'

'You choose.'

'The noise, the smells, the draughts.'

'Thank you.'

Yardley exchanged a bemused glance with the judge and then called Inspector Taylor, who said she hadn't even entered the building. Given the description of the body and her conversation with Mrs Sibhatu, she'd designated the flat a potential crime scene. Asked by Yardley about the importance of securing the premises, she said:

'You've only got one opportunity. If people were allowed to tramp in and out, the evidence would be fatally compromised.'

'Could you explain that, please?'

'It's very easy to leave traces of DNA. It's very easy to disturb existing evidence, critical evidence . . . the slightest interference can mislead the investigators.'

'Which is why you remained on the pavement?'

'Yes. I had no protective clothing.'

'Is that essential?'

'Absolutely. Shoe covers and gloves have to be worn, and if you touch anything the gloves have to be changed. It really is a desperately important exercise. The scene has to be kept sterile.'

'In relation to this case, to what extent had that objective been achieved?'

'It was as good as it gets. When I arrived the scene had only been accessed for a matter of minutes. Mrs Sibhatu had pushed open the bedroom door, but apart from that nothing else had been touched or moved. I then created a perimeter – or, more accurately, I formalised the perimeter imposed by the PCSOs.'

'Thank you. Remain there, please.'

Benson rose.

'You called DCI Goodshaw?'

'I did.'

'Do you know him?'

'No.'

'Did you mention Diane Heybridge by name?'

'I didn't.'

'Thank you, Inspector.'

Benson sat down, to another exchange of glances between prosecutor and judge. Yardley then listed the items of evidence that had been recovered by the forensic scientists. The picture was now complete:

Nobody involved knew Stainsby.

Nobody, at this point, had accessed the Police National Computer.

Nobody could have linked Diane to Stainsby.

Nobody had the motive or opportunity to plant any evidence.

Which is to say, if Goodshaw had decided that Stainsby had killed Diane by the time he went to Dover the next day, he certainly hadn't come to any such conclusion when he arrived at Heston Road. He hadn't even known her name. And by the time he did know, the SOCOs were in situ. The window of opportunity for a set-up had been well and truly sealed. There was no possible connection between 2009 and 2015. Which – according to the Crown – meant the hair, the ash and the cigarette butt could only have got there if Stainsby had done what he said he didn't do. Mrs Justice Fleetwood closed her laptop.

'Ladies and gentlemen, I think that's good place to stop for lunch.'

17

'How do you know she killed herself, Jane?' said Tess. 'I understand you may not like Stainsby, but he's on trial for *murder*. And if he didn't commit that murder—'

'He can still rot in prison. I can't tell you how good this feels . . . to know that I could get him out, and to not do it. I just want him to know he'll be in there because of me.'

If Tapster had been frightened to talk about the false alibi given in 2009, she'd bitten Tess's hand off when it came to discussing the death of her best friend in 2015. This was her chance to let the truth be known, aware that Tess would never be able to repeat it in a courtroom. And why tell it at all? Because there's no pleasure in living vengeance if you're the only one who knows what you're doing. Tess had followed Tapster all the way to her block of flats, up two flights of stairs, because the lift was broken, and to her front door, where, rather than getting the door slammed in her face, she'd been invited in.

Tapster should have been an artist. Maybe an interior designer. The armchairs were blue, the standard lamp was red and the cupboards were green. The door to the kitchen was striped like a zebra crossing. A huge mirror made the room seem larger and brighter. Tapster's love of space and colour made Tess faintly sad; there was a talent here, and it had probably gone unrecognised.

'We both felt bad after Stainsby got off,' said Tapster. 'Diane more than me. I'm not a bad person, but I just forgot about it. You've got to get on, haven't you? But Diane couldn't.'

For a couple of months she'd been in pieces. Couldn't pull herself together. That's when she went on those pills for the first time. But they didn't work. They messed with her moods. Made her feel worse. And that's when she started talking about killing herself.

'She'd come here and use my computer to find out different ways of topping yourself.'

'Have you still got the computer?'

'No. And if I had, I wouldn't give it to you. Remember what I said: I'll talk, but I won't admit nothing. I'll deny anything you say I said . . . but when this is all over I want you to—'

'I won't be telling Stainsby anything. You can tell him yourself.' Tess shoved Tapster back on track: 'Weren't you worried about Diane?'

'Of course I was.'

'But you let her research—'

'I didn't let her do nothing. I found it in the memory,

didn't I? The prompt thing in the search engine. She was doing it here because she didn't want Stainsby to know. And when I found out, I told her to come off them pills and get another doctor. I told her to forget about Foster but she couldn't.' Tapster bit her lip. 'She'd been looking at poison and drugs and drowning and hanging. There's loads of ways. And she went for hanging, didn't she?'

Tess just couldn't imagine the conversation. She'd wondered about ending her own life once, when she'd quit London for Strasbourg five years back, but it had been so abstract as to be nothing more than a symptom of extreme distress. Tess said, 'That was seven years ago, Jane. Didn't things improve?'

'Well, she stopped looking online. But that doesn't mean nothing. Thing is . . . she changed. She became odd, like.'

Tapster was seated, legs crossed, still clutching her copy of the *Sun*. And Tess had an inkling that she'd buy a copy every day and that she'd paste cuttings in an album. But for now the anger had been displaced by confusion.

'She started making up an imaginary life.'

'In what way?'

'I blame them pills. She became unreliable. Sometimes she didn't turn up on a Saturday night. She'd say she'd been feeling unwell. And then, sometimes she'd be high, walking fast and talking quick, saying that she was going to change things out there. She was going to do something good one day, she was going to make a difference to the world.' Tapster laughed, briefly and bitterly. 'She just wanted to be someone else. Get away from Stainsby. She even dressed up.'

'What do you mean?'

'What I said. She had wigs and hats and clothes picked up from Oxfam. Different pairs of glasses.'

'Seriously?'

'She kept the stuff here. In a box. Didn't want Stainsby

to know. And every now and then, when she was feeling bad, she'd come round and dress up and paint her face and head out. She'd borrow cars from people.'

'Did you go with her?'

'No. That was the point. She wasn't Diane any more. Just for one night she was a different person. She was Vicky or Sharon or Julie . . . with an imaginary boyfriend. She'd say, "I'm off to see Harry." And all because of that false alibi. Wanting to make up for what we'd done.'

'Have you still got the—'

'No. Diane chucked the lot before she went to London. When she left him she came here, you know? It was to me she turned when she'd had enough.'

Now tears broke out. Tapster's recollection released the grief that had been stifled by rage and the dark joy of knowing that Stainsby had been imprisoned.

'Most of the time she was normal. But then she'd flip and I couldn't reach her. She was talking rubbish and acting mad. And it's because she couldn't stand her life. Couldn't stand living with Stainsby. I mean, she only stayed with him because of his dad, Frank, who was a lovely man and loved her like she was his own, and needed her, and it was only when Frank died that Diane made a break. But it was too late. Her mind was messed up. I told her to stay with me. Not to leave Dover. But she wouldn't listen. Said she had to get away and start again and that I could come whenever I wanted and we'd go out on the town . . . but there was no way she was going to survive in London . . . not with her mind all over the place. Not without the Dover Five. Not without me . . . just like I can't get by without her. Cos we were mates, best mates, and now she's dead. She's gone. And I'm telling you, it all began when she met that bastard Stainsby. Being with him was one long suicide, only you couldn't look him up on the internet. There was Diane checking out hanging, and he was already around her neck. I'm sorry' – she threw the *Sun* on the floor and hid her face in her hands – 'I haven't spoken about this to no one and I wish I'd stopped her, kept her here, and looked after her like she looked after me, before she got screwed up by them pills.'

Tess went into the kitchen and returned with a glass of water. She sat on the arm of the chair, and something at once maternal and sisterly came over her, pushing the lawyer aside: she put a hand on Tapster's juddering shoulder.

'Will you show me some photos? I'd love to see Diane and the Dover Five in action.'

They laughed. Tapster told stories. And Tess was moved to see snaps of Diane fooling around. Touched to notice she was always beside Tapster, often with an arm around her neck. These were the good times; times when self-worth was flying high. Maybe too high to cope with the fall next morning.

But Tess was also glad to see pictures of Stainsby. There were photographs of him with Diane, sitting on the wall beneath that witch's hat in Pencester Gardens, and another of him falling in the Dour, pushed by his best mate Gary Bredfield, who'd done six months for possession with intent to supply, and who'd fancied Diane; and who'd matched Benson's description of the ex-con who'd had him thrown into the back of a van.

'I know you're sure Stainsby's innocent, Jane. But there's plenty of forensic evidence. What about that cigarette end? It was found by her feet.'

Tapster nearly smiled . . . like Stainsby when Benson had asked if he'd ever seen Diane eat a blood orange.

'She brought one to London, didn't she? She'd been looking up how to preserve forensic evidence as well.'

'What?'

'Yeah.' Tapster was triumphant, ecstatic and grief stricken. 'She kept it in my fridge in a plastic bag. And when she left for London she took it with her. She knew he'd come after her at some point. She knew he'd find an excuse . . . and she told me she was going to get her own back, for her and for me, and for loads of other people. She was going to do something big. Really big. She was going to put Stainsby away for life.'

18

After lunch Yardley called Milena Sibhatu, the neighbour who'd found Diane Heybridge's body, the woman who'd befriended Diane and could testify to her state of mind during the last ten days of her life. Aged thirty-seven, she had one son, an eleven-year-old called Jonas. She worked in the evenings as a waitress. She was from Asmara, the capital of Eritrea.

Benson looked up.

This last detail wasn't in the witness statement, and for an instant Benson was fishing in a bin for cigarettes, watched by a boy who'd got nowhere to play. Milena was almost certainly his mother. This was the boy schooled in diseases. Evoking Meersham, he'd scared Benson off.

'You met Diane Heybridge the day she arrived in London?'

'Yes.'

'This was Wednesday the twenty-third of September of 2015?'

'Yes. I was on the pavement arguing with the landlord, Mr Nesbit. She arrived with a single suitcase.'

Over the next few days, Mrs Sibhatu had helped Diane settle in. She'd invited her for lunch on Sunday. Conversation had quickly turned from leaking taps to future hopes. That Jonas would do well at school; that he'd learn who to follow and who to avoid; that he'd grow to be a man who told the truth, kept his word and was kind to his neighbour.

With his red pencil, Benson swiftly circled 'future', 'hopes' and 'neighbour'.

'After that lunch, Diane gave me a set of keys.'

'You arranged to meet again?'

'We did. I suggested we visit the Paddock Community Nature Park on the following Saturday.'

'That would be in five days' time; the third of October?'

'Yes.'

'Did you see her again, after that meal?'

'Yes.'

'How would you describe her state of mind during the time you knew her?'

'She was excited.'

Benson looped that word too.

'Could you elaborate?'

'She was like Jonas on Christmas Eve.'

'In what way?'

'Well, she said she hadn't ridden a bike since she was ten and she'd never been on a plane, so she'd bought herself a second-hand bike and she'd gone to a travel agent . . . she was planning a trip abroad . . . she was planning all sorts of things she'd never done before. Everything was new. She was impatient for tomorrow.'

'Within a week, Diane was dead. This defendant maintains it was suicide. What's your view, looking back?'

'It just doesn't make sense.'

'Why?'

'Well . . . no one kills themselves on Christmas Eve. Not when they know what's coming.'

When Diane didn't arrive at the agreed time, Mrs Sibhatu told Jonas to get well wrapped up and she went over with the spares. On entering the property she noticed an odour, at once familiar and unpleasant: faeces . . . which, it later transpired, had been a consequence of death. She'd also identified tobacco smoke, which had been striking, given that Diane had said she hated smoking and hoped never to see a cigarette again.

'I walked down the corridor and saw a flex tied to the bedroom door handle . . .with the other end looped over the top. As I got closer the smell got stronger. And when I pushed the door it jammed against something.'

Mrs Sibhatu swung her head to one side.

'Pause there, Mrs Sibhatu,' said Mrs Justice Fleetwood. 'Have some water. And take your time.'

'Thank you.'

It was dark inside and the light switch had been broken – said Mrs Sibhatu, on resuming her evidence – so she'd walked to the bed and found a wall lamp operated by a cord. She'd pulled it and turned around, and that's when she'd seen Diane, and her son standing in the room, looking at the body.

'I ran towards him and pushed him into the corridor.'

'How long were in you in the flat altogether?'

'Less than a minute.'

'At that point, you went outside and called the police?'

'Yes.'

'In due course, you spoke to Inspector Taylor. What did you say?'

'Well, the officers were wondering if it could be a suicide, so I said I couldn't understand why she'd put an orange in her mouth. I found that very odd.'

'Thank you, Mrs Sibhatu. Please remain there. Mr Benson may have some questions for you.'

Benson did. His eyes were on a few circled words. Strong words to be turned inside out.

19

Tess did her best to persuade Jane Tapster to give evidence, but she wouldn't yield. And it wasn't because she didn't fancy getting done for giving a false alibi. It was for Diane. She was helping her best friend get even. They'd got Stainsby off one charge and were now putting him down for another. It was an alliance that reached across the grave. Tess sat in her Mini and quickly sent some texts. First, to Archie:

> A fight took place on 6.2.2015 at the Twisted Wheel nightclub in Dover. Injured party: off-duty policeman John Foster. Case dropped on advice of counsel.
>
> Guy in van was Gary Bredfield. Did six months for possession.

And then to Benson:

> Stainsby was framed. Not by the police but Diane. Suggest a snifter at Grapeshots. 7pm? Hope all goes well, Tess.

It was only after sending the text to Benson that Tess noticed a warmer impulse had moved her fingers. The professional tone had gone to Archie. Why the hell had she done that? Tossing her phone onto the passenger seat, she switched on Radio London and caught the end of a row over Brexit. Then the announcer turned to another argument, the one connected to the Blood Orange murder, which had opened that morning at the Old Bailey.

William Benson, convicted of murdering Paul Harbeton and now representing Brent Stainsby, had been met by a crowd of protesters upon his arrival at court. Afterwards, Kenny Harbeton, the father of the victim, spoke to the assembled media, saying it was scandalous that a convicted killer could enter court and defend someone charged with the same crime. Paul had lost his life. Benson had kept his and was now earning a fortune. The family would be seeking an interview with Richard Merrington MP, the Secretary of State for Justice, as soon as possible. Kenny had the last word:

'He promised to act last year and he's done nothing. Benson's laughing all the way to the bank.'

Still on law and order, the announcer moved on to another case. A murder. By Limehouse Cut. Apart from an arrest, no details had been released. DI Susan Harvey was confident—

'Here we go,' said Tess, turning off the radio. 'The criticism, the abuse. The understandable indignation. It all starts again.'

The tabloids had been busy ever since they'd discovered Benson would be representing Stainsby. They'd focused on the tragedy of the girl from Dover. But the live issue was Benson from Spitalfields. His conviction. And the limits of rehabilitation. Sally was right: the Harbeton business was so much bigger than Tess. In fact, it was bigger than Benson, because whilst he'd won the argument, at law, to practise as a barrister, the court of public opinion had failed to settle on a verdict. Because Paul Harbeton was dead. And Benson had killed him.

Or had he?

Tess turned the key in the ignition and set off for London. Recalling the Limehouse business – or, rather, a few run-ins with the investigating officer DI Harvey – she turned the radio back on. But the item had been covered. The announcer had turned to other news. A prison officer had been stabbed at HMP Clayton Moor, near Halifax. The victim was in a stable condition. An inquiry was underway. In a separate development, a report from the Independent Monitoring Board on HMP Kingswood in Bristol had found that the influx of 'new psychoactive substances' along with reduced staff levels had led to the near collapse of order and a crisis in health management. The drugs, delivered by drones, were so dangerous and their use so prevalent that ambulances had been called to the prison up to thirty-five times per week. The Prison Officers' Association blamed this and other incidents on sentencing policy, along with savage cuts in funding since 2010, which had seen seven thousand experienced prison officers leave the profession. Greg Rawlings of the POA had sought another urgent meeting with Justice Secretary Richard Merrington, who'd said that he took the situation extremely seriously. A range of measures had already been implemented to support staff and prisoners, he said, 'but I accept more can be done'.

Accelerating along the A2 back to London, Tess could only find one glimmer of light in this dark and darkening picture. Merrington had too much on his hands to care about the scandal of William Benson. At least for now.

20

Benson proceeded like someone on a tightrope suspended high above Newgate:

'You entered the flat at roughly twelve-ten p.m.?'

'Yes.'

'Lunchtime?'

'We'd planned a picnic.'

'Could you hear music from the kebab shop below?'

Mrs Sibhatu seemed to listen once more. 'Yes.'

Benson was now very careful. He didn't mention the draught described by the PCSO, only its consequences: 'Smell the cooking?'

'I think so, yes.'

'Along with cigarette smoke?'

'That was for sure.'

'Was it fresh or stale?'

'I really wouldn't know.'

That was all he needed. Benson took a quick step forward before Mrs Sibhatu knocked him off the wire:

'The first time you had an intimate conversation with Diane was during that Sunday lunch?'

'Yes.'

'When you talked about the future?'

'That's right.'

'What about the past? Diane's past?'

'She didn't want to talk about it.'

'Didn't that strike you as significant?'

'No.'

'People usually get to know each other by talking about what they've done, not what they hope to do. But you didn't?'

'No. Because I understand how it feels to want to leave the past behind.'

'But if I was to speak on your behalf, Mrs Sibhatu, I'd need to know what you'd turned away from. Don't you agree?'

'Maybe.'

'To explain your hopes for Jonas, I'd need to explain why you'd left Eritrea.'

'Yes . . . you would.'

'And you have no idea why Diane left Dover, do you?'

'No. I don't.'

'And with great respect, Mrs Sibhatu, you can't speak for Diane. Any more than I can speak for you.'

'I wouldn't claim to.'

'But Mr Yardley has suggested that you can.'

Benson took another careful step, from a future without reference to the past, to hopes without reference to the future; the old hopes that Diane didn't want to talk about:

'Mrs Sibhatu, does it surprise you to learn that she told her GP that not having children was "almost unbearable"?'

Mrs Sibhatu wasn't surprised, but she'd hesitated before saying so, and at that moment Benson knew his intuition was right. Out of a desire to help the stranger, Mrs Sibhatu had not told the complete truth. She'd kept something back.

'When you spoke of Jonas and his future, how would you describe Diane's reaction?'

'Sad. I have to say, she looked sad.'

'You saw the longing?'

'I did, yes.'

'May I call it pain?'

Mrs Sibhatu nodded. And Benson made another hesitant step, hoping he wouldn't fall.

'When did you first sense that pain, Mrs Sibhatu? When you saw Diane arrive with a single suitcase?'

'Yes. But there's nothing wrong with that, Mr Benson. The same was true of me, once.'

'And many others,' said Benson, confident now. 'But I want the jury to meet the woman you met on the twenty-third of September last year. Without knowing why, you saw she was vulnerable and you pitied her?'

'I did.'

'Which is why you welcomed her into your family?'

'Yes.'

'Because she is your neighbour?'

'Yes.'

'Mrs Sibhatu, the person who'd come to London was impatient for tomorrow because she was desperate to get away from yesterday. That's what you recognised, isn't it?'

'Yes. But I recognised hope, too. Far more hope than pain.'

Benson steadied himself before posing his next question. He'd nearly reached the other side. The dizziness had gone. 'Forgive my directness, Mrs Sibhatu, but did you ever contemplate taking your own life?'

'No.'

'May I ask why?'

'Because I had my faith . . . and I had my son.'

'Thank you, Mrs Sibhatu.'

Benson had made it; and he couldn't have asked for more. Because Diane had come to Tottenham with neither of those. And the jury knew it. But the arresting similarity between the two fleeing women only took Benson so far, and potentially in a very damaging direction. He sat down hoping to God the jury hadn't noticed that Diane's escape from Stainsby – characterised as 'leaving Dover' by Benson – had been juxtaposed with Mrs Sibhatu's escape from extrajudicial executions, human rights violations and torture.

21

Crouched over the round table in a corner of Grapeshots, Archie could barely contain himself. Earlier that afternoon Rizla hadn't only managed to explain away the smoke – it could easily have risen from the shop below – he'd neutralised a key element of the prosecution case: the only instance when Stainsby had expressed an intent to kill. Benson, made uncomfortable by the praise of his clerk, went to the bar.

But Tess relished the moment, because Archie was talking to her as if all was forgiven. He'd called her Tess. By accident. But he'd done it. Caught up in his story, he'd dropped 'de Vere'.

Malcolm Hargreaves had been the Stainsby family solicitor. He'd handled all of Frank and Caroline's business and domestic affairs, from conveyancing to liquidation of assets. He'd had the painful task of managing the disintegration of their world. He'd also testified to the launch and sinking of Brent Stainsby and his Seafood Locker, an inherited client he clearly didn't like. Critically – for the prosecution – he'd been the executor of Frank's will. He'd arranged a meeting with Stainsby and Diane to explain the bequests and how they would be administered.

'This is when Stainsby and Diane find out there's thirty-odd grand coming to each of them,' said Archie.

'And Diane leaves him that night,' said Tess.

'Exactly.'

Taking his time, Yardley had then read out two agreed reported statements. First, after Diane had left him: 'I'll do time before she gets anything from my parents.' Second, after being arrested at Greggs for a public order offence: 'You won't see a penny of that policy and you will never, ever wear my mother's jewellery.' At this point, Yardley returned to Mr Hargreaves's evidence: that on hearing a payment would be made to Diane within three days, he'd said, 'I'll choke her first.'

Benson's cross-examination had been extraordinarily simple:

'Mr Stainsby is a big man, isn't he?'

'Yes.'

'There's a lot of muscle there and he's not the most tactful of men?'

'No, he's not.'

'His speech lacks ornament?'

'That's one way of putting it.'

'Were you intimidated?'

'Very much so. He was angry, leaning over my desk and pointing a finger at me. I can't say it was an agreeable encounter.'

'He was ranting about his father, wasn't he?'

'Yes.'

'Saying he'd never have made the bequest if he'd known Diane might leave him?'

'He expressed himself with fishermen's adjectives, Mr Benson. But I'll accept your version.'

'Speaking quickly, tripping over his words?'

'Very much so. And as I said to Mr Yardley, I could hardly catch them all.'

'Do you accept you might have dropped one or two?'

'Yes, I wasn't taking notes.'

'Caught one?'

'I don't follow your meaning.'

'Picked up a word he might not have said?'

'Yes, that's possible. He was, as you say, ranting.'

'How about a preposition? A word as small as "her"?'

'I'd need an example, but yes, it's possible.'

'I'm thinking of "I'll choke *her* first". Are you absolutely sure, without fear of contradiction, that he didn't say "*I'll* choke first"?'

Mr Hargreaves hadn't answered quickly enough. He'd paused to think, giving Benson the chance to add a rider: 'He was choking with rage, wasn't he?'

And the rider had slowed Mr Hargreaves down even more. He was wanting to be sure, because a lot hung on those three letters, H-E-R, maybe too much, and by the time he'd made up his mind it was too late to say anything else. His own hesitation had undermined his earlier confidence: 'I'm sorry, I can't be absolutely sure.'

And with that concession the previous admitted statements lost some of their bite. It had been a delicious moment.

'It's a crumb,' said Benson, returning with a G&T for Tess, a double port for Archie and a bottle of Spitfire ale for himself. To deter Tess from joining Archie in song, he reminded her that Hargreaves had also testified that Stainsby had been on the phone, wanting Diane's address, which he'd refused to disclose, and was ringing again within days of Diane's death, banging on about the insurance policy. 'It comes to me now, doesn't it?' he'd said. 'When can you get it back?'

'Which,' said Benson, 'just hammered home the prosecution case.'

The real issue for discussion, however, wasn't these small victories – which Benson described as straws in the wind – but Tess's visit to Jane Tapster. Her testimony, forever to be concealed, changed everything. And nothing.

'It never occurred to me that Diane might have planted the evidence herself.'

'Me neither,' said Tess.

'It explains why she went to London. If she'd stayed at home in Dover the forensic would have meant nothing. She'd thought it all through. Even down to getting work and starting a secretarial course. It's incredible.' Benson threw a packet of pork scratchings on the table. 'I'd have sworn Stainsby was guilty. And all along he's just been his plain nauseating self. I can't believe it. We're fighting for an innocent man.'

'Who's still nauseating,' said Tess. She took the slice of lemon from her G&T and ate it. 'Can't we just borrow Tapster's idea? Feed it to some witnesses and see if they bite?'

'There's no point,' said Benson. 'If we give the jury a choice between murder and a suicide made to look like murder by an abusive partner, the jury will opt for murder. If we give the jury a choice between murder and a suicide provoked by the abusive partner, they'll still go for murder.' He poured the ale into his pewter tankard. 'To show that we're sympathetic to Diane involves accepting that Stainsby was a complete bastard. To suggest Diane would have killed herself regardless involves asking the jury to be sympathetic to her abuser. Whatever way we come at this, Diane has it sewn up.'

'Don't forget the forensic, Rizla. You're knackered there, too.'

'Thanks, Archie.'

'Look, things aren't that bad,' said Tess. 'At least we can now forget about your man Bredfield. There's no half story or full story. He got it all wrong.'

'That's true,' said Benson.

'The case isn't complicated,' said Tess. 'We just can't win it.'

'Thanks to you as well.'

They raised their glasses and didn't speak for a while. When they did, it was Archie, returning to Bredfield. He'd done some research.

'For what it's worth, he's not from Dover. Lives down the road in Hythe. Used to work for Frank Stainsby until he got sacked. He's got a boat that he rents out for diving and fishing trips. Still does. Barely breaks even.'

Benson didn't seem to have listened because he returned, as if in reply, to that fight in the Twisted Wheel, and other research carried out by Archie. At Benson's request, he'd called the Dover CPS and obtained the name of the barrister who'd binned the case in 2009. She was called Pauline Osborne. She'd left the Bar three years back to run a pub in Tower Hamlets. Benson suggested Tess might drop in. Find out what she remembered.

'She'll know far more than Tapster.'

'And she won't talk. The conference was confidential.'

'All you can do is ask. That's what I say every time I stand up.' Benson glanced at his watch and frowned. 'Sorry, I have to go. Traddles calls. Do you know, he doesn't meow when he's hungry. He quacks like a duck. It's really disconcerting.'

After he'd vanished down Artillery Passage, Tess and Archie sat in silence. There weren't many other punters so the ongoing quiet became oppressive. Archie ate some pork scratchings while Tess turned a beer mat in circles. She tried to be cheery:

'Where's Molly?'

'Globe Town. A wrestling match.'

'Really?'

'She's a timekeeper.'

'She's not.'

'She is. Before that she was a referee. For twenty years.'

'You're kidding.'

'Nope.'

'God. Did she ever do the grappling stuff?'

Archie gave his glass of port a swish.

'He's got viewings for the boat already. Every day this week. That's why he's gone. He doesn't want you to know. He's embarrassed.'

'So why tell me, Archie?'

He drained his glass and called for some cheese and onion crisps and a pickled egg. 'Because I think you'd be upset if I didn't bring you into the family secret.'

22

Benson didn't like the spiv who paced around *The Wooden Doll* opening cupboards and drawers. His stomach leaned over his belt like a failed Yorkshire pudding. His hair was too long and his designer glasses had been conceived for someone half his age. A pointed shoe – probably Italian and put together from calves led to the slaughter by child slaves – was now pressing on Benson's pedal bin, moving the lid up and down.

'That's what a fish looks like out of water,' he joked.

'I'm afraid that item won't be included in the sale.'

'You were a fisherman, weren't you?'

'Yes.'

'Then a philosopher?'

'I dropped the subject at the end of my second year.'

Danny Weaver – he'd introduced himself with a moist handshake – gave a wink. The wink meant he'd read the newspapers. He knew who Benson was. He knew he'd been convicted of murder, studied law in prison and had come to the Bar. He was a fish out of water.

'Is it quiet around here?'

'Very.'

'No snoopers?'

'None.'

'Ever been broken into?'

'Never.'

'Is there an alarm?'

'No.'

'Any friendly neighbours who keep an eye on things?'

'I don't have friends and I don't have neighbours, and nobody's ever bothered me.'

Traddles slipped through the open door.

'Have you got a dog?'

'No.'

'I don't like dogs. They leave a smell.'

'There is no smell. Ergo there is no dog.'

'Good one. You've not forgotten the old philosophy. I just want to be sure, m'lord. That's what you say to a jury, isn't it, before they send someone down? They have to be sure?'

'It is and they do.'

Traddles had got the itch badly and he fancied his chances with Danny. He leaned on his sagging trousers.

With a kick, Danny said, 'Can I take some photos? There's only two online. The wife can be particular.'

'Your wife can come and look.'

'Another good one. No pictures, then?'

'No pictures. Are you finished, Mr Weaver?'

'Almost. Can we have a gander outside?'

They went on deck and Benson took him to the aft of the boat, and the bench with a view down Seymour Basin. Benson would sit here, going over his cases – when he had them – plucking sage or thyme from a cluster of earthenware pots. He'd smoke here, too, reading Frost or Yeats or Young, the poets who'd been his friends in prison. They'd written about important things: the scent of apples, an excess of love, a secret wood. They'd brought Benson a remembrance of forbidden sensations. They'd helped keep him alive. And it was here, at this bench, that he'd fish for his own words, keeping some and throwing others back, preparing to write his fragmented confessions. Evening light played upon the water. Flies skipped on the shadows. Benson loved this place. He needed it.

'Nice spot.'

'It is.'

'Why sell it?'

'A whim.'

'You'll take a sensible offer?'

'No.'

'You're short of the readies?'

'I mean what I say, ergo I want the asking price.'

'That's another good one.'

Benson led the way back to the wharf and the bank of trees that kept Seymour Road at a distance. Standing on the uneven stone flags, Danny hitched his trousers and nodded towards a wooden cabin.

'That's for the main bin?'

'Yes.'

'When's collection day?'

'Friday morning. I bring it to the main road on Thursday night. And now I'm afraid I must work.'

Danny's hands were in his pockets and his trousers had slumped again. He was heavy on his pointed feet and Benson feared a sting from a pointed tail.

'You're for Stainsby, aren't you? The Blood Orange murder?'

'I am.'

'Is he as evil as he looks?'

'If you've any more questions about the boat, just call the agent.'

'Is it difficult standing up for someone when you know they're guilty?'

'Don't forget to tell your wife she can come when she wants. But make your mind up. There's a lot of interest.'

Danny gave Benson's shoulder a slap. 'That's called side-stepping the question, isn't it? Neat move. If I ever kill the wife, I'll ask for you.'

'No, you won't.'

'Why not?'

'Because I'll be a witness for the prosecution.'

'Good one, Mr Benson. I like it. You're quick.'

* * *

After he'd gone, Benson went up the path between the trees towards the gate in the railings on Seymour Road. He kept back, watching his visitor walk a few yards down the pavement. After making a call on his mobile, Danny Weaver had another trouser-hitch, pressed his keys as if to switch from porn to Disney, and then opened the door of a lime green Audi. Before heading off, he threw the particulars of sale in a bin.

Sitting on the bench by his herb garden, Benson tried to make sense of his strange visitor. He'd asked all the usual questions of a purchaser but he evidently wasn't one. He'd no interest in when the bins were collected or whether Seymour Basin was a quiet spot or whether Benson had an alarm. His interest lay with Benson himself. And Stainsby. Which suggested that Weaver was a gutter hack. Confident he'd got the measure of the man, Benson called Archie, Tess and Molly, urging them to be careful. They, too, might be targeted. So keep schtum, he'd said. Then, leaning forwards, he began casting around for words. Words to say sorry to Eddie, who'd lost his memory; and to Paul Harbeton, who'd lost his life.

23

Merrington sat up in bed, stroking his thumb across the screen on his phone, rereading messages. He paused at one from David, sent after their row that morning, when he'd insisted on going to the Bailey for the opening of the Blood Orange murder: 'I love you, Dad.' He'd never say that to his face. Whenever they were in the same room, the history of conflict and expectation, mock disappointment and instinctive parental worry set them apart. David was confrontational; Merrington was flippant. They were both trying to find a new vocabulary for shared manhood.

And very different values.

That was the real area of contention. David was pulling away; going somewhere his father didn't like, and would never be able to like. Merrington could take long hair and not shaving. Just about. But the abandonment of conventions, the guardians of decency – and even Merrington didn't quite know what these were . . . it was a question of feel – left him terrified. The idea that David would join Benson's chambers, careless of a murder conviction, fully aware that in so doing he struck a blow against the things his father stood for – he made a stab at enumeration . . . Oxbridge, the Blues and Royals (not that he'd joined), Henley, walking before the umpire raised his finger, tea at four, warm beer, the list was endless and indefinable, but they were all . . . English, for God's sake, and protected by that wonderful word, *conservative* – the idea that David would join Benson was like a death. Benson's refusal to crawl under a stone for what he had done was emblematic of all that was wrong with modern Britain. Merrington tapped a message: 'Love you too, David.'

And he did. And he didn't want to lose him.

'Bad day?' asked Pamela, climbing into bed.

'Sort of. It's ironic, but life would be so much easier if I was allowed the duplicity permitted to the lawyers I represent.'

'What rot is that?'

'Well, darling, in a court, you argue your side of the argument, and nobody ever knows what you really believe. It's perfectly respectable to think the opposite of what you're saying. And nobody cares. It's not like that in politics. You're meant to mean what you say. You're meant to be principled. Remember, I'm a Right Honourable Gentleman.

And you can't be, not always. You have to lie . . . if only to yourself.'

Merrington had asked one of his aides to come up with an upbeat statement about what the department was doing: in effect, turning the crisis on its head, saying it was precisely because of these troubling matters that steps had been taken to ensure that Britain's prisons were cost-effective, modern and . . . Merrington deflected an arrow of shame: sure, he'd had a bad day; but damn it, he loved the dodging and weaving. He loved the sport. And he was good at it. He was a first-team player.

'Then cut the lying,' said Pamela, with feeling. 'Cut the cord, darling. You've had a good run.'

Merrington groaned and waited. She was about to raise retirement again. She was about to talk about spending more time together.

'You'll be sixty soon,' she said, her hand finding his. 'Why not hang up your boots? Take things easy? We could see each other more often . . . and for longer.'

Merrington's mother, Annette, had been saying the same thing. The two of them had formed a not-so-secret pact, because the refrain had been sung in unison since 2015, after the last election. No sooner had he won his seat for the fifth time – and been promoted from Education to Justice – than they'd begun urging him to leave the field altogether. It didn't make sense: after first winning his seat in '97, he'd spent thirteen years in the wilderness. Pamela, ten years his junior, had been the fire in his ambition, urging him on. She'd willingly sacrificed career and prospects, never once complaining. And then, in 2010, he'd finally got a job: Minister of State for Employment. They'd seen this as the beginning of his ascent. There'd been no talk of retirement at sixty. What he couldn't understand was this: Merrington was now perfectly placed to make a bid for the top job.

PM. He'd played all his cards right. He'd knocked Europe for years. He'd voted against the war in Iraq. He'd voted to leave the EU. And he'd kept out of the leadership battle after Brexit, because whoever won that scrap would pick up the ungodly mess of divorce negotiations with Brussels. No, his plan was to make a move when all the mistakes had been made. He'd be the safe pair of hands the country had been waiting for. And now Pamela, backed by his elderly mother, wanted him to pull up stumps and grow roses in their Sussex retreat. Take sherry on Sundays? Watch someone else pick up the ball? No thanks.

'Pamela, can I be honest with you? In a way that I can't be with the House? And colleagues? And my constituents?'

'Of course, darling.'

'To get where I am, I have waited. I've been patient. I've undermined rivals. I've backstabbed certain people before they backstabbed me. I've listened to what my leader wants to hear, and I've said it. I've listened to what the public want to hear, and I've said that, too, always being careful to stay on message. It's been a long journey, Pam.'

'I know. But that doesn't mean—'

'And you helped me wait and undermine and stab.'

'I know.'

'It's come at a price, Pam.'

'Which is why I've had enough. And I'm tired, Richard. I've lost what it takes.'

'But we've almost made it, my love. There's nothing else to be paid. It makes no sense to stop when the prize is within reach.' He squeezed her hand; until then his own had been lifeless. It was terrible really: without saying so, he was letting her know – still being honest – that his affection had a price, too. 'I'm here because Pamela Merrington believed in me. And I want to be here. And if I don't go on to the next stage, if I don't give it my best shot . . . I'll never know why we did what we did; why we set out on this road.'

Her hand had lost its strength, but she didn't pull away. She'd left it there. Which meant they were still on track. Still walking, side by side. He changed the subject:

'I know you'd never do anything to harm David, darling, but I think you ought to be careful with this Benson character.'

'What on earth do you mean?'

'You're not bound to defend him. Remember the Cab Rank Rule? It doesn't apply to you.'

She flinched as if stung. Merrington turned to her: she looked suddenly worried, her eyes wide with apprehension.

'Benson's narrative is an appealing one. He maintained he was innocent at trial and then admitted his guilt to get parole and come to the Bar. He's got the best of both worlds. No one knows what he really thinks . . . and no one knows if he killed this Harbeton fellow or not. Such people attract critics and followers.'

'Surely you can't hold it against me that I think he's innocent?'

'Absolutely not. But you might want to consider the implications of voicing that generous opinion here at home.'

'Why, for heaven's sake? It's the only place I've ever voiced it.'

'Because, my dear, David is listening. And David is thinking of coming to the Bar. And David is not beyond asking Benson if he can join his chambers.'

With the caution of a thief, Pamela slowly took her hand back. Then she said:

'Don't talk rot.'

Merrington left matters there. Her tone of voice said it all. She was appalled. He leaned over to kiss her forehead. The day had ended well, after all. Because Pamela would now do what he wanted her to do: she'd talk to David. She'd try to persuade him to take another road. She'd propose competing options, and none of them had come from Merrington. And as for Merrington, he had his own plans. For now, he was waiting to hear from Bradley Hilmarton.

Without another word, he turned over and switched off the light.

24

As soon as Tess got into Coker & Dale the next morning, she called Pauline Osborne, the brief from the 2009 case who'd become a publican. Curiously, she was more than ready to speak, agreeing to meet Tess on Friday – two days' time. Tess then went to the Bailey, sliding onto the bench behind Benson just as Yardley called his most important lay witness: Rosie Heybridge, Diane's mother.

Now began the long history of observed abuse. Her voice cracked with the guilt of a bystander who will forever wonder if getting involved would have made a difference. In her mid-fifties, her eyes were like wounds browned by infection. In a way, she, too, had died, and she'd prepared her corpse for inspection. She'd been to the hairdresser. She'd applied make-up to give colour. She'd put on some earrings and a bracelet.

She was eloquent.

Initially, Mrs Heybridge had thought that the defendant was simply unhappy. He'd lost his mother and he'd lost his job. She'd pitied him. But she'd soon learned that he was embittered. His words always had an edge, blunt and sharp in equal measure. And by being there, Diane gave him something to grind against.

'I recall one occasion when someone asked Diane if she'd ever like a couple of kids, and Mr Stainsby said, "Her oven doesn't work." Everyone in the pub had laughed.'

He'd made the remark a standing joke. Years later it turned out Mr Stainsby was sterile. He'd gone for tests. But the joke remained a standard. And Diane had said nothing. She'd protected him. When she'd started taking medication, he'd taken to tapping his head. It had become another routine, performed if she ever said something he didn't like.

'But she wouldn't leave him.'

'She said as much?'

'Yes. I asked her why not take off, and she said, "Not while Frank's alive." And I said, "But you deserve better than this, girl," and she said, "Don't worry, Mum, I've got plans." That was Diane. Putting her life off until tomorrow. Concerned for Frank when she should have been concerned for herself.'

Tess recognised the emerging pattern from her early days doing family law, a field of battle from which she'd fled as soon as possible. As with most abusive relationships, the abuser was dependent upon the abused. The attachment is an addiction. And Mr Stainsby, like all addicts, got a high from his partner's submission. He fed off her work, too. Mrs Heybridge had a flat in the same block as her daughter. From her balcony, she could see Mr Stainsby's refrigerated van in the car park below.

'And it was always there. Except that every now and then he'd vanish at night to do some deliveries. All he had was bit-work.'

'Any particular days?'

'There was no pattern to it, but the next morning the thing was back in the car park, gathering rust.'

Stainsby yelled from the dock. 'You're a liar. I was doing my best, right? I told Diane—'

Mrs Justice Fleetwood, with quite staggering patience, told

Stainsby to be quiet. To allow his legal representatives to speak for him. To remember that he, too, could give evidence if he wished. But the damage had been done. The picture evoked by Mrs Heybridge had come alive. Tess had seen him hitting Diane with words, the brute knowing she'd just soak them up. That she'd be there next morning, and the morning after. Mrs Heybridge's evidence had become a testament that couldn't be contradicted.

'He earned next to nothing, and yet he was always flush.'

'Meaning?'

'He'd pull out wads of notes, just to impress his friends. And he must have got the lot from Diane. He spent like there was no tomorrow . . . and it was Diane who'd done the work.'

Yardley was a good questioner. Throughout the morning and into the afternoon there was a subtle sense of momentum and of events gathering weight. He brought her to the death of Frank Stainsby, when Diane separated from the defendant and she started making plans. She decided to leave Dover.

'I said, "He might follow you." And Diane said, "I know he will. And so what? There's nothing he can do. It'll be hello, goodbye."'

Shortly after that conversation Mrs Heybridge had said farewell herself.

'She was so excited. Maybe it was my imagination, but she looked younger.'

'This was Wednesday the twenty-third of September, 2015?'

'Yes. I went with her to the station. She was only taking one suitcase and when I asked her why, she said, "I want everything to be new. I want no reminders." She got on the train and that's the last I saw of my Diane . . . she was waving like mad, crying . . .'

Yardley sat down, leaving that image of mother and child before the jury. Two women in tears. What on earth was Benson to say? Diane must have foreseen this moment. She'd planned it perfectly. No one could defend the man responsible for that final separation.

25

Helen Camberley QC – the barrister who'd defended Benson and been his guide and mentor once he'd decided to come to the Bar – once remarked, 'When you cross-examine, you're a grave robber. Get in, take the gold and get out. No hanging around.' When Benson came to his feet he was troubled by the advice. Because he was about to ignore it. If you don't know what you're looking for, the tomb must be rifled slowly.

'Your husband, and Diane's father, Colin Heybridge, died on the fifth of August 1987?'

'Yes.'

'He was killed in a hit and run?'

'Yes.'

'You were twenty-seven. Diane was nine.'

'That's right.'

'You have my sympathy, Mrs Heybridge, and I apologise for raising the memory. But the loss of her father had a profound effect on Diane, didn't it?'

'Well, of course it did. She'd adored him. He'd adored her. Her childhood came to an end.'

Benson knew of this because he'd scoured Diane's childhood looking for fault lines in her personality. He'd obtained her school reports. He'd found an old, faint crack.

'She went to see a counsellor?'

'Yes.'

'And she developed some understandable but worrying behaviour patterns?'

'This has nothing to do with Diane's murder. Nothing. I don't know why you're raking over something that will only upset me.'

'Please bear with me, Mrs Heybridge. Diane created an imaginary friend, didn't she?'

'Yes. So what?'

'What was the friend's name?'

'Harry.'

'And Harry would walk by her side and she'd talk to him? She made up stories and told them as if they'd really happened?'

'The counsellor said it was completely natural, Mr Benson.'

'I'm not suggesting it wasn't. I'm pointing out that when Diane faced unbearable unhappiness, fantasy replaced reality.'

'But only for a while. In fact, it didn't work.'

'No, it didn't, because on the twenty-sixth of September, almost two months later, she ran away.'

'You're trying to make Diane out to be mad, aren't you?'

'No. Where did she head for?'

'She took a train to London. But she didn't have a ticket. And she was only nine and the police were called. You're saying she ran away from me, aren't you? You're saying I couldn't cope? Because I'd started drinking? Because I needed a social worker? But that was only for a while. We worked things out. Everything turned out fine. We pulled through.'

'I'm not attacking you, Mrs Heybridge. I'm saying Diane ran away from real life because it hurt too much.'

Mrs Heybridge covered her face and Mrs Justice Fleetwood suggested a short break. After the jury had left court, Yardley came over to Benson.

'Where are you going with this?'

'Wherever it leads.'

'Is that what you learned in prison? To do anything to get out of a hole?'

'I learned that innocent people went down because the right questions were never asked in court.'

'Really? What happened in your case? Camberley missed a shot? Or were you banged up because the wrong questions produced the right result?' Yardley pursed his lips. 'I was warned about you, Benson. I was told you treated innocence like a dish cloth.' He came a step closer. 'Don't you understand? You can't wipe away guilt that easily. It leaves a stain.'

Benson watched him drift back to his place. An instant later Tess was at his shoulder, whispering urgently: 'There's no stain. I see no stain. He's just rattled. His best witness is falling to pieces.'

Benson couldn't face her. And he didn't have time to deal with the emotional turmoil. He ground his teeth and brought his breathing under control. By the time Mrs Justice Fleetwood came back onto the bench he was deathly cold, and Mrs Heybridge had returned to the witness stand.

'You mentioned wads of money?'

'I did.'

'Could you describe what you saw?'

'A thick pile.'

'How thick?'

'An inch.'

'The denominations?'

'Tens and twenties.'

'An inch of tens and twenties amounts to thousands of pounds, Mrs Heybridge.'

'It's what I saw.'

'Every few months?'

'Yes.'

'But Diane only earned £7.47 per hour, £179.28 per week and £8784.72 per year.'

'Then he must have got it from somewhere else.'

'But he can't have done. You said his van was rusting in the car park.'

'Maybe it wasn't an inch, then. Does it matter?'

'Yes, because you didn't see what you said you saw.'

'But everything else I saw was true. He bullied her. And that's why she ran away.'

Benson let the answer hang in the air. Then he moved in on the choice of words.

'Who said she ran away?'

'I meant she went to London to get away from him.'

Benson seemed to let the matter go. He sought common ground, if only for a moment: 'Diane was very close to Frank Stainsby, wasn't she?'

'Yes.'

'And his wife?'

'I really wouldn't know.'

'Were you jealous to see Diane finding her place in a family other than her own?'

'No.'

'Because yours – through tragedy – had been broken?'

'No.'

The punching denials couldn't be called lies; they were just a turning away from truths that no mother and widow could bear to contemplate. Without prising open the history of alcohol abuse and emergency child protection orders – about which he'd known nothing – Benson had evoked the consequences of Diane's shattered childhood. He went further, drawing out more resistance:

'Would you accept that Caroline became a second mother to Diane?'

'No.'

'That Frank became the father she'd lost?'

'No.'

'And that when he died, she'd lost her dad all over again?'

'No. Absolutely not.'

Benson paused. 'Mrs Heybridge, Diane took the train to London almost two months after Frank died . . . just like she'd taken a train to London almost two months after her father died. On each occasion, she only coped for two months.'

'No. You've got it all wrong.'

'You got it right, Mrs Heybridge. Diane was running away again.'

'Rubbish.'

'And she didn't run away from this defendant.'

'She did. She did.'

'No, I'm sorry, Mrs Heybridge, she didn't. She was nine again, without her father.' Benson paused and then repeated his message: 'She ran away from real life because it hurt too much.'

'No, no. Diane's childhood had nothing to do with her death, nothing.'

'She left with a single suitcase because she knew she wouldn't be needing anything.'

'How can you say that?'

'And when she said goodbye – and I am very sorry to say this, Mrs Heybridge; it gives me no pleasure – she was waving madly because she knew she'd never see you again. She'd made a choice as an adult that she could never have made as a child. This time she had a ticket. She'd decided to end her life.'

26

'How did you know about Harry?' said Tess.

She was like Archie after Benson's cross-examination of Malcolm Hargreaves on a phantom pronoun – the erasing of 'her' to produce 'I'll choke first'. Benson had given the jury a glimpse of a woman damaged without reference to Stainsby: he'd sought no sympathy for the man who'd made things so much worse, but that was the smartness of his questioning – he hadn't taken sides. And Tess had felt the jury tilt towards Benson. If it wasn't for the forensic evidence, they might just follow him.

'Harry,' said Tess. 'How did you know about him?'

'I didn't,' replied Benson, distracted. 'There was one line in a school report about an imaginary friend who was helping her. I wondered if she'd used the same name when things got too much with Stainsby.'

'The running away?'

'I went through the heaps of witness statements not relied on by the Crown. You know, the unused material. I found a remark from a neighbour.'

The day had ended with Mrs Heybridge leaving the court a reduced and confused woman, Benson frowning. A frown that only deepened when Stainsby, high on adrenalin, had said: 'I loved every minute of that, Mr Benson. I wish I could have filmed it. You know, for a souvenir. It was ace.' The guards had taken him back to the Green; and Tess had brought Benson to a side-street café near St Paul's.

'This is the first time I've been uneasy about the job,' he said. 'Stainsby might be innocent, but slowly, over time, he squeezed the life out of her. And here am I, trying to set him free, using her mother to help me do it.'

The waiter brought wine for Tess and water for Benson.

'You won't change your mind?' said Tess. 'Something stronger?'

He didn't hear. 'The only way I could get the jury to consider suicide was to show that Diane's vulnerability predated her relationship with Stainsby. So what do I do? I remind her mother that she failed her child. I link it to her daughter's death. No one's ever done that before. She'll never forget it.'

'That's not what you said.'

'That's the point. I got her to do it. And that gave it credibility.'

'You worked with the facts, Will. That's our job. Handling facts that aren't that nice.'

'But I want to get it right.' Benson became insistent. 'I don't want Stainsby to get off for the wrong reason and people to get hurt for no reason. That's why right reasons matter.'

'Will, I think you're forgetting something. Diane framed Stainsby. We're on the back foot but we're getting somewhere.'

'Yes. We're misleading the jury.'

'How so?'

'Diane was cracking up because she'd given a false alibi, not because of Frank's death.'

'What you put to her mother is still true.'

'But it's not the whole truth and nothing but the truth. So help me, God.'

Tess took the plunge. Ever since Tess had resumed a working relationship with Benson, her resolution to leave his past unexplored had been tested. The meal with Gordon, Archie's reprimand, the kick in the teeth from Sally, the condemnation of Benson in the media and, most recently, Yardley's unjust dismissal had incrementally worn down her resistance. The little that remained was now swept away by Benson's insistence that the truth, in fragments, could still be misleading.

'Will, you can't go on like this.'

'I'll come round. Molly says everyone gets off the canvas at some point.'

'I don't mean this trial. I mean you. I mean me. I mean everyone. You can't go on accepting responsibility for a crime you didn't commit.'

Benson had picked up his glass of water. He put it down again.

'What do you mean?' His voice was barely audible.

'You're always going to be misunderstood. Your motives will always be questioned. You'll always be in the dock. The suspicion will never go away. Not unless we do something about it.'

'Like what?'

'Reopen your case.' Tess's renewed declaration of faith in Benson had come out of nowhere: but it was honest: she saw no stain. Only a man who was passionate about the truth. She didn't know why he'd lied about not knowing Paul Harbeton, but she didn't care any more. She no longer wanted the confusion and uncertainty; or the little miracle of a reduced friendship. Sally was right. Benson couldn't fight for himself. He needed help. 'I don't mean publicly,' she said. 'I mean privately. You and I. Somebody killed Paul Harbeton and we can find him. And then—'

'Stop, Tess, please.' Benson had raised his hands as if to push her away. 'I've decided to leave the past alone. It's the only way I can move forward.'

'No, Will. It doesn't work.'

'It does for me.'

'Well not for me and not for those who care about you, and not for the clients who'd instruct you if only their solicitor could trust you. And it doesn't work for you either. I can see the cost. You carry guilt around as if it was your birthright. You can be free again, Will. You don't have to remain on the Numbers. God, it's the only way you'll ever stop smoking.'

Benson had paled. And Tess instantly recalled the agonising wait for the jury to return a verdict in his trial. He'd pleaded with her to believe in his innocence, and he was pleading again:

'If you care about me, Tess, promise me you'll never mention this again.'

He waited, staring hungrily. And the resolve which had only just taken hold of Tess began to waver. Benson leaned forward.

'It's not been easy, Tess,' he said. 'The case destroyed my parents. It wrecked my relationship with my brother. It brought the life I once had to an end. Everything fell to pieces. Can you imagine that?'

Tess couldn't. Sensing her admission, Benson pressed on:

'I went to prison with nothing but a crazy idea, an idea that you'd set on fire: you told me I could make it to the Bar . . . and you were right . . . in the end, against the odds, I actually did it. The flame didn't go out.'

Tess knew this; she was proud of her role.

'I've made a future I can live with' – Benson was nodding, still astonished at the outcome – 'in part, because of you. And I don't want to lose it.'

Tess remonstrated, but with failing conviction. 'I don't understand . . . reopening your case would simply—'

'Open a grave. My grave. And I can't go back there. When I admitted my guilt, I buried an innocent man. It was the only way to build a new life. To open that ground can only churn up everything I went through. The fight starts all over again. And what's the point? I'll never get back those eleven years . . . or my parents, as they were, or my brother, as he was. Everything's changed, and—'

'But if you're innocent—'

'It makes no difference. I've made my peace with the aftermath. I can handle the Numbers. I like the Numbers' – he paused, dragging a hand through his hair – 'I might even need the Numbers . . . the isolation . . . it's why I'm good in court. If I was fulfilled anywhere else, if there was no loss or remorse, I could lose my drive . . . my passion. The fire could go out. Don't let that happen, Tess . . . not after striking the match.'

Tess couldn't hide her capitulation; but Benson wanted more than a facial expression: he wanted words. He'd held on to what Tess had said once before, and he intended to do it again.

'Accept me as I am. Accept my choices. Promise me you'll leave my past alone.'

She had no will left. 'I promise.'

They finished their drinks, seeking relief with conversation about the man who'd brought them back together: Stainsby, in whose defence right reasons didn't matter. Benson insisted on settling the bill and then made a brisk exit towards Spitalfields. Tess watched him check his pockets as he walked, looking for a cigarette or a stub saved from a previous moment of weakness. After he'd rounded a corner, a line of Swift came to mind:

'Promises and pie-crusts are made to be broken.'

27

The problem with getting a kick in the teeth is that it tends to leave its mark on subsequent relations. So when Tess met

Sally at the Chiswick Community Centre later that evening, the memory of their previous conversation lay heavily between them. Ordinarily, Tuesday night was cocktails night, but Sally had been invited by one of her clients – a singer – to an amateur production of *The Pirates of Penzance*, and Tess had tagged along. They had front-row seats.

'I just love all that "Come, friends, who plough the sea" stuff,' said Sally who, thank God, had decided to dress low key rather than follow the theme of the evening. 'Takes me out of myself.'

'I'd have thought it takes you into yourself.'

'Meaning?'

'Well, it's all topsy-turvy, isn't it? It's a world of paradox and confusion.'

'Thank you so much.'

'I didn't mean that negatively.'

'Of course you didn't.'

'Honestly.'

They were saved by a conversation coming from the row behind. A man and woman were discussing the Blood Orange murder. But the man then shifted tack. His interest was Benson. Tess and Sally tuned in.

'His story doesn't hang together.'

'It does for me. He's innocent, but he had to admit his guilt so he can work. It's absurd.'

'Oh, you've swallowed that nonsense.'

'It's a fact, Charles. I read it in the *Guardian*.'

'It's what he says, and it's nothing more than a preamble to a misconception that no one's bothered to question.'

'Enlighten me.'

'He's told a truth: that he'd never have got parole if he didn't hold his hands up. And his chances of coming to the Bar – which were slim – would have been non-existent if he hadn't held them even higher.'

'You've just told mc a couple of truths.'

'The misconception comes next. He's implied that the Bar Council would shut him down if he now said he's innocent, and that's rubbish.'

'How do you know?'

'For God's sake, Judy, think it through. No one gets condemned for claiming they're innocent. If he was honest, he'd win some goodwill. He'd win mine. But he clings to this "I'm trapped" crap because he doesn't want his case reopened. If he stood up tonight and said "I didn't do this, and every hour when I'm not fighting for other people I'm going to be fighting for myself, and I won't rest until the Court of Appeal clears my name" he'd have a fan club before breakfast. But that's not what he wants. He doesn't want a new solicitor. He doesn't want a new barrister. He doesn't want the witnesses to be questioned again. He doesn't want a private eye looking for new ones. Because he doesn't want a clean bill of health. And that's why I don't trust him. Innocent people want their innocence, and he doesn't. He wants pity. And the kind of support that comes from a ravishing forty-something who reads the *Guardian* as if it was a fifth gospel.'

'You are clever, Charles. You should have been a lawyer.'

'Very funny.'

'I mean a proper one. In court.'

The curtain rose. And Charles, a keen G&S fan, though bruised by that last remark, eventually recovered his good humour and hummed along. Tess couldn't follow the show: her thoughts pursued Benson, who'd made her promise to leave his past alone, a promise that now seemed to be an act of collusion. Because Judy was right: Benson's situation was absurd. And there wasn't anything funny about it. There would be no final-act revelation making sense of everything. He was condemned to be misunderstood and maligned. With encore after encore of popular criticism. Unless someone acted on his behalf.

'Are you all right?' asked Sally when they'd followed the crowd outside.

'Yes. I'm fine. I'm sorry for what I said.'

'Why? It's true. I'm half bonkers, we both know that. However, paradoxically, you're the one who went into yourself.'

'I know.'

'Because of clever Charles?'

'No. Because of clever you. You've set me thinking.'

'About?'

'Benson needing me. Us.'

Sally came a step closer, speaking quietly. 'We go back to work? We find out what happened?'

'No, we won't.'

'Why not, for heaven's sake?'

'Because only a few hours ago I promised Benson I wouldn't. It was a moment of mysterious incoherence. Something that happened without any planning.'

When Tess got home she went to her desk in the sitting room, opened the bottom drawer and took out the souvenir given to her seventeen years ago by George Braithwaite after that week's work experience with Hutton, Braithwaite and Jones. At the time she'd been interested in shipping law, but she'd been lured into the Old Bailey with a promise of some excitement. That week had changed her life. In her hands was the brief she'd been given: *R* v. *Benson*. Given her promise to that one-time defendant, she ought to throw the damn thing in the bin . . . but instead she read it from beginning to end, recalling every twist and turn of the trial, and then went to bed. Lying in the dark she wondered what Sally might have uncovered. She'd called it significant progress.

28

Benson cried off. He told Archie he had too much to do. Important stuff. So Archie convened the Tuesday Club at the Pride of Spitalfields on Heneage Street in Benson's absence – apologies received and noted. On board *The Wooden Doll*, Benson fumbled with a tin of cat food, tripped over Traddles, and then grabbed the pad and pen. This time he didn't need to fish for words. They came flying out. That undertaking from Tess to leave his past alone had stirred up the sorrow and the shame. He'd never been so honest with himself. And that night he slept a different kind of sleep.

Next morning, he set off for the Bailey feeling obscurely cheerful. But when he reached the end of the road he realised he'd forgotten something. Reluctantly, he walked back.

According to Abasiama, it was the most important part of the exercise. He had to feed his confessions to the shredder, whether he liked it or not, and as each page got sucked into the whining plastic box he felt himself get heavier and heavier . . . until he felt heavier than the day before. And that wasn't the only outcome. Two hours later he met Tess outside the robing room, and when she squeezed his hand he pulled away, even though he wanted to leave it there. The impulse to withdraw from Tess, while simultaneously wanting to approach her, had intensified. Waiting in court for Mrs Justice Fleetwood, Tess leaned forward with various questions, but Benson couldn't reply easily. He gave closed answers.

Where did he get Traddles from? A sanctuary.

Has the Tuesday Club come up with anything? Yes, Bredfield vanished over the weekend.

Had he seen the Prison Officers' Association was threatening to strike? Before Benson could reply court rose and

– sparing Benson further embarrassment – Yardley was on the attack.

To reinforce the evidence of Mrs Heybridge, he called three members of the Dover Five: Samantha Hughes, Angela Wright and Cathy Dawson. One after the other, over a day and a half – Wednesday into Thursday – they told parallel stories of unpleasantness; of their dead friend's increasingly loveless relationship with the defendant. Benson didn't contradict them because it was all true. But none of them would accept that Diane's childhood had been traumatic; that the pain might have reached into the present. Put like that, without reference to Stainsby, their denials appeared defensive. Either they didn't know their friend or they were being disingenuous. Both explanations suited Benson's purpose. But his unease only deepened. These were the sort of relationships where you didn't talk about the bad stuff – it's how you survived: he did the same thing himself, but he'd still made their bonds look trivial. At the same time, and discreetly, he'd checked elements of Tapster's story.

Yeah, Diane had sometimes borrowed a car for the evening.

Yeah, she sometimes went solo.

Yeah, she used the internet to check out this and that.

And what of it?

And that was as far as he got, because none of them knew that Diane had sometimes dressed up for a night out with Harry, the nice guy in her life. None of them knew that she'd used Tapster's computer to investigate ways of dying. None of them knew about the plastic bag in Tapster's fridge. The gold remained buried.

All three witnesses recounted Diane's exuberant farewell party on the 22nd of September, when there'd been no hint of goodbye, just the promise of future laughs; and Angela

Wright mentioned an important detail that hadn't appeared in her statement: that Diane had suggested going to Malta for Christmas. Malta? Yep. With the Dover Five? You bet. A short break? Long enough to paint the place red. All of which sat ill with the idea of a woman who might kill herself, until Benson suggested that Diane might have misled them, hiding feelings that were spiralling out of control. Which provoked loud protestations. Too loud, because – Malta or no Malta – they didn't want to admit that Diane had endured problems they'd known nothing about. None of them had known just how much she'd wanted children. The surprise in Benson's voice was just this side of an accusation.

All three witnesses testified about the defendant's attempts to trace Diane, but it was only Dawson who told him where she'd gone:

'He turned up on Thursday night.'

'This was the first of October?' asked Yardley.

'Yes. And he said he wanted to make up with Diane, that he'd been in the wrong and that he was sorry for everything.'

'You believed him?'

'Yes, that's why I gave him Diane's address. He said he wanted to bring her his mum's jewellery. I'd no idea what he was planning.'

'Did he say anything else?'

'He told me not to tell anyone. That he was going to surprise her.'

Recalling the exchange, Dawson broke down because she was convinced she'd helped Stainsby murder her friend the next day.

'I'll never forgive myself.'

Attempts by Benson to suggest that Diane might have been suicidal – which, by implication, would have released Dawson from guilt – floundered, because Dawson's remorse was linked to a desire to punish herself, and publicly. She should never have given him that address and now she had to pay the price. She was ready to immolate herself. Diane? On the edge? No way. Diane had been strong. She'd been happy. She'd been full of beans.

'For how long?'

'Weeks.'

Benson frowned. 'Full of beans? Frank Stainsby had just died.'

And he left it there. On which note, with Yardley now seated, her ladyship adjourned the proceedings. Owing to a 'case management issue' in another trial, the court would not assemble until the following afternoon.

'Remember my warnings, ladies and gentlemen,' she said, closing her laptop. 'Keep your minds on the evidence presented in court. Ignore everything else.'

After a quick word with Stainsby – who was once more pleased with his brief: down in the cells, he'd held a thumb up and then a fist: 'You really got that Dawson cow' – Benson rushed his goodbye to Tess, unsettled by the mist in her eyes. And he was unsettled when, arriving at *The Wooden Doll*, he met Mr and Mrs Underwood, prospective purchasers who'd come for a viewing and had fallen in love with the boat even before stepping on board. After an enraptured visit, they looked at each other as if they'd just got married.

'We've been dreaming of something like this for years, haven't we, Tim?'

'Yes, darling.'

Tim turned to Benson. 'We're scaling down and getting out.'

'Of the rat race,' added Darling.

'We want a simple life.'

'And privacy.'

'And the sound of the canal at night. Do you know what I mean?'

Benson said he did.

'We're cash buyers,' said Darling. 'So there won't be any delays.'

They left for a sort of honeymoon, promising to speak to the agent first thing in the morning. But not before a short speech from the happy couple:

'I want you to know we think you're innocent, Mr Benson. If we didn't, we wouldn't be buying your boat, would we, darling?'

'No. Neither of us fancy sleeping in the same bed as a murderer, do we?'

Tim certainly didn't, and he went further: 'We wouldn't buy the boat if we thought Mr Stainsby was guilty either.'

Darling made the transcendental link. 'You're just the right man to defend him.'

'And for what it's worth,' said Tim, 'we're against capital punishment, aren't we?'

'We are. I mean, you'd be dead by now.'

Benson felt moved to join in: 'I would.'

The last word went to Darling: 'And if Mr Stainsby gets convicted, he'd be dead. That would be the two of you. Now, where's the justice in that?'

29

Tess spent Friday morning reviewing case files, trying not to hum tunes from *The Pirates of Penzance*. The one that kept coming back like an anthem from hell was 'A paradox, a paradox, a most ingenious paradox! Ha, ha, ha, ha, ha, ha, ha, ha, this paradox!' And when she wasn't humming, she was thinking of Benson's plight – his elected isolation – and her promise. She joined Gordon for a sandwich in the canteen, conscious that the review process would have to be done all over again.

'You're fond of bright colours, aren't you?' she said.

'Yes.' Gordon was bashful. His efforts had been rewarded at last.

'I'd like to introduce you to someone.'

'Really? Who?'

'An artist. I think you'd get on wonderfully. She's called Sally Martindale.'

The suggestion wiped the smile from his face. It was delicious and Tess, rather than rush, lingered over lunch, sharing a new-found enthusiasm for Cartier-Bresson. When Gordon had gone back to work – 'Terribly sorry, Tess, but it's a Supreme Court matter; tedious, frankly, but it's a groundbreaker' – she took a cab to the Crown and Thistle in Tower Hamlets, humming all the way.

Pauline Osborne had been the first member of her family to go to university. Her parents had come to London from Trinidad in the mid-fifties. They'd worked and saved and saved and worked, eventually buying a derelict chapel which they'd transformed into a very different kind of meeting place. When their only child had been called to the Bar they'd been speechless with pride.

'I never told them what it's like in practice. The anxiety. The stress. To be honest, I didn't know myself until I'd left. I found out the next morning, when I woke up feeling ten years younger.'

She'd started playing the piano again. She ate three meals a day. She went to bed at a decent hour. All those blue notebooks had been boxed away. But of all the cases that came back at night to disturb her, one in particular still made her skin crawl. It had never gone to trial. Why was she prepared to talk? Because it had to be connected to whatever was unfolding now at the Old Bailey.

'This was a very strange case. And it's not over. I'm sure of it.'

She made coffee, opened a blue notebook and went back to the beginning.

On the face of things, it was a simple matter. John Foster was a Detective Sergeant in the North Dover CID. He'd gone out for a couple of drinks at the Twisted Wheel on a Saturday night. Stainsby was alleged to have attacked him from behind, leaving him unconscious in a rear car park. The CPS had sent the file to Pauline Osborne because the police in Dover were screaming for a trial even though the evidence was weak.

'They wanted me to take the flak,' said Osborne, still troubled by the pressure of the conference. 'And I did. It's odd, I didn't feel uneasy then because I knew I'd made the right decision. But now I feel I'm partly responsible for that girl's death.'

The evidence had crumbled. A witness who'd seen Stainsby head out to the car park retracted her statement. CCTV footage went missing. There was no forensic and no motive. Other witnesses who'd seen Stainsby at the club were no longer sure it had been him. And then, just as the police were trying to persuade them to hold fast, Diane turns up with an alibi. A woman of good character, backed by Jane Tapster. More on her later.

'So the witnesses had been leaned on?' said Tess.

'No doubt about it.'

'Who by?'

'Hold your horses. We're not there yet.'

The SIO was a great guy. DI Peter Lambrook. He'd really

done his homework. And that's why everyone around the table knew that this seemingly straightforward case was something very different altogether.

'First off, there'd been another CID officer in the club. A Detective Constable called Steve Draycott. Who just so happened to be one of Foster's DCs.'

'Foster was his boss?'

'Yes. Led his inquiry team. And it just so happened that they were both at the Twisted Wheel on a Saturday night, the one not knowing the other was there.'

'That's not so strange.'

'Two blokes, drinking on their own?'

'If that's all you've got, no.'

'Well it isn't. Let me tell you what else Lambrook found out.'

Lambrook had checked the number plates on some of the vehicles in the car park. Picked up afterwards by people taking pictures on their phones. And Foster and Draycott weren't the only ones who just happened to be there.

'Have you heard of Terry Meersham?'

'No.'

'Well you should have done. He's the godfather of a London crime family. At the time – we're talking seven years back – he was known to be big on drugs. As you'd expect, he never got anywhere near the front line. All the dirty stuff was kept at a distance. So the big question was: what the hell was Meersham doing in Dover? All the more so because someone else just happened to be there. A Frenchman who moored his yacht in Rye Harbour. André Loupierre who, according to Interpol and the rest, was a major player in the Parisian underworld. Another guy who kept away from the trenches.'

Tess thought through the implications. Foster and Draycott must have been on an undercover operation.

'They denied it,' said Osborne. 'And so did their supervisor, a Detective Inspector. Ray Carlatton. Who Lambrook clearly didn't like. Point is, if Carlatton and his boys said nothing was underway, Lambrook couldn't contradict them.'

Tess was still working things out. 'Let me get my head around this. Stainsby – a small-fry out-of-work fisherman with a failing delivery business – is meeting up with senior crime gangs from London and Paris in a Dover nightclub?'

'Forget how crazy it sounds. Look at the evidence. It's what happened. And Meersham or Loupierre's people must have spotted Foster. Stainsby, who's on his home turf, has to sort it out. And he does.'

Had the case gone ahead, Pauline Osborne would have dropped the Section 18 and put attempted murder on the indictment. 'Foster was left for dead. Stainsby went out there to kill him.'

'What the hell was going on?' said Tess. 'What was this meeting about?'

'Lambrook didn't know. Interpol didn't know. But it wasn't drugs. The drug business from the coast into London was already covered for Meersham. No, something else was underway. Something with a continental dimension. Something new, or the big timers wouldn't have been there.'

'With Brent Stainsby at the table?'

'Maybe you need to revise how you see your poor little fisherman who lost his sheep. Or fish. Or whatever. He's kept a very low profile for a very good reason. Then and now. I just don't know what it is. And neither does Lambrook.'

'Does?'

'Yes. He rang me after the trial opened. He's got the same concerns as me. There's a sense of unfinished business.'

They were seated in the kitchen, a back room off the main

bar. Pauline Osborne's father had refurbished the place himself, helped by friends. But now the wallpaper was tired and the units were chipped and worn. Nothing much had changed since the seventies. To anyone else, the place needed gutting, but for Pauline it was comforting. She'd been born upstairs and, after the death of her proud, widowed dad, she'd decided to try to make a go of it. She was going to do music nights and poetry readings, and she didn't care if no one turned up. She was alive again. The weight of the Bar had been left behind. Except for this one unresolved case.

'I couldn't let it go to trial, even though Lambrook was confident Diane would withdraw her alibi under cross-examination. She was a good kid, he said. Not a natural liar. But we had no choice. The other witnesses were falling like flies.'

'Because the heavyweights had leaned on them,' said Tess, not asking a question.

'There's no other explanation. And do you know what Stainsby did, when Lambrook told him the case was being dropped? He smiled. And then he asked if he could have the photos of Foster as a souvenir.'

Tess didn't quite understand, so Osborne explained. 'The close-up medical photos for the proposed trial. He wanted a copy. He was telling Lambrook that he'd done the injuries.'

Injuries of such severity that Foster's personality had changed and he'd suffered uncontrollable bouts of panic and severe depression. His wife and kids had been through hell. Four years later, in 2013, he'd been found dead beside a multi-storey car park. He'd fallen. Suicide or accident or murder? With Foster's medical history there was no knowing. The coroner recorded an open verdict, which was kind, because on that basis, with no finding of suicide, the benefits of any life insurance policy would be paid out. And they were. Tess listened in horror, but her mind was on the primary argument raised by Osborne – and supported by Lambrook – that the death of Diane Heybridge might be connected to this secret history, which couldn't be true.

'I've spoken to Jane Tapster,' she said. 'And it's clear that Diane was falling to pieces. She planned her own suicide to look like murder. She framed Stainsby.'

Tess had stopped speaking because Pauline Osborne had gone back to her blue notebook, turning it around so Tess could read the neat handwriting.

'You can't trust a word that comes out of Jane Tapster's mouth,' said Osborne. And with a long, elegant finger she pointed at a word in the middle of the page, circled in red during that unforgettable conference when Osborne had been forced to let Stainsby go.

30

Benson took the call from Pippa at Barlow's Waterside Property Specialists late in the morning, just as his mind was gearing up to question Dr Lowmax, Diane's GP. Mr and Mrs Underwood had made a formal offer, she said. They'd reasoned that since most people – though not them – thought Benson was a murderer, the stigma ought nonetheless to be reflected in the sale. Would Mr Benson be prepared to accept a third off the asking price? It was akin, they said, to giving credit to the Underwoods for his admission of guilt.

'No,' he snapped.

'I thought not.'

The call left Benson depressed. And angry. He couldn't

escape the past – this he'd known and had long accepted; but he couldn't escape the leeches who fed off it either. And, unusually, he couldn't shed the turmoil when he entered court. His voice had an edge, though Dr Lowmax probably didn't notice because Benson began his cross-examination with a lamentation about the health service, GP contracts and the long hours of work. They'd been mourning friends, until Benson pointed out that Dr Lowmax's consultations with Diane had never exceeded eleven minutes.

'You diagnosed her as suffering from depression?'

'I did.'

'What kind? I don't see it in your notes.'

'What do you mean?'

'Reactive, physiological, stress-related, dysthymic . . . there are various types. The appropriate treatment varies according to the type. You didn't identify the type.'

'It's not in my notes, but I would have considered these matters.'

'In ten minutes?'

That had been the duration of the first consultation, when Diane had left the surgery with a prescription for fluvopram, a selective serotonin reuptake inhibitor, which had provoked instability, sweating and weakness. The subsequent consultation, where the change to certolfaxine was authorised, had lasted eight minutes. Diane had been back a week later, needing sleeping tablets to deal with the insomnia caused by the SSRIs. When pressed, Dr Lowmax admitted that in arriving at his diagnosis he'd only used the two questions recommended by the National Institute for Health and Care Excellence: have you often been bothered by feeling down, depressed or hopeless during the past month? Have you often been bothered by having little interest or pleasure in doing things during the last month? Diane had answered yes to both questions. Furnished with these bare concessions

– alleged Benson – rather than carry out a review of Diane's 'mental state and associated functional, interpersonal and social difficulties', as recommended by NICE, he'd simply written out a prescription.

'That's not fair. I tried to carry out the review, but Diane wouldn't cooperate.'

'Prior to considering medication, didn't you first consider conservative methods? Cognitive therapy? Talking?'

'Diane refused outright to discuss her problems with anyone.'

'How long did that conversation last?'

'Sarcasm is ugly, Mr Benson.'

'You suggested therapy, she declined the offer, you picked up your pen. Is that accurate?'

'You make it sound cavalier.'

'Quite right, Dr Lowmax. I'm suggesting you gave Diane Heybridge antidepressants and sleeping tablets as if they were fruit pastilles.'

'That's outrageous.'

'Is it? Your own evidence is that Diane asked for beta-blockers after a series of panic attacks in February 2009 and you gave her Blupanol. That consultation lasted seven minutes.'

'I didn't give them because she asked. Her request was incidental.'

'Did you determine why the attacks had taken place?'

'I'm at a disadvantage because I haven't recorded what she told me. I can't recall. My lady, please, this is many years ago.'

'You didn't enquire, Dr Lowmax,' said Benson. 'That's why it's not been noted. Just like you didn't explore the reasons for her depression and anxiety.'

'This is unfair. You're forgetting something: I specifically refer somewhere to . . .' Dr Lowmax asked if he could check his sheaf of records; and then, after some back and forth, as if vindicated, he read the relevant entry from January 2010. '"Finds not having children almost unbearable."'

This is what Benson had been waiting for; it's why he'd been rough-handed, wanting Dr Lowmax to lurch for those six words as if they were a shield. He said, 'My lady, the reference is at page fifty-six in File B.'

'Thank you, Mr Benson.'

'Is this your evidence, then, Dr Lowmax? Relying on your contemporaneous notes, the only clue you can provide as to the underlying cause of Diane's mental health problems was this issue of not having had children?'

Dr Lowmax had no choice but to agree. Otherwise he was just a vendor of sweets.

'As I say, she was insistent that she didn't want to talk about her feelings.'

Benson looked at the jury: 'But she never once – even remotely – implied that her depression and anxiety arose from her relationship with this defendant?'

'No, I never said it did.'

'Maybe not, but Mr Yardley would have you say otherwise.'

Benson paused and turned a page. He hadn't finished with Dr Lowmax. His eye was on his cheekbone, where the skin was tight and tanned.

'Do you see that cardboard box on the exhibits table?'

'Yes.'

'It contains the medication you prescribed. Blupanol, Fluvopram, certolfaxine, dorcarbamol, benzotriptyline and voltapromide. Two of those – Fluvopram and Benzotriptyline – had a very nasty effect on Diane.'

'Yes. That is why I modified the prescription. Despite your insinuations, it is a very delicate task finding the right treatment plan.'

'In the relevant sense, for Diane, these two drugs were lethal poisons. She shouldn't go anywhere near them.'

'Correct.'

'Then why didn't you take them back?'

Benson didn't hear Dr Lowmax's reply. It had been too quiet, and when asked to repeat it he'd made a stumbling defence of acceptable practice. But Benson had cut him where it hurts. He'd shown that Stainsby wasn't the only person who'd failed Diane. There were others, far less culpable and lacking malice, but still part of her tragic story. Even Diane's mother was among them. And the threesome from the Dover Five, whose love for their friend didn't include knowing what had mattered to her most. Benson – posing as Diane's defender – had nudged them all into the frame to explain why this vulnerable woman had been isolated, misunderstood, and was now dead. And by expanding the sources of heartbreak and spreading the responsibility, he'd taken some of the blame off Stainsby; which could only broaden the chances of an acquittal.

What a pity it had nothing to do with the truth.

'Will, let's go.'

Benson had felt a tug on his gown and he seemed to wake. Tess was at his elbow with Archie. The court was empty. Tess came close, her breath warming his cheek.

'We need to talk about Jane Tapster.'

31

'An informer?'

'On the books for years.'

'And she betrayed Diane?'

'For fifty quid.'

They'd settled on a corner table in a low-lit pub off Ludgate Hill. Archie had ordered a plate of toasted sandwiches and a round of drinks, with some crisps and nuts to keep them going. Then Tess had recounted Pauline Osborne's story. By the time she'd finished, Benson was altered, though he gave no hint as to why. As if needing confirmation, he went back to the beginning:

'Tapster was a registered informer?'

'With the police in Dover.'

Tess spoke to him as if he was far away, repeating some of what she'd said, not convinced Benson had absorbed the detail:

'That was one of the unanswered questions. How did DS Foster and DC Draycott know that Meersham, Loupierre and Stainsby were going to be in the Twisted Wheel that night? Someone must have told them.'

And while Foster and Draycott's boss, DI Carlatton, denied that an undercover operation had been underway, DI Lambrook was almost certain that couldn't be true. He'd checked the National Informant Management database and found Tapster's name. She'd been on the roster for ten years. He'd then gone over Carlatton's head and checked the payments register and, sure enough, the week before the meeting in question, Tapster had been paid £50 in cash. By DI Carlatton. Confronted with the facts, he'd said the disbursement related to another matter. He'd got shirty, too, saying all his operations were run according to the book. He'd never done anything off-piste. He'd made submissions to the National Informant Working Group, for Christ's sake. But Lambrook hadn't been impressed. Coincidence couldn't explain the concentration of criminals and police officers in the one building at one and the same time.

Archie said: 'Diane finds out that Stainsby's planning to

meet some serious criminals. She's worried and confides in Tapster. And Tapster tells Carlatton. And Carlatton sends in Foster and Draycott . . . but under the radar?'

'Something like that.'

'But Diane didn't say what was going on?'

'Well, we don't know. She might have done. At the time, everyone involved closed ranks. No one was saying anything. Lambrook was left out in the cold.'

'It's a cover-up,' said Benson. 'They botched an unauthorised operation and then pretended it never happened.'

'That's what Lambrook said,' confirmed Tess.

The waiter brought the sandwiches and drinks but Benson didn't seem to notice. He said, 'The CID had to watch Stainsby walk free after he'd beaten up one of their own?'

'Yep.'

'Where one of the alibis was a registered informer . . . who got her information from the other alibi?'

'Yep.'

'This stinks.'

'It more than stinks,' said Archie. 'Four years later, this Foster's found dead in a car park. Three years more and Diane's found hanging. A year later, Bredfield is driving around in a van scared for his life. And Stainsby's on the Numbers, convinced someone's out to kill him. That can't be a coincidence, Rizla. This case is bigger than we realised. Whatever happened in 2009—'

'Is irrelevant,' said Tess. After leaving Pauline Osborne, she'd come to a firm conclusion. '2009 is the case that stinks. Not ours. No one knows what happened back then because Foster is dead and Draycott and Carlatton have nothing to say. When Goodshaw began his investigation into Diane's death he contacted Peter Lambrook. And Lambrook sent him to Carlatton. And Carlatton repeated the same story. There'd been no unofficial operation in 2009. Now, that might be bollocks. But that doesn't mean there's a link between then and now. Which is obviously what Goodshaw believed, because the case against Stainsby went ahead on the available evidence . . . which pointed fair and square to a killing "out of spite and for money".' Tess reached for her drink. 'We need to be careful here. Pauline Osborne feels bad because she had to let a case go. Lambrook feels angry because Stainsby walked. They want to link then to now. Give it some meaning. Tie up loose ends. But they could be wrong. Coincidences happen.'

Archie wasn't convinced. 'Foster's death?'

'Don't argue with a coroner.'

'But why should Stainsby be scared?'

'Men who abuse women don't win friends in prison.'

'And Bredfield?'

'Half his brain's been cooked. Seriously, we need to keep focused. This case is as simple as it appears' – she turned to Benson – 'and you're getting somewhere, Will. Yardley's case is losing focus. Suicide is no longer some—'

'What about Jane Tapster?'

'Sorry?'

'Tapster. Lambrook must have grilled her.'

Benson didn't appear to have followed the argument; he was still slowly stroking his cheek, frowning to himself.

'He tried and got nowhere,' said Tess. She went back on the offensive. 'The reason we have to talk about Tapster isn't because she might know the answer to 2009 – she probably does and she ain't saying – it's because we can forget everything she told us. All that stuff about Diane having cracked up and her crazy plan to set up Stainsby . . . it was all self-serving. She didn't want me digging into 2009 because she's the one who tipped Diane over the edge. She was hiding her role. Giving us something big to swallow that could never be disproved, because she's the only one who claims to have seen her dressing up and putting a cigarette butt in the fridge.' Tess tried again to keep *R* v. *Stainsby* simple. 'Then is then, now is now. And, even if it wasn't, all that matters is the evidence in the courtroom . . . and I repeat, you're getting somewhere.'

'Which is why 2009 remains important,' insisted Benson. 'If Stainsby screws things up in the witness box, pretending he's never been in custody before, or whatever, Yardley will apply to call evidence about the attack on Foster. And at that point we might as well pack our bags and go home. So I want to know as much as possible.'

'But there's nowhere else to turn.'

'There is,' said Benson. 'Foster's wife.'

Tess laughed. 'You must be joking. We represent the guy who tried to kill her husband.'

'We need to find out why Stainsby was meeting Meersham and Loupierre.'

'No, we don't.'

'Foster may have told his wife.'

'You're not hearing me, Will. We don't need to know this.' Tess examined Benson's face. The strain of the trial was beginning to show. 'There's another reason, isn't there?'

'Yes.' Benson's voice changed; he made a sort of plea. 'Let's say I care about the evidence that never makes it before a jury. Like Bredfield said, if I'm going to try and get Stainsby off a murder rap, I might as well know what really happened . . . on the off-chance that then is linked to now. I just want to know what I'm doing.'

Tess was disarmed. 'Lambrook's got her number,' she said. 'I'll give her a call.'

They ate, going over the trial. Tess and Archie agreed. So far, things weren't looking so bad. The lay witness testimony had been completed and no one had left the court uncontradicted. Doubt was stirring amongst the jurors. Unfortunately, the largest obstacle – a body of interlinked scientific conclusions – was yet to be confronted. Come Monday morning, Yardley would start calling his expert evidence. How Benson proposed to get around the hairs, the ash and the cigarette butt found at Diane's feet – not to mention the binding of the limbs and spiking her food with drugs, along with the DNA on the electric cable – was anyone's guess. He remained quiet and remote. To draw him out, Tess said:

'Have you heard of this Meersham character? Apparently, he's a major player. High-end crime.'

'I've heard the name. Some while back.'

'Loupierre?'

'No. But I bet you he smokes Durand.'

And on that note, Benson glanced at his watch and said he had to go. Struggling into his duffel coat, he warned Archie that should he attempt to get from the Strand to Piccadilly later that evening, he'd better bring his wallet. Because Benson expected to own every street in between, not to mention a railway station, and it would cost him. Moments later Tess and Archie were alone, stubbing toast crumbs with their fingers.

'He takes Monopoly very seriously,' said Tess, her mind far from the game.

'Oh, he's ruthless,' replied Archie. 'Funny thing is, he thinks my sisters are bad, but he's far worse. He always tries to buy up one side of—'

'Something's troubling him,' said Tess, quietly, looking to Archie for an explanation. But the clerk who'd once been a cell-mate just licked his thumb. 'Don't worry. Something's always troubling him.'

32

'He's brilliant,' said Tess, later that night.

Because of *The Pirates of Penzance*, the ritual of cocktails on Tuesdays had been moved to Friday, and Sally had suggested the Callooh Callay in Shoreditch. It was a Lewis Carroll-themed wonderland, with purple furnishings and candles and – according to the glowing review in *Time Out* – a toilet hidden behind a secret door. Tess felt she'd tumbled into a dreamscape where everything was upside down.

'You read about these cross-examinations where the witness stumbles or folds, but nine times out of ten the questioner had loads of ammunition. Benson's got nothing.'

'So what does he do?'

'He gets inside them. He uses their past to his advantage.'

With Milena Sibhatu he'd used one word and its religious associations: 'neighbour'. Archie had found out she was an Oriental Orthodox Christian, and a one-time refugee, so Benson had drawn her into revealing what had prompted her compassion, the running away from a troubled past, which he'd then deflected from Stainsby by linking it to a stray word picked up in Dr Lowmax's medical notes. With Rosie Heybridge, he'd used nothing but a line from a school report, a remark in the unused material and a coincidence in timings: and all at once the jury sees Diane heading to London in a state and it had nothing to do with Brent Stainsby.

'Where's the truth in all this?'

'That's the trick. It is all true. It's what he does with it that counts.'

He makes unexpected connections. He puts things in a certain order. And no one stumbles or falls. The prosecution's own witnesses are seen to build Stainsby's case, and they don't realise what they're doing. It's as though he was hands-off.

'And that makes it real.'

Sally, dressed in a light blue dress (in homage to Alice) had chosen a Mad Baron – the nearest thing on the menu to a Mad Hatter. Tess had gone for a Runaway Man. They sipped their cocktails, no longer talking. After a while Sally said:

'I'm surprised at you.'

'Why?' Tess didn't like the tone. Sally was being serious. And these jaunts around London's cocktail bars were meant to be an upmarket version of a night out with the Dover Five. They talked serious, sure, but the object of the exercise was fun. Letting off steam. Even if that steam included the odd belch of jurisprudence.

'When I think back to that summer in Paris, all you cared about was justice. About the nightmare of guilty people being acquitted and innocent people being convicted. You wanted to get it right. I don't hear that voice any more. You're on about tricks and things seeming real and that doesn't seem to bother you.'

'It's not like that, Sally. It's more complex.'

'Really? Diane Heybridge was a real person. Her mother still is. So are the others. And they're just pieces on the board. You're getting a thrill from how they're moved around. It's horrible.'

Tess couldn't fight back because it was true. But in acknowledging the criticism, she realised it couldn't be said of Benson. He got no pleasure from what he was doing. Despite his own experience of the law in action, where the pieces had moved against him, he'd lost none of his idealism. She was about to say as much when Sally aimed a jab at those who wore wigs and gowns when fighting over the truth:

'I thought I was the one who dressed up and played the fool.'

Sitting on the District Line after a somewhat strained evening, Tess reached for a discarded copy of the *Standard*. A few pages in she came across an interview with Maureen Harbeton, the mother of Benson's victim. Tess had seen her in court every day during the weeklong trial. She'd shown none of the anger of her sons. Just inconsolable grief. Now, seventeen years later and just turned seventy, she'd stared into the camera, hiding nothing. Her eyes were still bleeding mascara. There'd been no closure, she said. Because even though Benson had admitted killing Paul, everyone knows he still claimed to be innocent – even if he'd never say so in public. 'So there's always this nagging thought in my mind, that maybe he didn't kill my son, and that means there's someone out there who did, and as long as they're living a normal life I'm stuck in the past. I can't get away from the day he died. The day they told me Paul had been found dead in Soho. It's like I've never buried him.'

When Tess got home she rang Sally to apologise, but things quickly went off track:

'So Benson cares about what really happened?'

'Yes.'

'And you do, too?'

'Absolutely.'

'Then what about his own case? Doesn't a grieving mother have a right to know the truth?'

Tess wasn't stupid. She could see through the argument. Sure, Sally cared about Maureen Harbeton, just as she cared for Rosie Heybridge, but her real concern was Tess, and her confused relationship with Benson. She wanted to go back to the beginning. To set in motion a process that would enable Tess to find out what she really felt. She wanted Tess to reopen their abandoned investigation.

'Tell me about this promise you made,' Sally said.

'I told him I wanted to reopen his case. He asked me not to.'

'What did he say, exactly?'

'That his life in court would be at risk if I dug up the past.'

'Abstract bollocks. Anything else?'

'That I'm the one who lit his ambition in the first place—'

Sally scoffed: 'And he begged you not to put out the fire? Don't tell me he said that.'

'He did, actually.'

'So you backed down?' There was a pause. 'Tess . . . are you still there?'

'I am; and I did.'

'Well you've made a mistake. Because emotionally damaged people rarely know what's best for them. Half the time, they're scared of getting better. They need to be challenged, not pampered.'

'He knows, Sally. And it's cost him dearly . . . and he wouldn't have paid the price unless he was sure it was worth it.'

Sally gave the point careful consideration, then she gave judgement. 'That's bollocks, too. You're colluding, Tess. He's got you exactly where he wants you.'

The line went dead. Tess couldn't think clearly. It was the old question that would never go away: had Benson been painfully honest or had he played her, knowing she'd do what he wanted? After pacing around for a while, unable to decide, she called DI Lambrook and asked for Mrs Foster's number.

33

Notwithstanding the threat to make central London his personal fiefdom, Benson cried off the Friday night Monopoly game. He cancelled all viewings of his boat over the weekend. And he ignored all calls from Molly and Archie. Hearing the name Terry Meersham had stunned him. For that figure, a shadow to Tess and everyone she'd met, was part of the darkness of his life. A man he still feared, even now. Because Terry Meersham had a hold on him. The same Terry Meersham who knew Brent Stainsby, whom Benson was defending. At every turn, he saw Skagman and Crazy Joe idling towards him.

It was only on Sunday afternoon that Benson managed to focus on the job at hand: how to undermine the forensic evidence. They'd left motive, means and opportunity behind. Now it was a question of science. So Benson scoured the reports once more, looking for weaknesses and data that would support Stainsby's limited instructions. By late evening, having found nothing, he began to panic. But then came the breakthrough that had eluded him for months. Reviewing his notes, he realised one of the experts had deliberately curtailed the scope of his analysis.

3.00 p.m. SOCOs take over crime scene.
Findings:

(i) Durand cigarette butt (+ DNA) on floor of bedroom by the body
(ii) 1 hair on armchair headrest (+ DNA)
(iii) Ash on same armchair, left armrest

Later at the lab:

(iv) 2 hairs on victim's cardigan
(v) 1 hair on inside of tape tied around the wrists.
(vi) Electric extension cable (+ DNA)

The scientists had produced their reports against the backdrop of Stainsby's initial and ludicrous denials. He'd denied going to London, never mind entering the flat; and that had prompted one expert, Dr Andrew Capicelli, to overplay his hand. He'd found a single hair on an armchair, along with some cigarette ash. He'd labelled these AC1 and AC2. He'd then, quite reasonably, thought of Locard's Principle of Exchange. As long ago as 1910, Edmund Locard had pointed out that when someone commits a crime, they always take something away from the crime scene and, more importantly, they always leave something behind. Relying, then, on Locard's dictum that 'every contact leaves a trace', Dr Capicelli had confidently stated that the defendant hadn't only been in the flat, he'd sat down and had a smoke. There was no doubt about it. The very idea was graphic. It had made its way into the media and the narrative fanned by the tabloids.

But there was another explanation for that hair on the headrest. And it wasn't mentioned by Dr Capicelli when he gave evidence on Monday morning.

Benson began his cross-examination, focusing on numbers:

'Dr Capicelli, how many hairs does the average adult male shed per day?'

'Gender isn't a significant issue, Mr Benson.'

'How many?'

'I'd say one hundred to one hundred and twenty-five.'

'That's roughly four per hour,' said Benson. 'Mr Stainsby was in Diane's flat for over three hours. That yields about twelve hairs.'

'It doesn't work that way, Mr Benson. Hairs don't shed like trains pulling out of Euston.'

The jury smiled.

'But they shed,' said Benson.

'They do. But not on the hour.'

A juror laughed. So did Benson. But the inevitable concession had been made. If Stainsby had been in that flat, he could have shed a hair *anywhere*. Relying on direct transference to put him in the chair was the mistake, because – and Dr Capicelli had to agree – the hair could just as easily have ended up on the headrest through secondary transfer – put there by Diane – after Stainsby had left the premises. Unfortunately for Yardley, Capicelli – broad-shouldered, with a squarish head – was the bullish sort; he stuck to his unimportant theory, observing that no other hairs belonging to the defendant had been found in the flat. And that gave Benson the opening he'd prayed for.

'Would you accept that Mr Stainsby might have shed at least four hairs while he was in the premises?'

'I only found one.'

'But in principle he could have shed others?'

'Yes. In principle. Not in practice.'

'Given that they might have been there, didn't you think to ask where they could have gone? Three of them, in fact.'

Dr Capicelli frowned and tried a joke. 'Who could I ask? Eddie Locard?'

'No, Dr Nadine Khan, the pathologist in this case.'

It was too late to repair the damage. Benson had given the jury an alternative explanation for the presence of Stainsby's hairs on Diane's cardigan and the inside of the tape that had bound her wrists – hairs that had been found prior to the post-mortem. By the same Principle of Exchange, Diane could have put them there herself, and Dr Capicelli's remonstrations to the contrary rang hollow. His exclusive reliance on Locard, as applied to Stainsby, had shown him to be biased, because he'd failed to apply the same principle in relation to Diane. This old-school expert had made an old-school mistake: he'd cosied up to the CPS.

'Dr Capicelli, have you ever read Part Nineteen of the Criminal Procedure Rules 2015?'

'I have.'

'Do you remember rule nineteen point two?'

'I'd need to check the wording.'

'Let me summarise. You are obliged to produce objective evidence, uninfluenced by the demands of litigation.' Benson paused as if to reload a sling. 'Let's consider the ash on the left armrest.'

He delivered short, fast questions and Dr Capicelli, keen to demonstrate independence of mind, cautiously affirmed – given the state of the windows – that the flakes could have been airborne, coming from the likely crowd of smokers gathered outside Alan's Kebabs on a Friday night, or indeed a Saturday lunchtime, a matter of hours before he'd arrived at the premises.

'Thank you, Doctor. No further questions.'

Benson sat down. The image of Stainsby manhandling Diane had been blurred. Now all that remained was to explain away the distinctive nature of the killing – the binding and the gagging – and, critically, the DNA (on the cable and the cigarette end) which put Stainsby in a room that he swore he'd never entered. But for the moment Benson was indifferent to the task ahead. He'd been paralysed by an eruption of memory. All he could see was Skagman and Crazy Joe. They passed on either side, brushing his shoulders. Skagman spoke:

'Two o'clock.'

So did Crazy Joe. 'The laundry.'

34

Linda Foster hadn't just left Dover. She'd left Kent. She'd brought her children, Beth and Bobby, to Great Dunmow in Essex. The pay-out on her husband's life insurance policy had bought an old cottage outside the market town. The thatch and windows needed redoing, and the plasterwork was cracked, but all that could wait. She'd got away from the place intimately linked to John's death. Or, to show what she thought of the coroner's verdict, John's murder. She'd bought some charm and some quiet. She'd got a job at the local library. She'd found a nice school for the kids. Things were getting better. They'd stopped asking questions about the nightclub in Dover. And that fall that didn't make sense.

'John loved the CID,' said Linda. The anger was right up against her front teeth. 'It was his life. All he ever wanted to do. He was ambitious and he worked hard and he believed he was doing something good. Making people's lives better. Helping victims. Protecting society.'

She was fine boned. She didn't need make-up, but she'd laid it on to recover some colour and contrast. They were sitting on a bench overlooking Doctors Pond, Tess aslant, Linda with arms folded tight as if to stop her guts from spilling onto the grass. On the far side, Bobby, now nine, and Beth, recently twelve – out of school to see their counsellors later in the day – were playing with a remote-controlled boat.

'It sounds idealistic I know, but it's true,' said Linda. 'If he'd stayed in uniform he'd have got promoted easily and he'd have worked better hours and there'd have been less pressure, but none of that mattered to John. He wanted to put bad people away. In the end the bad people pushed him off a multi-storey car park.'

Linda had not agreed to this meeting in order to help Tess understand how a mindless attack upon her husband in 2009 might be connected to a trial in 2015. This was her chance to send a message to the bastard in the dock, who'd beaten John out of the CID. Changed his personality.

Deprived Beth and Bobby of a normal father. And Linda of the man she'd loved. She was taking this slowly. Savouring the poison.

'John always did things by the book. If he ran an informer he followed the rules. He shared all the intelligence with everyone who needed to know. And what do you think happened, eventually? One of his own mates, another DS, used information from John to crack a case and get promoted. John stayed a DS and his mate became a DI *and* his supervisor. That's the CID for you. Guess who that was?'

'I've no idea.'

'Ray Carlatton. The same guy who, I presume, sent John to the Twisted Wheel, relying on a tip-off from a source that was never entered in the books. That's the CID for you. The guy who got the cream didn't follow the rules. He'd kept his source to himself. Didn't want anyone doing to him what he had done to John. If there was going to be any credit, he wanted all of it.'

Beth stayed close to Bobby like a shadow, watching him operate the controls, laughing when he laughed, touching him frequently as if to make sure he was still there.

'And when it all blew up in Carlatton's face, he just denied there'd ever been an operation. That's the CID for you. Break the rules and you get away with murder. John ended up in hospital with a fractured skull and permanent brain damage. I still don't know what the hell he was doing there. Neither did he. He'd lost half his memory.'

Tess risked a question. 'What about DC Draycott? He was in the club, too. Couldn't he help you? Tell you what they were up to?'

'Steve? He knew nothing. John wouldn't tell him. That's how Carlatton ran things. That's why Steve couldn't blow the whistle afterwards. He'd no idea why John had asked him to watch his back. He'd been totally in the dark. Couldn't prove that Carlatton had been in the driving seat. See how clever he was? And do you know what? Steve is still a DC and Carlatton's a DCI. A Detective Chief Inspector. Honestly, that's the CI bloody D. The ones who ignore the book end up writing it, shafting people who dare to do what they once did.'

Bobby had sent the boat racing towards the middle of the pond. He was pushing the range of the remote, chasing ducks; the signal could drop at any moment. Tess took the same risk.

'Linda, didn't John give you any hint as to why he was going to the Twisted Wheel?'

Thankfully, she replied. 'Yes, he did. He said he was on to something huge. It was going to change his career. His life. My life. The kids' lives. It was a turning point. He was right.'

After he came out of hospital John suffered constant headaches. He'd look out onto the sunlit garden, eyes half shut as the pain stabbed his brain. He dragged a leg. He'd blow up for nothing and throw his plate at the wall. His short-term memory was shot. Steve came every day. Took him to the clinic. Took the kids out. Took Linda out. Mowed the lawn. Fixed the gutter. Did everything he could. Him and John kept going over the Stainsby case – a case that should never have been dropped – trying to work out what had happened. They'd sit in the back room checking this, checking that. And Steve would head off with his homework. He got nowhere. But he helped John. Because as long as John and Steve were asking questions, Stainsby hadn't won.

'Do you know Dover?' asked Linda.

'I don't.'

'There was an old multi-storey car park behind the County Hotel. Disused. It's been demolished now. The place was used by dropouts and headbangers. Why would John go there in the middle of the night? He took a taxi. Went out while I was asleep. Didn't tell Steve. Some kids found him at three in the morning.' Her voice jammed and she squeezed herself tighter. She was looking at the pond and Bobby's boat, stranded in the water, drifting. Curious ducks were taking a closer look. 'It wasn't an accident and he didn't kill himself. Someone lured him out there. Presumably with the promise of information. And they killed him.'

'Do you have an idea who might—'

'It had to be Stainsby.'

'Do you have any evidence?'

'No. And guess what? He had an alibi. A scumbag called Bredfield.'

'But why would Stainsby kill your husband?'

'Why sound so surprised? He'd tried once, hadn't he? If John's memory ever kicked in he'd be a threat. I don't give a damn what the coroner says. I know and so does Steve. John would never take his own life. He loved me. And he loved them.' She pointed across the pond as if it was an ocean; as if she'd been deported and couldn't get home. 'He'd never have abandoned them. Or me.'

A gentle breeze nudged the boat towards the waiting children. They were patient, standing side by side, expressionless.

'The CPS should have put Stainsby on trial,' said Linda, the rage widening her throat. 'Made those witnesses turn up. Let the barrister have a crack at those alibis. But they didn't. Do you want to know why? The CPS were too worried about performance indicators. The percentage rate of convictions. And they didn't want to spoil their average. But the case should have gone to the jury. *They* should have decided, not some yes-woman from London. If they'd put Stainsby away back then John would be alive now, along with that woman who once lied for him.'

Tess wasn't going to defend Pauline Osborne. Justice denied is justice denied. The reasons don't count.

'Could you tell him? Tell him what he's done? To my kids and to me?'

Tess wasn't going to tell her that Stainsby had been pleased with himself; that he'd wanted the photos of the stitches and bruising as a keepsake. She said: 'I can't, Linda. The case was dropped and I'm his lawyer.'

She wasn't surprised; and her anger didn't burst out, as it must have done for years after Osborne's decision; it just slid back down to the bile in her stomach. A feat of control she'd learned for the sake of the kids; and her own sanity.

'Do you want my take on your trial?'

'Yes,' said Tess. 'I would.'

'Everything is connected. John and that poor woman knew too much. That's why they're dead.'

Linda didn't want Tess to meet her kids so she left her sitting on the bench. And Tess, cold and uneasy, watched them walk away, skirting the water's edge, Linda in the middle, holding the children's hands, Beth with the remote control and Bobby with the boat under his arm. Some ducks waddled after them, keeping a safe distance.

35

Benson was back in the laundry of HMP Codrington. He made his way past the caged, rumbling machines and the plastic barrows piled high with sheets and tablecloths from nearby hotels and restaurants. When he reached the far end of the room, he rounded a packed crate and saw one of Meersham's boys. He was seated on a stool, facing a portable

TV video player. Using a booted foot, he nudged a cassette lodged in the mouth of the machine. Gulls screamed over a high wind and the sea groaned in the distance.

'Sit down, Rizla,' he said. 'I've got something to show you.'

Benson looked over his shoulder as if to check where the screw had gone; but he only saw Archie . . . dear old Archie, who was struggling with a word puzzle hidden in a blue notebook. Needing help, he made a face – in prison Archie's questions had been maddening: on one occasion, Benson had solved an entire hundred-word grid, all through dictation – but a woman had entered the witness box. She was taking the oath. Benson turned to face her, forcing his mind into gear.

Dr Nadine Khan – a slight figure, but with a commanding presence – was one of the most important experts in the case. She dealt with death, and how people got there, whether by their own hand or someone else's. And she had never seen a case like this in her career. The taping of the hands behind the back, the consumption of mind-altering drugs and the gagging with a blood orange were all highly suspicious. There was an element of ceremony. And the combination of these various features persuaded her that murder was the most convincing explanation. Her conclusion had been supported by the finding of the defendant's DNA on the ligature along with three of his hairs on the body. That the latter may have been transferred by the deceased onto herself did not alter her view.

'This was a ritual killing. I can't seriously entertain any other analysis.'

Benson rose even before Yardley had sat down, determined to get in, grab what was needed and get out as fast as he could:

'You found this an unusual case?'

'Highly unusual.'

'But the use of gags and the binding of limbs is not unheard of, is it?'

'No.'

'It appears in the literature on suicide. These are techniques deployed by people who are determined to kill themselves. They prevent the person concerned from backing out of their decision.'

'I accept that, but this is an extreme example which strains comparison.'

'As extreme as the case of suicidal hanging reported by Marsh in 1982? Where a man bound his hands at his back and used a sock as a gag? Or the six cases discussed by Krzyanowski in 2002, all of which involved bound limbs?'

'I take your point, Mr Benson. The features we're discussing are not unprecedented. But there are other components in this case which make it distinctive. As I said to Mr Yardley, the use of a blood orange is altogether striking. It's not the sort of object you find lying around. Not the sort of item one would buy for the purpose, unless it had a private meaning. And this blood orange had been forced deep into the mouth.'

'She could have done it herself?'

'It's possible, of course, but we can't take this one element in isolation from the others. The binding is problematic, too. The tape had been wound very tightly around the wrists. Given the length of the deceased's arms and legs, getting her bound wrists behind her back would have required considerable contortion and strain. It's not quite Houdini, but we're not far off. These are all features of a singular nature.'

'That could, nonetheless, have been self-inflicted?'

'Yes, it's possible. Remotely. But the most reasonable

explanation is that the deceased was drugged, tied up and then suspended over the door.'

Benson had got as far as he could. Now it was time to get out.

'We're not going to agree on the meaning of these features are we, Doctor?'

'No.'

'And it's not because of the science; it's because of the psychology.'

'In what respect?'

'You underestimate the scale of Diane Heyward's desperation.'

'I'm not a psychiatrist, Mr Benson.'

'Neither am I. But it doesn't take an expert to recognise that a troubled woman might go to extraordinary lengths to make sure she died.'

'Perhaps not.'

'And use ritual to invest it with a meaning that no one else would understand.'

Benson sat down. He'd snatched what he could.

Yardley then called Dr Kate Sarsfield, a leading authority on DNA analysis . . . but Benson lost his grip once more. What could Stainsby offer Terry Meersham? And André Loupierre? Potted shrimps? Crabs? He ran a seafood delivery business that was going nowhere. So why have a meeting with him? The questions turned on a mental carousel, until all at once, over the hum of Dr Sarsfield's voice, Benson had a liberating insight. Something he should have seen right from the start. Regardless of what the answers might be, Stainsby had been protected back in 2009; and he wasn't being protected now. No witnesses had been intimidated this time. Which meant that Terry Meersham had no interest in this case. Then was then. Now is now.

'Mr Benson?'

Mrs Justice Fleetwood smiled. 'When you're ready.'

Benson seemed to float on air. He quickly established two points in Stainsby's favour: first, that the presence of the defendant's DNA on the electric cable meant nothing because Diane could have brought it with her from the shared flat in Dover; second, wherever else his DNA might be, it wasn't on the packets of Fluvopram and Benzotriptyline. Unlike Diane's. And that was the end of Benson's run. Because there was nothing he could say to contradict Dr Sarsfield's evidence on the Durand cigarette butt. Stainsby's DNA was on it and no one else's.

'The flex may have come in a suitcase from Dover, Mr Benson, but not this butt. It was perfectly formed. No creases, no folds. It lay where it fell and where it was found. Inside the deceased's bedroom. Beside a dressing table with a burnt edge. And near the door.'

'You exclude all innocent explanations?'

'I can't think of any.'

'But that doesn't mean there isn't one.'

Dr Sarsfield used a voice appropriate for a fairy tale. 'No Mr Benson, it doesn't.'

After Dr Sarsfield had left the court, Yardley announced that he wouldn't be calling any further lay or expert evidence. His final witness, to be questioned tomorrow, was the OIC, DCI Goodshaw. Assured by Benson that the defence was ready to begin, Mrs Justice Fleetwood thanked counsel and then adjourned the proceedings.

'I don't trust him,' said Archie, ambling with Benson back to chambers. 'He's a low-life and he's a liar. But I've got to admit, he sounds convincing.'

They'd paid a visit to the cells and Stainsby had sworn on his mother's life that he hadn't smoked in the flat, that he couldn't have left a burning cigarette end in Diane's bedroom.

'I know what you mean,' said Benson. 'Truth has a ring to it. And of all his crazy denials, that's the one that troubles me most. Because I believe him.'

Over tea and Jammie Dodgers, Benson listened to Molly read out various newspaper cuttings. The commentaries were unanimous. The Blood Orange murder, once thought to be an open-and-shut case, had turned out to be a far more involved affair. Because William Benson had shown Diane Heybridge to be a less than simple character. More significantly, Benson had managed to defend an abusive man while respecting his accusers. The phone kept ringing, too. Archie was taking bookings.

Now that the prosecution case was all but closed – and Meersham's shadow had withdrawn – Benson felt exhausted. His work was almost done and, cycling home, he had to admit he was pleased: he'd listened to Molly and made himself Diane's defender. At each turn, he'd glanced at the jury, and they'd been uneasy, wondering what to think. Arriving at Seymour Road, Benson dared to believe that Stainsby might just have a chance. The only problem – and it was a big problem – was that cigarette end. But if—

Benson wobbled, hit the kerb and nearly fell off his bike. Parked outside the railings, by the gate that led to *The Wooden Doll*, was a cherry red Mini Cooper S. A 1964 classic. It belonged to Tess de Vere. The driver's door opened and she appeared, leaning over the roof, and for a moment Benson thought he stumbled into a photoshoot for a glossy magazine. She looked sensational.

'Aren't you going to invite me in?' she said.

36

'Whatever else,' said Tess, '2009 casts a long shadow.'

Benson was frying sausages and bacon on the Aga while Traddles, already fed, wound himself between his feet, apparently asking for more. Every now and then Benson's phone made a light buzz, but he ignored it.

'Do you like baked beans?' he asked.

'I do, but I avoid them.'

Benson, a sensitive advocate, didn't ask why.

'Tomatoes?'

'Yep.'

'Mushrooms?'

'Yep, yep.'

He went to the fridge, took out a brown paper bag and threw it at Tess. 'Wash and slice, please.'

Standing side by side at the work surface – Benson slicing tomatoes, Tess slicing mushrooms, the phone buzzing and Traddles getting underfoot – Tess resumed her diagnosis: that 2009 was best forgotten about. Expecting resistance from Benson, she'd rehearsed her argument all the way back from Great Dunmow: Pauline Osborne, DI Lambrook and, most tragic of all, Linda Foster were all desperately trying to redeem the past by finding something significant in the unfolding trial. But the evidential link wasn't there. A lawyer, a policeman and a victim had made the same mistake: they'd let suspicion grow until they'd lost the ability to question themselves; they'd lost the ability to doubt. The need to find meaning had led them all to clutch at the senseless murder of Diane Heybridge. Linda Foster had even added another murder – that of her husband. Guesswork, imagination and credulity – the wise men of the possible – had soothed the agony of not knowing.

'And even if there is a connection, it goes no further than altering the alleged motive. Like Archie said at the outset, Stainsby could have been silencing a former alibi. It changes nothing for his defence.'

'Eggs?' said Benson.

'Please.'

'Any preference?'

'Fried.'

Benson went back to the fridge, followed by Traddles. 'You're right,' he said. 'We know as much as Yardley now, and if a wheel comes off, that's all we need. As you say, our defence remains the same.'

Benson set the table while Tess prepared the plates, but unfortunately, when sliding an egg onto a plate – abstracted by Benson's sudden and unexpected willingness to let 2009 go – she broke the yolk. Benson examined each portion and frowned:

'Now we've got a real problem.'

'I'll have it.'

'No, I will.'

'Seriously, I don't care.'

'That's not true.'

'They're cooling as we speak.'

'Okay, we'll do what my brother did when we were kids.' Benson picked up a knife and broke the other egg. 'Problem solved.'

Tess made a light cough. 'I would have preferred one of us to have it whole.'

'That's not true either,' said Benson. 'One of us would have spent the entire meal looking at it. Honestly. I've been there. Ask Eddie.'

Benson frowned again and Tess tried to see into his fractured eyes, but he looked away. And then, all of a sudden, like a bottle knocked over and spilling water, he began emptying himself in sudden bursts. Once, when Benson was eight, Eddie had dared him to walk on a frozen lake – it was a lake in the grounds of Lushmead's, a hotel near Brancaster, not far from home – and he'd walked about ten yards when there was a sudden crack and Benson dropped into the freezing water. He'd gone right under; and when he came up, his head had hit the ice. By the time he'd found the hole and surfaced, he could barely breathe.

'I thought I was going to die. I tried to yell out but I couldn't, and then I saw Eddie coming for me. He'd found a branch and it was like in the films – he lay down and pushed it towards me and I somehow got out.'

Benson was blinking quickly, as if he was still eight, wet and shivering.

'Before that, I couldn't stand him. But afterwards . . . we were inseparable. We were going to sail to Canada. Become Mounties. We were going to travel round the world and learn Russian and Japanese. We were going to find a desert island and live in a tree . . .'

'What happened, Will?'

Tess knew about the Lushmead Hotel. It was mentioned in the pre-sentence report prepared after Benson had been convicted. Tess had read it only recently, the night she'd seen *The Pirates of Penzance*. She'd been haunted by 'a paradox, a paradox, a most ingenious paradox', fighting to concentrate; but now her mind was clear and still. Two years after that near-escape, when Benson was ten and Eddie was nine, they'd been playing in the grounds again, this time with a friend, Neil Reydon. They'd been riding their bikes towards that same lake. Daring each other to get as close as possible without falling in. Slamming on the brakes at the last moment. Inexplicably, come Eddie's turn, he'd set off down a path towards the main road. A Citroën people carrier had come around the corner.

'What happened, Will?' said Tess. 'Tell me everything.'

'The trial happened.'

'Your trial?'

'Yes.'

Tess didn't understand. Benson looked up, and for once he didn't turn away. The blinking had stopped and his eyes were like cups of water. Tess couldn't stop herself. She reached over and caught the first tear with her thumb.

'Come here,' she said.

Benson didn't move. So Tess stepped closer, one hand finding his neck . . . but then, outside, there was a thud. Heavy steps sounded on deck and the cabin door, ajar as usual, swung open.

'I do beg your pardon.'

It was Archie, red-faced and panting.

'What's the point of having a mobile phone if you never answer it? Have you seen the news?'

Tess and Benson both said no, moving apart as if to deny they even knew each other.

'What news?' added Tess airily.

'About the riot. In Kensal Green. The prison's out of control.'

The workshops had been set on fire. Two officers had been taken hostage. The wings were barricaded.

'The listing office called,' said Archie, taking more bacon and sausage out of the fridge. 'The trial's adjourned, at least for tomorrow because they can't get Stainsby to court. He's stuck in a war zone. We're on holiday.'

And that wasn't all. Archie was holding something back and he didn't reveal it until the table had been set and they were all seated, cutlery in hand.

'Remember Gary Bredfield? The guy who was scared for his life? Well, he's just been found dead in Rye Harbour.'

* * *

Tess didn't even wait to get home. When she'd dropped Archie off at Congreve's, she sat in her Mini and rang Sally. She didn't even know what she was going to say. How could she explain the distance she'd travelled? Too many people remained in a twilight world, ghosts of who they might have been, crippled by what they'd done or what had been done to them, joined at the extremes by grief but unable to grieve properly, because grief, to have an end, requires a submission to reality, and reality had been turned on its head. What did Mrs Justice Fleetwood tell the jury? 'Keep your minds on the evidence presented in this court. Ignore everything else.' It was true and it was false. Sometimes you had to look elsewhere.

Sally answered.

'I've been an ass,' said Tess.

'Meaning?'

'I listened to a damaged man when I should have listened to you.'

Sally didn't reply immediately. When she did, she chose her words carefully.

'And would that have been out of compassion?'

She'd left the alternative, love, unstated, which only served to give it more prominence.

'I don't know,' said Tess. 'And, for now, I am not sure that it matters.'

'What does matter?'

'The truth. The whole truth, and nothing but the truth. It's the only thing that will set everyone free.'

'Could you be a little more specific?'

'My place, tomorrow. Lunchtime. We're going to find out who killed Paul Harbeton.'

PART THREE

War zones

Benson went to the laundry and the screw, clearly terrified, just let him in. He was a new guy, not much older than Benson, and to Benson's eyes the sort of gangling kid you saw in the supermarket stacking shelves over the summer. He looked the other way, too ashamed to find out if Benson viewed him with pity or disdain.

'Sit down, Rizla, I've got something to show you.'

Benson had walked the length of the room and rounded a crate stacked high with sheets. There he'd seen Roy – one of Meersham's boys – seated on a stool. He'd used a foot to push a cassette into a portable TV video player.

'I said sit down.'

Roy pointed at a second stool, and Benson slowly lowered himself, listening to the cry of the gulls and the rush of the wind, recognising the Fisherman's Quay at Brancaster Staithe. Recognising Neil Reydon pushing Eddie in his wheelchair.

'He's not in a good way, is he?' said Roy.

Benson could only whisper. 'No, he's not.'

'Can he walk?'

'Yes, a bit.'

The film had been taken from a parked car with the window wound down.

'What about his memory? Is it getting any better?'

'I don't know. I think so . . . we're not in touch.'

'That's sad, Rizla. When you've done your bird, you might go visit him. Try and patch things up. That's my advice.'

Roy wasn't a big man, like Crazy Joe or Skagman. He

had no tattoos either. But there was something hard about his features and voice, and the look of wet slate in his eyes.

'That's assuming he's still in one piece,' said Roy.

'Please leave him alone. He's—'

'Take it easy, Rizla. I'm not the problem here, you are.'

'What do you mean? What have I done?'

'For someone who wants to be a lawyer, you're not that clever, Rizla. It's not what you've done that interests me, it's what you're going to do, or not do. That's the problem. Or might be a problem. It's up to you.'

'What do you mean?'

'You and I are going to work together, okay, Rizla?'

'Okay, sure. But—'

'You're going to do what I say, when I say and how I tell you to do it. Do you understand?'

'Yes.'

'And as long as you're a good lad, Eddie's going to be just fine. He'll still walk a bit and his memory won't get any worse. And when you've done your time you can go and make up. But if you mess with me, just once, or if I think you've messed with me, I'm going to show you another video, and you'll see your brother getting the sort of pasting you've never even dreamed of. Have you got that, Rizla?'

Benson's chest was tight and he couldn't speak easily.

'If you're going to be one of them barristers, Rizla, you'll have to speak up. I'm only going to ask you twice. Do you understand?'

'I do.'

'No. I need some volume. And I want a bit more respect, Rizla. Try, "I do, my lord."'

Benson just got it out. 'I do, my lord.'

'You're halfway to the Old Bailey, Rizla. You're going

places. From now on, that's what I want you to call me. Got it?'

'Yes.'

'Pardon?'

'Yes, my lord.'

'Good. We're in business. Be in the library at twelve o'clock on Friday. Court adjourned.'

Benson went back to his cell. He climbed onto his bunk and folded himself up in anguish. When it was time for bang-up – the time he normally wanted to scream, when he heard the lock turning – he didn't even notice the crashing of doors and the shouting. Manchester had a fit of coughing, spat into his mug, and cleared his throat.

'You got any family out there, Rizla?'

'Yes.'

'Well, come on.'

'My mum and dad.'

'Anyone else?'

'My brother.'

Manchester took a puff of Ventolin and then a match flared.

'I lied, Rizla.'

'What about?'

'My family. I haven't got one. My wife's not waiting and I don't have a son. Not any more.'

'What happened?'

Manchester sucked in the smoke and held it tight in his big lungs. 'I killed him.'

37

Forget the briefing from G4S, who ran HMP Kensal Green. Or the briefing from his own department. Or that of the Metropolitan Police. Merrington had gone online and seen for himself. Prisoners had taken selfies and posted them on Facebook. Instagram. Various websites had made compilations. The whole world could see a prisoner holding keys taken from a warder. Another three were wearing helmets looted from the security equipment store. Some were in warders' uniforms. There were videos, too. Of prisoners drinking hooch. Smoking spice. Beating someone with a broken chair. Lighting fires. Smashing the place to pieces. Twitter had gone crazy with prison officers giving real-time commentary and family members expressing fear for their loved ones trapped inside.

This was the fourth major disturbance at an English prison in five months. Only this time Merrington had been warned. By the Independent Monitoring Board. So he'd need to do a bit of dodging in the morning. For now – after midnight and home at last – another matter required his attention. There was a tap on the outside door to the kitchen.

Bradley Hilmarton, suited in grey herringbone, looked pleased with himself.

'Someone paid for his law degree, his Bar course and all ancillary expenditure. That's about twenty K. They bought him accommodation. He chose a boat – seventy-five K. Throughout the Bar course, pupillage and first year in practice he received twenty grand per year. After that he was meant to be financially independent. He set up his own chambers in 2015 because no one would have him. That said, the word on the street is that he played the system, doing his three years so he could then work on his own, which is what happened. Either way, the same someone bought him a library. Another ten K. He paid for the refurbishment of Congreve chambers with a loan, so we can assume the gravy stopped running as soon as he set himself up. In all, that's a hundred and sixty thousand quid. It's a lot of money.'

'How was it channelled?'

Merrington poured out two fingers of the Talisker he reserved for special occasions.

'Through George Braithwaite. His solicitor. Benson signed undertakings promising never to try and find out the identity of his benefactor. If he did, the cashflow would stop. Now the payments are over, it's a matter of honour.'

'So we're dealing with a single benefactor, not a few?'

'Exactly.'

'Who is it?'

'I don't know.'

Merrington gave a wooden smile. This was the one bit of information he wanted. Hilmarton still looked pleased with himself.

'Our source tells us the set-up was very carefully handled. The initial meeting between the benefactor and Braithwaite didn't occur at the office. It took place elsewhere. Presumably Braithwaite's home or some other secure location. No fees were billed. Nothing was entered in the firm's public records.'

'Is that legal?'

'Yes. He wasn't even charging. Did it pro bono. And clients are entitled to anonymity. All the money was above board. Paid into the firm's account by a company set up for that purpose.'

'Who were the directors?

'I don't know. Not yet. Because we don't have the company's name. But we're on to it. Our source is reticent. But legal secretaries don't earn—'

'I don't think I want to know.'

'Of course.'

Merrington took a big nip. 'Why work pro bono, if the client can afford to pay fat fees?'

'Good question.'

'Do you know the answer?'

'No. But it tells you something about Braithwaite. Apparently, he was shocked to discover who it was that wanted to help Benson. For some reason, having met them, he didn't want paying.'

Merrington wasn't satisfied with that outcome. He took a bigger nip.

'But what about money-laundering regulations? Law Society rules governing client relations? There must be more paperwork.'

'There is. All kept in a safe. And we can't get access to that. For now.'

'So we've no idea if the money was clean, or who it came from.'

'No. But, given George Braithwaite's reputation, I would be staggered if it was dirty. He's old-school and highly respected. And as for the benefactor, it's not some crook Benson met in prison. I think we're looking at a well-off liberal-minded philanthropist. Someone who believes in second chances. Or someone who's done time themselves and wants to take a swing at the system. There are endless possibilities.'

'But why the secrecy?'

'My question is, who is it secret from? And the answer to that is Benson. This benefactor doesn't want Benson to know who they are. It's not about avoiding public flak.' Hilmarton made a reassuring smile. 'Don't worry. We'll get the name eventually.' He reached for his scotch. 'There is a rumour. At the Bar.'

'As to who it might be?

'Yes.'

'Well, who is it?'

'Helen Camberley. The silk who defended him in his trial.'

Merrington knew the name and face, and not just because of her link to Benson. She was a vocal critic of his department. One of those tiresome sages who brought indignation to *Question Time*. 'That would explain Braithwaite not taking a packet,' he said.

'It would,' replied Hilmarton. 'And she's got an interesting personal history. High-flyer from the start, when it wasn't that easy for women. Worked every hour God sent. This much is common knowledge. What's less well known is what happened on the home front. Her son did four months in a youth custody centre.'

'When's this?'

'Back in the eighties. Possession with intent to supply. Cannabis. When he came out he was branded. Had always wanted to be a lawyer like his mother. Now he didn't have a chance. Or he thought he didn't. Kid killed himself at sixteen, and Helen chucks herself into work and prison reform. The theory goes that in making Benson her protégé, she was redeeming the son who'd lost his way. In a sense, she'd failed them both.'

'It's poetic, at least.'

'It fits. And it's what Benson thinks. It's what he's said to those who've got anywhere near him.'

Merrington, however, had his eye on the ball, not the poetry:

'I won't cut Benson down through Camberley, that's for sure.'

'No. Whoever it is, I don't envisage anything to substantiate bringing the profession into disrepute, or dishonest or discreditable blah blah. He doesn't even know who it is, so he couldn't be blamed if it turned out to be one of the Krays.'

'No, Bradley, you're wrong there. It would help a great deal. If Braithwaite's been forced to act as an intermediary for a criminal concern, financing Benson's training and set-up, that paints Benson as their player. That's a good headline. He'd never shift the suspicion. So find the name.'

'We will.'

'Check if Benson served his time with any big-time villains.'

'I know the routine.'

'Indeed you do. Sorry. Is there anything else? What about how he runs things?'

'All above board. You can't fault him. But it's an unconventional arrangement.'

'In what way?'

'Everything he earns is divided three ways, between him, his clerk and his typist. They're a sort of collective where no one is more important than anyone else.'

'Dear God. "Everyone's a somebody, and no one's anybody."' Merrington reached for the Talisker. That was right up his son's street. Pamela would like it, too. People who think kindness won't mix with competition or merit usually do. 'Well, keep at it, Bradley – for the moment we've got nothing I can work with. And I need something.'

'I haven't finished.' Hilmarton held out his tumbler; that self-satisfied smile had broadened. 'You know Benson studied philosophy?'

'My wife reminded me only recently.'

'Well, I've been wondering if he ever read Rousseau. Or even Augustine.'

'What are you talking about?'

'They both wrote "confessions". Heart-searching, painfully honest expositions of what they did, and why, and what they thought about the mess of their lives, looking back.'

'And?'

'So did Benson. He didn't publish his, though, he fed them into a shredder. But with patience – and a software package – you can piece them back together.' Hilmarton gave his glass a gentle swirl and smiled. 'You can forget about Benson's benefactor. You've already got everything you need. Do you have any ice?'

38

Benson, unexpectedly, found himself getting angry. He'd gone to see Abasiama intending to recount developments as if he were a geographer describing a puzzling change in topography. He took her round the changes, but as he spoke it dawned on him she knew this new territory. She'd seen it before. Possibly been there. She'd set him up.

'It's those confessions,' he said, all at once.

'What do you mean?'

'Ever since I started writing down what I dare not say – like you told me – I've started falling to pieces.'

'Are you sure?'

'Bloody right I'm sure.'

She'd braided her hair with coloured bands of cotton and then wound the lot into a beehive. Long earrings reached her shoulders. Her wrists were heavy with metal bangles. As always, the box of tissues and that cactus were on the table between them. For the first time, and obscurely, he understood the choice on offer: two types of pain.

'All that shredding business the next morning, it leaves me feeling worse than before, which at first I didn't mind, but now other stuff's been happening.'

'Like?'

'Well, I used to go into court and argue a case not caring whether it was true or not . . . but now I'm finding it hard to remain detached. I don't want to twist anything anyone says. I don't want to lead them into an alley and slam the gate, not unless I'm sure I'm on to something that's true.'

'You call that a problem?'

'Wouldn't you?'

'No. I would call that being human. I would have thought that makes you a better advocate.'

'But my job isn't to care about what's true. My job's to argue one side of the coin.'

'You can still care how it spins and lands.'

Benson felt another flush of anger. Because it wasn't just his work that had been affected.

'I used to be able to put things in different compartments. Feelings. Memories. And leave them there. The other day I broke an egg yolk. And the next minute I'm crying, telling Tess all about my brother. I haven't cried in years. I've tried, you know . . . I've got down on my knees and I've tried to force the things out of my eyes, and I'm dry, dry like the Sahara; I just don't have any, not any more . . . and there I am, looking at a full English, and they appeared out of nowhere. I thought I was going to crack up completely, but Archie appeared and saved the day.' As Benson spoke, he was ambushed again. Those same tears made a heave towards the surface; he felt the weight behind them; there was more water than sand. 'Oh God, no, I can't let this happen . . .'

Benson didn't expect words of comfort, like 'Yes you can,' because that wasn't Abasiama's way. She might not even think crying was a good idea. Everything had its proper time. And this wasn't Benson's. He capped the flow, twisting himself in his seat as if to get some leverage on a handle. Then he looked up, over the tissues and the cactus.

'You did this on purpose, didn't you?'

'No.'

'But you knew it would lead to this. To my breaking down.'

'You're not breaking down.'

'I am. I'm losing control of myself.'

'No, you're not. You're finding yourself.' She moved her wrist and a bangle flashed. 'You still have the choice, Will. You've always got the shredder.'

Benson wondered if this was what an interrogation centre might look like. Because, with his back to the window, there was nothing to distract the eye. No pictures or sculptures or mementoes. No books. No interesting furnishings. Nothing. Just Abasiama. She said:

'Have you been depressed lately?'

'Nothing big.'

'Any panic attacks?'

'No.'

'Anxiety?'

'Just what comes with the job.'

She paused, and Benson seemed to hear the tape rewind to that moment of collapse over a fry-up, when he'd nearly spilled out everything he'd chosen to hide.

'You almost picked the fruit.'

'I knew you were going to say that.'

An authentic life, she'd once said, was like a fruit in a tree.

'You'll never know what it tastes like—'

'Unless I take the risk. I know.'

'It might not be bitter.'

'And it might not be sweet.'

'I never said it would be.'

'Have you given any thought to Eddie?'

The question gave Benson a jolt. 'I think of him all the time.'

'I mean, have you ever considered that a false life for you might mean a false life for him? That he might need the truth more than you need to hide it?'

And again Benson felt that Abasiama had set him up. That maybe she'd been planning this since he'd first come to seek her help, an ex-con unable to close doors or stop smoking. She'd dealt with neither complaint, focusing instead on Benson's family; on the trial; and the slow annihilation of self-esteem behind a locked door. She'd disentangled the panic, the depression and the anxiety, never once mentioning 'therapy' or 'rehabilitation' or 'recovery'. Instead, she'd told him about the fruit in the tree; and they'd stood beneath the branches, looking up; and they'd talked about Benson's freedom to choose. But she had never suggested that Benson's picking it might be necessary for someone else; for one of the victims in his life.

'Why do I come and see you?' he said.

She didn't ponder that one for long. 'Every con likes a visit.'

39

Compassion without limit as opposed to love. Tess had never thought that the one could masquerade as the other. And now that Tess had effectively admitted that the distinction might well be relevant to her relations with Benson, she couldn't face Sally, who'd raised the matter, without feeling a degree of embarrassment. It turned acute when, having met to formally reopen the investigation into Paul Harbeton's death, Sally asked if there'd been any 'developments'. None, sighed Tess, feigning impatience, mindful that her reaching out to Benson could easily have morphed into one of those line-crossing moments. Mercifully, Sally let the matter drop. Instead, upon Tess's invitation, she turned to the task in hand, outlining the methodology she'd followed under Gordon's enthusiastic supervision.

It had been faultless.

She'd taken the evidence given during the trial. She'd taken Benson's lie that he'd never met Paul Harbeton before. And she'd brought the two together as if they were pieces of a jigsaw, trying to make them fit.

'We both know the facts,' said Sally. 'There's a scrap outside the Bricklayers Arms. Twenty minutes later Paul Harbeton is found dead in Soho by a motorcycle despatch rider called Michael Lever. Remember the name. Just around the corner, sitting on a doorstep with blood all over his face, is Benson, who's seen by a taxi driver, a terribly nice chap who insists on driving him to A&E at University College Hospital, where dear old Benson lies to the doctor with some crap about falling over. Which is different to the crap he gives his girlfriend about being mugged by some hobbledehoy in Lambeth. Can we just assume he's innocent for this meeting? Good. He's lying from the word go because he doesn't want to make any reference to this fight at all. Doesn't want anyone to ask him what the rub was between him and Harbeton. Bear in mind, if Benson is innocent, he wouldn't know that Harbeton was dead until he was picked up by the rozzers a few days later.'

'You've lost me,' said Tess. 'Why is that significant?'

'Because it means Benson was hiding the rub even when he thought Harbeton was alive and nursing a hangover.

There was no need to. He could have told his girlfriend, but he didn't. And he only hid it afterwards because it would have given the police a motive for the murder he hadn't committed. That's why he lied his balls off from then on. To the police. To Camberley. To you. To everyone.'

'That's a good point.'

They were working in Tess's sitting room. The papers in the case were laid out on an oval dining table made longer by an extension leaf. Tess was seated. Sally was standing on the other side, leaning on the sideboard.

'At first, I focused on that poor man with the surgical scars all over his head. You'll remember him well.'

Tess did. She'd been on her way home late at night when a man who'd been tracking her and Benson throughout the Hopton Yard killing trial – always at a distance; always watching and waiting – suddenly appeared out of the darkness. She'd felt no fear because there'd been no threat. He'd been cowering, squinting with pain from a headache, and he'd come with a message for Benson.

'Basically,' said Sally, 'it's "Thank him for killing that bastard Paul Harbeton. You beat me to it."' Now this is the point: he had memory problems. Just like Benson's brother. They'd both been brain damaged. Now, Harbeton, of course, had been a volunteer with various charities. And if you look them up, you'll see they're all concerned with memory-related conditions. The patients all need help coping. None of them can remember very much.'

Tess nodded and said, 'Harbeton worked in Norwich in 1992. He volunteered at the Radwell Clinic when Eddie Benson was there. He'd have been thirteen at the time.'

'The obvious inference is that Harbeton was exploiting these people in some way,' said Sally. 'Financially, sexually, I don't know and I don't care. The point is, Eddie must have remembered something and told his brother—'

'Which explains why Benson went looking for him in 1997. He went back to the clinic.'

'Exactly. Only Harbeton wasn't there and the manager had no idea where he'd gone. Interestingly enough, they'd got rid of him for borrowing money from a patient, only, of course, they'd not be able to prove anything, because people with brain injuries can often remember things that never happened . . . which rather suggests this Harbeton was probably a bad guy.'

'Who probably took advantage of Benson's little brother.'

'Which I would have thought was a strong motive for murder.'

'It is.'

'And which explains why Benson would want to hide it,' said Sally. 'Not just to protect himself, but to protect Eddie, who's got a secret that he doesn't want all over the papers. You know what this sort of thing is like. The victims just don't want to talk about it. Eddie probably hadn't even told his parents. Just his big brother.'

Tess looked at the papers on the table: the neat piles of evidence that had put Benson behind bars for eleven years. It could all have missed the point. 'If you're right, Sally, they were both compromised. Benson couldn't say anything without incriminating himself and exposing his brother. His brother couldn't say anything without giving the police the motive they were looking for. What a bloody mess. Benson must have gambled on getting acquitted.' But then Tess had a sudden lapse into doubt. 'But if Benson went looking for Harbeton in 1997, that suggests he found him in 1998. Which in turn means he was out for more than an argument.'

Sally shook her head. 'I contacted the three charities where Harbeton volunteered in London. Benson hadn't come asking questions. Also – if you remember from the trial – there was no suggestion that Benson had contacted Harbeton's employer. And he would have done. The visit to the Radwell had been an impulse. That's where his search ended. Benson left Norfolk, came to London in search of wisdom and a pint, and who should walk through the door but—'

'Paul Harbeton.'

'Yep. These things happen, Tess. And Benson gave him a mouthful, got a headbutt back, and that's as far as it went. Except Harbeton ambles into Soho and so does Benson. It was one of those Cartier-Bresson moments – not so magic this time – when everything came together.'

Tess moved away from the table. 'I need a break. Let's get the pasta going.'

They ate pretty much in silence. Tess was thinking as much about Sally as about Benson. During the Hopton Yard killing trial, Sally – after analysing Benson's handwriting – had concluded that he was a broken man who kept the fragments of his life apart, never bringing them together because he couldn't face the truth about his past. And while Tess might have scorned the methodology, she'd been obliged to endorse the conclusion. The picture drawn by Sally had been accurate. But now they were wondering if she'd depicted not so much a perpetrator evading guilt as an innocent victim captured by a quirk of circumstance. When the coffee was made, they got back to work.

'If Benson had a motive to kill Harbeton, so did many others,' said Sally. 'Unknown victims and unknown friends or family who might have found out what he had done. I'd come to a dead end. I couldn't find these people. And they weren't going to come forward.'

'So what did you do? You said you'd made significant progress.'

'Be patient. I had lunch with Gordon. Who wore blue and terracotta. Looked like Monet's kitchen, which I've never—'

'Who recommended you forget Benson's story and look at everyone else's.'

'That's right. I worked my way through the witness list. Traced their whereabouts. Checked their background. Found out what they'd done since the trial.'

'And?'

'I tried to get in touch with Lever, the despatch rider.'

'And?'

'I got his girlfriend instead. Ex-girlfriend, in fact. Tracy Patterson. And she tells me she's got something significant to say.'

'To say? She hasn't said it?'

'No. She wants paying.'

'How much?'

'A thousand quid.'

'Bloody hell.'

'That's not all. She wants immunity. In writing.'

'She's been watching too much television. We can't offer immunity from prosecution. Only specified prosecutors can. And you wouldn't get an immunity notice for something like this anyway. What did you say?'

'I said I'd get back to her.'

'And you didn't?'

'No, because you asked me to drop everything. But I did have tea with Gordon. And Gordon says I should scare the living daylights out of her.'

'That's not a bad idea. You've got her address?'

Sally smiled. 'Tess, I know where she was born. You think I don't know where she lives?'

40

The Tuesday Club had a members-only car. A battered Fiesta with 210,000 miles on the clock. After leaving Abasiama, Benson booked it and set off for Brancaster Staithe, calling to warn his dad when it was too late to turn back. Having parked beside The Crab Hut, he walked onto the Fisherman's Quay, among the rusted oil drums, heaped nets and thick ropes. Lobster pots had been stacked beside the low wooden sheds. Feeling a sort of delirium induced by hope, Benson sat on the keel and waited. And sure enough, at the expected time, he saw Eddie in his wheelchair. Neil Reydon had brought him on to the quay.

'It's been seventeen years, Eddie,' said Benson eventually.

Benson never thought he'd utter such words. He never thought he'd see his brother again, but now here they were, face to face. He'd spent hours rehearsing that opening phrase, desperately hoping that Eddie would relent; that he'd cut short this second stretch – an indeterminate sentence that was so much harder to endure than the first. As he'd got closer to home, panic had set in. He'd thought he might be sick. But then, on reaching the coast, he'd seen the sea . . . the endless sea, which had always made him calm. And hope had fluttered in his stomach.

'Seventeen years,' he repeated. 'It's a very long time.'

There'd been no shaking of hands. No playful thump to the shoulder. Neil Reydon had walked out of earshot. He'd lit up and was now smoking by the sheds.

'I know. And you chose this, Will.'

Like Benson he had black hair, but it was long, and tied back in a ponytail. His voice was slow, and he blinked with the effort. They'd last seen each other on the 4th of

July 1999. Eddie had been twenty, Benson twenty-one. Now they were both in their mid-thirties. The years between had contracted into nothing. And nothing had been resolved.

'Why are you here?'

'I've got something to say.'

'It's too late. You had your chance. We all had a chance.'

Eddie had begged Benson to admit his guilt. He'd refused. Eddie had warned him what would happen if he didn't change his mind: that he'd never speak to him again.

'It's never too late, Eddie.'

'Really? Because, at last, you've got something to say? You silenced me just when I was able to talk again. You shut me up.'

'I'm sorry, Eddie, but—'

'No, Will. It's me who has something to say. I've been thinking, too, over the years. And this isn't just about me and you—'

'Let me speak, please,' said Benson. He was beginning to vanish inside his head. He was looking at Eddie from afar. His voice barely rose over the wind. 'I want to go back to the beginning. Tell you everything. Everything I've run away from. And—'

'Sorry, I don't want to listen, not now.'

'Eddie, I—'

'No. You plead not guilty for the trial. You admit everything afterwards. Then you tell Mum and Dad you're still innocent. Have you any idea what your screwing around has done to us all? Not just to me, but to Dad? Have you any idea what it did to Mum?'

Benson wanted to shout his brother down; but he couldn't. He was such a great distance away. And he had no authority. Eddie had it all. Benson knew he had to listen.

'Dad tells himself every day you didn't kill him. It's taken years off his life. Because he'd lost me in the accident and he lost you in a courtroom.'

'Don't, Eddie, please. Don't say this.' Benson wanted Eddie to come out onto the ice again. To hold out a branch and save him.

'Mum never got over it.'

'Please.'

'She got cancer.'

'I know.'

'But the cancer was nothing. The radiotherapy and the chemo were nothing. The thing that ate her up was doubt. You should have heard her talking to Dad. Tearing herself apart. And in the end—'

'Eddie, stop.'

'You bloody killed her. She died not knowing, and you could have told her outright. She'd have forgiven you anything. I would have done, too . . . and then' – Benson flinched from a gust of wind. It rattled the lines against the masts and the flags flapped like clapping hands – 'and then, after all that, you didn't even come to the funeral.'

'A screw messed up the paperwork. He did it on purpose. I tried to—'

'You couldn't face Dad. You couldn't face me. You daren't leave the prison. Because you were safe in there. Safe from real life. Safe from what happens when a family has to make sense of a murder.'

Benson breathed in deeply and then seemed to go under. Everything he'd planned to confess sank slowly into darkness.

'Go on then,' said Eddie. 'You've come all this way – let me at least hear you say it.'

But Benson was lost, to Eddie and to himself. He was beneath the ice, unable to move, far from the hole that would allow him to return to the surface. Eddie waited, head aslant, watching him more with contempt than curiosity.

Then, with a shrug, wheeled back a couple of yards and called Neil, who quickly came over, offering to shake Benson's hand, though clumsily and without conviction. They'd left talking about the Canaries' next match. It was an away game.

Once they were out of sight, Benson stumbled to the place where Meersham's people must have been hiding when they'd filmed his brother. When he'd located the spot – a track by the wooden sheds – he looked towards the empty quay, listening to the wind and the cry of the gulls.

'You don't know the half of it,' he murmured.

Jim, Benson's dad, was worried about Brexit. The UK fishing regions had voted heavily in favour of leaving the EU. They'd wanted to regain control over UK waters. Jim's mates had all said Britain could become another Norway. Exporting fish left, right and centre.

'I wasn't so sure then, and I'm not so sure now.'

They'd gone out in *Dalston's Girl*. Just a few miles offshore. The wind had lost its strength. The waves were calm, gently lifting and lowering the boat, with the odd slap to show who was in charge. The sky was darkening and the banks of cloud had turned purple.

'The problem was always quotas and equal access,' said Jim. 'I told you that when you were a boy. The EU policy was a total disaster for us. And—'

'Dad?'

'Yes?'

'You know I'd've come to Mum's funeral if the paperwork hadn't vanished?'

'Of course I do, son.'

'I handed it to my personal officer and he just—'

'Will, don't you worry about nothing. I understood. Everyone did.'

Jim was quiet and so was Benson. They looked over the blackening waves. Then Jim said:

'The thing is, fish stocks are in shared waters. We're tied into EU coastal states. Most of what we catch is exported and—'

'Did she believe in me, Dad?'

'What are you on about?'

'Mum. Did she believe in me? Did she believe I was innocent?'

'Look, lad, she never went to bed without going on her knees. She prayed that the culprit would own up. Face the music. Set you free. That you'd make it home in one piece.' Jim cut the engine and *Dalston's Girl* gave a sigh. 'You shouldn't have gone to see Eddie. I warned you.'

'I just wanted to make up. Tell him that . . .' Benson couldn't get the words out. He was still beneath that thick lid of frozen water. And the coldest part of him was fairly sure he preferred this hidden death to what might happen if he told the truth. Had Abasiama been here, too? Did she really think it was better for Eddie and his dad to find out that so much of their shared personal history – the years of confusion, heartbreak and pain – had been constructed upon a single lie?

'His mind doesn't work properly,' said Jim, turning to his son. 'You said you were guilty, lad, and he's latched on to that. You can't reason with him.' The deep creases in Jim's face contracted as if the wind and rain had come blasting off the sea. His mouth narrowed to pull in some air. 'You've got to understand that Eddie's never recovered. He changed. When he came home, he wasn't the same lad who'd gone cycling round Lushmead's. He's still angry, Will. He doesn't know why he went tearing towards that road rather than the lake. He doesn't know why he hit that car. And I . . . and I don't know why I let you both go there. You were ten and he was nine . . . I should have been with you. It's my fault, son. All this is down to me, and you mustn't go blaming yourself or him for—'

Benson grabbed his father. He couldn't listen and he couldn't bear to see him cry. Not this man, who'd faced every storm without complaint. They held on to each other, like two men who'd agreed to drown. After a minute or so, Jim stuck out his jaw and gave the engine a turn.

'The EU is going to want access to UK waters,' he said gruffly. 'Otherwise they won't let us sell in Europe at zero tariffs. And all that's going to be part of the bigger deal . . . and who are we? Just a handful of fishermen. No one's priority.'

On his way home, Benson cried. He made loud gasping noises and at one point, stupidly, he'd turned on the windscreen wipers because he couldn't see clearly. But a tiny part of himself was watching: the deep part that had devised desperate strategies to try to limit the trauma of life in a locked cell. And he realised that he'd been broken. That he'd broken himself. He'd followed Abasiama's advice, and now he couldn't get back to the numbed existence he'd known only a few weeks ago. He couldn't avoid the pain, and it was searing.

41

'You're the one she knows,' said Tess, after ringing the bell, 'so you speak first.'

It was a neat and tidy two-bed ground-floor flat at the end of Glenville Road in Brixton. Tracy Patterson, now aged forty-three, lived here with Scott, her husband of three years, who was presently somewhere in Spain. He worked for a removals business and quite a few Brits were coming back home. At the time of Paul Harbeton's death she'd been Tracy Stewart, aged twenty-five, living with Mickey Lever, a freelance motorcycle despatch rider whom she'd met the year before. They'd been together for fifteen years. Until Tracy met Scott and finally got married. Scott, unlike Mickey, had wanted kids. They'd adopted a boy, who was now at school. Such was the lowdown delivered by Sally while Tess had driven, brooding on the Harbeton family.

'This is Tess de Vere,' she said. 'She's a solicitor of the High Court. Presently with Coker & Dale. You've heard of them?'

'No. Like I said, I want a grand, and I want immunity.'

'We'll come to that in a moment.'

Tracy remained standing behind an armchair, arms tightly folded, a cigarette in one hand. Tess and Sally had sat down, allowing their host to at least feel she was in a dominant position.

'Please tell us what you know.'

'Sorry, I've got nothing to say. Not yet.'

'You told me you have information that may be relevant to the death of Paul Harbeton. What is it?'

'I told you what my conditions were. You said you'd think about them. Have you made up your mind or not?'

'Well, I was about to draw out my savings when Miss de Vere told me there was a problem.'

'What problem?'

'I'll let Miss de Vere explain, but it turns out – from what you've said – that you've committed one or two crimes of a relatively serious nature.'

'I'll deny everything.'

'You can't. I recorded our conversations.' Sally took out her phone and gave a sample; Tess took over as Tracy stared open-mouthed across the room.

'I'll spare you the technicalities, but you ought to be aware that withholding information from a criminal investigation is a grave matter, especially when you were interviewed by the police and gave a sworn statement that you now contradict. A man spent eleven years in prison. If it transpires that—'

'Okay, stop. Let me think.'

'If you get arrested, social services are going to be involved. Along with the adoption panel and the guardian *ad litem*. I really wouldn't want that. Which is why I'm prepared to hear what you've got to say without, in the first instance, calling the police. I might be able to help you, Tracy. Sit down. Telling the truth is never a big deal. It just feels like it after nigh on twenty years.'

'Well, that was a damp squib,' said Sally.

'I'd hope for a lot more.'

'And to think I might have paid up.'

It turned out that Lever had given Tracy a present about two months after the Harbeton business. A silver bracelet with imitation stones in it. At least that was how Lever described it. He'd bought it in Camden market. It was old and the catch kept popping open, so Tracy took it to Evington's, a jeweller's in Victoria. And the jeweller looked it over and said it wasn't silver, but platinum, and the stones weren't glass but diamonds. It was an antique and worth at least a thousand pounds. Tracy confronted Mickey and he eventually admitted that he'd found it that night in Soho. Three or four yards from the body. He'd picked it up and said nothing to the police when they'd arrived. Tracy then kept it, not wanting to pay for a repair, in case the owner was trying to trace it, and she only got rid of it in 2013 – fifteen years later – when she'd married Scott. She'd sold it to Evington's for twelve hundred quid.

'I'm sorry, Tess.'

'Don't be daft, it's material evidence. From the crime scene.'

'It's almost certainly irrelevant.'

'It's possibly significant. And that's what this game is all about. Chasing the possible.'

They'd left Tracy reassured that social workers weren't going to turn up with a guardian *ad litem*. Tess, being ponderous, was driving slowly through South London. She turned on the radio to catch the news. The disturbance in HMP Kensal Green had not yet been resolved. Eight public-sector Tornado squads were ready to be deployed along with thirty riot police and ten canine units. Trained negotiators were endeavouring to secure the safe release of the two guards taken hostage. When questioned in the Commons, Justice Secretary Richard Merrington refused to confirm he'd been warned about the need to take urgent action at this specific prison. Addressing the wider crisis, he said, 'Our prisons face a number of unusual challenges that won't be resolved instantly. But we are committed to delivering a modern, efficient service designed to protect society and help prisoners turn their lives around.' In respect of the current incident, he added, 'The cost to the public purse will, of course, be met by our private-sector partners.'

'So what do we do now?' asked Sally.

'We go to Evington's.'

42

Benson went straight to Helen Camberley in Hampstead. He was like a boy in need of home; and Benson's home was the law. And he was Camberley's bastard son. On his account, she'd taken criticism and abuse right from the start. Friends and colleagues, two Lord Justices of Appeal and the Master of the Rolls had all urged her not to harm her own reputation. They'd said befriend a black sheep, for sure, but not *that* one. She'd refused. She'd gone further. She'd said that, given a chance, Benson could rise to the top of the profession. Which, frankly, had been imprudent. Because it gave the whisperers – those confiding types whose self-esteem thrives on the decline of their peers – a chance to say that Helen was losing her judgement. For Benson, it mattered not whether she was right or wrong. She'd given him hope. She'd been there when Eddie had turned away, and when his parents hadn't known what to think.

'You've not done too badly,' she said, pouring coffee. 'The evidence against Stainsby is overwhelming, but you've raised some reasonable questions.'

Benson had hoped he'd got further than that. Helen's cool analysis brought him down to earth. She led him from the dining room into a conservatory that overlooked the back garden. At seventy-four, short and slow-gestured, it was difficult to imagine her immense presence in court.

'Yardley painted a fairly black-and-white picture of a vulnerable girl being caught up with an abusive man. You've filled out some detail. We've got a deeper appreciation of her character, her past. She's something of a mystery. Misunderstood by her friends and family. Let down by those who might have helped her. But she remains an abused woman. She remains vulnerable. You can't escape that.'

This isn't what Benson wanted to hear. He'd thought Stainsby might just get off. He'd even felt a flicker of dark excitement. Before sitting down, Helen went to a bookcase stacked with vinyl records and pulled out a tatty cover. The needle went down and Maxine Sullivan gave 'Loch Lomond' a bit of swing. Benson's foot began to tap, but he was distracted. Helen had moved much more slowly than usual; she'd frowned when lowering herself into the armchair.

'How do you find Yardley?'

'Difficult. Can't read him. Looks at me as if he's seen all my sins. He only speaks when he has to, and then he's aggressive.'

'That's not surprising.'

'Why?'

'Do you know anything about him?'

'No.'

'Before coming to the Bar, he paid his way playing poker. Banned from casinos in Deauville, Monaco, St Tropez . . . can't remember the others.'

'Because he cheats?'

'Because he's good.'

Throughout his pupillage, Helen had often used games to teach the art of advocacy. Chess and billiards in particular. She'd likened questions to moves and shots. They had to be built on each other. She'd tried with poker, too, but Benson just couldn't get the hang of it. The vocabulary alone had left him confused.

'You haven't played a card that he hasn't thought about,' said Helen, frowning once more. 'Nothing has surprised him.'

'Really?'

'I've no doubt. He knew about Diane's troubled childhood.

He knew the Dover girls would fight points they should have admitted. He knew the GP would clutch at a single word in his notes. He knew Capicelli would stick to his pointless theory. He saw it all coming.'

'Then why not neutralise them in advance, or repair the damage in re-examination?'

'Arguments are best won when there are two sides. Juries don't like it when it's obvious, because they take what they're doing very seriously. They can begin to doubt just to be fair. Like I said, Yardley started in black and white. He left the colour to you. But it's his picture.'

Helen had said poker isn't really about chance – about the right cards coming together at the right moment. In the long run, as the night wears on, it's about psychology and probability.

'He's been playing around with me?'

'No. He's just laying the evidence on the table. He knows your hand, that's all.'

Once, Helen had spent an evening trying to explain a blind defence. It was a way of exploiting an aggressive player. Rather than fold a weak hand, you had to call or raise. Benson had gone home unsure about the ploy in poker, but clear about what to do if he ever had a weak case and an antagonistic opponent: raise the stakes.

'I don't have anything.'

'Pardon?'

'Sorry, Helen, I was just thinking about a blind defence. How can I turn this to my advantage?'

She smiled, with affection and a hint of pride. 'The case isn't over. Just keep your eyes on the table. See what turns up. Give nothing away.'

Helen had given him some comfort; but then, grimacing, she walked over to a sideboard, opened a mahogany box and took out a couple of cigars.

'You can't win them all, Will. He secured his case right from the start.'

'How?'

'By closing down any possibility of fit-up. He showed you his hand at the same time.'

'Which is?'

'The cigarette butt Stainsby denies smoking, in the bedroom he denies entering, at the feet of the woman he denies killing. It's a full house. Speaking of houses, what's all this about you selling your boat?'

'Don't worry about that. What about you? Are you all right?'

Helen forced a smile. 'I've never been better.'

The moral of the story, thought Benson, is don't go home. Real or adoptive, just keep away. Because whether you're feeling high or low, don't think for a moment that those who've shared your growing pains will tell you what you want to hear. They'll tell you things you hadn't even thought of. Things you don't want to know. They'll hit you with a crowbar. And Benson, heading back to the only other home he had, was acutely aware that the place was for sale and the only other occupant was a cat who cared for nothing but his next meal. But thought of the boat brought back Helen's fretting over Benson's finances, and their parting shortly afterwards. She'd been pale and unsteady on her feet. The conversation about the trial had tired her . . . and this was a woman who'd often kept Benson up all night, drinking and smoking, while they'd discussed the finer points of cross-examination technique. At the door, she'd kissed and held on to Benson as if she'd had something else to say; she'd looked uneasy . . . but Benson couldn't think about the matter. Outside Seymour Basin, blue lights flashing, was a police car. Two officers were standing on the pavement talking to Archie. Behind the car was a van. And beside the van stood a couple of armed figures in black.

'Why have you got a mobile phone?' asked Archie. 'You never answer.'

'What's happened?'

'There's been a development in the case. You've been advised to sleep at my place.'

PART FOUR

The case for the defence

'You're a minute late, Rizla.'

'I'm sorry.'

When Benson went to the library – as instructed – he found it empty save for Roy, who was already there, seated by a window reading The Cathedrals of France *by T. Francis Bumpus. The slate in his eyes shone.*

'What did you say?'

'I'm sorry, my lord.'

'That's more like it. Don't ever make me wait again. Now, Rizla, we need to change the books in here. Get some stuff in that the boys'd like to read. Thrillers. True crime. Comics. Do you understand?'

'Yes, my lord.'

'Good. Now, I'm going to give you a list of charity shops in London. And you are going to write to them asking for donations. Not money. Books and comics. Got it?'

'Yes, my lord.'

'But first, you go to the governor. You tell him about your project. You get permission. Okay?'

'Yes, my lord.'

'This is easy, isn't it? Now, pick up the pen.' Roy nodded at the library counter. There was a pad and a pen ready for use. 'Ready? Off we go.'

And Roy, looking out of the window, listed five shops in different boroughs, giving their addresses, complete with postcodes. When he'd finished, he said:

'Sort this out within a week. When the first parcel comes, you let me know.'

On his way out he tossed The Cathedrals of France *into the bin; and then he came back.*

'Neil Reydon, the guy who looks after your brother. Have you seen Michelle, his kid sister?'

'I have, my lord.'

'She's fit, isn't she?'

'Yes, my lord, she is.'

Benson did as he was told; and after the first parcel arrived and cleared security, he told his lordship, who came to the library and counted out twelve books. He checked the titles, put them in alphabetical order by author, and then pointed at a pencil. Benson had to write the number 10 on the inside cover of the first book, 20 on the second, 30 on the third, and so on. When he'd finished, his lordship dictated a list of ten names, which Benson wrote on a sheet of paper.

'You put these books to one side.'

'Yes, my lord.'

'These guys are going to come looking for something to read. You give them a book out of the box. It doesn't matter which one. You show them the number. You rub it out. You tick the list. Got it?'

'Yes, my lord.'

'Any questions?'

'None, my lord.'

'Good. Let me know when the next parcel arrives. Court adjourned.'

Benson's Books, as the scheme came to be known, was a real hit. People who didn't normally read had started giving it a go. The governor was pleased. So were the prisoners. Except for one. Owen 'Manchester' Kennedy.

43

Merrington was High Church. But he kept that sort of thing firmly in place. Any God discourse was for Sundays, and ideally with a lunching vicar who had a baptism at three. However, he made exceptions. And today was one of them, because in his hands was a godsend.

Hilmarton's team hadn't finished. But what they'd managed to put together was beyond Merrington's wildest expectations. Benson's confessions knew no bounds. And he was never satisfied with a first helping of remorse. He'd come back for seconds. And thirds. He'd explored what he'd thought. What he'd said. What he'd done. And what he'd failed to do. The whole shebang. And to think, there was more to come.

Merrington stood at the window in his office, looking towards St James's Park. The trees that had looked tired only last week seemed to have remembered the coming spring. It was going to be a good day.

The serious disturbance – Merrington was careful to avoid the word riot – at HMP Kensal Green had been resolved. Tornado teams had swept in and done the business. The hostages had been freed. The prisoners had surrendered. No staff had been injured. The ringleaders had been isolated and 144 inmates transferred to other prisons. And Merrington had used the glut of airtime to speak reform, revitalisation, investment and security. He'd blamed 'black mamba' psychoactive drugs, too. The drugs he'd been warned about in the report that he wouldn't admit to having read.

Yes, it was going to be a good day.

Pamela had been talking to David over breakfast. She'd been suggesting legal work in a UN agency. She'd stressed the humanitarian focus. He'd been interested. They'd talked internships in Rome. And Merrington had said nothing, listening while he'd read the *Telegraph*.

For a Wednesday, there was a lot to thank God for. Odd, really, that top of the list wasn't a quelled riot or his deft moves to invert his own department's failures. It was the soul of William Benson in the palm of his hand.

How it had got there couldn't be put down to chance. It had been a divine act. Overwhelmed by curiosity, Merrington had invited a breach of the protocol established with Hilmarton – that he must always be kept in the dark. He'd asked how the confessions had been obtained. And the most delicious part of the answer was this: Benson himself had supplied Hilmarton's agent with all the information he required to effect an invasion of privacy . . . and to do so without breaking the law.

'He was completely unsuspecting,' Hilmarton had said. 'He told our man there was no dog, no alarm, no watchful neighbours. Told him when the bins went out and when they were collected. In the end, no trespass or break-in was necessary. Our man bagged the goods when they were no longer on Benson's premises. They were on a public highway, in a bin belonging to the local authority.'

Merrington had joined in the fun. 'But taking the contents would still be theft. The rule on abandonment requires more than throwing something away.'

'I know, and that's the best bit.' Hilmarton had grasped some nuts from a bowl. 'According to our legal people, the shredding would be enough to demonstrate that Benson had intended to get rid of his property.'

'Which means there would be no dishonesty in taking it,' Merrington had added, wishing he'd always asked how Hilmarton's people did what they did. The finding out had been exhilarating. In a sort of quid pro quo, Hilmarton had then posed his own, tentative question:

'Why are you so against Benson? I know he's an embarrassment . . . you dropped a planned law and all that, but I get the impression there's something else . . . something personal.'

Merrington had thought of David. An innocent, decent, ambitious young man who was still as impressionable as a boy. An idealist who could easily be led astray. Like all those Cambridge spies, seduced by an impossible utopia. They'd ended up gay, drunk or exiled.

'Nothing personal, Bradley,' Merrington had replied, selecting an ascending tricolon. 'I'm only concerned for my office, my party, and the people we serve. I can't tell you how grateful I am for your help.'

As it happens, he'd given Merrington a new problem. The sort of problem he liked best.

How was he to use what he'd discovered? A less experienced man would act immediately. He'd pick up the phone and set in train a sequence of events that would lead to Benson's moral destruction. But Merrington was not a novice. Armed with more than he could have hoped for, he intended to cause more damage than he'd originally thought possible. And that would require not just careful planning, but thought. Meditation. Perhaps prayer . . . if God was willing to share some of the vengeance He claimed as His own. And if He wasn't, well, Merrington would keep what he had to himself.

'For now, Benson, you can enjoy your career,' he said, returning to his desk. 'Fly as high as you like. But you're finished. Take it from me.'

This much was sure, though Merrington wouldn't make a single move until he'd discovered the identity of Benson's benefactor. If God was in his heaven, their days were numbered too.

44

Benson was brought to the rear entrance of the Bailey by an armed police escort. There, outside Number 2 Court, he met a baffled Tess, who'd been offered identical protection. The electric atmosphere overrode the memory of their last meeting – another charged moment – which now seemed unreal, a flash of life that had died away. All that remained was a hint of self-consciousness, instantly dispelled when Yardley emerged from a conference room and invited them to join him.

'What's going on, Andrew?' said Benson, throwing his wig on the table.

'Goodshaw doesn't take risks.'

He picked up some documents with green covers and handed then to Benson and Tess, along with various applications to serve statements at short notice and amend existing court papers.

'I got these last night. I took one look, tried to contact you both, failed, and then Goodshaw sent an email to the cluster manager. Out came the guns.'

Yardley had given Benson two notices of additional evidence, numbered NAE1 and NAE2.

'You'll want an adjournment,' said Yardley. 'I'm instructed to oppose.'

Benson flicked through the pages, wondering why he hadn't seen this coming. There'd been enough clues. All it had required was a little imagination.

'I'll take instructions.'

Benson left the room but Tess called him back. He'd forgotten his wig.

* * *

They went down to the cells. While waiting, Tess made small talk, trying to ease the tension. Your wig must be over a hundred years old. It is. Where did you get it from? Camberley . . . it was her grandad's. But it's got your initials inside . . . WB. Yeah, it's a coincidence. That's nice. And then they were back to work. Stainsby was brought in.

Since the beginning of the trial, Benson had kept conferences short, recoiling from the praise and complaint. Now it was time to look Stainsby in the eye for as long as he could bear it.

'I told you the place was going to blow, didn't I?' he said when the guard had shut the door. 'I told you I was at risk, didn't I? But you wouldn't listen. You—'

'Be quiet, Mr Stainsby. What matters is what you didn't tell me. Read these, please.'

Benson passed over the two statements and glanced at Tess. Together they watched him pale. They watched his lip curl and his teeth appear. They watched his eyes flicker . . . with disbelief and anger and impotence.

'They're trying to shaft me. I'm saying nothing.'

'Then you will be convicted.'

'They can't prove half of this.'

'No, they can't. But the half they can is all they need.'

'I've got a right to silence.'

'No, you haven't.'

Benson stood up and leaned against the chipped wall, looking down on Stainsby. He was like a bleeding animal caught in a trap. He was crouched. His eyes were wild.

'I want you to listen to me very carefully, Mr Stainsby.'

But Stainsby didn't hear. He was trying to make sense of the last sixteen years of his life. Trying to understand what had been going on. His jaw made minute movements as he rehearsed some ugly conversation in his head. He was shouting and swearing. His fists had clenched.

'Mr Stainsby, listen.'

He looked up, his mouth half open.

'Even without this evidence, you're going to be convicted,' said Benson. 'We've had a decent run, but you're facing a life sentence with a seventeen-year tariff. Maybe more.'

'I'm admitting nothing.'

'You don't have to. But what you do have to do is listen to me. And then you have to decide if you trust me. And if you trust me, you have to decide if you want to follow my advice.'

Stainsby looked at Tess; and Tess nodded. Benson returned to the table.

'Do you play poker, Mr Stainsby?'

'Yeah.'

'Well, I suggest we raise the stakes.'

45

Tess thought Benson had lost his mind. He was right: if there was an adjournment, there was nothing Tess could track down to undermine the evidence now presented by the Crown. In the circumstances, they might as well deal with it immediately. In fact, said Benson, now was the best time, because it allowed him to exploit the lack of warning. So far, Tess had concurred. It was the next proposal that stunned her. She wondered what Mrs Justice Fleetwood would say.

The jury were kept out for the application to admit the evidence. Yardley apologised. And he accepted that the witnesses would have to explain their conduct and face severe censure from her ladyship and, no doubt, Mr Benson. But what they had to say was of such importance that the trial could not continue without them.

'You are taken by surprise, Mr Benson?' said Mrs Justice Fleetwood after Yardley had sat down. She'd listened without interrupting, but it was clear she hadn't been impressed.

'I am.'

'I imagine you want me to discharge the jury?'

'No, my lady.'

'But you resist the application?'

'No, my lady. The application is unopposed.'

Benson hadn't warned Yardley; and for one who was normally inscrutable, his guard dropped: this wasn't what he'd expected. He'd smiled. Mrs Justice Fleetwood remained impassive:

'You seek an adjournment?'

'No. I am ready to proceed, my lady.'

Mrs Justice Fleetwood removed her glasses.

'Forgive me, Mr Benson, I assume you have taken instructions on the matter?'

The question was code between Bench and Bar. It meant, had Stainsby insisted on proceeding against Benson's better judgement? Benson clarified matters:

'Yes, my lady. My client is content to follow my advice. Here is the amended defence statement.' He handed a copy to a clerk and to Yardley. 'It consists of a bare denial. There is nothing else Mr Stainsby can say to assist the administration of justice.'

Mrs Justice Fleetwood looked worried. She was wondering if Benson, through inexperience, was making a catastrophic mistake.

'You appreciate, Mr Benson, that there is hearsay upon hearsay in both these statements. There is much that is arguably irrelevant and deeply prejudicial to your client. I have the discretion to exclude it. You do not ask me to do so?'

'No, my lady, I don't. On the contrary, I respectfully submit it is essential that the jury hear what these witnesses have to say, subject to a warning from your ladyship that nothing has ever been proved against my client, and that the allegations are vigorously denied.'

'Very well, Mr Benson. You have conduct of the case.'

Benson turned around and leaned towards Tess.

'Trust me,' he whispered. 'This is our only chance.'

46

Given the circumstances in which the new evidence would be heard – from behind a screen – the locus of the trial was transferred from Number 2 Court to Number 16 Court. In the former, the witness box was right beside the jury, in full view of the public gallery. In the latter, it was situated on the other side of the room, almost beneath the gallery itself, where screening from the public was possible and evidence could be given in open court without exposing a witness to identification. Once the jury was seated, Mrs Justice Fleetwood explained the need for the arrangements, and then gave the background to the testimony they were about to hear, subject to the warning requested by Benson. Two witnesses, designated A and B, were to be called, she said. 'Treat their evidence no differently to anything you've heard already.' Just then, Benson caught Yardley's eye; and Yardley, aggressive and confident, held Benson's gaze until Benson, being an amateur, looked away. Seconds later, Yardley called Witness A . . . Detective Constable Steve Draycott.

And at last the secret history of Diane Heybridge came to light.

Benson listened from afar. Occasionally he glanced at the autopsy photographs, trying to picture the young woman deceiving everyone, from Stainsby to her pals in the Dover Five. Yardley kept his questions simple so that the jury followed each step.

In February 2009 Draycott's boss, DS John Foster, received a tip-off that the leaders of two major criminal gangs had planned to meet at the Twisted Wheel nightclub in Dover. One was from London: Terry Meersham. The other, André Loupierre, was from Paris. That was all that Foster had said to Draycott. And Foster, contrary to regulations and guidelines, decided to mount an unofficial surveillance operation. No details were entered into the force computer systems and Foster's superior, Witness B, had not been informed. Foster did, however, ask Draycott, to accompany him.

'He asked me watch his back.'

'Did you?'

'I tried. The place was crowded. There was a lot of noise . . . and I let him out of my sight.'

Foster had been found unconscious in the club's car park following an attack. The defendant was the prime suspect and he was duly arrested. Shortly afterwards, Draycott received a call from Diane Heybridge. She wanted to see him in private. They'd met at night in Pencester Gardens.

'She said that the defendant and a friend, Gary Bredfield, had been trafficking migrants from Calais to Britain, using a small rigid-hull inflatable boat. They'd been bringing ten people at a time and charging three thousand pounds a head. The crossing took about forty-five minutes. They'd targeted the smaller ports on the south-east coast, or isolated beaches, and the defendant was using his van to transport the migrants to nearby railway stations with a connection to London.'

'How did she know this?'

'She'd become suspicious about the defendant's spending and his vanishing. So she'd borrowed a car and followed him. She'd seen the boat beach near Lydd-on-Sea. Most of the passengers had been women and children. She'd heard them speaking a foreign language. And she'd seen them get into his van.'

'When was this?'

'2008.'

'Which was shortly after he'd set up his business, Stainsby's Seafood Locker Ltd?'

'Yes. According to Diane, it was just a front.'

'How frequent were these crossings?'

'She estimated he'd done three by the time she spoke to me.'

'Where did the three thousand pounds figure come from?'

'She'd eavesdropped on the defendant and Mr Bredfield. There'd been an argument, because Mr Bredfield was only getting eight hundred pounds for each job.'

'Did she know the purpose of the meeting with Meersham and Loupierre?'

'Yes. She said the defendant couldn't spend the money he was earning. He needed it laundered. He'd hoped to integrate himself into a bigger operation. And they were keen to take advantage of his frequent crossings of the Channel. Meersham was prepared to pay Mr Stainsby to bring people who couldn't afford the fee, people selected by Loupierre . . . in effect making those migrants indebted to them. Once in the UK they would have to pay back Meersham once they'd found work. Work he'd help them find.'

'How did Diane know this?'

'More eavesdropping. She said the defendant thought she was stupid. Had never taken her seriously. His only precaution was to shut the door when he was on the phone.'

Unfortunately, Diane had believed that simply by telling DC Draycott what she'd discovered, Mr Stainsby, would be imprisoned for the foreseeable future.

'It was a total mess,' said Draycott. 'DS Foster had been seriously injured. He couldn't remember why he'd been at the Twisted Wheel. He hadn't seen his attacker. His operation didn't officially exist. And Diane wasn't willing to give evidence about the trafficking. She wouldn't go on record. She didn't understand how the courts worked. I told her that to put the defendant away, ideally, we'd need to mount a full undercover operation to gather extensive evidence, not just of the defendant's activities but of those with whom he was working. On both sides of the Channel. We'd need photographs, recordings, surveillance logs, forensic evidence, the lot . . . she was devastated.'

DC Draycott had drawn up a report of the meeting but he'd then heard that Diane had come forward as the defendant's alibi for the attack at the Twisted Wheel.

'She was obviously terrified. So I binned my report. I didn't want to contradict her . . . and, anyway, I couldn't refer to what she'd told me without revealing my own presence in that club with DS Foster. Like I said, it was a total mess.'

'So what did you say to Witness B?' Who, of course, was DCI Ray Carlatton.

'I said nothing about Diane; and I said I hadn't even known that DS Foster had been in the nightclub. I said I'd been there on my own for a pint and a dance.'

'You lied?'

'I did. To protect the reputation of DS Foster, who'd been brain damaged in the attack. And to protect the defendant's girlfriend, who I believed to have been the original source, and who I now judged to be at risk if her role became known to the defendant.'

'And the defendant walked free?'

'Yes, he did.'

Benson looked at an autopsy photo. Dr Khan was right. The manner of death – murder or suicide – had been ritualistic. Diane had been a gentle, pretty girl. She'd had brown eyes and short auburn hair. The harsh light of the camera's flash had accentuated that delicate hint of red. The grimace of death, once the blood orange had been removed, was like a stifled shout. The creases around the eyes belonged to a smile.

'I next heard from Diane in September of last year.'

'The date, please.'

'Monday the twenty-first of September.'

'My lady, that is the day before Diane's farewell party with her friends. She went to London on Wednesday the twenty-third.'

'Thank you, Mr Yardley.'

Diane had phoned Draycott to say that this time she'd nailed it. She'd been very excited. Falling over her words. For the past six years she'd been monitoring the defendant's activities. She'd taken photographs and filled out surveillance logs and collected forensic evidence. She'd compiled a dossier linking the defendant to Meersham and Loupierre. She wanted to give it to Draycott.

'What was your reaction?'

'I was stunned.'

'Did you believe her?'

'Frankly, I wasn't sure. And yet it was a weird thing to make up. We arranged to meet.'

'When?'

'Sunday the fourth of October. That gave me time to sort out the paperwork. I wanted things done official this time.'

'Who chose the date?'

'I did.'

'Where were you to meet?'

'London. She didn't want anything happening in Dover.'

Having put the phone down, Draycott had spoken to DCI Carlatton and told him not only what Diane had said, but what had happened with Foster and Diane and himself in 2009.

'What was his reaction?'

'He went ballistic. Not least because he'd backed me and Foster during the Twisted Wheel investigation. He'd been deceived into misleading a major inquiry that had collapsed for lack of evidence.'

But Carlatton agreed that the meeting should go ahead, and the usual protocols regarding covert human intelligence sources – CHIS – were to be implemented immediately. That meant carrying out pre-registration checks, a risk assessment and a source evaluation process. Draycott was to be the handler and Carlatton, as the controller, was to be responsible for general oversight. These procedures were never completed. Because the meeting in London never took place. Ten days after making that arrangement, Diane Heybridge was dead.

Yardley broke from questioning. 'My lady, a decision was subsequently made not to cooperate with the murder investigation carried out by DCI Goodshaw. That decision was made by Witness B and I would respectfully suggest that he is the best person to deal with the matter.'

Mrs Justice Fleetwood agreed and Yardley surrendered his witness to Benson.

47

'Are you any good at maths, Witness A?'

'Not really.'

Draycott reminded Benson of those jaded entertainers who appear on the working men's club circuit. He looked like he enjoyed a pint and was used to an aggressive reception from the usual troublemakers. Benson intended to oblige.

'Well, let's do some together. Three trips carrying ten people a time, each paying three thousand pounds a head – either from their own resources or thanks to Mr Meersham – yields ninety thousand pounds.'

'Yes.'

'With two thousand, four hundred going to Mr Bredfield, that leaves my client with eighty-seven thousand, six hundred pounds?'

'I'll take your word for it.'

'You haven't done the calculations?'

'I recognise we're talking significant figures.'

'They're highly significant. Because if – as Diane said – my client went back and forth across the Channel, three times a year for six years, assuming prices remained the same, he'd have netted five hundred and twenty-five thousand, six hundred pounds.'

'Yes.'

'That's a lot of currency. Pounds, euros, whatever.'

'It is.'

'Have you looked for this heap of notes and coins?'

'Yes.'

'Did you find it?'

'No.'

'Did you look for the other heap of paper, that dossier?'

'Yes.'

'Did you find it?'

'No.'

'Witness A, until this morning, my client was understood to have killed Diane Heybridge because he wanted to get his hands on an insurance policy that it now turns out he wouldn't need. You've come forward at the last minute to suggest he killed her because he'd found the dossier?'

'I don't know, Mr Benson. I'm simply telling the court what I was told.'

'Don't be disingenuous. You're changing the direction and meaning of this trial. As you ought to do, if what you say is true.'

'It is true.'

Benson came at Draycott from another angle.

'You never carried out the risk assessment on Diane Heybridge, did you?'

'No.'

'So you wouldn't have known that she'd been reliant upon antidepressant medication?'

'No.'

'That, as a child, she'd been deeply affected by the loss of her father?'

'No.'

'That she'd coped by making up stories?'

'No.'

'That not having had any children had been an unbearable loss?'

'No.'

'That Frank Stainsby, another father figure, had died in July 2015, two months before she contacted you about a dossier concerning the trafficking of – as it happens – distressed women and children?'

'No.'

Benson pondered the chronology with the jury. Then he said:

'Witness A, Diane wouldn't have passed the risk assessment, would she?'

'I can't say for sure, because it wasn't carried out.'

'You couldn't rely on what she said, not because she was a liar, but because, when distressed, she was a fantasist?'

'Without a completed assessment, I'm not prepared to say.'

'Even though the police in Dover and London never found anything to substantiate what she'd alleged?'

'Not finding isn't the same as not existing.'

'Witness A, you're a highly experienced officer in the CID. Can't you see what has happened? Diane Heybridge first contacted you in 2009 after my client had been arrested for an alleged assault upon John Foster. By that stage, the police had interviewed her. They'd told her that my client had been at the nightclub at the same time as Mr Meersham and Monsieur Loupierre. They'd been looking for an explanation. Looking for a connection. Diane simply went home and made one up. The trafficking story was pure invention. And she gave it to you, rather than the police investigating the assault, because she didn't want to face any questions.'

'But why make up anything?'

'Your risk assessment would have given you the answer. She wanted shot of my client but she was trapped because she wouldn't leave his father. This trafficking story was her way of getting rid of someone who'd never taken her seriously and who thought she was stupid. Someone who'd repeatedly wounded her dignity.'

'The assessment was never carried out and I'm not prepared to guess its outcome.'

'Are you prepared to tell us what Interpol had to say?'

'About what?'

'This high-level meeting at the Twisted Wheel between a washed-up fisherman and two giants of the crime world. Interpol had no idea what was going on either. Correct?'

'Correct.'

'There'd been no intelligence suggesting that my client was involved in the trafficking of migrants?'

'That doesn't mean he wasn't doing it.'

'Answer the question.'

'There was no such intelligence.'

'And there was no intelligence linking my client to Meersham and Loupierre?'

'No, there wasn't.'

'Thank you, Witness A. Now, let's return to what almost certainly happened. Once you'd told Diane that the trafficking story, on its own, wasn't enough to remove my client from her life, she returned to reality. She went back to the police and admitted that my client had been with her at the time of the attack.'

'It remains possible that your client compelled her to cooperate.'

'Did she tell you anything to justify that?'

'No.'

'Then spare us your guesswork when it doesn't suit your argument.'

Benson poured himself a glass of water. When he next spoke the tone of indignation had disappeared.

'Let's come forward six years, and to this dossier that no one has found – the idea being that Mr Stainsby destroyed it before or after he'd killed Diane Heybridge. Are you with me?'

'Yes. But I haven't said that.

'No, but Mr Yardley will.'

'Okay, I understand.'

'This time the trafficking story had the foundation it lacked before?'

'Yes.'

'But Diane wanted you to come to London to collect it?'

'That's right.'

'If you'd carried out your risk assessment, wouldn't you have at least considered, after her sudden death, that Diane might have killed herself intending to frame my client?'

'Why would I think that?'

'Because you'd been given the motive – just like she'd tried to give you a motive for the attack in 2009? She'd told you about an incriminating dossier.'

'I'm sorry, but that wouldn't have crossed my mind.'

'And because you were meant to find her body, suspended on an electric cable that she'd brought from Dover, a cable that she knew would have my client's DNA on it?'

'I wouldn't have thought that either.'

'And because – out of suppressed anger arising from years of humiliation and ill-treatment – she'd also brought a cigarette end used by my client and placed it at her own feet?'

'No, Mr Benson, I can't say I'd have thought of any of these things.'

'Because you didn't carry out the assessment?'

'I'm sorry. These appraisals aren't child's play. They're serious evaluations of a potential covert human intelligence source. And Diane was dead before it could be completed.'

'Completed? It didn't even begin. And it didn't begin because you thought Diane Heybridge was speaking complete nonsense.'

'That is not true.'

'Ten days passed. And you did nothing.'

'I spoke to my superior.'

'Who demanded urgent action. You did nothing.'

'I planned to meet her first.'

'You didn't even do the maths.'

'That could wait.'

Benson sighed.

'Have you been suspended from duty, Witness A?'

'Yes.'

'You're facing disciplinary proceedings?'

'Yes.'

'Because you concealed evidence and lied to your superiors?'

'Yes.'

'Why should the jury trust you now?'

'Because I could have kept quiet but I didn't. I've come forward and hidden nothing.'

Benson cocked his head as if he'd heard a plate drop. And the cheer that followed the crash.

'Nothing?'

'No.'

'Forgive me for being blunt. John Foster got beaten senseless because you didn't watch his back?'

'I've accepted that. I've never forgotten what happened.'

'You're here today, halfway through a trial, because by repeating Diane's crazy story you hope to get my client convicted for the murder of Diane Heybridge.'

'Why would I do that?'

'Because you're trying to make it up to Linda, John Foster's wife, and his two kids, Beth and Bobby. You want to bring them a scalp.'

'That is untrue.'

'It's shameful, Witness A.'

'I would never try and mislead a court.'

'Why's that? Because you draw the line at suppressing evidence and lying to your superior?'

* * *

Benson sat down. It would be wrong to say he'd seen a flicker of light, because everything to do with Stainsby was dark. But he'd seen the beginnings of a possible acquittal. He'd felt the nettle sting of excitement.

48

Tess hadn't anticipated Benson's cross-examination. Its shape had emerged like a quick sketch drawn by one of the surrealist painters she'd seen in Montmartre with Sally. A wholly unexpected image had emerged from swift, confident lines . . . based on something that was familiar: the narrative of Jane Tapster, which had seemed to be self-serving, but which Benson had now taken and reworked to Stainsby's advantage, adding the Interpol detail from Pauline Osborne. It had been brilliant. The court rose for lunch. Benson, shunning compliments, went to the library to prepare, and Tess and Archie shared a sandwich convinced that Benson's argument wasn't just a clever move, but the truth: that everyone involved in Stainsby's life, up until now, had got almost everything wrong. The willingness to believe anything bad about a bad person had got Diane Heybridge's story off the ground. And Benson – taking an insane risk – had caught her out.

'When did you first learn about the Twisted Wheel fiasco?' asked Yardley when the court reconvened.

Witness B – Carlatton – looked intimidated and he hadn't even been questioned yet. Unlike Draycott, he wasn't at ease in public. He leaned towards the screen, lowering his neck into the collar of his clean white shirt.

'Monday the twenty-first of September 2015,' he said. 'The day Diane Heybridge had called Witness A out of the blue with fresh allegations. Witness A had then come to me.'

'Getting on for seven years later?'

'Yes.'

'We've been told you went ballistic.'

'That's an understatement.'

Yardley took Carlatton through the layers of rage and disappointment and the subsequent arrangement to deal with Diane Heybridge as a CHIS. Eleven days later DC Draycott – who'd gone to London as planned – had learned that she was now dead and that a murder investigation was underway. Carlatton had reached the most delicate part of his evidence. The decision not to cooperate with the Metropolitan Police.

'I am responsible for that error of judgement.'

'Tell us your reasoning.'

'The most problematic aspect of the Twisted Wheel incident was that DS Foster was the victim. He suffered significant head injuries. We knew very early on that the damage was permanent and that his career in the force was over. That's a heavy price for a mistake. To that extent, while I was angry, I understood Witness A. He'd been following DS Foster's orders in 2009. And he'd wanted to protect DS Foster's reputation. He'd been concerned that any financial payments that might arise – either from insurance or the Criminal Injuries Compensation Board – might be compromised if it was known that, in effect, DS Foster had been the author of his own misfortune . . . running a highly dangerous operation without appropriate planning and authorisation. And let's not forget, he had a wife and two young children. So, yes, I understood why Witness A had misled me.'

'You recite that argument as if you found it compelling.'

'I did. Which is why I did the same thing as Witness A and misled DCI Goodshaw when he came to Dover.'

'But this was a murder investigation?'

'I know. Which is why I was almost paralysed beforehand.'

'You were aware of a potentially significant lead.'

'I was.'

'So why follow in the footsteps of Witness A?'

'Because – and I say this not to prejudice the defendant – I thought the evidence against him was devastating. I thought, to be honest, that the defendant would plead guilty, either at the first opportunity or at the beginning of his trial. And I thought, what is the point of revealing a botched-up unauthorised operation from 2009 where no one knows what happened or why, and risk Mrs Foster having to return monies that she has received, when Mr Stainsby is going to plead guilty anyway?'

'And that was the totality of your reasoning?'

'No.' Carlatton turned to the judge. 'My lady, DS Foster subsequently died in a fall. The circumstances suggested suicide, but the coroner returned an open verdict. That was in 2013. Mrs Foster and her children went through hell, having been there once before in 2009. The last thing I wanted to do was cause them more pain by publicising the biggest mistake her husband – and their father – had ever made.'

'So why did you change your mind?' asked Yardley.

'The defendant didn't plead. And I thought, if he's acquitted I'll never forgive myself for having withheld potentially significant information.'

'As a result, do you now face disciplinary proceedings?'

'I do.'

'Please wait there, Witness B.'

49

'My client's grateful that you don't seek to prejudice his defence.'

'I don't.'

'I accept what you say. In fact, Witness B, he relies upon your integrity.'

DCI Carlatton looked uncomfortable. Cross-examining barristers don't usually compliment police officers. Tess wondered what Benson had planned.

'You took your time, though.'

'I waited until the prosecution case was almost over.'

'I see. Mr Yardley enquired about your reasoning. Might I do the same?'

'Of course.'

'I want to ask you about this missing dossier compiled by Diane Heybridge that proves my client was exploiting mothers and their children . . . and a few men.'

'Yes.'

'It is difficult to imagine a graver allegation.'

'I agree.'

'We're not talking about simple trafficking, we're talking about migrants who have been targeted for what they have to offer criminal interests.'

'I agree.'

'Certain people can afford to pay the traffickers. Others cannot. As Witness A told us, it is this second group who are vulnerable to exploitation.'

'That's right.'

'Please tell the jury what usually happens once such individuals reach the UK.'

'They're forced into menial work.'

Benson demurred. 'Let's use the word slavery, Witness B.'

'Absolutely. It's slavery.'

'And others can be forced into prostitution.'

'Yes, that's right.'

'It goes without saying that fraudulent benefit claims will be made where possible and every penny will go to the traffickers?'

'Correct.'

Benson took a sip of water. 'In the light of these considerations, and having heard about this so-called dossier, have you at any time, then or since, contacted the Modern Slavery Human Trafficking Unit?'

'No.'

'The National Crime Agency?'

'No.'

'Immigration Enforcement?'

'No.'

'The Border Force?'

'No.'

'You appreciate, Witness B, that I am referring to those agencies brought together in June 2015 to form Project Invigor, the UK's Immigration Crime Taskforce?'

'I do.'

'It's the largest in Europe.'

'So I understand.'

'You attend its meetings and are on the distribution list for intelligence briefings?'

'Yes, I am.'

'And at no point since the twenty-first of September 2015 did you think it prudent to inform your colleagues about the allegations made by Diane Heybridge?'

'No, I did not.'

'Because they were wild?'

'They were certainly . . . unusual.'

'You didn't take her seriously for one moment, Witness B. She'd messed your officers around in 2009 and now she was doing the same thing in . . .'

Just then, Tess's phone vibrated. She'd received a text. Glancing down, stunned, she saw it had come from Linda Foster. It said:

Ask DCI Carlatton if he knew Diane's codename.

Tess froze. How did Linda Foster even know that Carlatton was in the witness box? Her mind went blank . . . she saw her walking beside a pond followed by ducks, a bitter woman with something to be bitter about; a widow for whom justice was an empty word; a mother whose kids were still in counselling . . . Benson had finished. Yardley had no re-examination and Carlatton, relieved his ordeal was over, was about to leave the court. Tess lunged forward and tugged Benson's sleeve and whispered the question.

'Just one moment, your ladyship,' said Benson. 'There's one final matter.'

50

Archie got the round. But Tess insisted on paying. They were both quietly elated. Quietly because Benson didn't like effusion. And quietly because the trial wasn't over. They weren't home yet. But a win was in sight. An unexpected, unbelievable win.

They were seated at their corner table in Grapeshots. People had come over to congratulate Benson and shake his hand. They'd seen the news coverage of the Blood Orange murder. Others had read the *Evening Standard*. And the story was the same: Benson had stunned legal commentators with his decision to allow in evidence which – on a reading of the statements – would guarantee the conviction of his client. One pundit had commented that Mrs Justice Fleetwood would have excluded it all if Benson had made the application. But he hadn't. And within half an hour the Crown's case had been turned upside down. Not just the case they'd argued from the outset – murder out of spite and for money – but the new one, introduced by another police force: the murder of a rogue informant. The effect of Benson's cross-examination of Witness A wasn't simply to show that the prosecution was in disarray; he'd hammered home the defence that had never changed: that Diane Heybridge was a tragically damaged woman . . . in a way that couldn't be laid at Stainsby's door.

They were on to a win.

DCI Goodshaw had given evidence after Carlatton. Stainsby's interviews had been read out. Certain parts had been played to the jury. The lies had poured out, with swearing and threats, but the effect now was not of a guilty man trapped in a corner but of a potentially innocent man trapped by his former girlfriend. Benson had kept his cross-examination brief. He'd not bothered to highlight the anger and frustration felt by DCI Goodshaw on discovering he'd been misled by a fellow senior officer. He'd left unexplored North Dover CID's shocking lack of professionalism. Benson had done nothing to distract from the impression he'd already made on the jury about the woman who'd probably killed herself. Everything else was irrelevant. Benson's management of the evidence had led one wag to observe that the person who'd really made a big mistake was Andrew Yardley. He should have left Witnesses A and B out in the corridor; by bringing them to the table he'd failed to see the weakness in his own hand. As a result, he'd closed the prosecution's case as if the game was already over.

Yes, they were on to a win.

'But why did Linda Foster send that text?' said Archie. 'What was she after?'

The answer to her question had been a straight 'No.' Carlatton didn't know Diane's codename. In fact, he didn't know if she'd even been given one. He hadn't checked the force computer because he'd no reason to look. His oversight duties had never got underway.

'I don't like it,' said Benson. 'And if I'd known she'd asked you to ask me, I wouldn't have put the question.'

'I'm sorry,' said Tess. 'I lost the plot. Carlatton was halfway out of the door and I just felt for her . . . She's got no answers; and I thought why not give her this one? It's insignificant.'

'But she's in Great Dunmow and yet she knew I was cross-examining Carlatton. Which means Steve Draycott must have told her. It was Draycott's question.'

Tess hadn't thought of that.

'So what's Draycott up to?' asked Archie.

'I don't know,' said Benson. 'But it points to something bigger than the trial.'

'You're wrong,' said Tess. 'News sites are following the case in real time. That's how she knew. It's part of her fixation with 2009. She wants to link Carlatton to the informer who gave the tip-off about the pow-pow at the Twisted Wheel. She's clutching at anything that will help her prove that Carlatton sent her husband in there – which we know he didn't. Let it go, Will. It's nothing.'

'But Diane wouldn't have had a codename in 2009. And according to Osborne, the likely informer was Tapster.'

'She's not rational, Will. She's been to hell, remember. The third time was today, when Carlatton, backed by Draycott, went public with her husband's stupid mistake.'

Benson nodded; but he didn't look entirely satisfied.

Archie took the ball and ran: 'I'm with Tess, Will. Forget it. Just look at what's really happened. Stainsby's almost free. He's heading home to his miserable life under a stone. He didn't kill her, Will. You've shown that. And no one saw that coming.'

Stainsby had been ecstatic. He'd almost hugged Benson

in the cells. He'd completely forgotten his usual refrain, that someone was trying to kill him. He could see the opening door and he was desperate to get through it. And he wanted to go out in style. He couldn't wait to give evidence tomorrow morning. He'd been brash and vengeful and Benson had had to urge him to calm down.

'I'm starving,' said Archie. 'I've been seeing pies and peas for the last half hour.'

Tess was about to suggest pies and peas at her place when Benson made his usual excuses. He had work to do. The cat was calling. It seemed an age ago that Benson had been slicing tomatoes; he'd been . . . accessible, for once; and abruptly vulnerable. She had been wanting to pull him towards her ever since. But he'd withdrawn again, frowning about evidence. After he'd gone, Archie, sensing Tess's disappointment, leaned forward confidentially.

'He's got a buyer.'

'For his boat?'

'What else?'

Tess had forgotten; and the forgetting shamed her. 'Oh God,' she said. And then she marvelled. 'How does he do it? How does he focus on a case as if nothing was going wrong in his life?'

'Because he's someone else in court,' said Archie. 'He comes alive for the client. Even somebody like Stainsby.'

51

A detective inspector specialising in organised crime had briefed Benson after the close of the day's proceedings. He'd explained that any potential link to Terry Meersham's operations justified extreme caution. Accordingly, he'd offered

Benson a personal panic alarm the size of a USB key. It was extraordinary, he'd enthused. Thanks to Bluetooth technology and an integrated GPS, once activated a signal would . . . but Benson had politely cut him short. He'd be just fine. Because, ironically, Terry Meersham would have been very pleased with Benson's cross-examination of Draycott and Carlatton.

'Well, it's funny you should say that, because one of the lads said you had to be on the payroll.'

'Which lad?'

'It was a joke, Mr Benson.'

'It's oral defamation, Detective Inspector. Tell him I didn't laugh.'

The buyer for *The Wooden Doll* was a twenty-six-year-old city trader called Hooper who'd seen more possibilities with the wharf than the boat. He'd come for one last visit with a few friends who kept referring, reverentially, to the Consortium. Benson left them to it, heading into the kitchen where, taken aback, he walked into a kind of fire . . . the recollection of a thumb upon his cheek . . . a hand on his neck. Disorientated, he went back outside, only to recall the sight of Tess leaving, walking through the trees. She'd left quickly. After Hooper and Co. had gone – not quickly enough by half – he went to his bench by the herb garden, feeling cold and empty. The desire to confess had gone. Instead, he worried about Stainsby, hoping that he'd get through his examination-in-chief without alienating the jury.

Which he did. Just about.

He accepted that the Crown's original case looked devastating. He'd treated Diane badly for years. He'd been angry. He'd wanted all of the insurance policy. He'd made threats. He'd gone looking for Diane. He'd brought her medicines to London when she didn't want them. And then he'd lied like there was no tomorrow. But he hadn't killed her. He hadn't known which drugs would cause which reaction. And as for the trafficking story, Stainsby had been shocked by the allegation, but in the end, that was the sort of thing Diane did. He'd tapped his head. She was just like her mother. It's why she'd needed pills.

Then it was over to Yardley and Benson held his breath.

'Who is Gary Bredfield?'

'He's a mate.'

'A dead mate?'

'Yes.'

'For your ladyship's note, Mr Bredfield's body was found three days ago in Rye Harbour. It seems he'd fallen into the water while under the influence of alcohol and drugs. The death is not being treated as suspicious.'

'This is the gentleman referred to by Witness A?'

'Yes, my lady, in respect of an argument with the defendant regarding the division of monies arising from trafficking.'

'An alleged argument, Mr Yardley.'

Yardley politely agreed and then resumed his questioning. 'You don't sound especially distressed, Mr Stainsby.'

'We'd fallen out.'

'When?'

'A few years back.'

'Why?'

'He owed me money. And despite what you've been saying, I haven't got very much. And that argument never happened, right? If Diane heard anything it was me asking Gary to pay up.'

'He ran a business renting out a boat to divers and fishermen?'

'Yeah.'

'What make of boat did he use?'

'How would I know?'

'Size?'

'Can't help you.'

'Where did he get it from?'

'You'd have to ask Bredfield.'

'I can't. When did you start smoking?'

'When I was eight.'

Benson didn't like this. Stainsby wasn't thinking. The petulance made him smile, and it was ugly. He was convinced Benson had already got him off and now it was time to hit back. But most worrying of all was Yardley's instantaneous shift in direction – dropping the boat for smoking. Benson couldn't guess the reasoning. And Yardley's tone had changed, too. He was now doing the maths with Stainsby, just like Benson had done the maths with Draycott. Only Yardley wasn't deriding. Just curious. Stainsby agreed he was a heavy smoker, buying two packets a day. It's how he'd coped with the stress of unemployment and the loss of his dad's business, and his mum's cancer and his dad's collapse. Yes, it was expensive, but he'd needed them. Still did; Christ, he was struggling. Still without a future and banged up for something he hadn't done. And no, he'd never tried to stop. Yardley was sympathetic. He calculated that Stainsby had smoked more than 290,000 cigarettes over the previous twenty years. One every fifteen minutes. Yardley made a face:

'Except for one night?'

'What do you mean?'

'When you went to London to see Diane.'

If Benson could have placed his head in his hands he would have done so. Because Stainsby's remonstrations simply didn't make sense. He'd never once *not* smoked in Diane's presence. For someone who'd never stopped he'd have been craving within half an hour. And he'd been with

Diane for about three hours. You'd had a curry, Yardley whispered. And a beer. David Bowie was playing . . . and you didn't want a smoke? Yardley kept circling, coming back, tightening the ridicule until – as Benson anticipated – Stainsby snapped.

'Okay, I had a fag. I had one. Only one.'

And then Yardley went to work again. 'Only one? Why?'

And Stainsby spouted more rubbish. About knowing Diane didn't like it – which was not a credible explanation, because it had never stopped him before. But Stainsby wouldn't give another inch. His shoulders were hunched as if to push back, and he raised his voice.

'I had one and only one, and I didn't even finish it, right? I lit up in Diane's and I chucked it away when I got outside.'

Yardley watched the judge note the answer. Then he said, 'Please look at page thirty-seven in File A.'

The file was handed to Stainsby and he found the relevant page.

'My lady, these are the start-up costs of Stainsby's Seafood Locker Ltd.'

'Thank you.'

'Mr Stainsby, would you be so kind as to read out the second item on the list. After the refrigerated van. Centre of the page.'

Benson looked, panic entering his mind. The document was nine years old. Benson had glanced through it once, months ago. He'd had no reason to think it might be significant. Now he stared at the entry, understanding why Yardley had taken a risk in calling Draycott and Carlatton.

'Speak up Mr Stainsby, I didn't hear.'

'It says, "RIB Neptune 460. Ten-passenger. Number: WPM36L."'

'This is a rigid-hull inflatable boat?'

'Yeah.'

'It's registered for use at sea with the Small Ships Register?'

'Yeah.'

'Under whose name?'

'Mine.'

'Why was Gary Bredfield using it?'

Stainsby's teeth appeared. 'Because I was helping him out. He was broke too.'

Yardley closed the file. 'You told this court you'd no idea where he got the boat from. You lied. Again.'

'Look, I don't trust you. Not you, not the police. You'd use it against me. That's why I said nothing.'

'He owed you money?'

'Yeah. Eight hundred quid.'

'Then why not take your boat back?'

'Then he wouldn't earn nothing, would he?'

'But Mr Bredfield's business has never earned a penny. Not in nine years.'

Stainsby stuck his jaw out. 'I'm not playing this game. I tried to help a mate and I'm saying nothing else.'

'Just like you tried to help Diane by bringing her medicines to London?'

'Yeah, actually.'

'That's another lie.

'How do you know?'

'Because you never tried to get them to her when she was still in Dover.'

'I didn't know where she was.'

'All you had to do was ask your solicitor, Mr Hargreaves.'

'Never occurred to me.'

'Mr Stainsby, you lie every time you open your mouth. But I think you've told a single, important truth. You smoked one cigarette. Because you were desperate.'

'So what?'

'You left it behind.'

'I didn't.'

'You placed it on the dressing table in Diane Heybridge's bedroom, where she'd gone to lie down.'

'I didn't go in her bedroom and she didn't go to lie down. I lit up, smoked about half and then I left.'

'You then bound her wrists and forced a blood orange into her mouth.'

Stainsby stood defiant, shaking his head.

'And after you'd hanged her – and only you know why, whether it was for the insurance policy or because you'd found some kind of dossier – you left the cigarette behind. It fell from the dressing table to the carpet. Where it was found the following afternoon.'

'I chucked it on the pavement.'

'Then how did it get back upstairs?'

'How the hell would I know?'

'You're the only one who can know, Mr Stainsby. It's your cigarette. And your DNA's on it. Yours and yours alone.'

Yardley had finished. And so had Benson. He'd daren't re-examine Stainsby for fear of what he might say. Having long ago decided not to call expert evidence of his own, and since no one was prepared to come forward to contradict the evidence of mistreatment, Benson rose to utter the words he'd been rehearsing ever since that first conference in HMP Kensal Green. It was a relief to get them out:

'My lady, that concludes the case for the defence.'

52

Yardley's speech was brief and masterful. He didn't dwell on the motive. He didn't focus on the emotional abuse. He didn't even bother to anticipate Benson's argument that Diane had been psychologically compromised since childhood; that she'd sought revenge by contriving her suicide to look like murder. He just focused on the lies. He listed them one after the other, starting with the denial that he'd even gone to London. The climax was, paradoxically, a truth forced out of him at the last moment. That he'd smoked in the flat. Topped off with another lie: that he'd thrown the cigarette away outside the front door. By the time Yardley came to that last assertion it sounded simply implausible. People finish cigarettes and then say goodbye; they don't leave while smoking. But the most devastating effect of Stainsby's admission – and, cleverly, Yardley left this unstated – was that Benson's adroit removal of the smoke and ash as damning factors now appeared as cheap tricks. The defence Benson had constructed out of nothing now seemed not just flimsy but contrived.

Benson's speech was brief, too. He began after lunch, trying to summon the woman who'd made up a friend called Harry. A woman who'd learned to cope with reality by creating fictions. But the point had lost its force. Yardley had placed considerable emphasis on the crime scene. And the light was bright. It no longer quite mattered what Diane's childhood had been like, or even how bad a partner Stainsby had been . . . or what the motive might have been. The problem was the cigarette end. Because even if the jury still accepted that the smoke and ash had been carried into the flat on a breeze, there was no explanation for how that butt had come to land by Diane's feet. The concessions forced out of Dr Capicelli counted for nothing. Because that cigarette end – without a contrary explanation – put Stainsby in the one room he denied entering. It was Yardley's best point, and he'd protected it, right from the start of the trial. He'd excluded any tampering with the crime scene.

Everything presented to the jury after that had just been window-dressing. Camberley was right. Yardley had played with Benson – even with the late calling of Draycott and Carlatton. The issue had never been a change in motive or the massive prejudice that might arise from an unsubstantiated allegation of trafficking. All he'd wanted was the lie about the boat. Which he'd then used to underline the lie about the cigarette. If poker was the best analogy, Yardley had banked on those two cards coming his way; and they had done.

After a short break, Mrs Justice Fleetwood began her summing up of the evidence. And Benson listened, feeling the case had slipped through his fingers; that perhaps it would have slipped through his fingers regardless of anything he might have done or said, because, in truth, the most damning evidence had fallen from Stainsby's hand and there was nothing Benson could do to remove it. The words of Archie Congreve came to mind:

'Don't forget the forensic, Rizla. You're knackered there, too.'

The phrase stayed with Benson after the court rose. Because he went to see Mr Edgeworth, who said much the same thing, though for different reasons and with respect to a different subject. Hooper's offer had come in 5K below the asking price, which Barlow's thought was fair enough. Benson couldn't concur. But he had no room for manoeuvre. The Whitechapel Building Society was no longer prepared to wait for its money. So he went home and called Braithwaite, asking if he'd handle the conveyance.

The next morning, Mrs Justice Fleetwood continued her careful review of the evidence. And while Benson wrote down every word, his mind was elsewhere. Not, this time, on how the trial might have slipped through his fingers, but

Terry Meersham. His presence lay upon the case, like a stain on the carpet of Diane Heybridge's seedy flat. Benson almost had a sense that Meersham was watching him write, still draped in that gold dressing gown, flanked by his grinning minders.

'Do you know what smoking causes?'

Benson nodded.

'Do you?' His fine lips stretched even thinner. 'You've heard of peripheral vascular disease?'

Benson nodded.

'Furring of the arteries? Weakening of the oesophagus?'

Meersham stared at him, white with rage.

'Brain aneurysms. Cellulite. Stained teeth . . .'

Benson sat bolt upright. Mrs Justice Fleetwood had completed her summing up. She was now giving instructions to the jury. They would shortly go out and they'd only come back to deliver a verdict. No more evidence could be received. But Benson's memory had stirred. His open hands seemed to hold an article he'd once read: 'Children, trauma and evidence: the potential suppression of truth' by T. Maddison et al.

'My lady,' said Benson, quickly rising. 'Please forgive my interruption. May I raise a matter with the court before the jury retires?'

53

The press is often unfair on judges, thought Tess. A few wacky dicta from a handful of celeb cases and the entire profession is branded out of touch or eccentric. In fact, the greater part of them are wise. They've seen everything – at the Bar and on the Bench. Very little surprises them, and in this particular case, Benson's application to cross-examine a witness who hadn't even given evidence-in-chief, after the closure of both the prosecution and defence cases, was received with benign curiosity. After considering the only authority on the question – *Sanderson (1953) 1 All ER 485* – and listening to Yardley's impolite remonstrations, Mrs Justice Fleetwood gave Benson leave to reopen the defence case. TV monitors were installed in the court while an appropriately trained officer and social worker went to bring the witness.

Over lunch Benson deflected all Tess's questions, preferring instead to talk about a fascinating article he'd once read while in prison. Apparently, children sometimes handled trauma by removing themselves from an event, reporting information as if they were a bystander and erasing their own actions. As a result, vital evidence known only to the child could be inadvertently passed over. But what was most interesting was this: since the child was not being deceitful, all it took was a few targeted questions and out it came. Tess agreed it was thought-provoking. But so what? And then Benson dropped his guard:

'I'm chancing my arm. But I think I know what really happened.'

At 2.15 p.m. the screens flickered into life and Jonas Sibhatu looked into the camera that linked him to Number 16 Court.

Jonas had been with his mother when Diane Heybridge's body had been discovered. He'd given a statement, like his mother. And its content, though briefer, was entirely consistent with that of his mother's. Which is why there'd been no reason to get him down to the Old Bailey and face questioning. But Benson had a hunch; and her ladyship thought the jury ought to know if he was right. As a preliminary, Benson established that Jonas had no idea what the evidential issues in the case might be. His mother, his school and Alex, his counsellor, had all cooperated to ensure that he'd been shielded from any discussion of the trial. He knew it had opened. He knew a man had been charged with murder. There, mercifully, his knowledge ended. Benson became matey:

'Jonas, what does your mum think of smoking?' he asked. His wig was off and his tone came from his own playground years.

'She thinks it's really bad.'

'Yes. Well, it is. That's why they put those warnings on the packets.'

'That's what my mum said.'

'Just in case there's anyone on the jury who doesn't believe us, could you tell them the sorts of things that can happen?'

The eleven-year-old was shifting in his seat.

'Your breath stinks.'

'Anything else?'

'Weak bones.'

'Some of the jurors are looking worried, Jonas. Give them some more. What about heart attacks?'

'The chance of having one is doubled.'

'Come on Jonas, we're winning.'

'Your skin will turn grey and you'll get wrinkles.'

'Who taught you all this, Jonas?'

'My mum.'

'Why?'

Jonas didn't answer and Mrs Justice Fleetwood, now more grandmother than High Court Judge, told him not to worry. That he wouldn't get into trouble for anything. But this was a critical moment: neither Benson nor the judge had suggested any reason why, even though it was now obvious to the jury. After a long silence, he said it:

'Because I'd been smoking with my friends. But I don't want to say who they were.'

'And I won't ask you, either,' said Benson. 'However, I do want to know where you got the cigarettes from. Did you steal them?'

'No,' said Jonas, still shifting. 'I've never stolen anything. But I've borrowed without asking . . . and my mum says that's just as bad.'

'Did you ever borrow money from your mum's purse without her knowing?'

'Never.'

'Then how did you buy the cigarettes?'

'I wasn't buying them . . . I was just picking ends off the floor.'

'By floor did you mean street?'

'Yes.'

Tess felt as if Benson had brought the defence case to the edge of a cliff. Either a kite was about to fly, or it would just float down into the sea. If Benson was nervous, he hid it well. Still matey, he said:

'Before your mum went over to Diane's flat, she told you to get yourself well wrapped up.'

'Yes.'

'What did that mean to you?'

'Hat, coat, scarf and gloves.'

'Did you put that lot on?'

'Yes.'

'And then you came outside?'

'Yes.'

'Did you go straight into the flat?'

'No.'

'What did you do?'

'Just waited, pretending to play football.'

'Head down, eye on the ball?'

Jonas smiled. 'Yes.'

'Did you see a cigarette end?'

Benson hadn't cushioned the question. And Jonas, curiously, stopped shifting about. The drama of the morning and the cameras had made him completely transparent. He just said, 'Yes.'

'Did you pick it up?'

'Yes.'

'And then you went into the flat, looking for your mum?'

'Yes.'

'With the cigarette in your hand?'

'Yes.'

Jonas spoke as if in a trance, relieved that someone else was putting words to what he'd done. Only – and this was the irony – his relief went no further than admitting that he'd picked up another fag end. The greater worry was for those friends his mother didn't really like; the ones who'd been leading her son astray. He'd no idea that the entire trial had turned on what had been found at Diane Heybridge's feet. Benson's voice had a waver when he asked the next critical questions:

'Did you ever smoke it?'

'No.'

'Why not?'

'I dropped it . . . when I saw my mum's friend on that door.'

54

Both Benson and Yardley were given the chance to address the jury once more. But it was only Yardley who felt obliged to do so, recalling the evidence against Stainsby that he'd not bothered to emphasise first time around. Which made him look as if he was trying to correct the list of a ship that just might sink. Or was he simply underlining points that the jury had already decided were of decisive importance? Benson couldn't be sure; and Camberley had always said never, ever think that a jury can't surprise you. They can and they do.

Now began the long wait. And as usual it was a torment. Made worse by another encounter with Yardley after the jury had filed out to begin their deliberations. They'd only spoken to each other three times and they'd got exponentially more insulting.

'You knew Sibhatu had picked up that cigarette.'

'No, I didn't.'

'You met him in the street and you quizzed him then.'

'I certainly did not, and if you think I did you should have asked him when you had the chance.'

'Expose what you'd done in public? Place the kid at the centre of a controversy? I wouldn't do that, Benson. Because, as you well know, it wouldn't change anything.'

Benson made to leave, but Yardley grabbed his arm at the elbow:

'You got past Fleetwood but you didn't get past me. You knew Stainsby had smoked in that flat—'

'I did not.'

'—and your ploy from the outset was to hold back on the kid until the very end. You exploited him. Do you know what that's called, Benson? It's called child abuse.'

When Yardley had gone an usher and the shorthand writer came over like a secret delegation:

'Forget him, Mr Benson,' said one.

'He's always nasty when he loses,' added the other.

* * *

But Benson hadn't won, not yet. And during the long wait he realised he'd never be a winner, regardless of any jury's decision. He'd always be someone you couldn't quite trust. There'd always be a question over every innocent mistake or afterthought. He'd always be the sort of opponent you were warned about. Because he was a wolf in sheep's clothing. A killer who'd denied or admitted his offence depending on the direction of the wind.

After three hours, the jury reached a verdict. The court reassembled. The foreman, a man in his sixties, stood and faced the clerk.

'Have you reached a verdict upon which you are all agreed?'

'We have.'

'And what is your verdict, "guilty" or "not guilty"?'

Benson barely heard the reply. His eyes had landed upon an autopsy photograph of a part-time worker at Greggs who'd left Dover and come to London in a hurry. The ligature marks on the neck were deep. But it was the smile creases around the eyes that upset him. The ambiguity was unbearable. In the great game of life, had she won or lost? Had she found something to smile at, however small and insignificant, before the light faded? Or was it a jolt in the facial nerves kept in place by the rigor?

Stainsby shouted out. In triumph. Benson was suddenly alert, and time shot forward as if its brakes had failed. He seemed to fly through events. The shorthand writer was smiling; Mrs Justice Fleetwood was telling Stainsby he was free to go; then she was thanking the jury; and then, after the opening and closing of doors, Benson came to a shuddering standstill and Tess was at his side.

'You did it,' she said.

'Did what?'

'You won, for God's sake.'

Benson wrapped up his brief. He just wanted to go home.

55

Stainsby had wanted to leave the Old Bailey by the front door. He'd been itching to face the cameras. And he'd set off without thanking Tess or, indeed, Benson, who'd gone to the robing room to change out of his wig and gown, and his collar and bands – the protective equipment that sterilises the connection between an advocate and the person he represents. When he emerged, Tess suggested they leave by the rear entrance where, unfortunately, a couple of photographers were waiting. They tracked them for a few yards, Benson, with head lowered, not giving them what they wanted. It was only when they got to Congreve Chambers, after a largely silent walk, that his face relaxed. Molly opened the door:

'I'll make tea, Mr Benson.'

Benson sat behind his desk. Tess took an armchair and Archie leaned on the old radiator by the window.

'I'm glad we didn't get rid of these,' he said, tapping the ironwork.

'Me too,' said Tess.

'You can't get them any more.'

'No.'

'I used to sit here while my sisters gutted the fish over there. Great days. And my dad would be out front, telling the punters what to look for when—'

Benson spoke. 'Bredfield was missing for a week.'

'Yes,' said Archie. 'Went on a bender.'

'He turned up floating in Rye Harbour.'

'Yes. And?'

'He lived in Hythe.'

'It's only half an hour up the road.'

'Rye Harbour is where Loupierre moored his yacht back in 2009.'

Tess glanced at Archie. And Archie spoke for them both: 'Forget it, Rizla. The case is over.'

Benson nodded; then he said, 'I got a call when I was in the robing room.'

'Who from?'

'Cruncher.'

'Who's Cruncher?' asked Tess.

Archie explained. 'He's in the Tuesday Club. A wizard. Computers and maths. Turned down an approach from GCHQ. Unfortunately, he went and cracked into—'

'And Cruncher told me he'd found a link between Diane Heybridge and John Foster.'

The case might be over, but Tess was now interested; and so was Archie.

'They were at primary school together. In Dover.'

'Is that it?' Archie wasn't impressed.

'And Diane contacted him through Facebook in January 2008. Just the once. Things could have ended there. They could have met. Cruncher didn't know.'

Tess immediately saw the significance of the date. 'That was the year before the meeting between Meersham and Loupierre at the Twisted Wheel.'

'Exactly,' said Benson. 'Which suggests that Diane may have become an informer well before Stainsby tried to hook up with the big players. It would mean that Diane had been tracking him for over a year, and that she only got in touch with Foster once she knew she was on to something serious.'

'And he ran her off the books until the thing blew up in their faces,' said Archie.

Benson nodded. 'That's what it looks like.'

'No, it doesn't,' said Tess. 'That's what it *might* look like.'

She knew that post-mortems after a verdict were always a dodgy activity, especially when much of the wider background would always remain obscured from view. Yardley had been right: with a murder – with any kind of violence – what really matters is a tight focus on the mechanics of the attack; motive was a swamp. God alone knew what really lay beneath that shifting surface.

'Stainsby was acquitted, Will,' she said. 'Even if all this went before the jury, it doesn't change a thing. He's a dark guy in a dark world. Diane Heybridge got pulled into his darkness, and for reasons I'll never understand she stayed there. All that's true. And maybe he did dark things. But the jury weren't sure he killed her. He had to walk. That's justice.'

Tess had wanted to prevent another layer of self-disgust settling on Benson's shoulders. She'd been so impassioned she hadn't noticed that the door had opened and Molly had entered the room.

'Mr Stainsby's here,' she said. 'He'd like to say thanks.'

56

Benson shook Stainsby's hand. But he wasn't offered a seat; and Tess and Archie remained standing. And for a moment, Benson was abstracted. His palm felt wet. He held his hand slightly away from his side as if it might stain his trousers.

'You pulled me out of the fire, Mr Benson. I've told all the papers you're the best.'

Benson didn't acknowledge the compliment. He just took in the borrowed suit that was too small; and the tight white shirt; and the large knot hanging loose below the open collar.

'I like the way you kept saying "my client". You were saying we're in this together.'

He was chewing gum, moving it around his mouth through an excess of energy.

'Which was great. Because I don't think the jury liked me that much.'

'They set you free, Mr Stainsby,' said Benson coldly.

'Yes, but that's all thanks to you.'

'It's thanks to the evidence.'

'Nah, you're being modest. I reckon they looked at me, and they looked at you, and they thought, Them two aren't that different. And I bet—'

Tess intervened. 'Mr Stainsby, we're very busy. If you don't mind, we have to get back to work.'

'Sure. I just wanted to say thanks. Shake the great man's hand. You know what I mean?'

'Yes.'

'One reporter called you The Magician. Because you pulled that kid out of a hat.'

'Is that everything?' asked Tess.

He idled, chewing, his eyes flicking from Benson to Tess and back again. 'There's just one last thing. Do you remember our first conference, Mr Benson?'

'Yes.'

'Well, it's the only time you brought the papers . . . you know, all that crap sent over by the CPS.'

'It's the evidence compiled by the Crown.'

'Yeah, I know. But in the end it was all a waste of paper, and I was just wondering' – he let his eyes drift over to Benson's desk – 'do you reckon I could I have a souvenir?'

'Meaning?'

'You had a book of photos. You know, the pictures taken by that Paki doctor.'

Benson's throat contracted. Stainsby was sending them a

message. If Benson and Tess had thought that their achievement was to get a loathsome but innocent man off a murder charge, well, he was putting them straight. He'd killed her; and he wanted them to know it. He was wide-eyed, still looking from Benson to Tess and from Tess to Benson.

'You bastard,' whispered Tess.

'Please, Miss de Vere, mind your language. You're my solicitor. We've got through this together. Do I get my photos?'

'No.'

He didn't want them, Benson was sure. All he was after was this, the sight of his representation, Benson and de Vere, sickened by their role in his acquittal. He was smiling . . . just like Meersham. And Roy. And Skagman. And Crazy Joe. They'd all smiled when tasting their power. And now Stainsby was tasting his, chewing violently, making sure there was no doubt in anyone's mind as to who'd won and who'd lost. Diane, his weak-headed girlfriend, had spent six years trying to nail him. And she'd failed. More than that, he'd put her down, and no one could touch him. Suddenly Benson felt blinded: not by rage, or disgust, but something comforting, only he didn't know why. The reason slipped out of reach just as he tried to grasp it. He pointed vaguely to the doorway.

'Get out, Mr Stainsby. Now.'

'Hey, not so fast. Today's my day. Don't spoil it.'

Tess said, 'It's time to leave.' And Archie, fists clenched, took a step forward.

'Okay, okay. I know when I'm not wanted.'

The show was over, so Stainsby sauntered towards the exit, but not before he'd made a mock lunge, with a wink, for Archie. On reaching the door the smile returned, broader this time. 'If they ever try and put me down for something else, I'm coming to you, Mr Benson. Like I said, you're the best.'

After he'd gone, Molly came back into the Gutting Room. No one else moved. It was as though Diane was present . . . at the beginning of her post-death ordeal, her body exposed on a mortuary table. But there was nothing to be done and nothing to be said, because her killer would never be brought to justice. The only activity and sound came from Molly as she collected the cups and saucers, placing them neatly on a tray. When the tinkling came to an end, she spoke:

'Mr Benson?'

But Benson had slowly sat down. He was trying to understand that sudden consolation which had departed as quickly as it had come, only to leave him empty and depressed. He couldn't revive the insight. But the experience had been real. Under its influence, Stainsby had appeared insignificant. A shell. There'd been no—

'Mr Benson?'

He seemed to wake. 'Sorry. Yes?'

Molly waited until she was sure Benson was listening carefully. Then she said, 'You were sitting here only a short while ago – do you remember? – and you said you had to win the sort of case where everyone knows the defendant's guilty, and you don't want to win, and you shouldn't win, but somehow you do.'

'Yes, I remember.' Molly had quoted him word for word.

'Well, this is what it feels like.'

Benson raised an eyebrow. 'I don't like it.'

'No one does.'

Molly didn't sound especially sympathetic; just practical. 'You'll have to get used to it. Because there are lots of folk out there – evil people, who do evil things, shattering good people's lives – and they'll never plead guilty when they're caught. They'll use the system, and they'll use Miss de Vere, and they'll use you. And all you can do is believe in their innocence, because one day someone will come along, and they'll look and behave no different, only they'll be as honest as the day is long, but no one in their right mind would believe them . . . and you could save the day. It's worth the candle, don't you think?'

'Yes, Molly. I do.'

'Good.'

And she left the room, the cups and saucers tinkling. But the remembered conversation wasn't entirely over. Back then, prior to the trial, Molly had said something else. She'd been cryptic, saying that justice doesn't always finish with the jury's verdict, but Benson couldn't recall exactly what came next. A reminding voice came from the kitchen:

'And as for Mr Stainsby and all the others like him . . . they can go to hell.'

PART FIVE

Her life meant nothing

Benson sat in a stupor before Mr Fitzsimons, the governor.

'Your good work was exploited, Mr Benson. And now someone is dead.'

With a sigh of resignation, he explained what had been done before the books had come into Benson's possession. A given page had been soaked in a liquid form of herbal ecstasy. Dangerous stuff. Very dangerous. Creates a sense of intimacy. Heightens sensory experiences. A few hours of euphoria. Things you don't get in prison, so you can understand the appeal. But it contains ephedra. And that's a stimulant that can kill.

'All those donations were spiked, we think. Because they've all got a missing page.'

Benson was staring back, unable to process what he was hearing, so Mr Fitzsimons explained.

'You put the paper in your mouth and off you go. Or you sell it. Which is what happened here.'

A twenty-two-year-old on remand had bought a trip for ten cans of tuna. He'd had a heart attack. If only he'd put up with the waiting. The CPS had decided to offer no evidence. Notification came through while he was in hospital. Life's like that, sometimes, isn't it? Things line up. You'd think it was planned.

'Don't blame yourself, Mr Benson. Prisoners like you, with initiative, are vital for the well-being of the community. But there's always someone out there ready to subvert a worthwhile idea. We'll have to ban books and letters now.'

Benson tried to recall the dead man. He was Benson's age. He'd denied two counts of criminal damage. It all turned on ID at night. His name was Parker.

'The person responsible has admitted everything, Mr Benson, but I'm moving you to another prison. Someone will blame you regardless of the evidence . . . but I suppose you know that already.'

'Who was it?'

Benson's mind was fogging. It couldn't be his lordship.

'I'm sorry to say it was Manchester. Owen Kennedy. And while he won't name names, at least we've got the guy who organised the spiking. He'll be interviewed and charged later today, but I want you out of here first. Get ready. Just say you're being ghosted.'

Benson went back to his cell. A guard waited outside while he packed his things. Manchester watched, wheezing and smoking. The tension between them became excruciating. Because Benson knew that all the evidence pointed to him. His lordship had seen to that.

'Why, Manchester?'

'I'm never going to get out of here.'

'What are you talking about? You were up for parole.'

'Parole's never meant nowt to me, lad. And anyway . . . I've got cancer.'

He said the word as if he'd won the lottery.

'I've cleared everything with Meersham. Just do your bird. Then start again, Rizla. Live your life. Get married. Have some kids. And whatever you do, don't lay a finger on 'em.'

The guard came in, stifling Benson's reply. All they could do was shake hands.

57

She might be ninety-one, but Merrington's mother, Annette, had the spirit of a woman in her late teens. Her life was almost over but she lived each day as if there was simply more to come. It had to be her faith – that was Pamela's view. She'd married the Rev Gilbert Merrington and together they'd preached the Kingdom throughout the age of war and genocide that had defined their lives. She was an inspiration. And she'd come for dinner, invited by her son. He hadn't seen her for months. Her presence alone created a sense of occasion. David even had a shower. And Pamela looked radiant. Conversation soon turned to the Blood Orange murder.

The verdict wasn't so much controversial as the starting point for a wider debate about the ability of the law to comprehensively do justice to the facts. Stainsby's emotionally abusive conduct had been admitted. But the jury had accepted Benson's argument that the bruised reed had already been broken. But where did that leave the bruising? No judgment was passed upon it because it did not constitute a separate offence. It had simply been a part of the grammar of Stainsby–Heybridge relations, to which she had consented. Or had she? And either way, could suicide be so cleanly separated from its surrounding circumstances? Circumstances in which Stainsby was the dominant figure?

The discussion had also inevitably focused on Benson as Stainsby's advocate. He'd negotiated very difficult territory without once underplaying the reprehensible behaviour of his client or diminishing the experience of his victim.

'They're calling him The Magician,' said Annette.

'Who are "they"?' enquired Merrington cheerily. Ordinarily

the word, used in this way, annoyed him; but tonight, he'd made an exception.

'The media, darling,' said Pamela.

'And the people,' added Annette. 'He's pulled off the most astonishing win.'

Pamela glanced uneasily at Richard. 'Yes, he has.'

Certain papers – papers that mattered – had taken the opportunity to point out that the Justice Secretary had once tried to silence this man. What had happened to those promises? Had those undertakings to the Harbeton family been quietly forgotten? Would any other legislative proposals be shelved the moment convenience outweighed principle? It was precisely these questions, and the humiliating commentary they generated, which had hardened Merrington's resolve to ruin Benson. That, and the threat he posed to his own family, for David, notwithstanding Pamela's valiant attempts to point elsewhere, still looked to Benson for inspiration. Annette, it seemed, couldn't see the problem.

'And he's got star quality, too,' she said. 'Would you be so kind as to fill my glass, David? Where was I?'

'Star quality.'

'That's right. But without the self-importance one associates so often with members of the legal profession. That's what marks him out. Your father always said, "Humility grows best in the garden of an outcast." Do you remember, Dicky?'

'Yes, I do,' said Merrington. He'd hated that diminutive all his life. 'And I always thought: what a pity for those who belong. There's no virtue in keeping the rules.'

David had his own view. 'He's made the Bar cool.'

Merrington couldn't stop himself. 'Cool?'

'Yes. He's turned the known order upside down. He's not interested in silk or becoming or judge or making a heap of money. He's rap in a world that hasn't even heard of Elvis.'

'David's right, you know,' said Annette. 'And my generation thought Elvis was terribly dangerous.'

'Because he was, Gran. And Benson is now.'

Merrington had seen Bradley Hilmarton that morning. They'd gone for a stroll in St James's Park. Bradley had chosen his words carefully:

'Now that you've got Benson's confessions, we may as well draw the investigation to a close.'

'You're hiding something, Bradley, I can tell.'

'Not hiding, Richard, just keeping things simple.'

'You've traced his benefactor?'

'Yes. And you might as well let it go.'

'Why?'

'The money's clean.'

'So what?'

'Well, you won't be able to use the information against Benson.'

Merrington offered Pamela some more saltimbocca. 'It means "leaps in the mouth", darling. Which I always thought was a God-awful name for a dish. The idea of something jumping . . . it makes me think of a toad. And a toad behind my teeth—'

'For heaven's sake, Richard, stop.'

David and his grandmother were still singing Benson's praises. How he'd brought a gust of fresh air into a fusty room dominated by public-school types who make jokes in Latin.

'Well, someone out there must be very pleased with themselves,' said Merrington, serving tongs in hand.

'Who, darling?' asked Pamela, still mindful of that toad.

'Whoever financed the return of the prodigal.'

'What rot are you on about now?'

'Benson, my dear. Someone forked out something like a hundred and sixty thousand smackers to set him up. They must have thought he had enormous potential. To make the Bar cool, I imagine.'

'As much as that?' asked Annette, surprised.

'Absolutely.'

Bradley had sat down on a bench. Merrington had joined him, and together they'd looked at the lake. A couple of swans had cut through the water and, almost miraculously, they'd turned their heads at the same time to gaze at the two men. It had been a startling moment.

'I suppose it was some celebrity?'

'No.'

'A member of the party?'

'No . . . but it will complicate your life, politically, if you knew. So how about we just draw down the blinds?'

Pamela couldn't eat the saltimbocca. She was thinking of slime and boils and spawn. Annette was still remonstrating. 'Is that what it costs these days to come to the Bar?' And David had a view, too: 'He's been worth every penny.'

The swans had turned away, again in unison, suggesting synchronised disinterest.

'Tell me, Bradley. I thrive on information that other people think is useless.'

'All right, then. You.'

'What do you mean?'

'Ultimately, you paid for his training. You set him up.'

'Don't be bloody ridiculous.'

'Your father left a small trust fund. Your mother's a trustee. She's got wide-ranging powers. Whatever she doesn't spend goes to you. She gave the lot to Braithwaite to give to Benson. Well, not the lot. There's five grand left.'

Annette turned to Pamela. 'Is that what it'll cost David to become a barrister?'

'Don't worry, Gran,' said David. 'There are loans.'

'Oh, I don't like loans. Gilbert always used to say, "Never borrow. Only spend what you've got." It's a good rule.'

Merrington couldn't agree more and he said so.

'Anyway, your father's got plenty of money,' said Annette. 'He'll look after you . . . won't you Dicky?'

58

'Her life meant nothing,' said Benson.

He'd once more withdrawn from the fight for real estate, public services, utilities, and railway stations. Instead, overwhelmed by thoughts on the harshness of chance, he'd gone to see Abasiama.

'Everything was fine. Then her father gets killed in a hit-and-run . . . and that driver will be out there now, living his life as if nothing had happened. Thankful to have got away with it. Probably followed the trial and didn't make the link. But that death destroyed Diane's mother. And it devastated Diane. There was no one there to hold her hand except Harry, who didn't exist. He helped her with her homework. Walked with her to school.'

Then there'd been the social workers doing their best. There were meetings about possible foster placements. And a new vocabulary for Diane and Harry. EPOs. Interventions. Child protection teams. The protocols and procedures designed to limit the harm. The next support group had been the Dover Five. Although they'd known little of the pain that the social workers had done their best to contain. It had worked, though. Singing in the street. Laughing. Happy hours. A bit of dancing. And then she'd met Stainsby.

'I don't know why she stayed with him,' said Benson. 'She

told everyone it was because she didn't want to leave him while Frank was alive . . . but even Frank did nothing to protect this girl who loved him. He must have known. He was another one who was too caught up in his own problems to see that something bad was going on. Something seriously wrong. But by then, there were no social workers and no interventions and no procedures. She just put up with him. And only one word ever made it on to paper. "Unbearable." She'd been talking about the longing for children . . . but if that meeting had gone on for longer than a few minutes the rest might have come out. The longing for a family. For a man who loved her. For some fun in the evenings. But even then, what could the GP have done? Change her prescription?'

Abasiama listened without reacting and without enquiry. But her attentiveness was a like a magnet, drawing out Benson's troubled thoughts.

'You know, I'm struck by something. The only person she turned to was someone she'd known at primary school. From the time before her dad died. When life had been normal. When her mum put her to bed without stinking of booze. She contacted a kid who'd grown up to be a policeman.' Benson could just picture it: Diane trawling through the names, the photos and the comments. 'I just wonder, is this a boy she'd liked? Was John Foster the good-looking kid at the back of the class? Is that what kicked off the fantasy?'

Because there had to have been a heap of invention. There was no dossier. No money. No corroboration from any agency dealing with trafficking. Diane must have learned about some grubby drug deal between Stainsby and Bredfield and then pumped it up into something far more serious. Got herself some excitement and attention. And who knows, maybe Foster remembered Diane as the good-looking girl who sat at the front of the class. Whatever happened, he never bothered to register Diane in the usual way. Because he'd picked up at their first meeting that she wasn't the usual type of informer. Maybe he'd sensed her vulnerability. Doubted her claims. He'd probably gone to the Twisted Wheel to find out if she could be trusted, only to stray onto the patch of the big boys who'd been planning a major deal. What a bloody irony. Diane's mind games had distracted Foster and Draycott from what was really going on. The summit between Meersham and Loupierre had been about drugs, not trafficking.

'I really think she went to London to start over,' said Benson. 'To get free of Stainsby. Perhaps the Dover Five, too. She'd planned a future. She signed up at a secretarial college in Harringay. She'd bought herself a bike.' Benson recalled the flat and the posters of Big Ben and Piccadilly Circus. 'And all she got was ten days.' Benson didn't know what else to say, until he'd said it: 'Thank God she met Milena Sibhatu.'

Benson's bodyweight had seemed to increase. He felt heavy in the chair and he looked at Abasiama as if he might need help standing up.

'Whatever the true motive might be doesn't really matter. In the end, a long history of emotional abuse culminated in violence. When he could no longer control her, he took her life away . . . the little that was left, the little that he'd allowed her to keep. He killed her. He effectively told me he killed her. And I got him off.'

Abasiama nodded. It was a rare gesture.

'And I did nothing wrong. Everything I did in court was . . . my duty. My duty to the evidence. My duty to the client. But I can't escape a sense of responsibility.'

It was all down to those damned confessions. Benson knew it and Abasiama knew it. Not so long ago, he'd found it easy to simulate passion, conviction and determination, not caring if his defence in a case was true or false. He'd gone into court detached from the world outside. And that's where he'd flourished. But that person had gone.

'You find that painful?' asked Abasiama. It was the first time she'd spoken.

'I'd call it profound unease. Which is painful, yes.'

'Is it the kind of pain you want to avoid?'

Benson didn't have to think for long. 'No. Not at all.'

He owed Diane that much.

59

The Blood Orange murder acquittal had left Tess feeling dirty. It was the right result – as lawyers always say – because it was the jury's verdict. But Stainsby's gloating implication that he'd murdered Diane, just as he'd implied having tried to murder DS Foster in 2009 – and may well have done in 2013 – had removed the barrier of ignorance which allows a lawyer to walk away from a case without feeling involved. He'd done that on purpose. Part of his victory over Diane was to make sure that even his defenders knew that the suicide story had been bogus. That his plan had worked.

Tess had called Benson late that night. They'd stayed on the line for over an hour, though Tess did most of the talking, trying to scrub off a sense of responsibility. Stainsby had done nothing except watch, she'd said with her feet up, drinking a gin and It. She and Benson had done everything, in his name. They'd been his dupes . . . possibly willing dupes, for they'd willed into existence a credible defence. Benson had been consoling, but whatever he said to reassure her could only reveal his own unsettled conscience. They were in this together. Which had a certain intimacy. Tess had put the phone down asking herself a question. Sally's question. And Lionel Bart's. 'Where is love?' Could it come from . . . confusion?

The answer to that lay in the future. And she was glad to leave it there. The task of the moment was to trace the history of a bracelet found near the body of Paul Harbeton and sold, years later, to Evington's in Victoria. Accordingly, Tess and Sally found themselves in a cramped back room where Mr Butterworth, the manager, checked the shop's records. And sure enough, the bracelet had been purchased, but subsequently sold on to a Mrs Dillon, who lived around the corner in Pimlico. She was a regular client. And charming.

And she was also at home. A white-fronted Edwardian terraced house with a blue door, set back behind iron railings that had survived the munitions requirements of the Second World War. She'd received Tess and Sally, waving away offers of identification. The word of Evington's was enough: Mr Butterworth had called ahead, explaining that a lost property investigation was underway. In her eighties, she was the last of her generation. The rest of her family had moved on.

'My father flew a Spitfire,' she said, shutting the door. 'He was one of the Few.'

And it was only forty minutes later, after tea and biscuits and a discourse on Operation Sea Lion – 'That was Hitler's plan to put us all in chains, Miss de Vere' – that she opened the lid of a small green box and took out the bracelet.

'I buy myself a little treat every year. Try it on.'

Tess did.

'It's lovely,' she said, turning it around her wrist, her thumb counting nine twinkling diamonds.

'If the owner wants it back,' said Mrs Dillon, pouring more tea, 'we'll have to come to some sort of understanding. As my father used to say, look after the pennies and the pounds will look after themselves. But you have to look after the pounds as well.'

'Of course you do. May we take some photographs?'

Mrs Dillon agreed, and then, after an hour on the Dam Busters, Tess and Sally made to leave.

'You really should insist on identification, Mrs Dillon,' said Tess, taking her hand. 'You can't trust everyone.'

Mrs Dillon tightened her grip. 'But everyone must trust someone, young lady. And I'd rather take my chances than live in fear every time there's a knock on my door. That's what my father died for, you know. I'd just turned eleven . . . in spring, 1943. A Tuesday.'

Tess and Sally then went straight to Marylebone. Because, engraved on the inside edge of the bracelet, was the name of a jeweller, R. J. Shipton, along with an identifying number: MJB27. Shipton's was a well-known family business that specialised in platinum, while gold and silver, trading from a magical universe of creaking display cabinets, dark green baize and worn leather chairs. The owner, Anthony Shipton, a tall, thin man with round glasses, was more than happy to dig out the old ledgers. He found the likely year and then laid it on a glass-topped table, peering at the entries on the yellowed paper while turning the pages and talking.

'It was made by Manny Brewster – that's MJB. He made stuff for royalty. My great-grandfather, Henry, knew him well. He had a basement workshop over in Clerkenwell. Very popular with lawyers . . . especially the Gray's Inn lot, who were just around the corner. We get pieces coming back, even now. For repair. They tend to – ah, here we are.'

Mr Shipton turned the ledger around and pointed at a line of immaculate copperplate.

'It was made for Arthur Wingate in 1918. And that's typical of the period. Henry even wrote down the purpose of the commission: an eighteenth birthday present for Elsie Wingate. His daughter. Those were the days. It makes everything feel so personal, even after all these years. It's over to Microsoft Excel now. No pen and ink. We print everything off, but it's not the same, is it?'

Sally photographed the entry, but Tess, frankly, was losing heart. And she said as much to Sally when they found a coffee shop and split a jam doughnut.

'We can track the bracelet from a Saturday night in 1998 through to now. But what about 1918 to 1998? That's eighty years. Elsie must be dead by now. So it's changed hands at least once. Anything could have happened . . . she was forty-odd during the Blitz. Maybe she was in France with the SOE. Maybe she dropped it in Paris and—'

'Maybe it's been handed down from girl to girl,' said Sally. 'Maybe it's been kept in the family.'

Tess had to agree. It was worth another shot or two. There were other archives: census records, the electoral register, school admissions lists. All sorts. And the search had already been narrowed down because Henry, of course, had noted the address of his client. Mr and Mrs Wingate, along with Elsie, had lived in St John's Wood. At 15 Clifton Place.

'Leave it to me,' said Sally.

60

Benson was nonplussed.

He'd gone to Field Court, behind Gray's Inn, to the offices of Hutton, Braithwaite and Jones for a meeting with his solicitor that he didn't want, because its purpose was to finalise the sale of his boat. Solicitors for Hooper and his vague consortium had sent over some pre-contractual enquiries and Benson was now obliged to deal with them prior to signing the agreement. But on entering George Braithwaite's cubbyhole of an office he suspected events were about to take a surprising turn in direction because Braithwaite, predictably stiff in a starched collar and a silk university tie, had looked vaguely cheerful.

'Do sit down, Will,' he'd said.

Benson had done.

'Before we proceed, I ought to inform you that I have been contacted only half an hour ago by a party who has decided to take an interest in your affairs.'

'Yes?'

'And they have informed me that I am to offer you the sum of twenty thousand pounds, to be used as you see fit and without oversight from me. It's an arrangement I have never encountered in my professional life.'

Benson hadn't replied.

'Do I need to repeat myself, Will?'

'No, Mr Braithwaite.'

Benson instantly recalled a very similar conversation that had taken place years ago, when he'd been in the Green for just over a week. Braithwaite had come on a visit to inform him that funds had been made available to transform his life. There'd only been one condition: that Benson should never try to establish the identity of his benefactor. He'd signed undertakings to that effect.

'The same conditions apply,' Braithwaite said; for he, too, was remembering that dark moment. On that occasion he'd been uneasy; this time he'd nearly smiled. And Benson had only ever seen Braithwaite smile at a menu.

'May I ask if the person concerned is the same as before?'

'You may.'

'Well . . . is it?'

'No.'

'They're different?'

'It's axiomatic.'

Once more, Benson was stumped. Who on earth could it be, if it wasn't Helen Camberley? Only Archie and Molly knew he owed eighteen thousand pounds to his building society, and that his building society had threatened to send in an enforcement officer. Neither of them had money to spare. There was only one possible explanation: Braithwaite must have been talking to people.

'How do I express my thanks?'

'In this particular instance, I imagine it's by remaining on your boat.'

Benson reached for a pen. 'Why does anyone look out for me, Mr Braithwaite? I'm "The Man Everyone Loves to Hate".'

But Braithwaite, being Braithwaite, took the question narrowly and declined to answer for fear of breaching the terms of his own engagement. After signing the undertakings, Benson carefully tore up Hooper's papers and threw them in the bin.

Benson dawdled all the way home, along Rosebery Avenue into Finsbury, and then cutting across the City Road towards the Albert Canal. He tried to take an emotional inventory, but failed to arrive at a simple understanding of himself. He felt a kind of grief for Diane Heybridge, but there was nothing he could do to change his role in the violation of her memory. He grieved for the loss of his brother, knowing he'd never receive his forgiveness. He grieved for his mother, who was dead, and his father who was alive, neither of whom had known what to forgive, but who'd struggled on, loving and forgiving, without rhyme or reason, because it was in their blood. And he grieved, in a way, for Tess – or was it for himself? – because he could never allow her to get near him. Not after what he'd done.

But this wasn't the entire picture. Beneath the powerlessness and grief and loss, he was vibrant and alive. He could feel all this pain; pain built up over so many years, and suppressed, and which was now coming to the surface like fizz in a glass of hooch. Pain he was no longer frightened to endure. A synthesis of mood and feeling was simply impossible . . . because, notwithstanding the agony, Benson felt happy too. He was coming home. To himself, as he was; not who he'd once been or who he'd liked to have been.

And there, at the railings, sat Traddles, ears twitching.

Then Benson slowed. Because parked down the street was a blue van. The same battered blue van that Bredfield had driven. The engine growled and the vehicle pulled away from the kerb, heading towards him, gathering speed, the gears whining. Benson was paralysed. The thing was going to mount the pavement, he knew it. There was no escape. He thought of his dad, who blamed himself, wrongly . . . and then the van flew past him.

But two things happened in quick succession. First, Benson glimpsed a face he thought he knew at the wheel – the face of a much older Skagman. And secondly, at the very moment of passing the rear doors opened and a naked body tumbled onto the road, rolling like a carcass dropped from a butcher's van.

And then Benson was alone. He'd cried out, but no one had heard, and now the street was eerily still. Slowly, in a trance, he walked towards the heap in the gutter with its splayed arms and legs. He stopped at the broken feet, and he stared, his mind blank, absorbing the red and blue of the blood and bruising. Without warning, his stomach heaved and he buckled over, retching, a hand on one knee.

Stainsby had been right. Someone out there had wanted to kill him.

61

Benson needed company. He might have detested Stainsby. And, his shock and disgust having subsided, he might even have felt the stirring of animal instinct: a brutal and brutalising satisfaction that retribution had come to a heartless man whose crimes had gone unpunished. But that didn't mean he could easily forget the sight of his disfigured corpse. So, after the police and ambulance had gone – after a new crime scene had been opened on his own doorstep – he called Tess and Archie. He said the same thing to both of them:

'Get yourself over here, and quick.'

Tess and Archie were on board *The Wooden Doll* within the hour. Between them they brought an Indian takeaway and some beer, not quite noticing that they were reconstructing Diane's last hours. Somehow, the blunder brought her along too. She was there in the galley, in the shadow of Stainsby's murder, puzzling over Benson's philosophy books while they huddled around the table, discussing anything but the killing. Except that Benson wasn't truly present. His mind kept drifting to the killer. And the meaning of what he'd done.

Benson's vague identification of Skagman, someone he'd last seen sixteen years ago, had no evidential value whatsoever. Meersham, of course, knew this. He'd have taken legal advice before ordering the delivery of Stainsby's body. What had been the message? Benson had no doubt. He'd drifted back onto Meersham's wing. And Meersham was telling him what can happen if you forget who owns the place. That he still owned Benson. And Eddie. The threat was like a calling card, and Benson was convinced that at some point he'd be hearing from his lordship.

'A penny for your thoughts.'

Tess had spoken, and softly. She'd touched his arm. But Benson couldn't share his thoughts. He wasn't prepared to reveal that he'd once been one of Meersham's dealers. That he was part of the chain that had killed Dominic Parker, an innocent kid on remand – a kid whose background he'd researched upon release. The parents had separated a couple of years after the death. A young sister, Gemma, had become a social worker. At different times Benson had nearly stopped them in the street, as if he might hand out some kind of glossy leaflet. He'd wanted to clear Manchester's name, tell them what he, Benson, had done, and tell them about Meersham and Eddie, and the bent screws, but he'd always clammed up, taking the stairs to the Underground instead and heading back home. If there'd been a leaflet, it would have ended up on the floor with all the other bogus deals. No, he couldn't share those thoughts, not for a penny, not for a lot more.

'Sorry folks, my mind's all blank.'

'Well, I'll tell you mine,' said Archie. 'I'm sad.'

'Why?'

'I was looking forward to having a magician in the house. He pulls money out of a hat.'

Benson laughed and Tess wondered who the genie had been, shelling out twenty grand as if it was short change. They started guessing. Only Benson, at last easing up, dropped out of the game. Because, glancing over Archie's shoulder, he'd seen a man emerge from the cluster of trees between the boat and Seymour Road. He walked onto the wharf and stray orange light from the streetlamps caught his face.

'What's up, Rizla?'

Benson hesitated over the name. He thought of a working men's club in Norwich, a watering hole for his dad when he was away from the coast.

'I think Witness A might want a beer.'

62

Tess brought over a chair. But no one was talking. The silence carried so many questions that even Steve Draycott didn't know where to begin. Eventually, scratching the back of his head, he said:

'Look . . . you've played a big part in what's now happening. Maybe the most important part. I just thought you ought to know the full story. Diane's story. Because she's about to bring the roof down.'

'Roof?' said Archie.

'Yep. Here and in France. Over there it's *toiture*.'

Draycott nodded at a beer and Archie flipped the cap. They'd all been standing but now they sat at the table cluttered with aluminium trays, shattered poppadums and beer bottles. After clearing away the empties, Benson had to object. 'We haven't played a part in anything.'

Draycott gave another nod. 'You asked Carlatton Linda's question. And that was the clincher.'

'About Diane's codename?'

'Yes.'

'He said she never had one.'

'Well she did. It was Blood Orange.'

A very different silence now bound them together. And when the questions came blurting out, from Tess, Benson and Archie, Draycott just sipped his beer. When he put the bottle down he went right back to the beginning, to the year that Frank Stainsby (Dover) Ltd collapsed. 2002. The year the Stainsby family home was sold and Diane's boyfriend had to sell his car at auction.

'Stainsby worked on other people's boats for the next four years, remember? He took jobs in Kent, Suffolk and Norfolk? Well, that's when he spotted the opportunity. The French Red Cross had already opened a refugee camp in Sangatte in '99. By the time Stainsby was doing bit work, migrants had been storming the Tunnel, there were jungle camps all around Calais . . . and we now know he went there. We know he met up with low-level operatives of Loupierre.'

'How?' asked Tess.

'There's been an ongoing investigation into Stainsby and his associates since Diane's death. Since the dossier arrived at Linda Foster's and she gave it to me, and I went outside the force.'

Tess, like Benson and Archie, abandoned any attempt to piece things together. They let Draycott explain what had happened, Tess acutely aware, now, that Stainsby's trial had been unfolding against the backdrop of a wider, and covert, inquiry that couldn't be compromised by the demands of Stainsby's prosecution, and that had somehow come to a climax when Tess had been sent a text by Linda Foster. Knowledge of a codename had been the critically important piece of evidence . . . for charges that hadn't yet been formulated.

'Diane contacted John Foster in 2008. She'd been tracking Stainsby for a year. And for reasons I didn't understand at the time, John ran her secretly. He didn't want Carlatton to know, and he wouldn't tell me anything either. What I said in court was the truth. He just wanted me to cover his back. As you know, I didn't.'

Draycott took a swig of beer. The big questions in the

aftermath were these: how the hell had Stainsby known there was a copper on the premises? And how did he know that the copper in question was John? Someone must have identified him. But only three people knew about the undercover operation: Diane, John and Draycott, and they were obviously beyond suspicion. Who, then, could have found out? And how?

'The attack on John was investigated by DI Pete Lambrook. And he discovered that Carlatton had paid an informer fifty pounds the week before the attack. Carlatton said it related to another case . . . but this informer was Diane's best friend. Jane Tapster. One of the Dover Five. And an examination of her computer showed that Diane had used it to contact John through Facebook – looking back, she was obviously hiding what she was doing from Stainsby. It looks like she used Tapster's flat as a kind of safe house, where she could speak freely.'

'I can see where this going,' said Tess. 'Tapster knew that Diane was communicating with Foster, a policeman . . . and she told Carlatton.'

Draycott nodded. 'That's what we now think. And Tapster was listening in on Diane, just as Diane was listening in on Stainsby.'

'And Tapster was passing it all on to Carlatton.'

'Exactly.'

Benson had to interrupt. 'Hold it. Are you saying Carlatton's bent? That he had dealings with Stainsby?'

'He's certainly bent,' said Draycott. 'But his link was with Meersham. At the time there was no proof.'

'You've got the proof now?'

'It's all in the dossier . . . but we're getting ahead of ourselves. What you need to understand is that much of what I'm telling you now has been worked out backwards, starting with Diane's murder. At the time of the attack in the Twisted Wheel, I had no idea what was going on. I didn't suspect Carlatton of anything. And when Diane contacted me a week or so afterwards, I thought she was off her head. I thought the trafficking story was incredible and, as I said in court, I told her if what she'd said was true we'd want heaps of evidence, linking all the main players. She was distraught. I never thought I'd see her again. Could you pop another beer there, Mr Congreve?'

'It's Archie, Mr Draycott.'

'And I'm Tess.'

63

Benson slipped into a reverie. He looked beyond the huddle to the galley, imagining Diane. Attracted by its title, she'd pulled a book off a shelf. She wasn't listening to Draycott, because she, of all people, knew what had happened next. And so did Benson. How she'd gone home to Stainsby, found herself pressured into becoming an alibi, and then wondered if the best way out wasn't death. She'd toyed with the idea. She'd come close to the fire, weighing up hanging and drowning. But then – and Benson knew what this felt like – she'd found something deep inside herself. A strength that she'd never known was there, not even after her dad had died and her mum had fallen to pieces. She'd reached the bottom of the pit and she'd made a decision. To put Stainsby away. And to save all the children she'd never had. Benson looked at her more closely. She was reading *Ethics: Doing the Right Thing* by Julia Moore. Going by her facial expression, she couldn't understand a word.

Draycott spoke: 'When she contacted me in September 2015, I didn't take her seriously. She said she had a mountain of evidence. That she'd done everything I'd said would be needed.'

Draycott had listened in amazement. She'd bought a tracking device and a camera. She'd not only followed Stainsby on his operations with Bredfield, she'd followed Stainsby into London. She'd taken the addresses where trafficked migrants had been housed. She'd collected forensic evidence that linked people together.

'She asked me not to tell Carlatton because she'd sent him anonymous tip-offs and nothing had been done. And I looked at my diary and made an appointment.'

'Ten days later,' said Tess.

'Yep. Ten long days.'

Draycott lost his momentum; and Benson said:

'But you thought, this is 2009 all over again, we can't have another operation running off the books. So you went to Carlatton.'

Draycott nodded. 'And if I hadn't done, if I'd waited to look at the dossier, Diane would still be alive.'

He'd told Carlatton all about 2009 and Diane's reappearance out of nowhere. And as Draycott had explained in court, Carlatton hit the roof. But he'd authorised Draycott to take matters forward, recording data on the force computer in the first instance, not the National Informant Management database. He didn't want to commit himself until he knew that Diane was going to be a reliable source of intelligence. He wanted to see the dossier.

'I created a file. And I gave her the name Blood Orange, because I'd just eaten one. Ten days later she was dead.'

'Who else knew the name?' asked Tess.

'No one. I didn't tell Diane. I didn't tell Carlatton. But Stainsby had found out. And Stainsby could only find out from someone with access to the force computer. And someone who knew that Diane had just been registered locally as a source of intelligence. It's at this point that Goodshaw comes down from London making enquiries about Diane, and Carlatton decides – for Linda Foster's sake – to say nothing about 2009 or Diane's call to me six years later. And, of course, I'm going along with this because I wanted to protect John, so I delete Diane's file a couple of days after she died. It was as though we'd had nothing to do with her.'

'But what about the dossier?' asked Benson.

'I assumed the thing just didn't exist. There was no mention of it in the Stainsby investigation. But then I got call from Linda Foster. It turned out Diane had sent it to her. With a note. Saying she'd completed what John had set out to do. Off I went to Great Dunmow.'

And Draycott's heart had sunk. The 'mountain of evidence' was useless. The surveillance observations, without Diane to explain them, might as well have been used to light the fire. But then he came across notes of the tip-offs sent to Carlatton. And photographs of Stainsby with various people in London, all of whom could be traced through existing intelligence records. And, stapled to a plastic bag with a cigarette butt inside, a single photograph that made him freeze.

'It was Carlatton meeting someone in a Dover café. One of the people pictured with Stainsby in London.'

'Who?'

'A guy called Roy Chalker. I didn't recognise him, obviously. I had to go looking in the files. But when I found him, I realised Diane had stumbled upon something big.'

Roy, thought Benson. Roy whose eyes were like wet slate. Roy who'd insisted on being called His Lordship. Draycott confirmed the link:

'Because Chalker is one of Meersham's lieutenants. And that meant Carlatton had a connection not just to Chalker but, potentially, to Meersham's network as a whole.'

'What's with the cigarette butt?' asked Archie.

'Chalker's DNA is on it. It backs up the photo.'

Benson spoke as if from a distance. 'But without Diane being alive to prove it, they'd just go on the fire with the surveillance notes. The whole dossier goes on the fire.'

'Yep,' said Draycott. 'Except I now know for sure that Carlatton was bent.'

And, more significantly, Draycott instantly identified the possible chain of causation that had led to Diane's murder. If Carlatton had warned Chalker about the dossier, and mentioned the codename that had just been entered in the force database, then it was entirely possible that Chalker had turned on Stainsby and told him to sort this out . . . just like he'd been told to sort out Foster in 2009. And Stainsby, being an idiot, had gone too far. He'd use that blood orange, presumably as some kind of in-joke to please Chalker and Meersham, relying on the fact that his trafficking business enjoyed police protection.

'Once I'd seen that connection I went outside my force. I didn't know how high the corruption might go, so I contacted Surrey and they took over. They initiated Operation Springtime.'

'But that was a year ago. Why not blow the whistle immediately?' asked Tess.

'Two reasons. First, the aim was to bag the lot of them, not just Carlatton, and that meant mounting a significant investigation . . . Remember, everything in Diane's dossier was inadmissible. It was a starting point to get hard evidence that would stand up in court. Second, we couldn't act immediately. If Carlatton was confronted with the photo he could easily say he was recruiting an informer. Our best bet was Stainsby himself, while Springtime was underway. Once he'd been charged we were hoping he'd try and cut a deal. We expected a call from you, even during the trial. To say

Stainsby was prepared to talk for a new identity . . . but he hung in there. He seems to have thought he'd win brownie points from Terry Meersham by keeping his trap shut. Didn't realise he was dead from the moment he put that blood orange in Diane's mouth.'

Benson had his eye on that all-important chain of causation. 'If you didn't tell Carlatton Diane's codename, how would you prove he knew it, and could have passed it on to Chalker?'

'That was the main question. I'd checked his laptop. And he'd accessed Diane's file once. The day I created it, presumably wanting to know what I'd written up. So he definitely knew the name. And no one else would have had a reason to look it up, not yet.'

'So it was down to you and Carlatton,' said Benson. 'You were the only ones who could have passed the codename on to Meersham's people.'

'That's right. But to clinch the case against Carlatton – according to our lawyers – we needed a lie that could be shown to be a lie.'

Which is why the decision was made to try to ambush Carlatton during the trial. In the first instance, Draycott forced Carlatton's hand. He insisted that they contact DCI Goodshaw and the CPS, and reveal what they knew about Diane Heybridge. As a result, statements were duly prepared and Yardley was informed.

'The tricky part was getting you, Mr Benson, to ask a specific question. Springtime officers couldn't approach you directly so it was decided to get Linda Foster to send that text to Tess while you were on your feet. Cut down your thinking time. Thankfully the ploy worked.'

'Because Carlatton not only denied knowing the codename,' said Tess, 'he denied ever checking the force computer.'

Draycott raised his beer. 'And that's all you need for an interrogation. A couple of good lies under oath. And a dossier on the table that you don't even open.'

Benson glanced again towards the galley. Diane, being polite, had kicked off her shoes before putting her feet on the sofa. She'd dozed off and the book had fallen to the floor.

'Has he been arrested?' asked Archie.

'Yes. They've already got more from him than they'd ever have got out of Stainsby. He's singing like a canary.'

Tess raised her beer too, only she was querying: 'Does Springtime reach as far as Paris?'

'Absolutely. And beyond. There's going to be a series of coordinated arrests. I'll keep you informed. And on that note – a breach of secrecy that would finish off my already wrecked career – I'll be off. Thanks for the beer. And thanks for asking the question, Mr Benson.'

'I've got one more.'

Benson was still looking at Diane. At last he'd been able to imagine her face without the contortions brought about by death. The deep marks had gone from her neck. The lines around her eyes had been smoothed away.

'Did Foster have a codename too, back in 2009?'

'Yes. Diane liked the idea.'

'What was it?'

'Harry.'

64

There'd been no celebratory meal after the Stainsby acquittal. But the arrest of the people that Diane Heybridge had watched and tracked was a different matter. And so, having been warned by Draycott in advance, Tess invited

Benson, Archie and Molly to her place. They gathered around the television screen at 9 p.m. for the culmination of what had been a month of coordinated police activity in three countries.

There were no cheers. No clinking of glasses. No commentaries. They just watched as news crews captured the moment when Terry Meersham and a number of his associates were taken into custody. Similar footage showed the arrest of André Loupierre in Paris and other individuals in Italy. An international migrant trafficking operation had been broken, and for once specialist law enforcement units in Britain, France and Italy had been able to detain not just the couriers but the organisers, the top-level criminal gangs who so often evaded detection.

There was no mention of Carlatton. Which is what you'd expect. Because it was clear to everyone crouching forward in Tess's sitting room that once confronted with the evidence against him – evidence collected by Springtime – he'd taken a route very different from Stainsby. He'd elected to disclose everything he knew and, as a result, pins were falling. Big pins. In due course, he would testify against his co-conspirators and then he'd have to do his time and vanish off the face of the earth. He'd get a new identity, but life as he'd known it was over. Same for his family, who were now in protective custody.

'Apparently, Meersham had a hold over him,' said Tess, who'd spoken to Draycott that morning. 'Right from the beginning of his career. This Roy Chalker had told Carlatton if he didn't drop an inquiry into a drugs deal, they'd maim his daughter.'

'I bet they would have done, too,' said Archie.

'Oh yes. These are hard, hard people. Carlatton had thought they'd forgotten all about him. But when he made detective inspector, Chalker came back.'

'So he was trapped.'

'Yep.'

'And he turned a blind eye to Stainsby's activities.'

'A lot more than that. He fed Chalker information on the work of the Immigration Crime Taskforce. Basically, every time Stainsby did a crossing he'd known in advance where the patrol boats were going, where the Border Force were operating, what Immigration Enforcement were doing – the lot.'

But information is often a two-way street. And just as Carlatton was feeding data to Chalker, he was collecting it too. Information on how Meersham operated, along with the what, where, when and why. And once Meersham had been lifted he'd squealed, which, to quote Draycott, had brought the roof down.

'He's after a shorter sentence,' said Tess, 'but the rest of the crew will want deals as well, so we can expect them to start tearing each other apart. Opening cans of worms we don't even know about. This is just the beginning for Terry Meersham.'

'Haven't they got some kind of *omertà*?' said Archie.

'Sure. But all that goes out of the window once you've got the boss. And they've got the boss. By the time he ends up in court, he'll be looking at a two-page indictment and a whole-life tariff.'

Benson hadn't said anything. He'd been watching the images flicker across the screen with unblinking eyes. Finally, he leaned back and said, 'Diane did this.'

And that was no exaggeration. Her dossier might have ended up on the fire, but that one photo connecting Carlatton to Chalker had been the keystone which, when removed, had – to quote Draycott once more – brought down not just the roof, but the *toiture*. In due course, it had pulled down a *tetto* as well, which suggested Loupierre's people had buckled pretty fast in relation to their Italian connections.

'Where's the money?' asked Archie. 'If Stainsby was piling it somewhere, wanting it laundered, and couldn't spend it, then it should still be out there.'

'Keep watching,' said Tess, pointing at the screen.

According to Draycott, Springtime investigators had postponed looking for the money until after Stainsby's trial. They'd hoped he might crack under the strain and offer Queen's evidence, at which point disclosing its hiding place would have been integral to any potential deal. Pending the outcome, they'd been hamstrung, because any attempt to find it would have warned Carlatton that the dossier did in fact exist and that an outside force was operating on his patch. Now that Stainsby was dead and Carlatton had been arrested, the search had begun in earnest. Tess said nothing more. Eventually, the newsreader explained:

Officers had searched Stainsby's old boat shed and seized over half a million pounds in mixed currencies. The various notes had been concealed in small plastic bags and then hidden in the soil pipe of a disused toilet. The irony was lost on no one save perhaps Stainsby's ghost. Filthy money hidden in a filthy place.

'It seems Chalker, on Meersham's orders, was stringing Stainsby along,' said Tess, after she'd turned off the news. 'They'd never intended to launder the money for him. They'd kept him tied into the operation and dependent on them. The thinking is that they'd never have trusted him and would probably have killed him at some point once Carlatton could no longer provide the cover they needed.'

'He was a dead man long before he put that blood orange in Diane's mouth,' said Benson. 'He was dead from the moment he met Meersham.'

Tess had gone into the kitchen to check the oven. She'd

prepared something to please Archie. But when she returned Molly, who, like Benson, had said very little, now gave a loud sigh. And if there was any sense of quiet celebration, she put it very much in perspective.

'They got Meersham,' she said, coming to the table, 'but there are plenty more like him. And plenty more like Stainsby . . . but there aren't many like Diane. Maybe there are no Dianes.'

Tess put on some music. Jason Mraz. 'Details in the Fabric'. And she lit a candle and pointed at the chairs, saying who was to sit where. She'd bought some flowers and she'd made some bread. She'd done her best to mark the occasion, but it wasn't really working. Archie tried to lift the mood. He clapped his hands and gave his plate a nudge.

'What's for dinner, then?'

'Pie and peas,' said Tess.

65

Sally was an excitable type. As a result, Tess tended not to take too seriously her bursts of enthusiasm. Not immediately. For Sally could easily find a painter or photographer simply wonderful after an exhibition, only to revise her opinion once the initial fervour had died down. The same could be said of her engagement with information, as opposed to visual data. Her response was equally swift and she frequently arrived at conclusions which, in quieter moments, were found to be unsustainable. It was her climbdowns that appealed to Tess. For they were always graceful, demonstrating the keen intelligence that ultimately kept her emotions in check.

With these considerations in mind, Tess sank into an armchair in Sally's drawing room. She'd come to Chiswick

Mall, by the Thames, after an excited summons. It was evening and the lights south of the river were shimmering on the water.

'The bracelet was made by Manny Brewster in 1918,' said Sally, by way of recap. She was standing by the window, looking out onto the narrow street between her house and the railed gardens on the other side. 'And the client was Arthur Wingate.'

'Who wanted a bracelet for his daughter's eighteenth,' said Tess.

'That's right. It was made for Elsie, who was born in 1900, and she grew up in a rather grand house in St John's Wood.'

The walls of the drawing room were covered with paintings, sketches, and photographs. All sorts of styles picked up from all sorts of places. There were sculptures, too – again, unusual things snapped up during adventures at home and abroad with Tess. Sally's life was all around them; along with a part of Tess's. There was that surrealist sketch from Montmartre. The public disorder charge sheet, now framed, issued by the police in Vienna. And, with its own lighting, a half-brick displayed in a glass dome that had once held a stuffed owl. It had come flying through Tess's window during the Hopton Yard killing trial when, as it happened, she and Sally had met to begin their investigation into Benson. At the end of that first line of inquiry, they'd been convinced of his guilt.

'Elsie subsequently married a chap called Wilfred Baker. That was in 1924. Now, Wilfred was a barrister. And he'd been called to the Bar in 1923. But for now, it's Elsie that interests me. Elsie Baker.'

'Go on.'

Tess had noticed that Sally's tone belonged to the post-climbdown calm, when she'd reached conclusions that were difficult to undermine. The excitement had been reserved for the summons alone.

'Elsie didn't hang around on the maternity front. She had a child in 1925. A girl. And that girl's name was – or perhaps I should say *is* – Annette. So now we're interested in Annette. Annette Baker.'

'Who did Annette marry?' asked Tess, sensing the flow of Sally's research.

'An Anglican cleric. High Church. Something of an intellectual. Did theology at Oxford but in the end opted for pastoral work. He was twenty-eight and she was twenty-nine. This was 1954.'

'What's his name, Sally.'

'Well, he's dead now. *Crockford's Clerical Directory* has him down as the Right Rev Gilbert Merrington DD. So we're now interested in Annette Merrington.'

Sally looked away from the river and met Tess's gaze.

'Did you say Merrington?' said Tess.

'Yes.'

'The same family as the Justice Secretary? The man who wants to shut Benson down?'

'Annette is his mother. She and Gilbert had one child, in 1956. He was baptised Richard, went to Peterhouse, Cambridge and entered Parliament in 1997, when he was elected Conservative MP for Hampstead and Highgate.'

Tess could no longer remain sitting. She stood up and began pacing the room, but she was unable to organise her thoughts. Sally, still calm, had already covered the ground.

'Richard married Pamela Longhirst in 1994. Which means that Pamela, to state the obvious, is Annette's daughter-in-law.'

Tess was on track now. The bracelet could have moved from Elsie to Annette to Pamela. She thought out loud.

'Paul Harbeton was found dead in Soho in November 1998.'

Sally had already anticipated Tess's thought processes, because they'd been her own.

'By then Elsie was dead, Annette was seventy-three and Pamela was thirty-one.'

'So we're talking about Annette or Pamela,' said Tess. 'One of them could have been present in Soho at the time Paul Harbeton died. The bracelet was found by Michael Lever three or four yards from the body.'

Ironically, it was Sally who cut the wild thinking down to size. 'Slow down, Tess. One of them could have been there, that's for sure. But it could have been hours beforehand. Or a day beforehand. It proves nothing. And anyway, it doesn't follow that the bracelet was in the possession of either woman. They could have dropped it elsewhere, someone different found it, wore it, and they lost it because—'

'There was a faulty catch,' said Tess. 'That's how it got lost in the first place. The damn thing could have been found and dropped over and again. You're right. It proves nothing.' Tess fell back into her armchair. 'But it's one hell of a coincidence that someone in Merrington's family might know something about a death that put Benson in prison for eleven years.'

'Might be implicated,' corrected Sally quietly.

The thought silenced them both. Sally turned to the window, her eyes once more on the twinkling lights and dark shadows of the river, while Tess thought of Benson. He'd served more than eleven years. His life had been destroyed. He couldn't even look Tess in the eye without running away, inwardly, to some other cell which he'd never leave, because he'd admitted his guilt. The private claims of innocence meant nothing. He was a murderer. He had the mark on his forehead. He'd never be free.

'That's not where the coincidence ends,' said Sally. 'But let me first observe that despite its value – sentimental and financial – no one has reported this bracelet missing. Not in November 1998. Not before and not since. As far as the police are concerned it hasn't been lost.'

'Which means the Merrington family never made an insurance claim,' said Tess, seeing a fresh angle. 'Whoever it is didn't want to tell the police when and where they might have lost it . . . because they knew it would put them by the body.'

'As I say, we may be talking implication, not just knowledge.'

She came away from the window and sat down opposite Tess, crossing her legs and reaching for the martini she'd poured but left untouched.

'Now, back to coincidence. Remember Wilfred Baker?'

'Yes,' said Tess, feeling strangely alert. 'He was a barrister. And he married Elsie.'

'That's right. Now Wilfred came to the Bar in 1923. He joined a set of chambers in the Temple. Smollett Court. His pupil master was a legend. Edward Grace KC. Appeared against Marshall Hall. A friend of Norman Birkett. Was a prosecutor at Nuremberg. All of which is totally irrelevant.'

'Tell me what is.'

'Edward Grace married a porcelain-faced beauty called Charlotte. And they had a daughter Vivian.'

Tess waited for Sally to take a generous sip of her cocktail.

'Vivian tied the knot when she was twenty-four. Who she married is interesting. He was a barrister too. Same chambers as her father and Wilfred. And his name was John Camberley . . . whose daughter, Helen, grew to be one of the most distinguished QCs at the London Bar.'

For a time, Tess said nothing; she knew she'd need to write all this down. And then examine the timeline and the arrows in the family trees. But she didn't need to know the detail to appreciate that everything about Benson's trial now looked radically different.

'That's the kind of coincidence defence lawyers dream about,' said Tess at last. 'The family that owned the bracelet found at a crime scene has a hidden connection to the woman who represented the person charged with the crime. That can't be chance.'

Sally nodded slowly. 'If these elements made up a picture, I'd say it wasn't finished.'

'And it isn't,' said Tess with conviction. 'The answer to everything will be in the relationships and in the geography – who was where and when. Sally, you might have done it. You might have found the key that will open the door to Benson's prison. I don't know what to say.'

Sally thought for a moment. Then she became mischievous.

'If we crack this, just give me the credit,' she said. 'And if it turns out that compassion fuelled your engine, just step to one side, will you? Because if you're not interested, I might be.'

66

The dumping of Stainsby's body in front of Benson had generated considerable press attention. A lawyer who'd simply done his job had been subjected to unprecedented, not to mention grotesque, intimidation by criminal interests. Benson was seen, for once, as a victim. And while he shunned any sympathy, the effect was to subtly distance Benson from his own wrongdoing. The scandal of his past had lost some of its force. As a result, the phone wouldn't stop ringing. Archie was having trouble covering all the bookings. You might need to take someone on, he'd said, exasperated. You've crossed the brow of the hill, chipped in Molly, warming a teapot. You're just going to move faster and faster now. But Benson was looking backwards, not forwards, and, one day when a trial came out of the list, he told his clerk to get his coat on and together they went to Dover in the Tuesday Club's rattling Fiesta. On arriving, Benson bought a bunch of roses and one of tulips, and then they went to the cemetery on the Old Charlton Road.

Diane's grave was a simple black stone, marked with her name, the dates and a cliché: 'Loved and never forgotten'. But clichés are clichés because they are true. The earth, still high, was covered with flowers from her mum and customers from Greggs, and, of course, the Dover Five, who'd obviously decided to keep their name rather than drop the number to Four. Benson laid the roses on the pile and then stepped back. There was no message on the card. Because there was too much to say.

'Meersham had a hold over me, too,' said Benson at last.

'Since when?' Archie was incredulous.

'Right from the beginning. My first year of bird.'

'What did he do?'

'I don't want to talk about it, Archie. It's part of the bad stuff we leave inside. But he would have come for me, one day. Like he came for Carlatton. And I don't know what I would have done. But I've been spared all that. And you've been spared anything I might have done. Because of Diane. She saved me and she saved what we've started.'

There was a strong wind and it rushed into the trees. The clouds were low and rolling, blown apart. Gulls swooped and cried. Benson stepped forward again and laid the tulips by the roses. He was thinking of all those people who would never know what Diane had done for them.

'Diane didn't just tip off Carlatton,' said Benson. 'She alerted agencies working with migrants in London. Some of those women and children were picked up before Meersham's people moved them on. Among them were Milena Sibhatu and her son.'

They'd eventually been granted asylum. Milena had been an English teacher in Asmara. After her husband's execution, she'd fled the country with Jonas. All she'd brought was what she could carry.

'How did you find this out?' said Archie.

'Draycott. It's all in the useless dossier. He thought I'd want to know. And I did. It's changed my understanding of Diane's last week alive.'

Benson saw her now, arriving in Tottenham and meeting Milena . . . Milena who'd finally made it to the other side of despair and whose son would one day grow to be a good man. He could see Diane's face and auburn hair. He could almost feel the electricity in her movements. She was living intensely. For the moment. She'd bought a bike. She'd brought home some holiday brochures. She'd been like Jonas on Christmas Eve, all the while knowing that she'd probably never see Christmas.

'Did you ever wonder why Diane sent the dossier to Linda Foster?'

Archie hadn't. And Benson had been kind to Draycott by not raising the question with him.

'She'd known Draycott hadn't taken her seriously. Any more than Stainsby had ever taken her seriously. He told her to wait *ten days*. When she put that phone down, she'd known he'd go to Carlatton. She'd known that Stainsby would somehow be warned. She'd known that he'd come for her.'

Archie put an arm on Benson's shoulder. 'She'd known this, too, Rizla: she'd known she was the winner.'

The remark struck Benson forcibly. This, in the end, was the reward for goodness. A special kind of knowledge. Not protection from harm. Or any hope of praise, because you might not live to receive it. And all at once Benson understood why he'd been strangely consoled at the very moment Stainsby had shown himself to be a wicked man. Set against Diane's moral depth, the evil he embodied had no content. There was nothing there. For all his monstrous acts, he was just a silly man in a silly suit playing a silly game.

'Thank you, Mr Congreve,' said Benson. 'You've solved the puzzle.'

67

They spoke of Diane all the way back to London. How this gentle, fragile woman had brought about the downfall of so many dreadful, abusive men. How she'd appeared to be weak, when she'd been incredibly strong. How she'd seemed to have been overwhelmed by circumstances when, in fact, she'd taken control of them. By some strange alchemy, when Benson pushed open the door to Congreve Chambers he felt a journey was complete. Not just Diane's, but a part of his own.

'Where've you been, Mr Benson?'

Molly had a certain authority that went far beyond her role as office manager, typist, tea-maker and expert on evidence.

'We went to Dover.'

'You went to Dover. Well, you've obviously forgotten we're all meant to be in Shoreditch. It's Monopoly night.'

And that meant Archie's four unmarried sisters, Dot,

Joyce, Betsy and Eileen were probably cooking up some game plan while they waited.

'We've got to get going,' murmured Benson.

They took a bus up Brick Lane and then ran to the customary venue, the overheated parlour of an old people's home off Old Nichol Street where CJ, Congreve senior, aged ninety-seven, reigned as the eldest resident. In deference to his years and long experience of commerce – he'd run Congreve's for nearly four decades – the role of banker always fell to him. And he always drifted off within five minutes of the start of play, only surfacing from a dream to blurt out his side of a phantom conversation. Which explained why he was gently snoring when Benson's token – the boot – landed on Chance before he'd got halfway round the board. Benson stared at the words on the card and then, resigned to confront his past once more, he let Joyce take over. There was cheering and laughter as she intoned the instruction with judicial pomp:

'Go to jail. Move directly to jail. Do not pass "Go". Do not collect two hundred pounds.'

'Serves you right,' said Dot.

Archie was indignant. 'He didn't do it.'

'Throw away the key,' cried Betsy.

'Bastard,' said Molly.

Eileen was more generous. Like her brother and sisters, she was fond of pies and cake. Even her voice was well-rounded. 'I've got a "Get Out of Jail Free" card,' she said. 'It's yours, Mr Benson.'

'Eileen, you're a ministering angel.'

'For five hundred quid.'

'You're not serious.'

'All right then, seven-fifty.'

'You're a fat fiend. I'd rather serve my time.'

For now, the Congreves, Archie and Molly were allies, so

Eileen won a coarse cheer, and Benson went directly to jail. He did not pass "Go". And he did not collect £200. But he did have a visitor. Sort of. In a cell once more, his thoughts turned to Tess.

Since the Blood Orange murder, she'd been sending him lots of work. Theft. Criminal damage. A mixed bag of basic crime, usually with Basil, rather than Tess, in attendance. On the occasions they'd met, she'd been polite and purposeful; the conversation had never strayed far from the case; she'd made no reference to his past conviction; and, critically, she'd kept her promise to leave his past alone. In effect, he'd got what he'd been looking for. A species of detachment. Only—

'C'mon, Rizla,' said Archie, giving a prod with his elbow. 'Your turn. Throw a double and get out of there.'

Benson tried – insofar as one can ever try with dice – and failed.

'Six-fifty?' asked Eileen, commiserating.

'Get stuffed.'

Still locked up, Benson returned to his reverie. Yes, he'd got what he was looking for . . . only he didn't really want it. He kept waiting for those stray questions, that passing reference, and, most obscurely of all, a hint that maybe she'd broken her promise. He was drawn to this last like a moth to a flame, knowing it could only entail a kind of death. Only recently, he'd told her about the letter he'd received from David Merrington. That's right, he'd exclaimed. The son of the Justice Secretary. He'd written asking if he could spend a week in chambers. Shadowing Benson. And Benson had told Tess, expecting her to pace the corridor, urging him to be careful, warning him that hostile scrutiny of his past could only increase . . . that he'd never be truly free as long as his conviction stood unchallenged. But she'd only gone to first base, and rather casually at that, advising caution.

There'd been no insistence in her voice. Benson still hadn't decided how to respond, and that was largely because he'd wanted Tess to be part of the decision. Which made no sense, given his—

'That'll be one pound, four shillings and sixpence,' said CJ, opening his milky blue eyes. 'Atlantic cod doesn't come any fresher.'

'We've gone metric, Dad,' murmured Betsy, stroking his bony hand; and then, much louder: 'I suggest you sling our Eileen a monkey, Mr Benson. That's cockney for five hundred nicker.'

'I won't give her a cow's calf.'

Which was fifty pence. Benson preferred to take his chances. And ultimately luck was on his side. By the time CJ had been wheeled to his bedroom and an inventory taken of cash and possessions, Benson had become a very wealthy man. In the dog-eat-dog world of investment and speculation, he'd devoured everyone. Except Archie, who'd gone under through self-inflicted bankruptcy. Benson dawdled home, however, feeling empty. Because even if all that money had been real, he couldn't buy a smidgen of insistence for someone else's voice.

'She sounded excited,' said Archie on Monday morning when Benson, after a subdued weekend, arrived at chambers. 'She wants you to call her back.'

Benson went to the Gutting Room and rang Tess immediately. Still in his duffel coat, he stood by the window, listening intently, watched by Archie and Molly. There wasn't much back and forth, so when Benson put the phone down, Archie was the first to speak:

'What was all that about?'

'She's going to instruct me in another murder.'

'Which one?'

'She called it the Limehouse case.'

'Never heard of it.'

'Me neither.'

Archie glanced at Molly. 'Why the excitement?'

'She says something doesn't feel right.' Benson sat down, still toggled up. 'The facts look simple but she's convinced there's more to it than meets the eye. It's just a feeling, but . . .' His voice trailed off and Molly had a guess at what might have come next:

'But if anyone can get beneath the surface it's you?'

'Yes,' said Benson after a fitting pause. But he thought: does it get any better? This was a case for Tess, not Basil. He'd get her insistence without any threat to himself. Her determination, in all its shades, would be directed entirely towards the coming trial. Benson's third murder trial within two years of going it alone. Another story of life cut short, where the claim to innocence would bring out the hidden secrets of the guilty . . . if Benson did his job properly. He didn't know whether to be scared or to celebrate. His schooling as a defender was taking place faster than he'd ever anticipated. There'd been insufficient tuition in those quieter instances of heartbreak.

'I warned you,' said Molly, arms folded as if to contain her pride. 'From here on in, things are only going to move faster. You're a name, Mr Benson. You're a name at the London Bar.'

Acknowledgements

My thanks go to the following: Ursula Mackenzie; Richard Beswick, Zoe Gullen and Grace Vincent at Little, Brown; Victoria Hobbs, Jennifer Custer and Helen Ferey at A.M. Heath; Conrad Williams at Blake Friedmann; Her Honour Judge Penny Moreland; Professor Nick Hardwick, Chair of the Parole Board and formerly HM Chief Inspector of Prisons; Françoise Koetschet; Sabine Guyard; and Joseph Dublin. I'm also grateful to Dr Ian Evett CBE and Dr Sue Pope of Principal Forensic Science for guidance in relation to a plotline subsequently abandoned. Needless to say, I thank Anne, for endless support; and patience, when asked if she wouldn't mind listening to yet another revised sentence . . . or paragraph.

Representations regarding the law, criminal procedure and the prison system are mine.

About the Author

John Fairfax is the pen name of William Brodrick, who practised as a barrister before becoming a full-time novelist. Under his own name he is a previous winner of the Crime Writers' Association Gold Dagger Award and his first novel, *The Sixth Lamentation*, was a Richard and Judy selection.